My Own World

Mike Holmes

First Second
New York

First Second

Published by First Second
First Second is an imprint of Roaring Brook Press,
a division of Holtzbrinck Publishing Holdings Limited Partnership
120 Broadway, New York, NY 10271
firstsecondbooks.com
mackids.com

Library of Congress Control Number: 2020919548

Our books may be purchased in bulk for promotional, educational, or business
use. Please contact your local bookseller or the Macmillan Corporate
and Premium Sales Department at (800) 221-7945 ext. 5442 or by email
at MacmillanSpecialMarkets@macmillan.com.

FIRST
EDITION

First edition, 2021
Edited by Mark Siegel and Jill Freshney
Cover design by Kirk Benshoff
Interior book design by Molly Johanson
Color assistance by Jason Fischer
Printed in China by 1010 Printing International Limited, North Point, Hong Kong

Penciled, inked, and colored digitally in Photoshop CC 2014
using a Cintiq 22HD display on a 2015 iMac.

ISBN 978-1-250-20828-6 (paperback)
1 3 5 7 9 10 8 6 4 2

ISBN 978-1-250-20827-9 (hardcover)
1 3 5 7 9 10 8 6 4 2

Don't miss your next favorite book from First Second! For the latest
updates go to firstsecondnewsletter.com and sign up for our enewsletter.

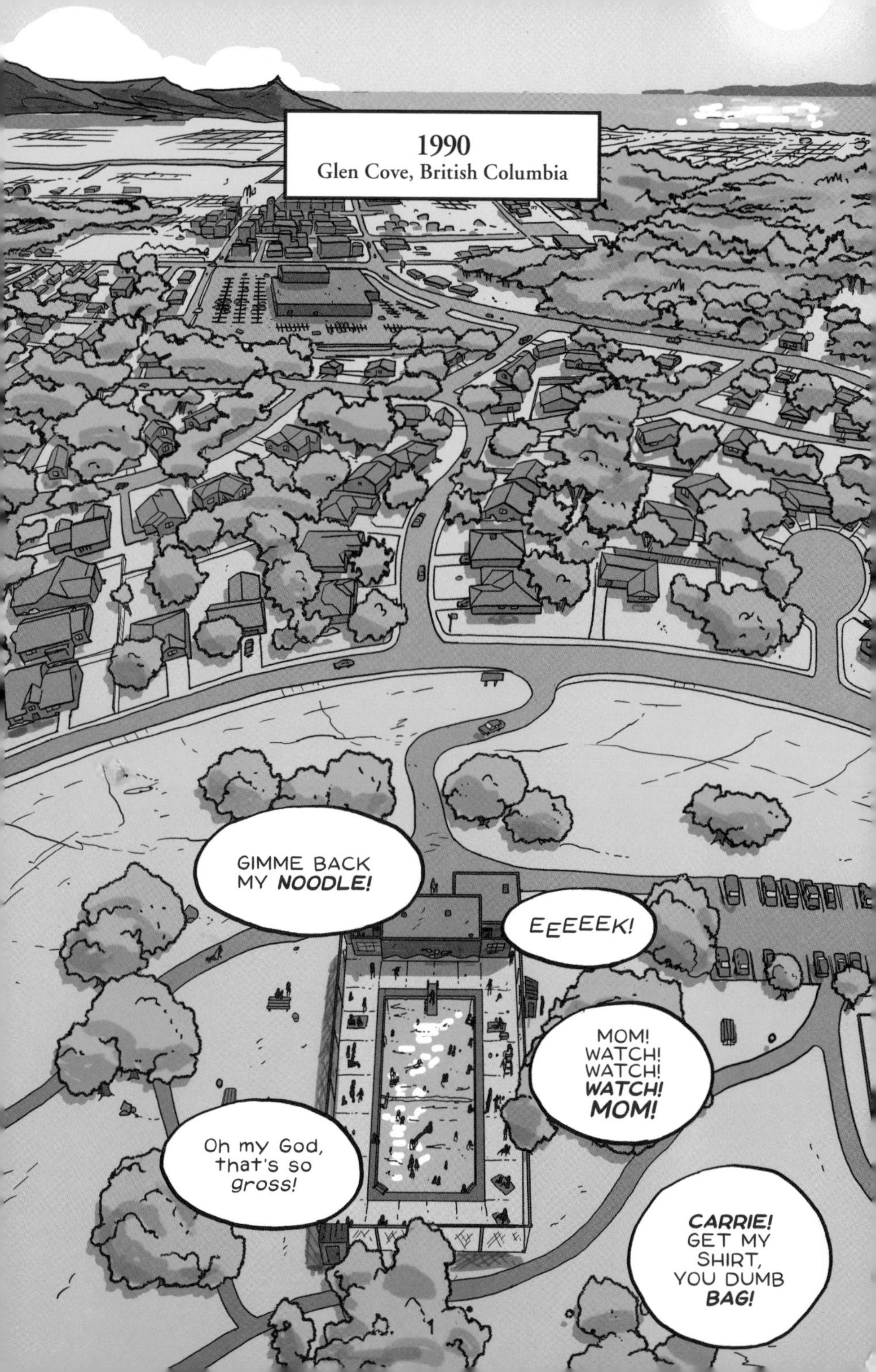
1990
Glen Cove, British Columbia
GIMME BACK MY NOODLE!
EEEEEK!
MOM! WATCH! WATCH! WATCH! MOM!
Oh my God, that's so gross!
CARRIE! GET MY SHIRT, YOU DUMB BAG!

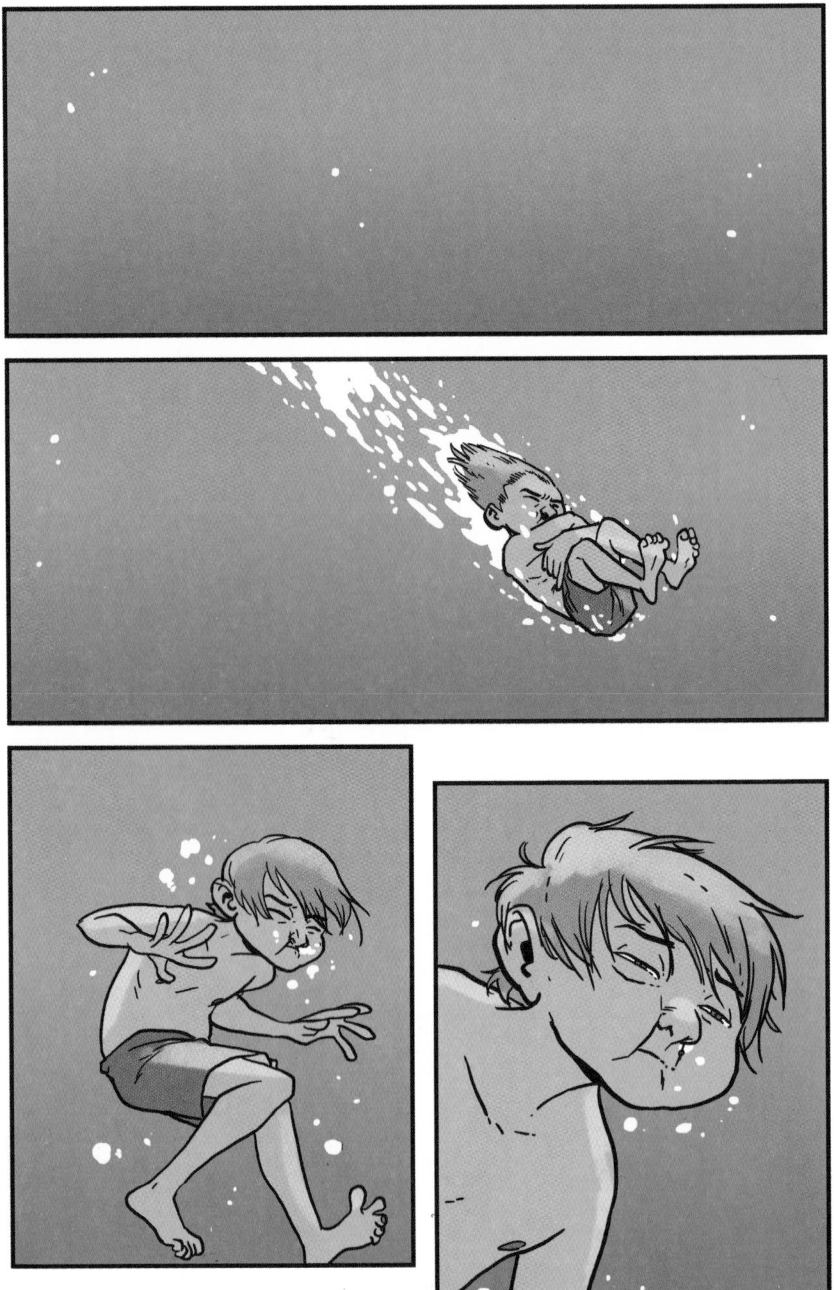

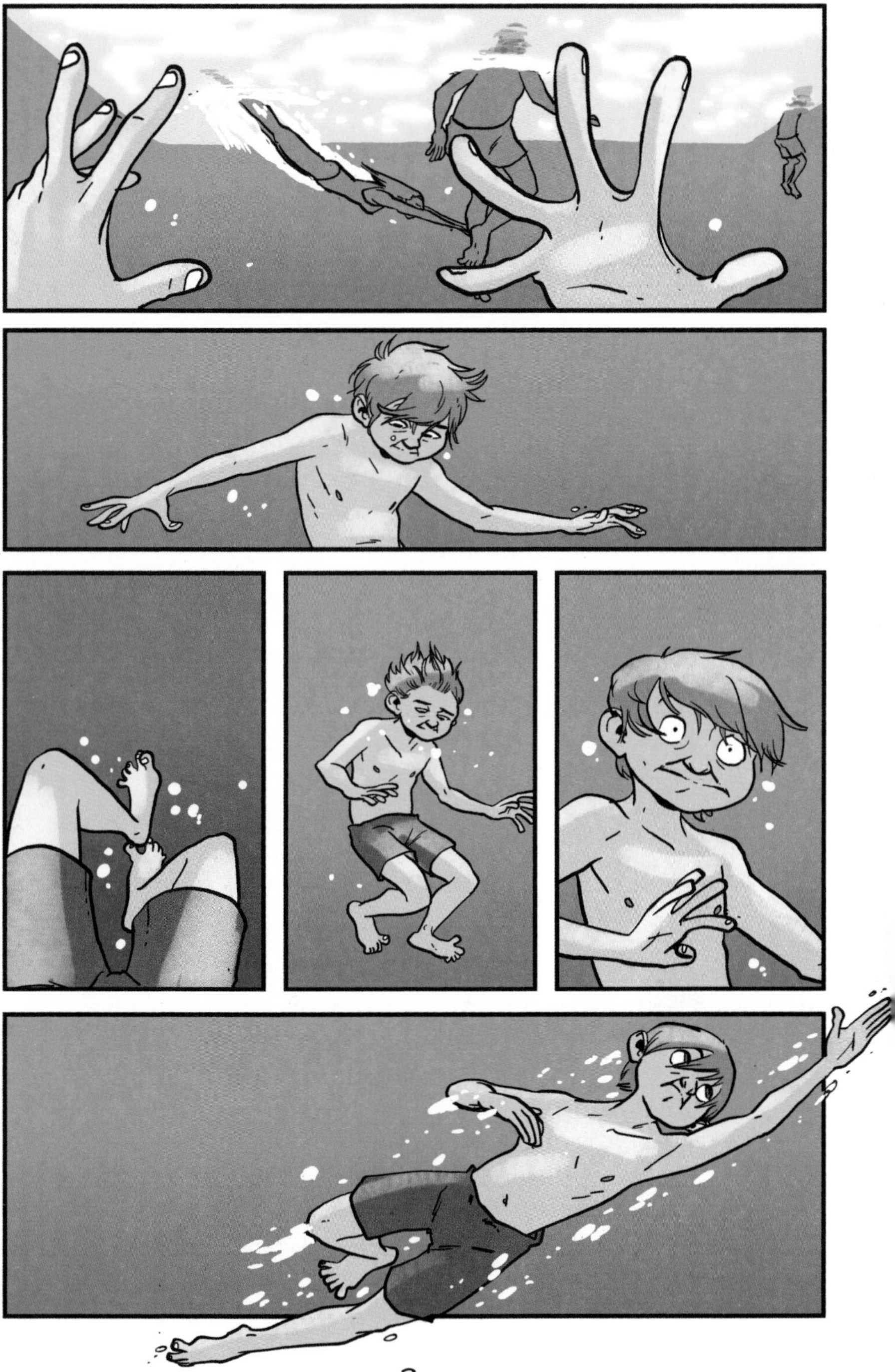

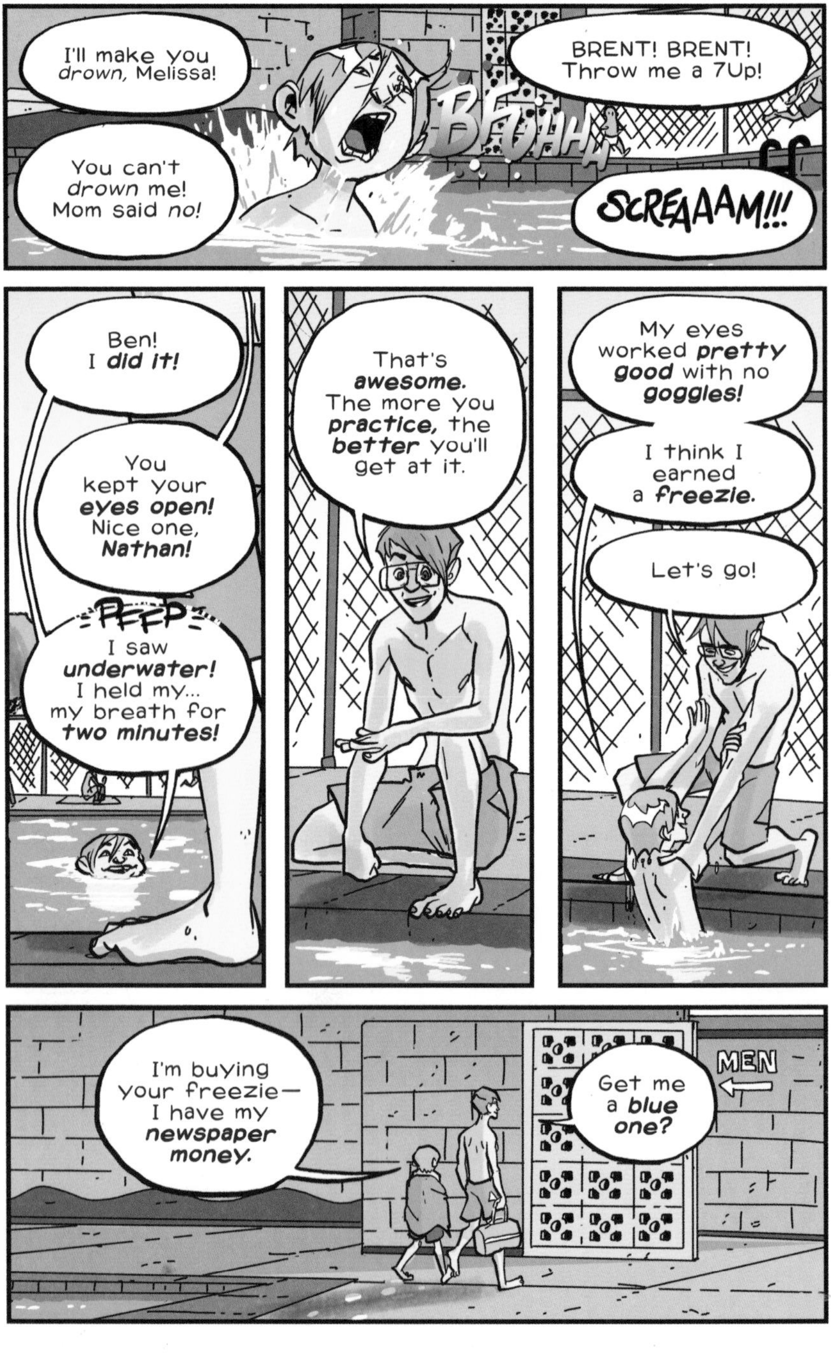
I'll make you *drown,* Melissa!
You can't *drown* me! Mom said *no!*
BFOHHH
BRENT! BRENT! Throw me a 7Up!
SCREAAAM!!!
Ben! I **did it!**
You kept your **eyes open!** Nice one, **Nathan!**
PFFP
I saw **underwater!** I held my... my breath for **two minutes!**
That's **awesome.** The more you **practice,** the **better** you'll get at it.
My eyes worked **pretty good** with no **goggles!**
I think I earned a **freezie.**
Let's go!
I'm buying your freezie— I have my **newspaper money.**
Get me a **blue one?**
MEN

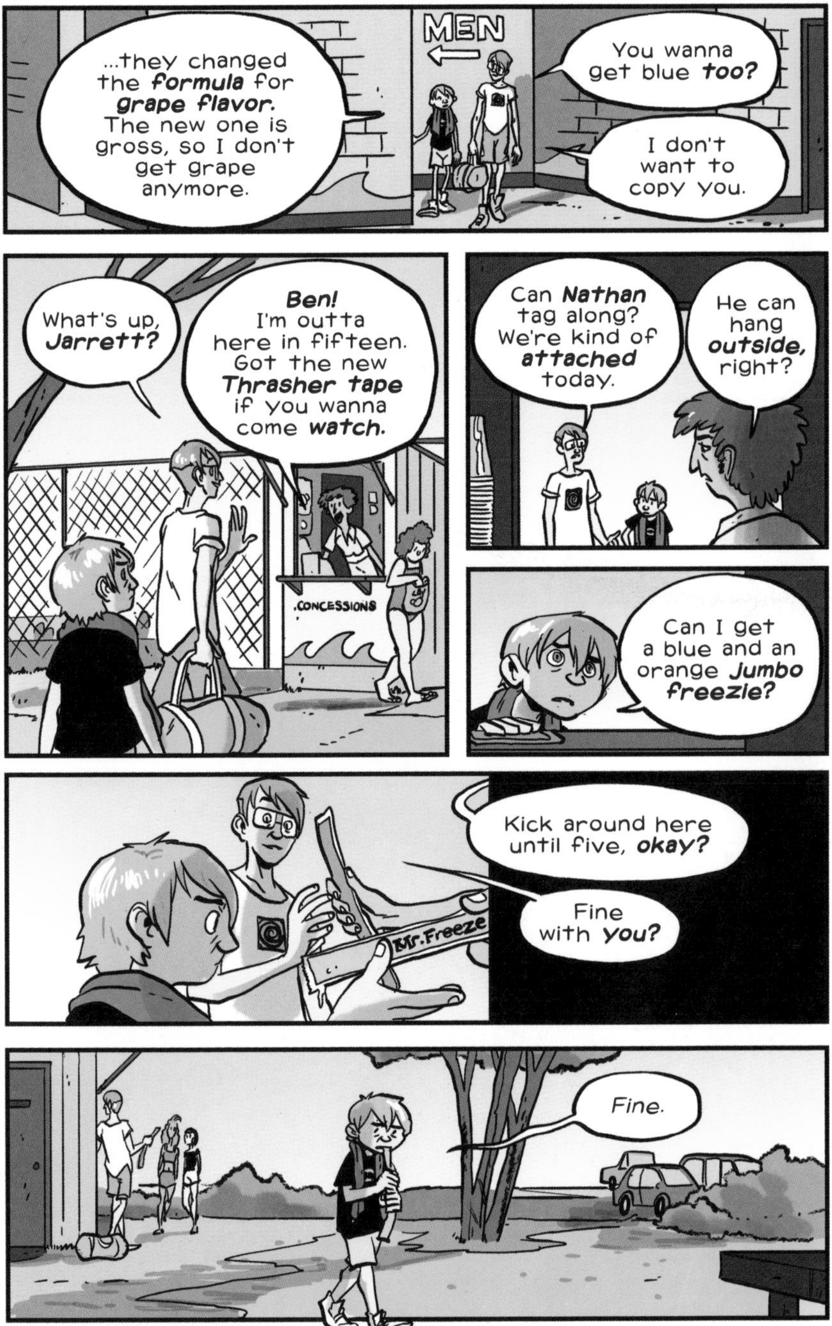
...they changed the formula for grape flavor. The new one is gross, so I don't get grape anymore.
MEN
You wanna get blue too?
I don't want to copy you.
What's up, Jarrett?
Ben! I'm outta here in fifteen. Got the new Thrasher tape if you wanna come watch.
CONCESSIONS
Can Nathan tag along? We're kind of attached today.
He can hang outside, right?
Can I get a blue and an orange Jumbo freezie?
Kick around here until five, okay?
Fine with you?
Mr. Freeze
Fine.

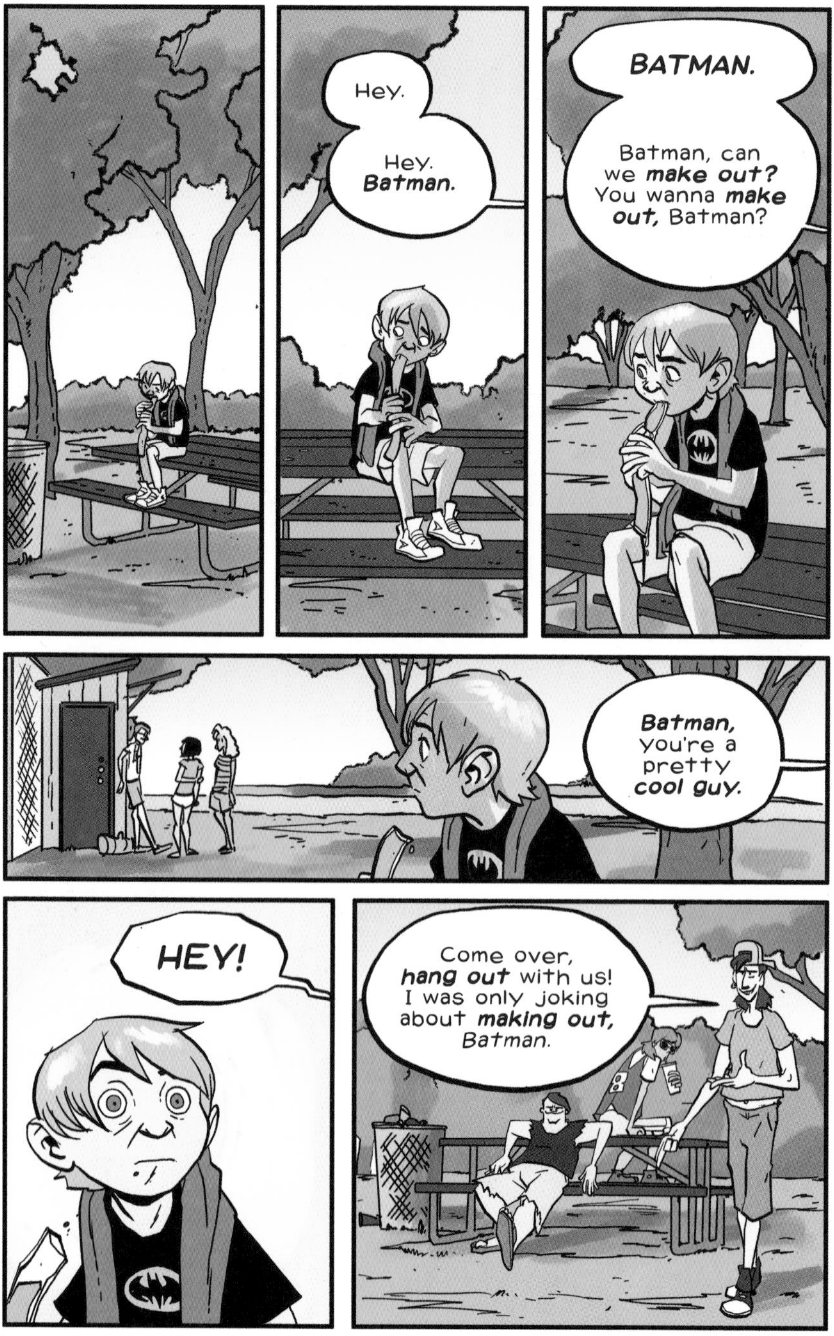
Hey.
Hey. Batman.
BATMAN.
Batman, can we make out? You wanna make out, Batman?
Batman, you're a pretty cool guy.
HEY!
Come over, hang out with us! I was only joking about making out, Batman.

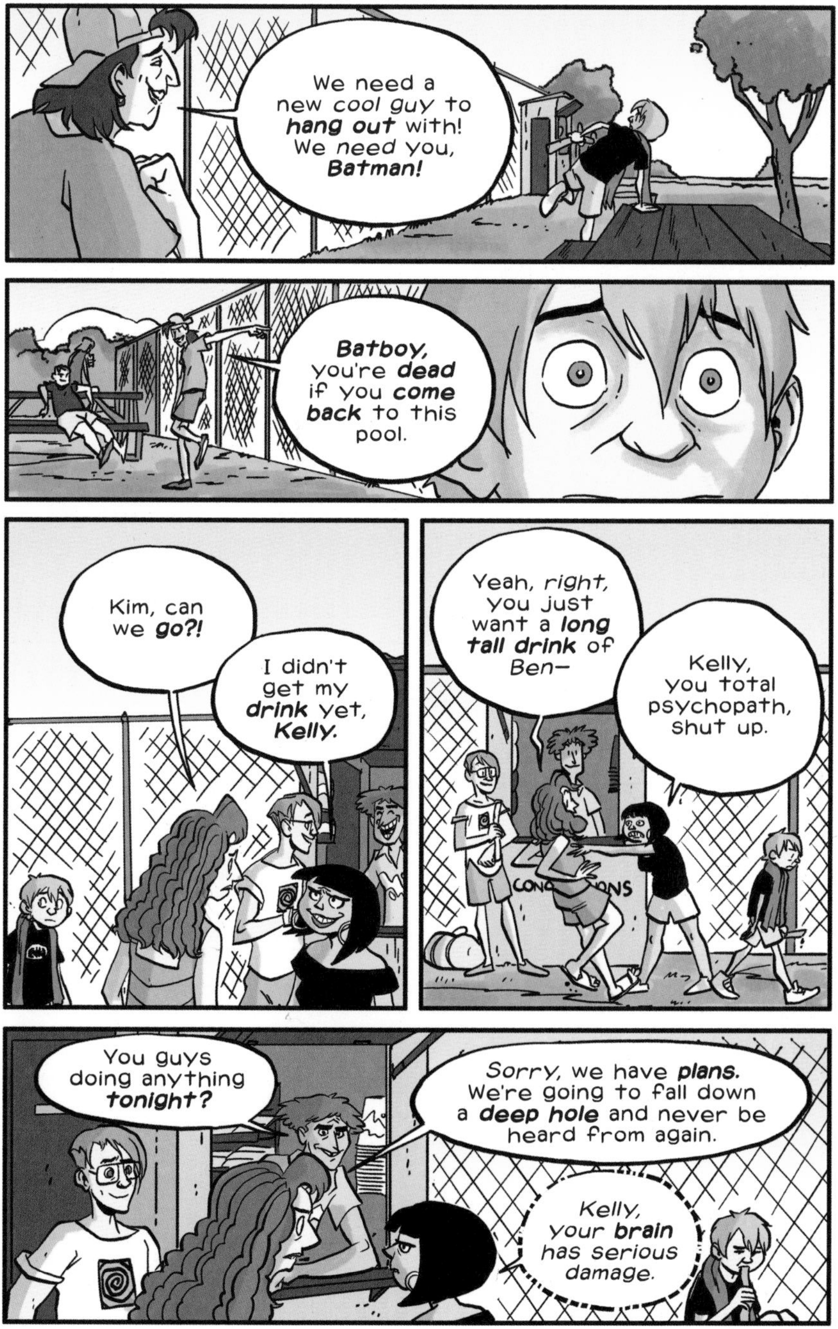
We need a new *cool guy* to **hang out** with! We *need* you, **Batman!**
Batboy, you're **dead** if you **come back** to this pool.
Kim, can we **go?!**
I didn't get my **drink** yet, **Kelly.**
Yeah, *right*, you just want a **long tall drink** of *Ben—*
Kelly, you total psychopath, shut up.
You guys doing anything **tonight?**
Sorry, we have **plans.** We're going to fall down a **deep hole** and never be heard from again.
*Kelly, your **brain** has serious damage.*

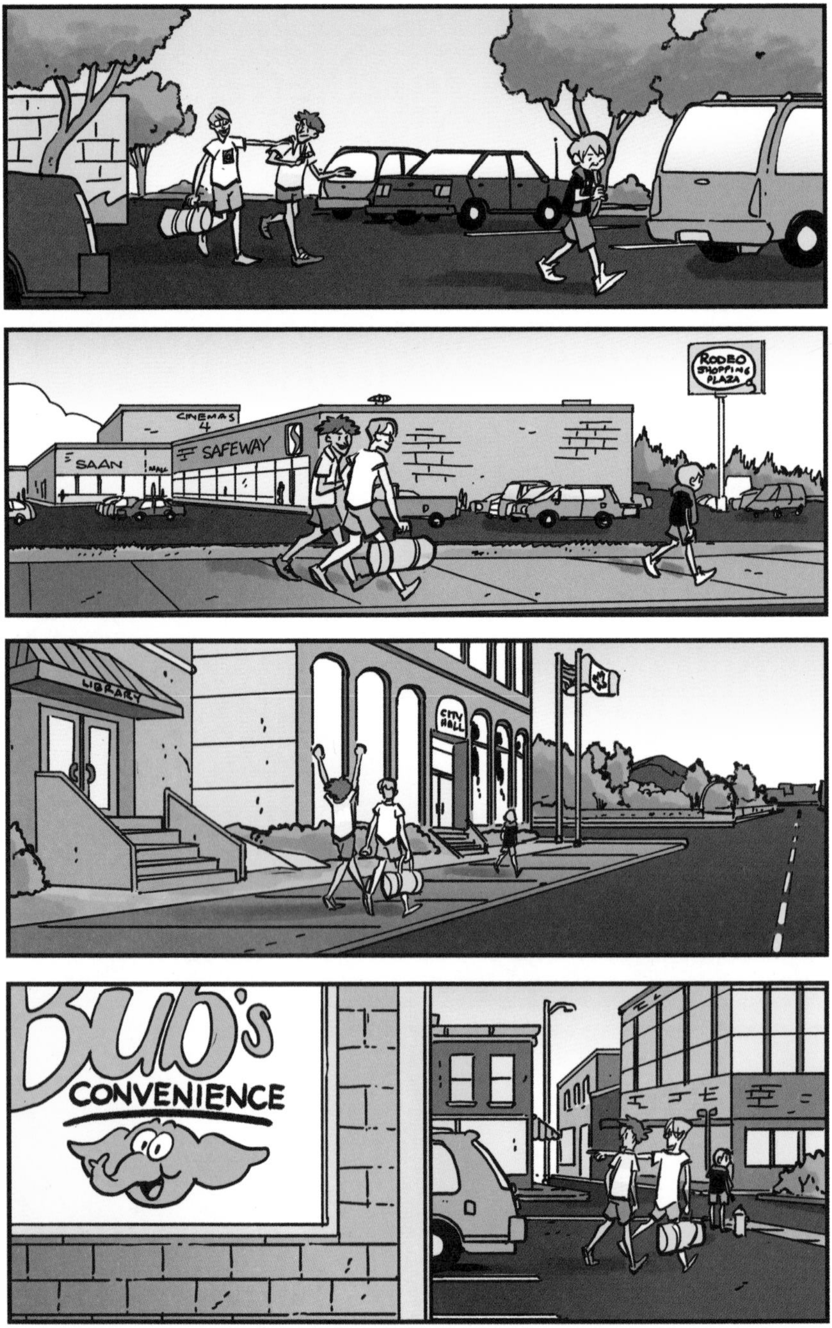

RODEO SHOPPING PLAZA
CINEMAS 4
SAAN
SAFEWAY
LIBRARY
CITY HALL
Bub's
CONVENIENCE

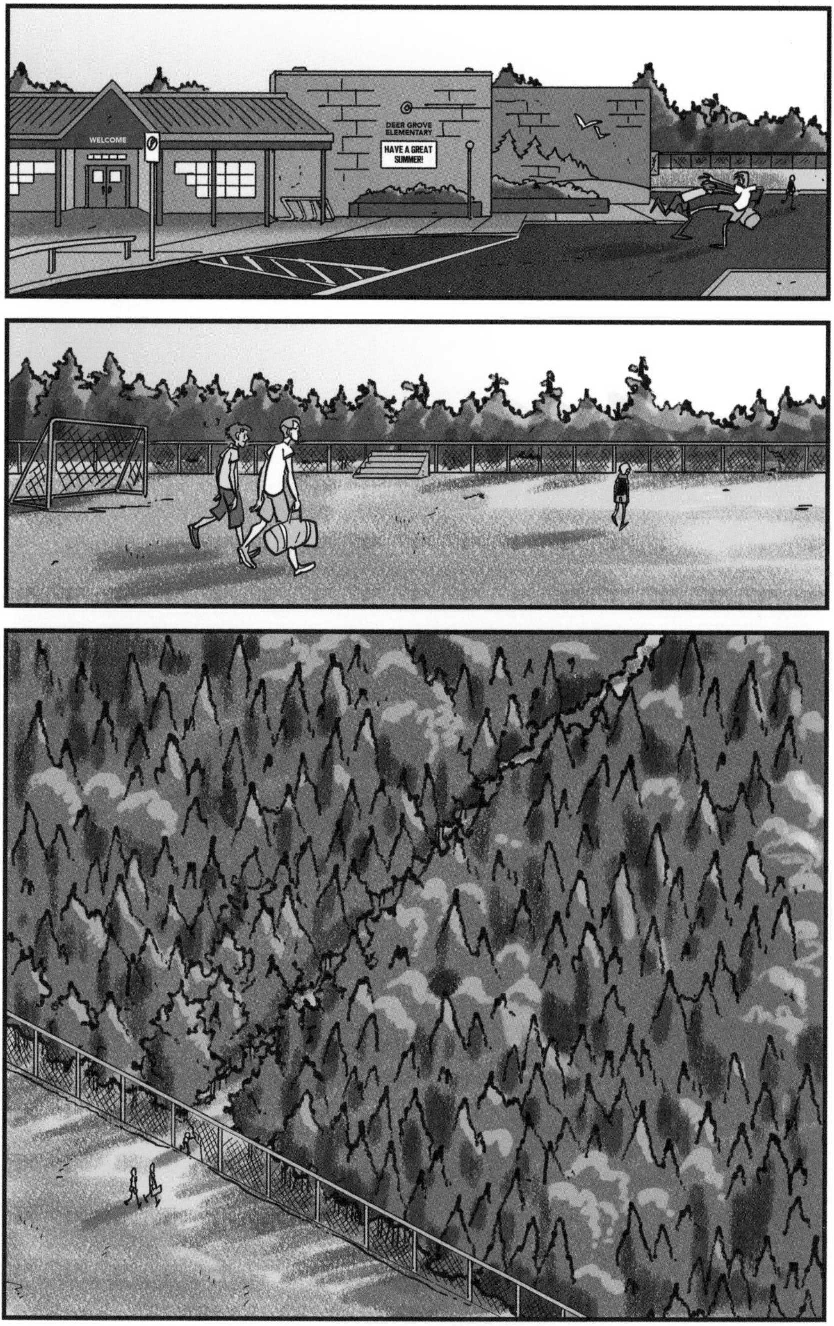
WELCOME
DEER GROVE ELEMENTARY
HAVE A GREAT SUMMER!

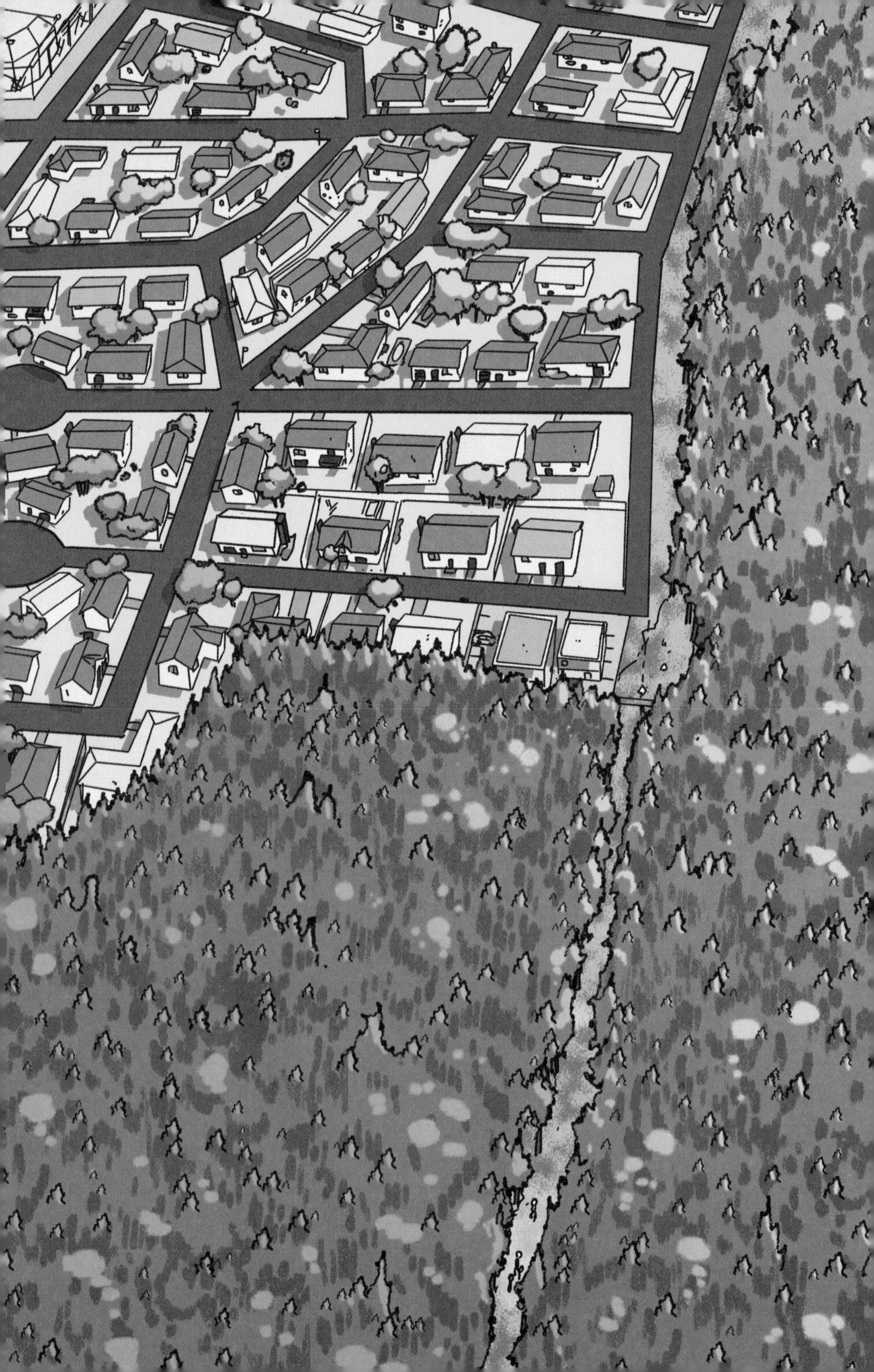

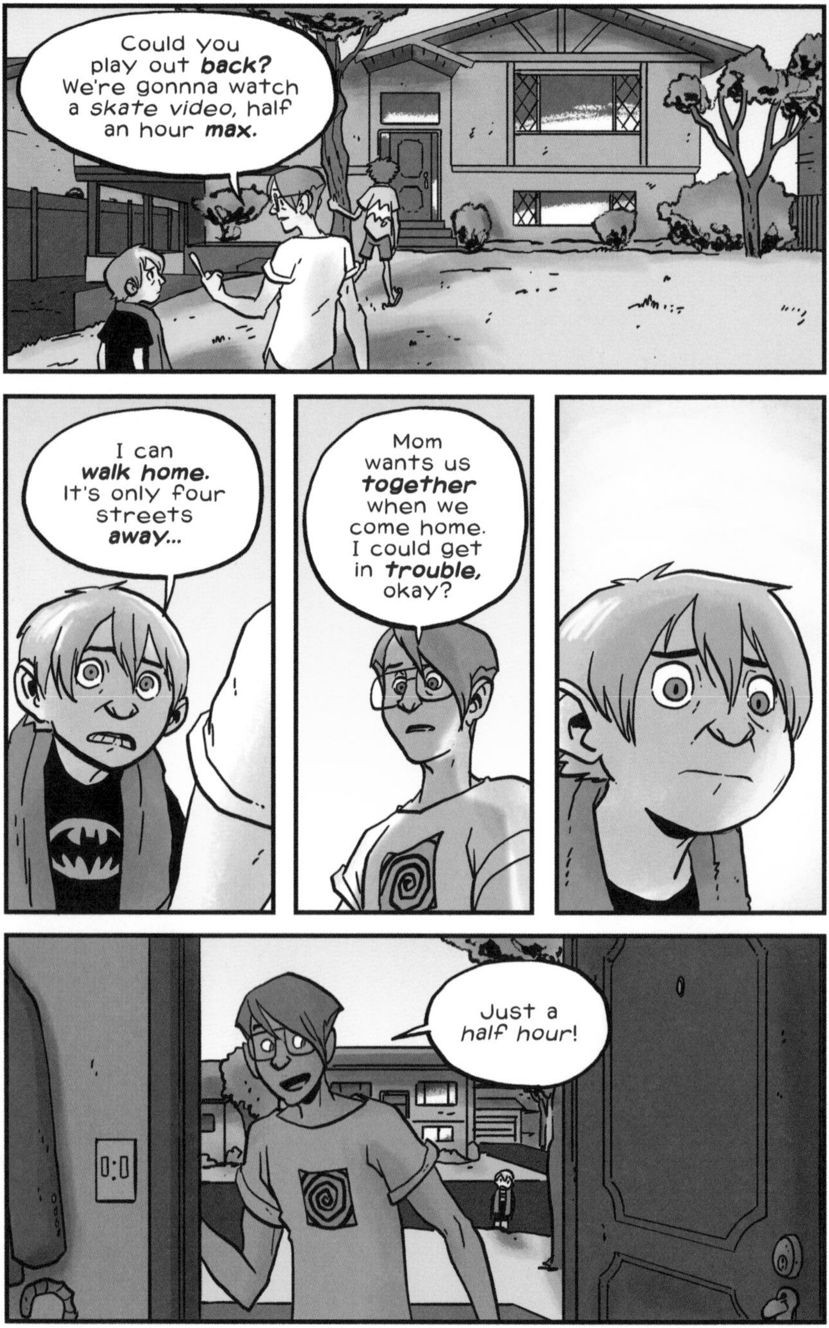
Could you play out **back?** We're gonnna watch a *skate video,* half an hour **max.**
I can **walk home.** It's only four streets **away...**
Mom wants us **together** when we come home. I could get in **trouble,** okay?
Just a *half hour!*

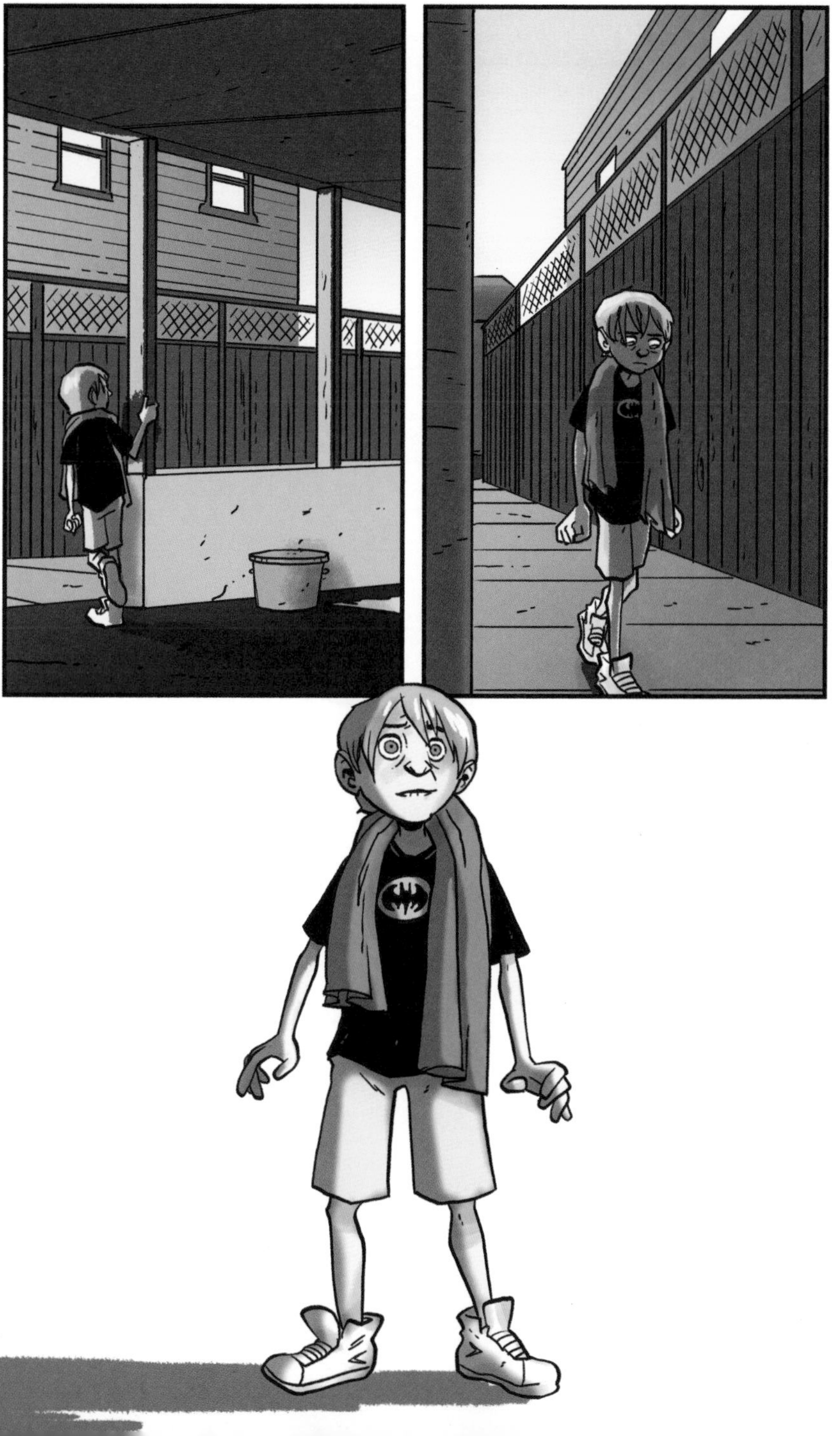

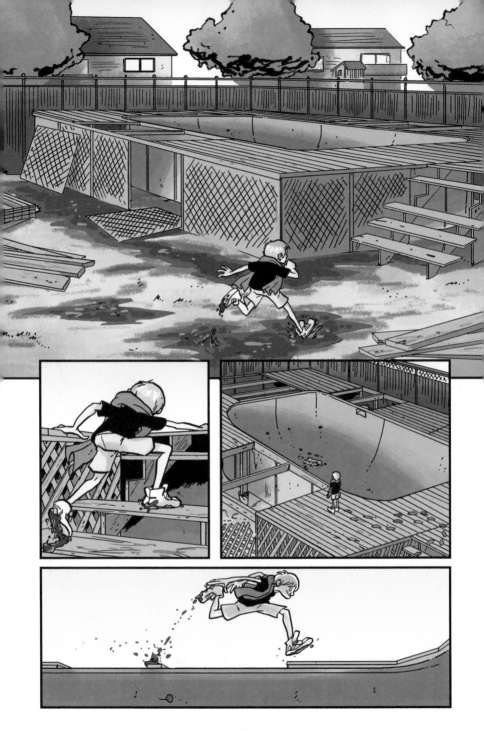

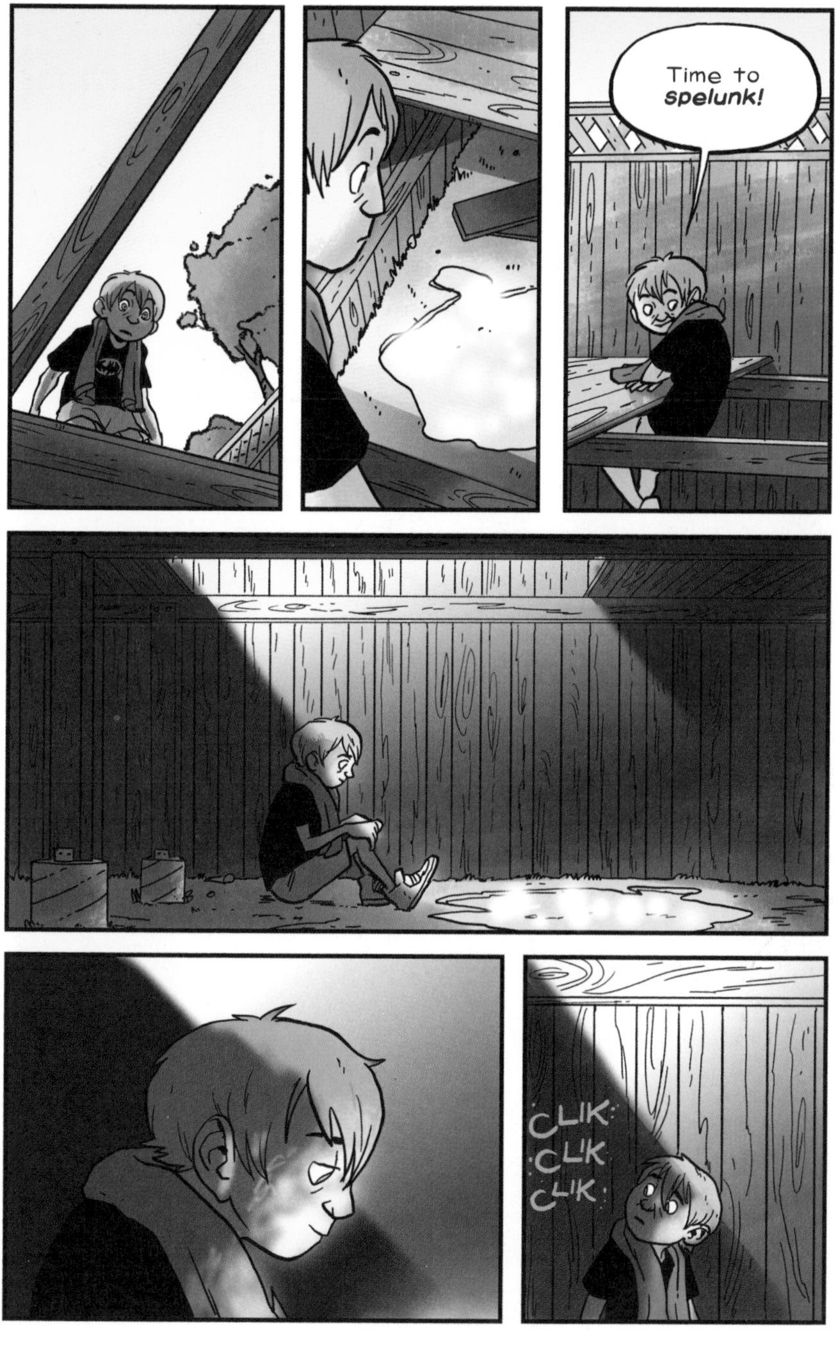
Time to spelunk!
CLIK CLIK CLIK

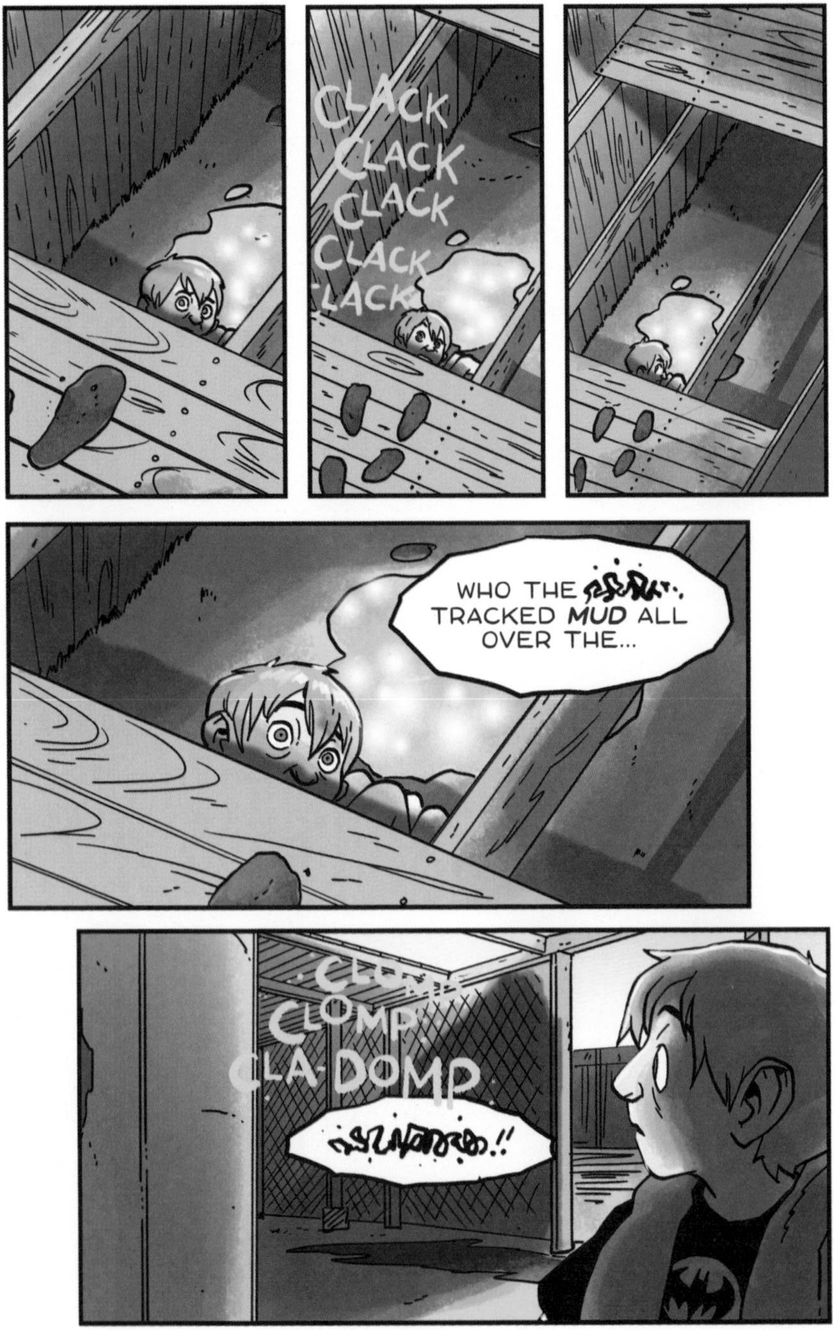
CLACK
CLACK
CLACK
CLACK
CLACK
WHO THE
TRACKED MUD ALL
OVER THE...
CLOMP
CLOMP
CLA-DOMP

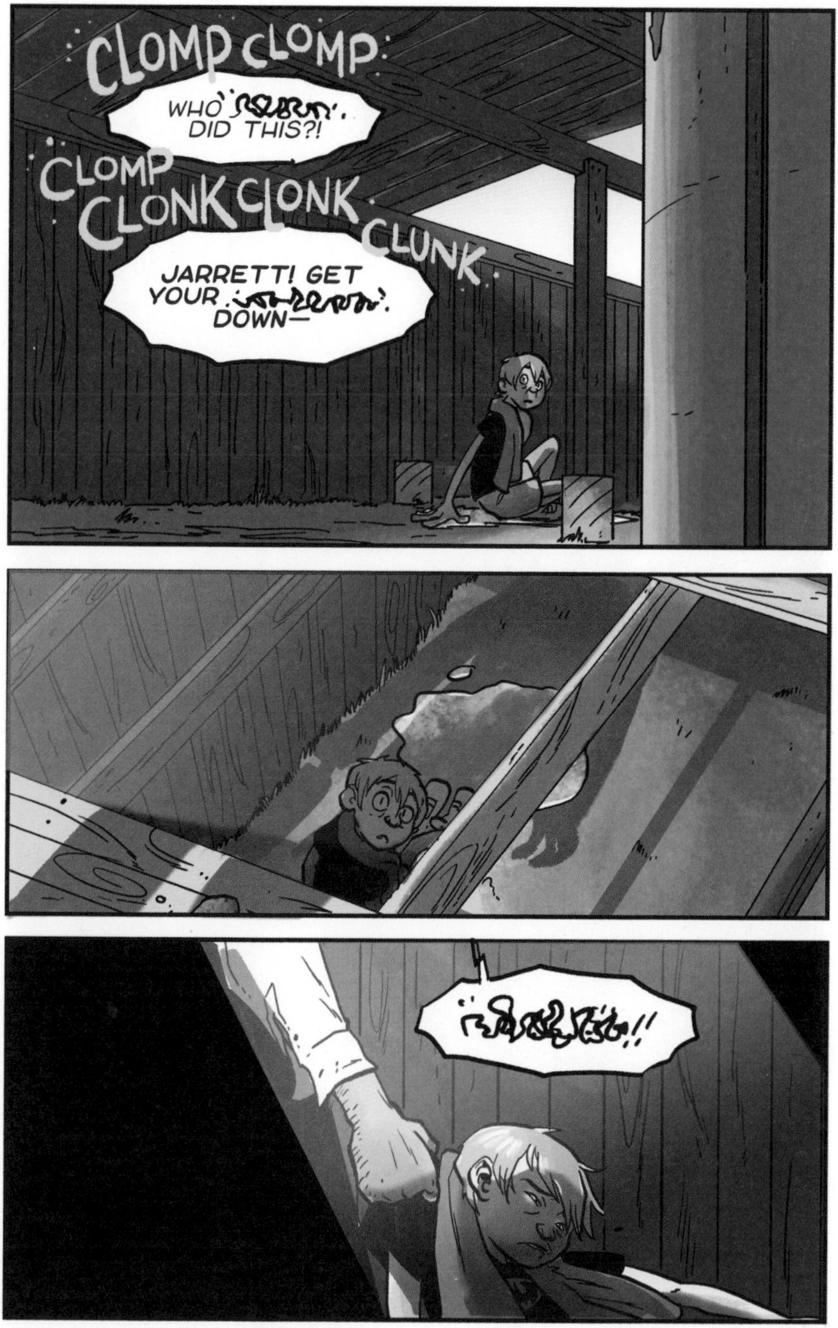
CLOMP CLOMP
WHO ... DID THIS?!
CLOMP
CLONK CLONK
CLUNK
JARRETT! GET YOUR ... DOWN—
!!

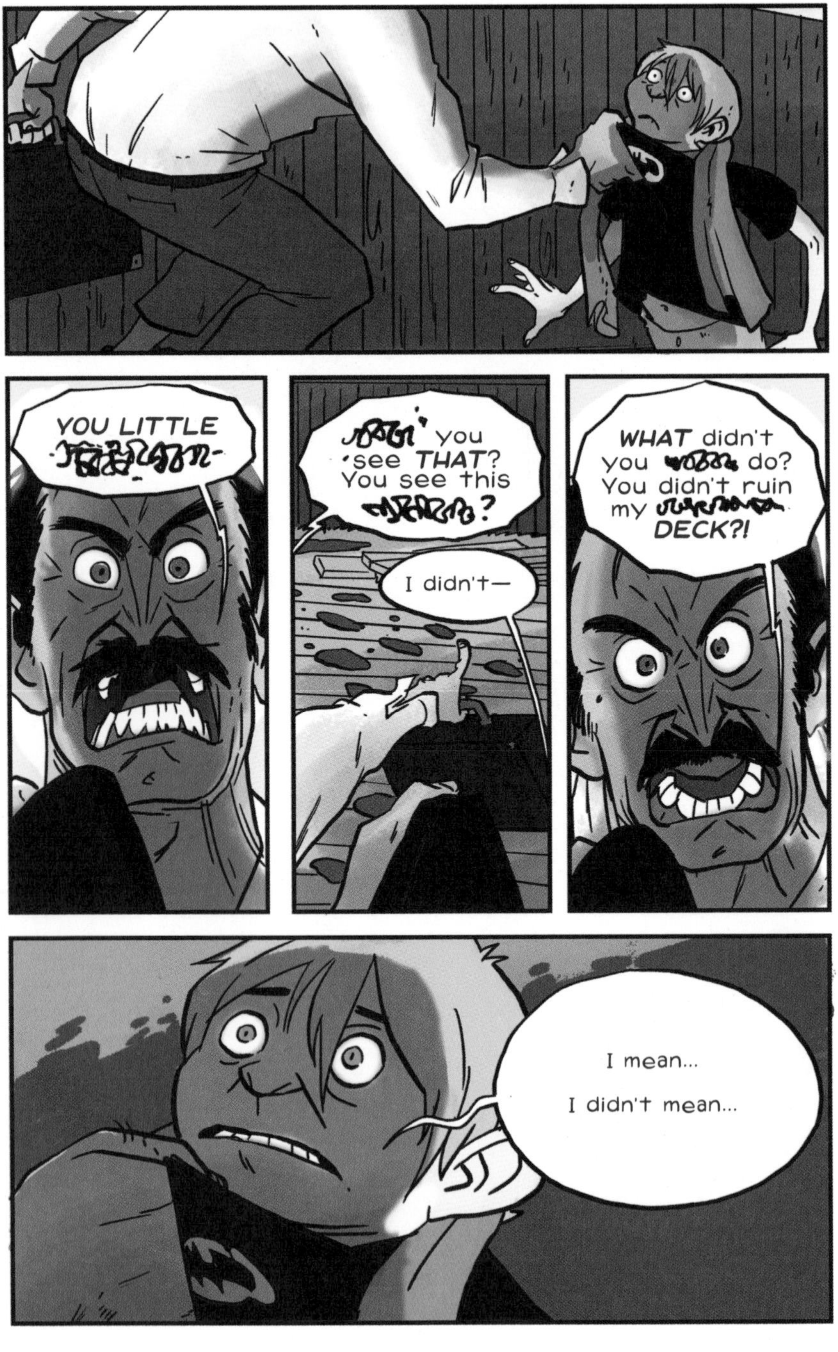
YOU LITTLE
you see THAT? You see this ?
I didn't—
WHAT didn't you do? You didn't ruin my DECK?!
I mean...
I didn't mean...

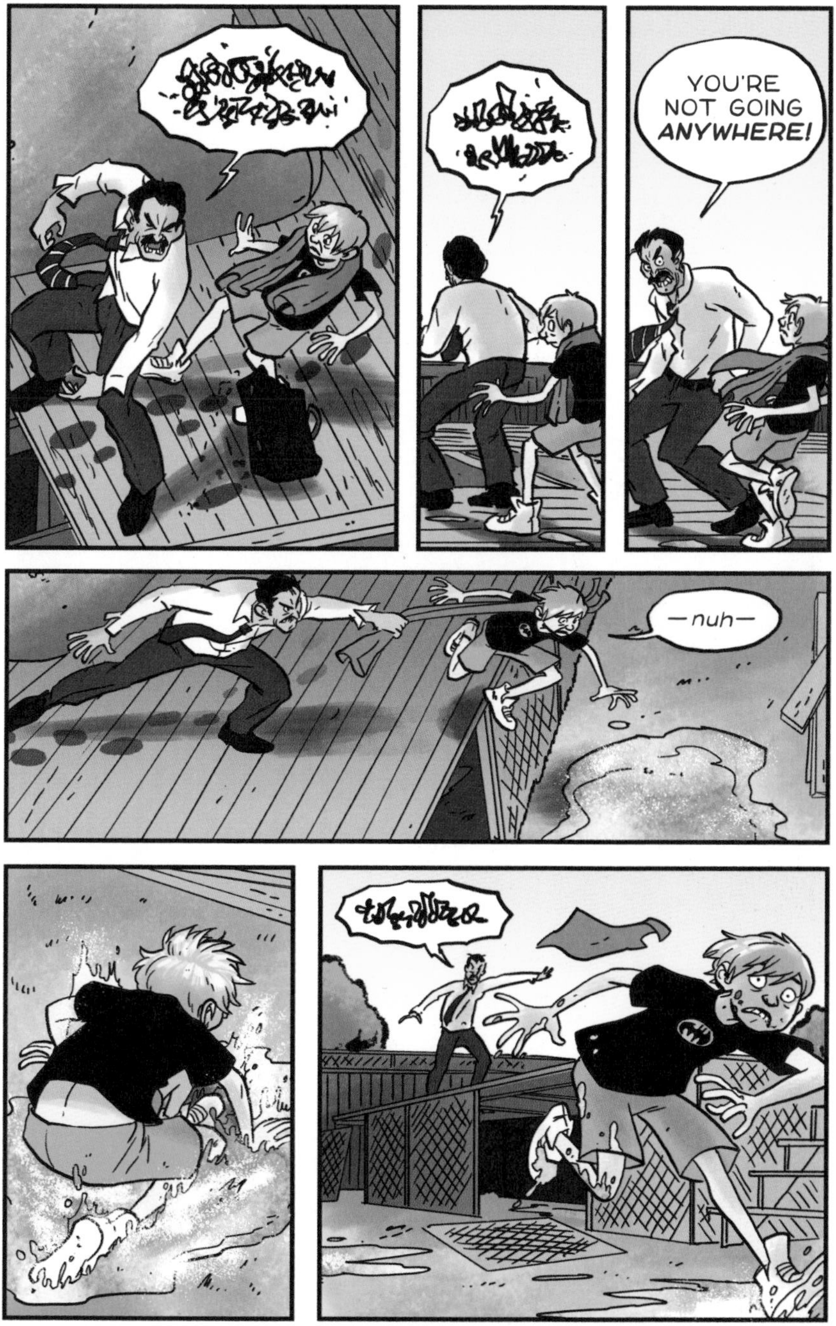
YOU'RE NOT GOING ANYWHERE!
—nuh—

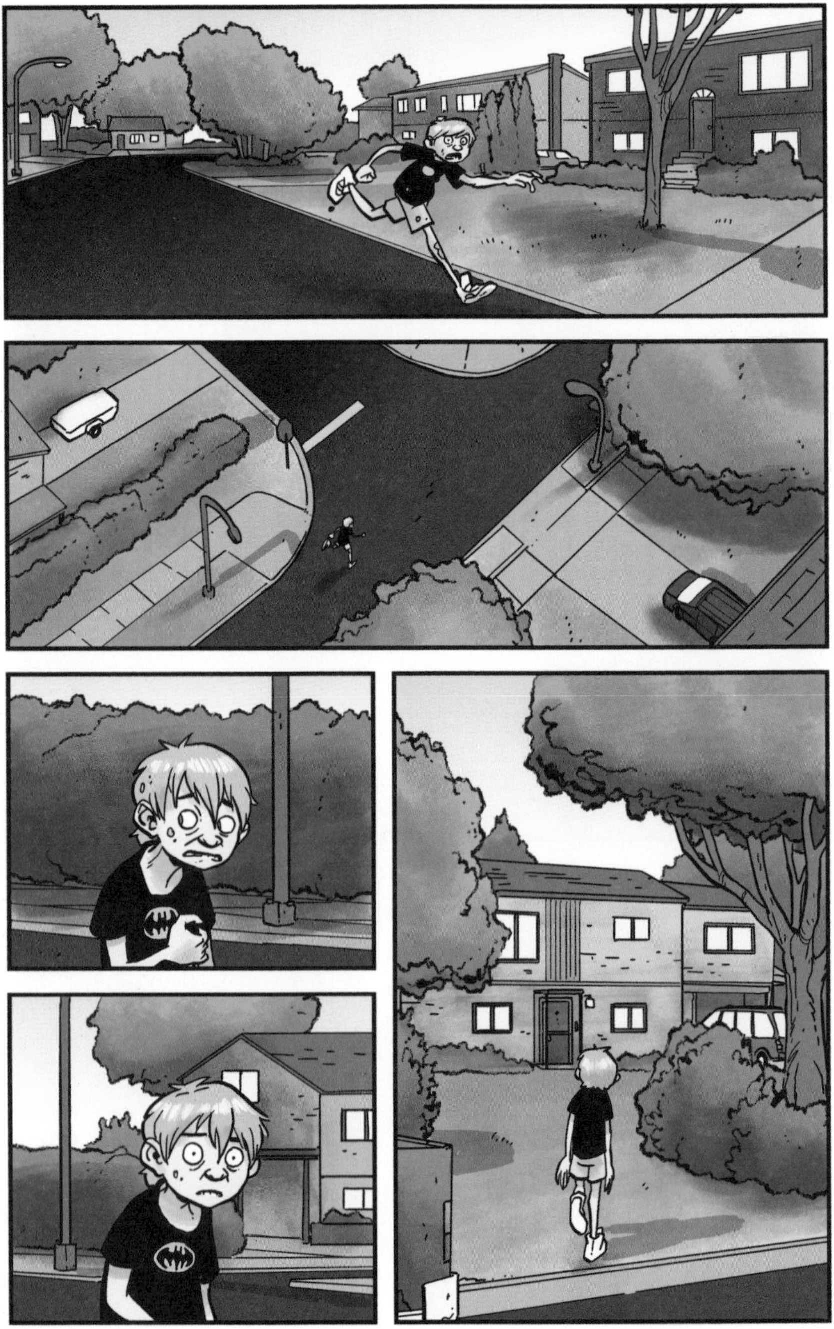

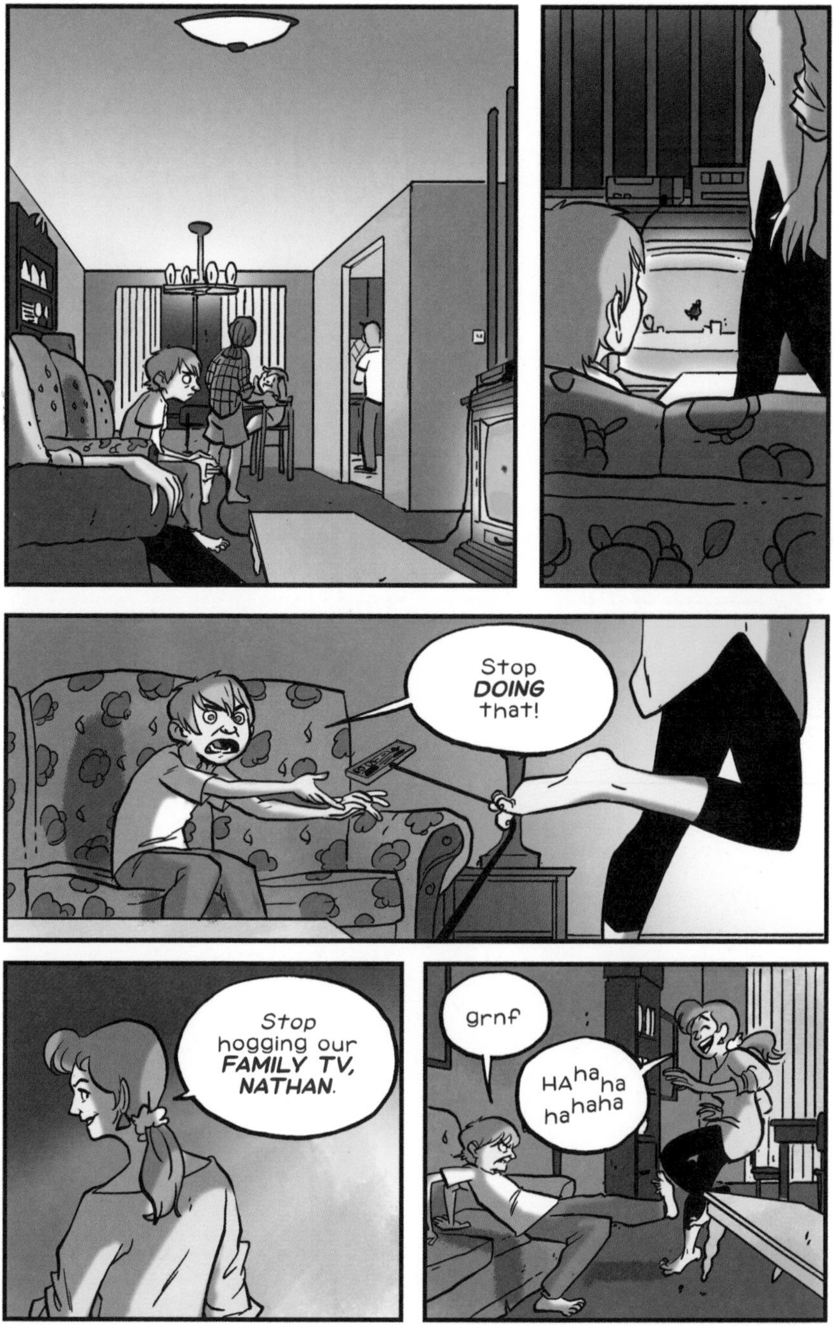
Stop
DOING
that!
Stop
hogging our
FAMILY TV,
NATHAN.
grnf
HAhaha
hahaha

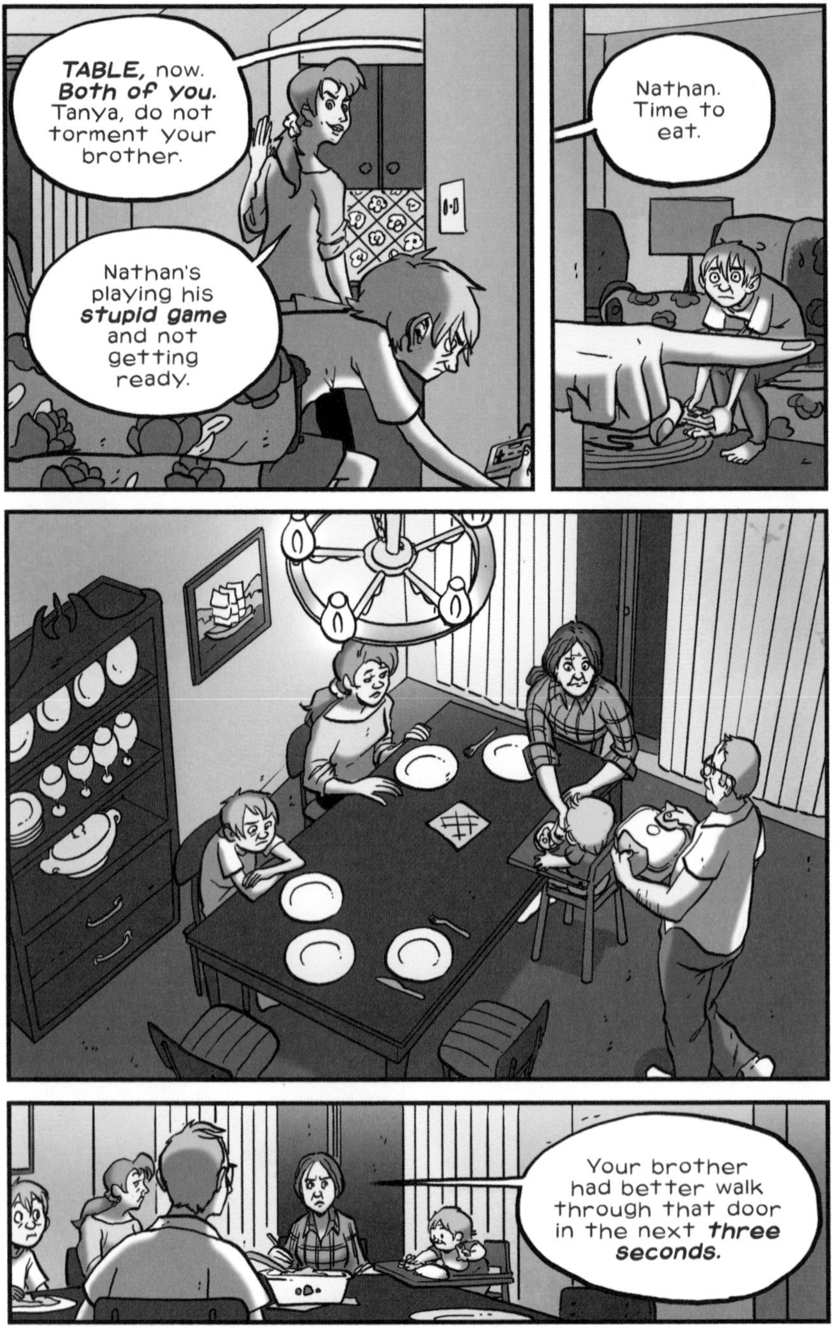
TABLE, now. ***Both of you.*** Tanya, do not torment your brother.
Nathan's playing his ***stupid game*** and not getting ready.
Nathan. Time to eat.
Your brother had better walk through that door in the next ***three seconds.***

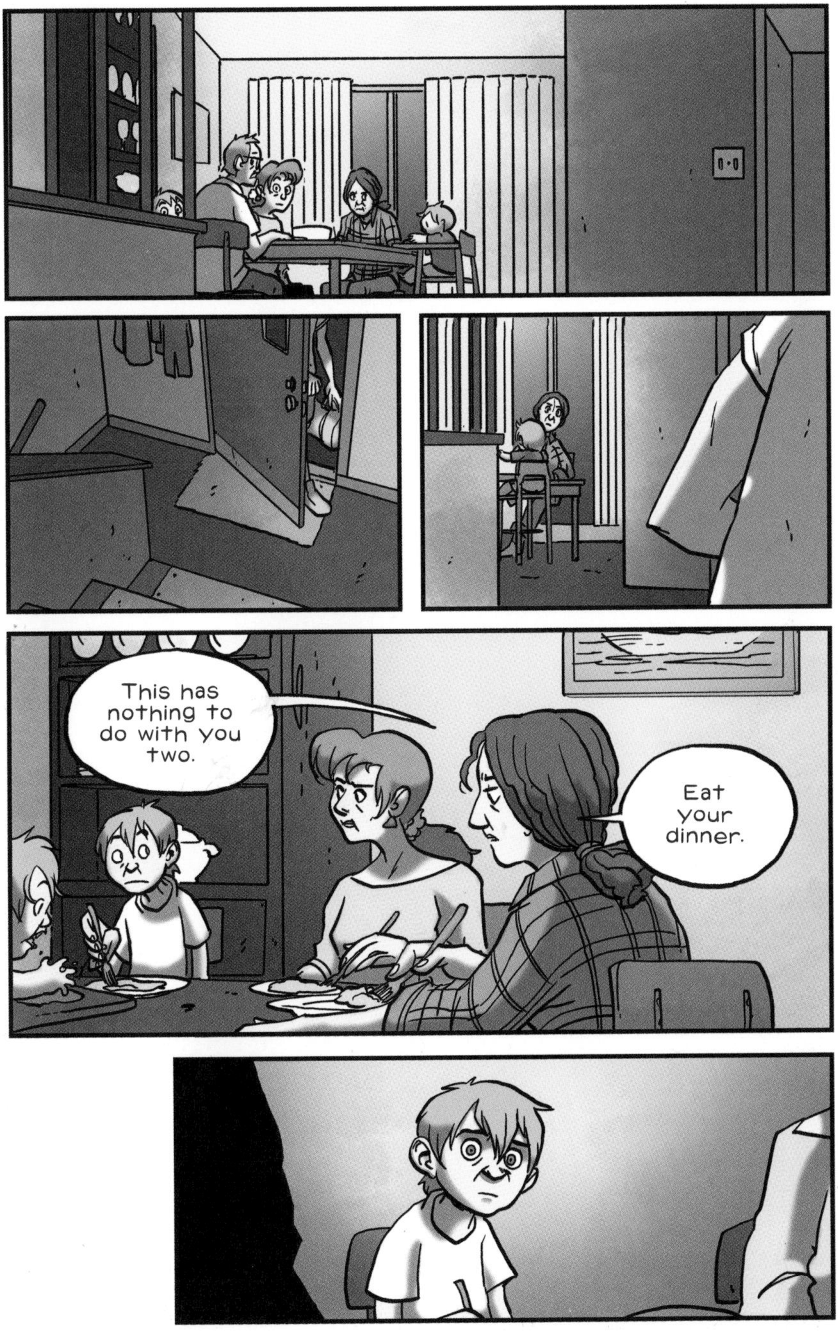
This has nothing to do with you two.
Eat your dinner.

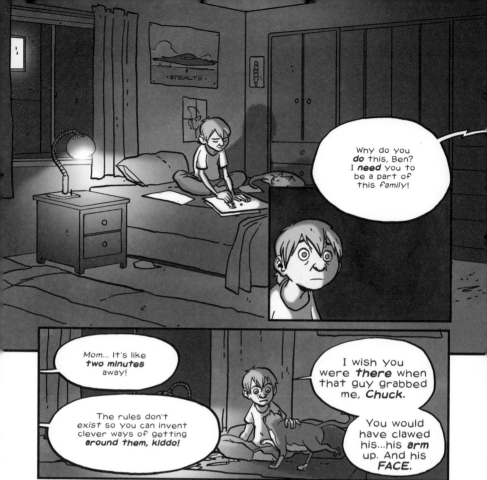

Why do you **do** this, Ben? I **need** you to be a part of this **family**!

Mom... It's like **two minutes** away!

The rules don't *exist* so you can invent clever ways of getting **around them, kiddo!**

I wish you were **there** when that guy grabbed me, **Chuck.**

You would have clawed his...his **arm** up. And his **FACE.**

You're my **only** best **friend.** You **understand** me.

DO not— **EVER**— leave your brother again.

I didn't **leave** him! He was—

BEN! NEVER! Do you understand?!

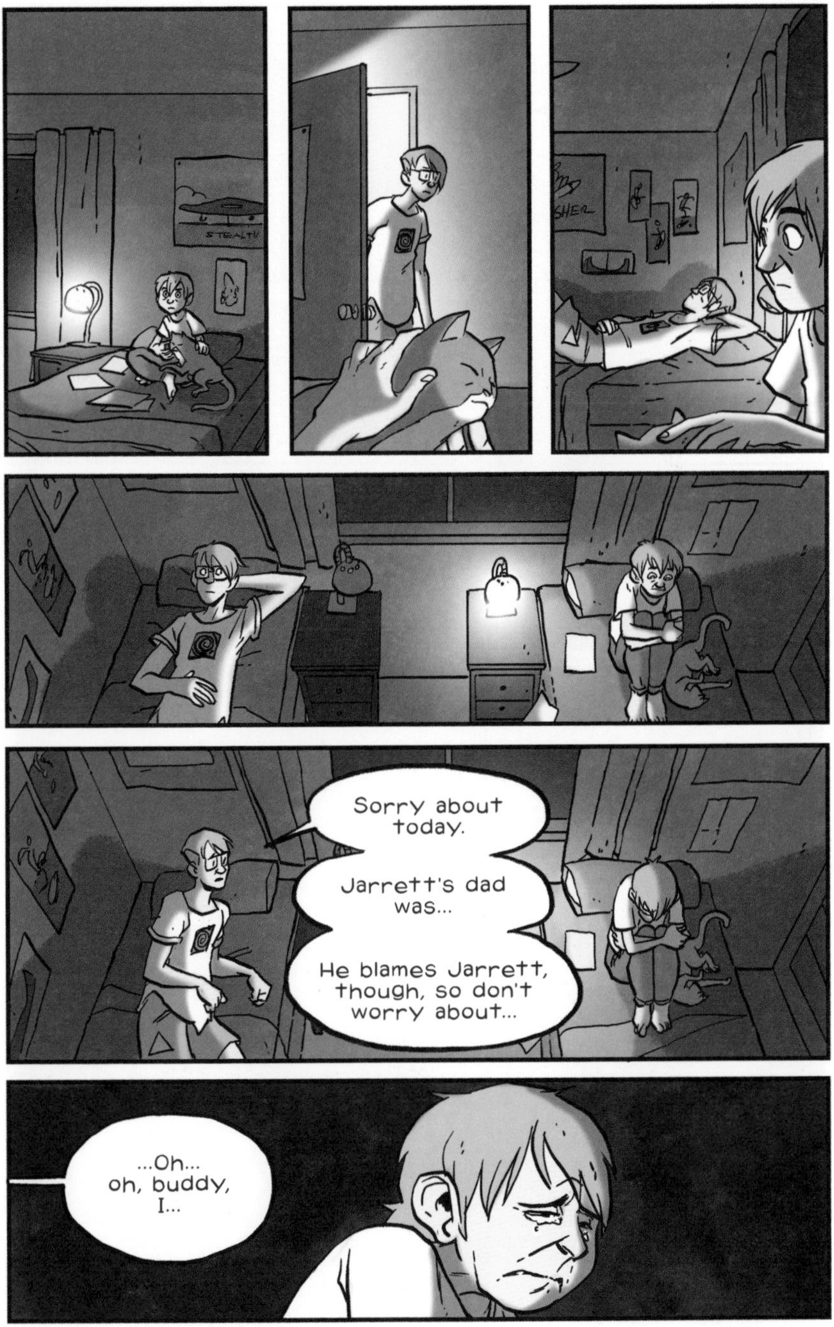
Sorry about today.
Jarrett's dad was...
He blames Jarrett, though, so don't worry about...
...Oh... oh, buddy, I...

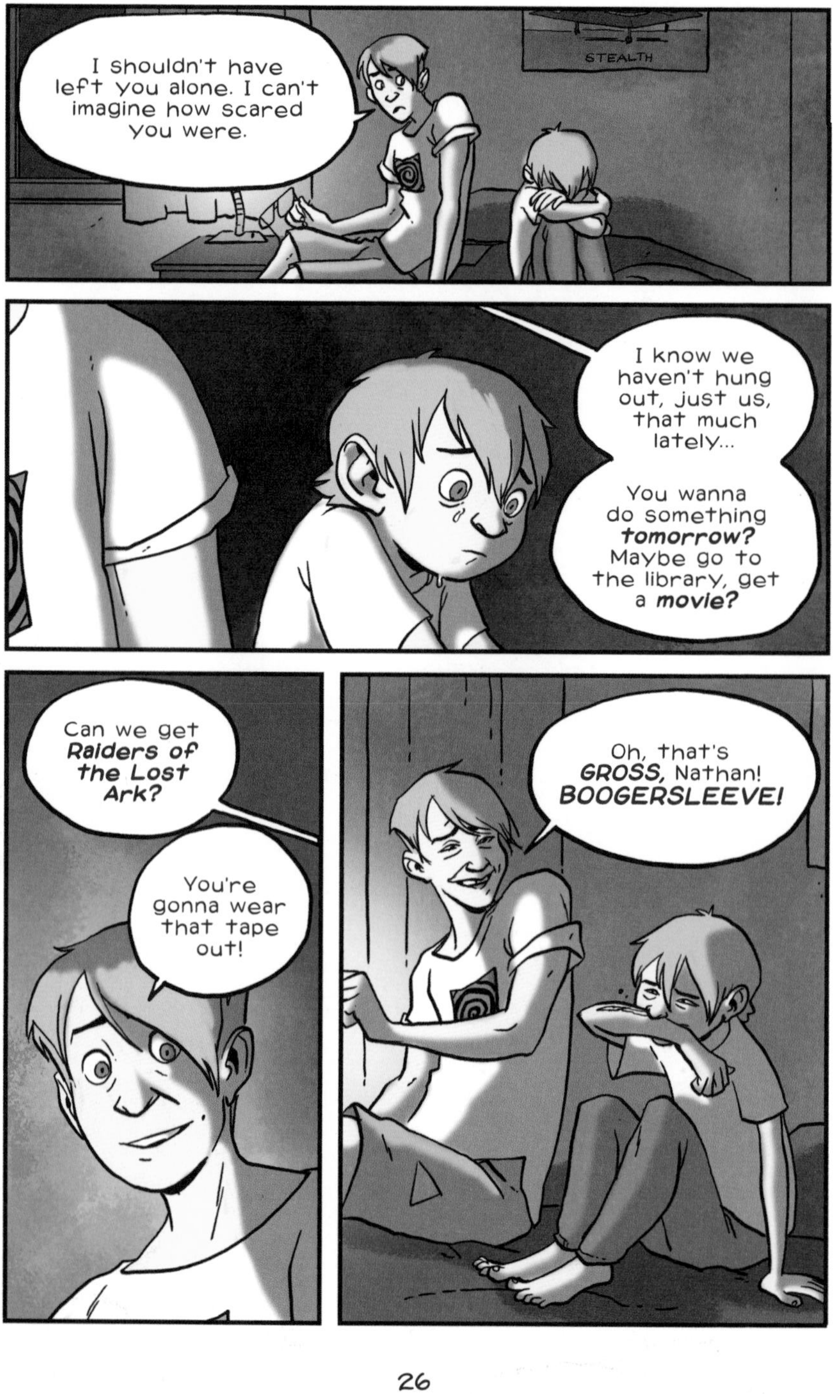

STEALTH
I shouldn't have left you alone. I can't imagine how scared you were.
I know we haven't hung out, just us, that much lately...
You wanna do something ***tomorrow?*** Maybe go to the library, get a ***movie?***
Can we get ***Raiders of the Lost Ark?***
You're gonna wear that tape out!
Oh, that's ***GROSS,*** Nathan! ***BOOGERSLEEVE!***

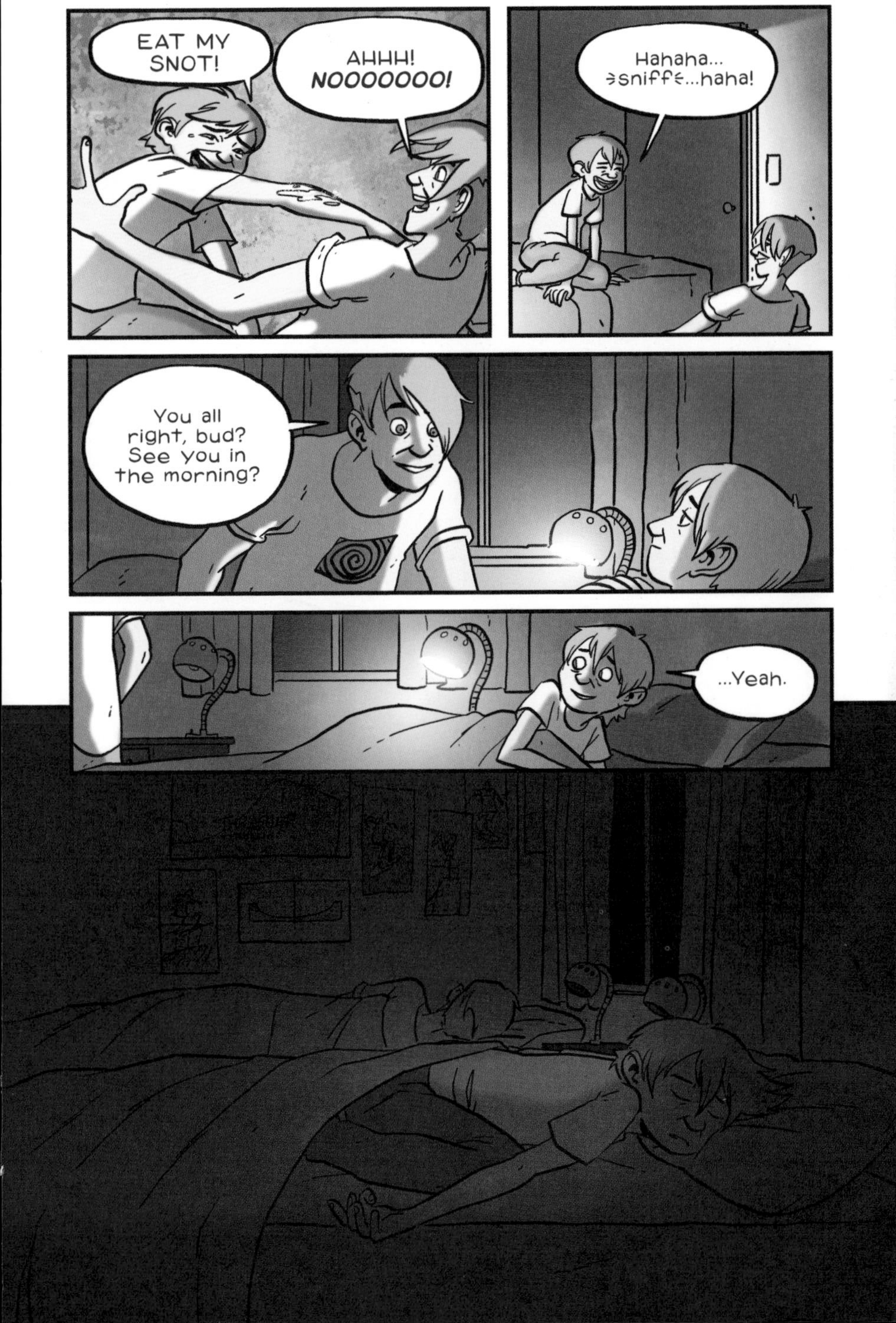
EAT MY SNOT!
AHHH! NOOOOOOO!
Hahaha... ≥sniff≤...haha!
You all right, bud? See you in the morning?
...Yeah.

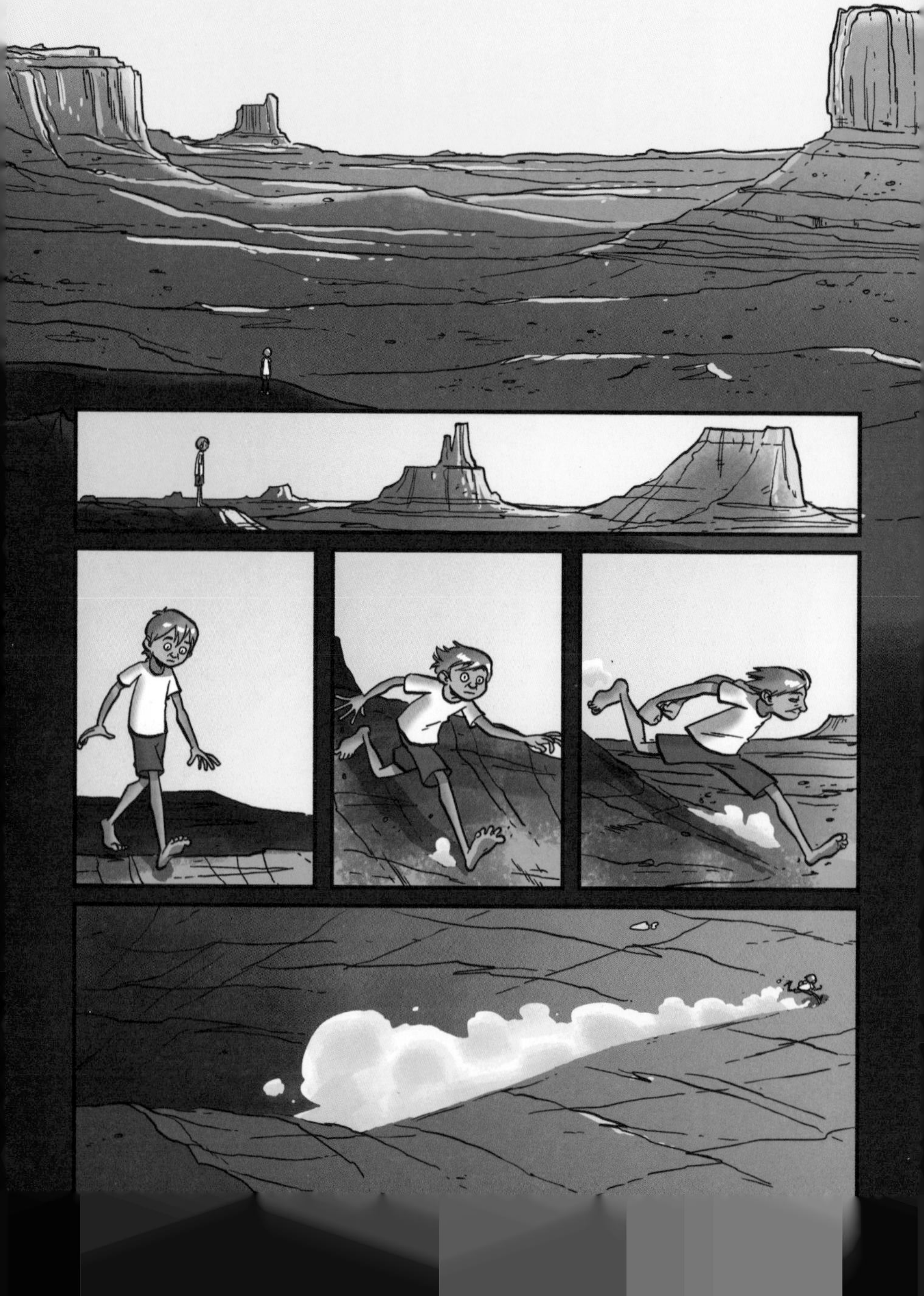

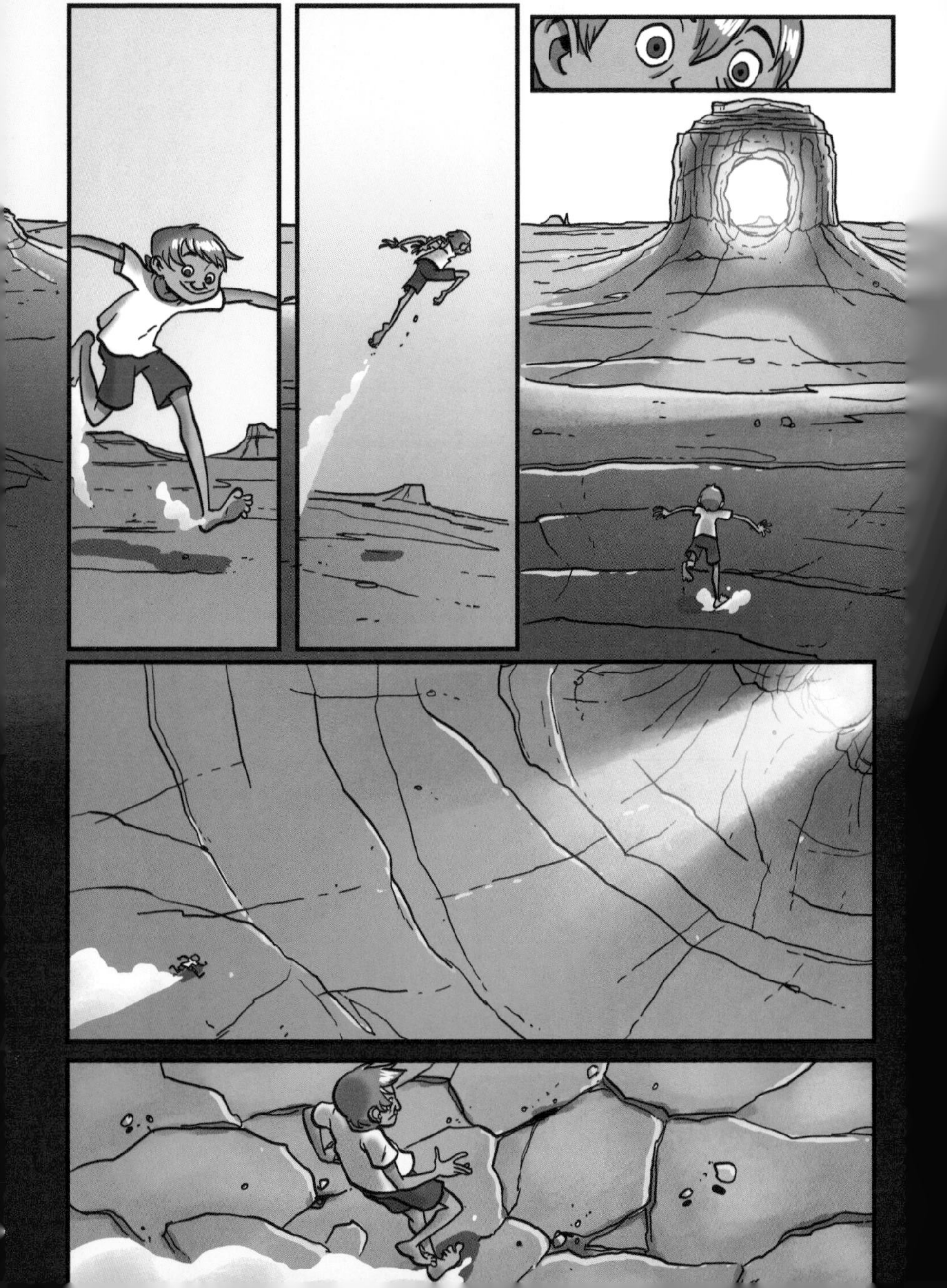

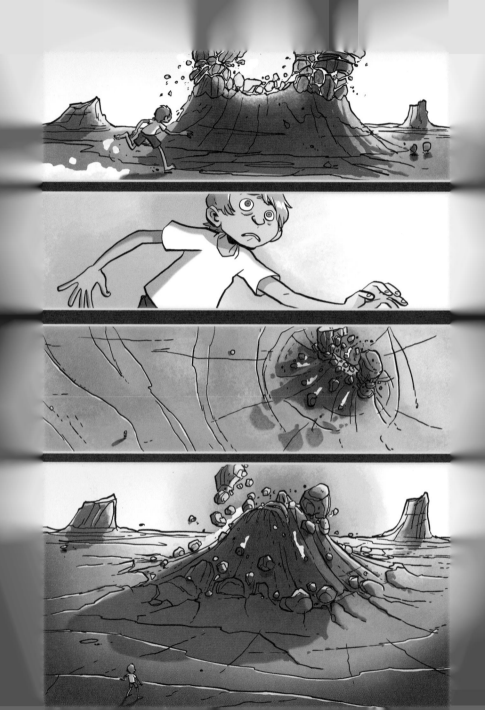

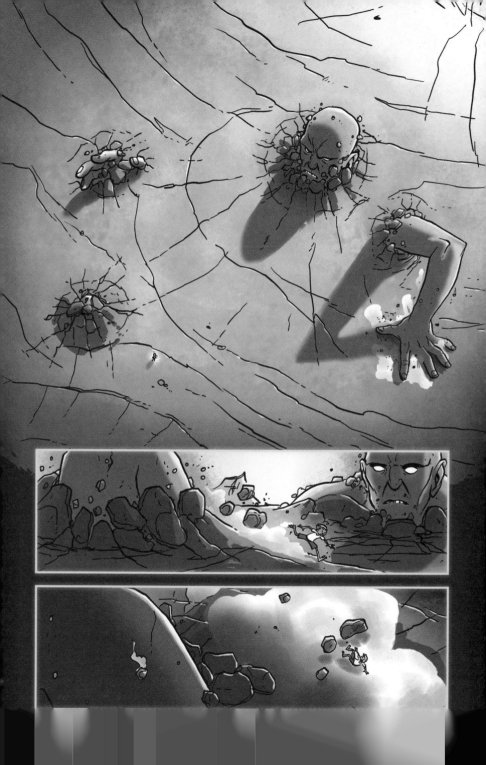

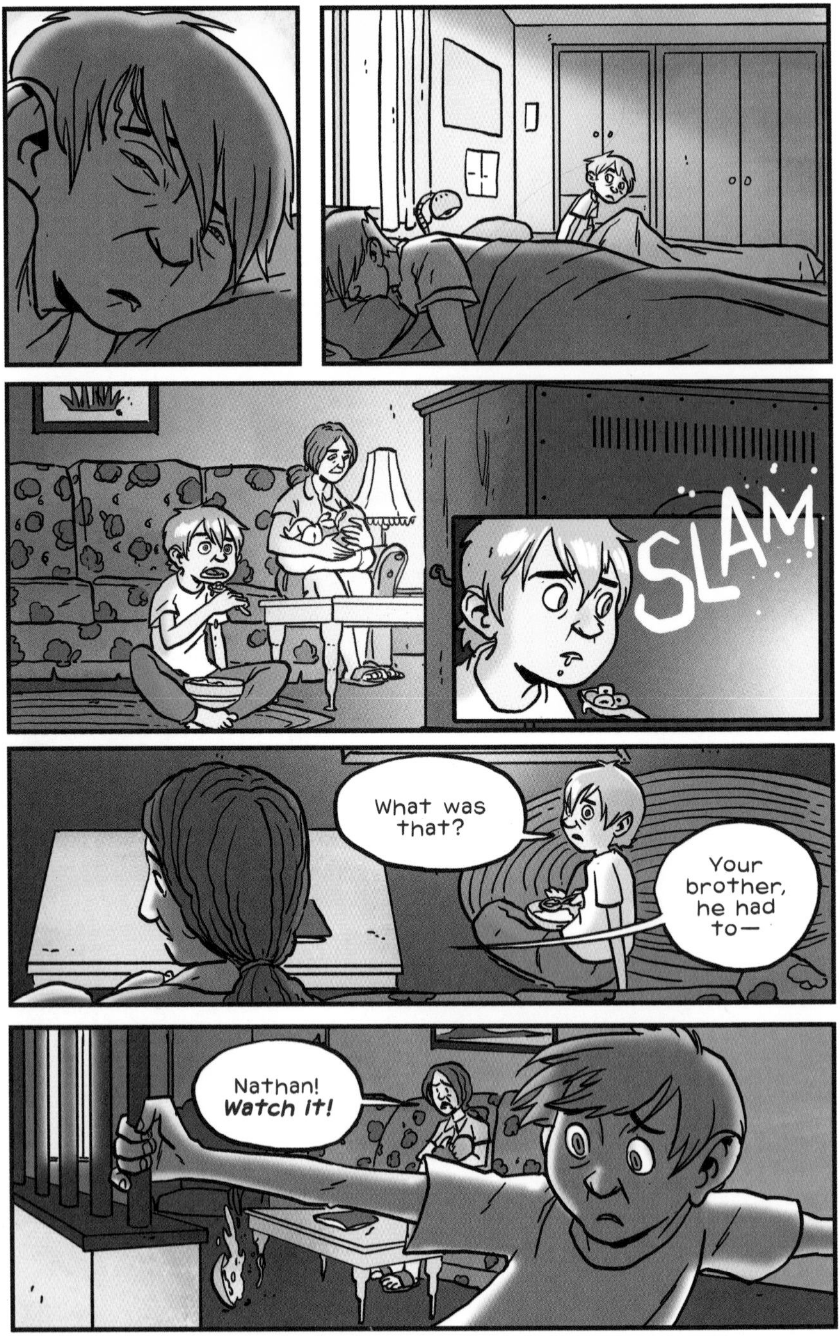
SLAM
What was that?
Your brother, he had to—
Nathan! **Watch it!**

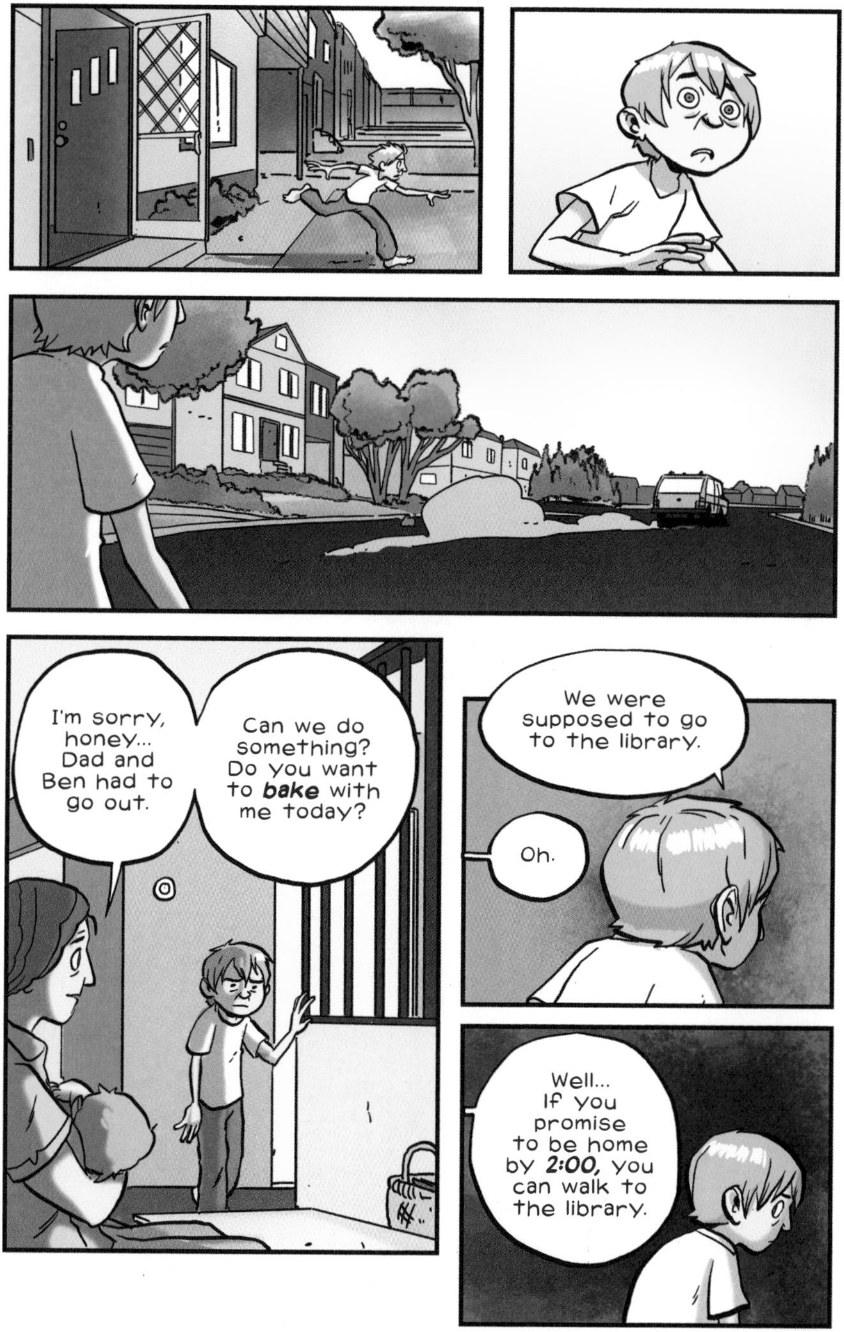
I'm sorry, honey... Dad and Ben had to go out.
Can we do something? Do you want to **bake** with me today?
We were supposed to go to the library.
Oh.
Well... If you promise to be home by **2:00,** you can walk to the library.

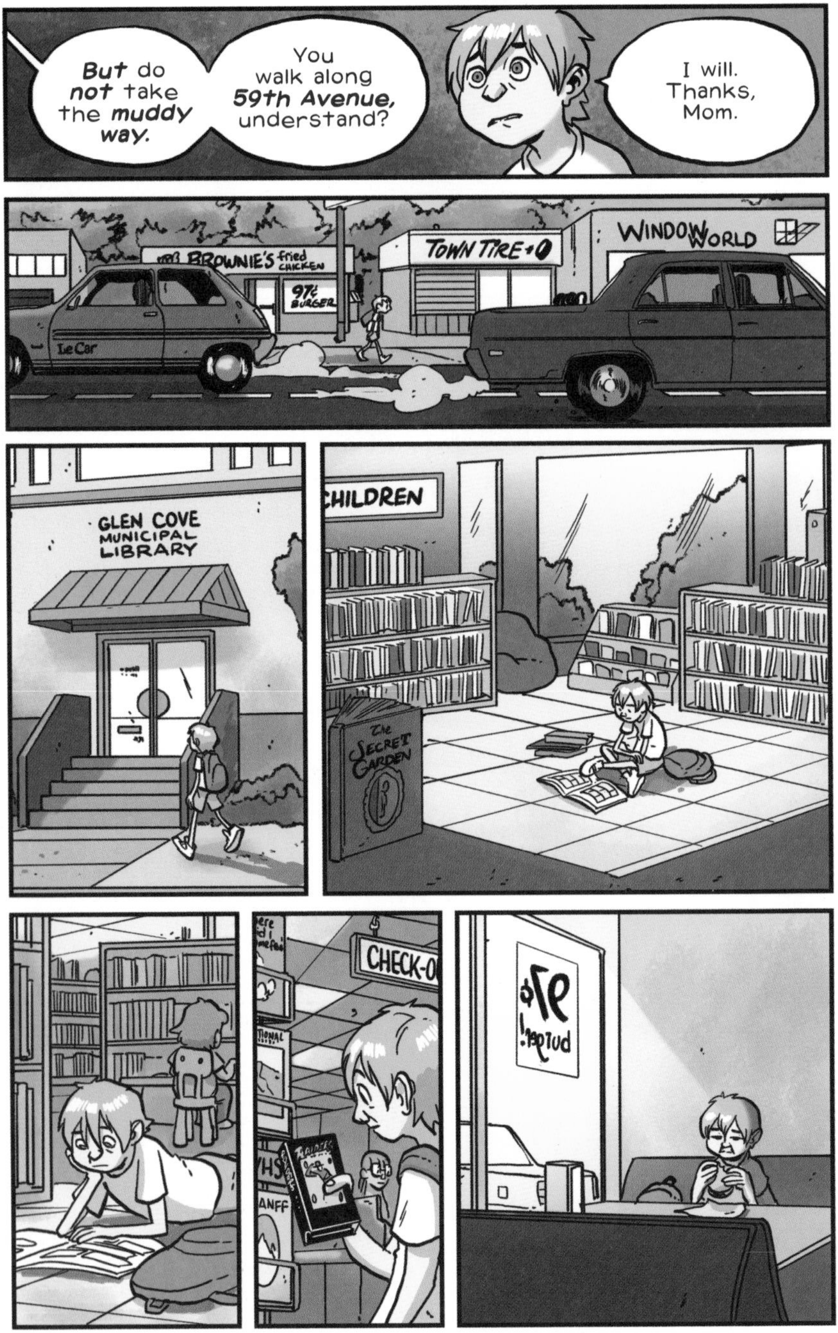
But do not take the muddy way.
You walk along 59th Avenue, understand?
I will. Thanks, Mom.
BROWNIE'S fried CHICKEN
97¢ BURGER
TOWN TIRE
WINDOW WORLD
Le Car
GLEN COVE MUNICIPAL LIBRARY
CHILDREN
The SECRET GARDEN

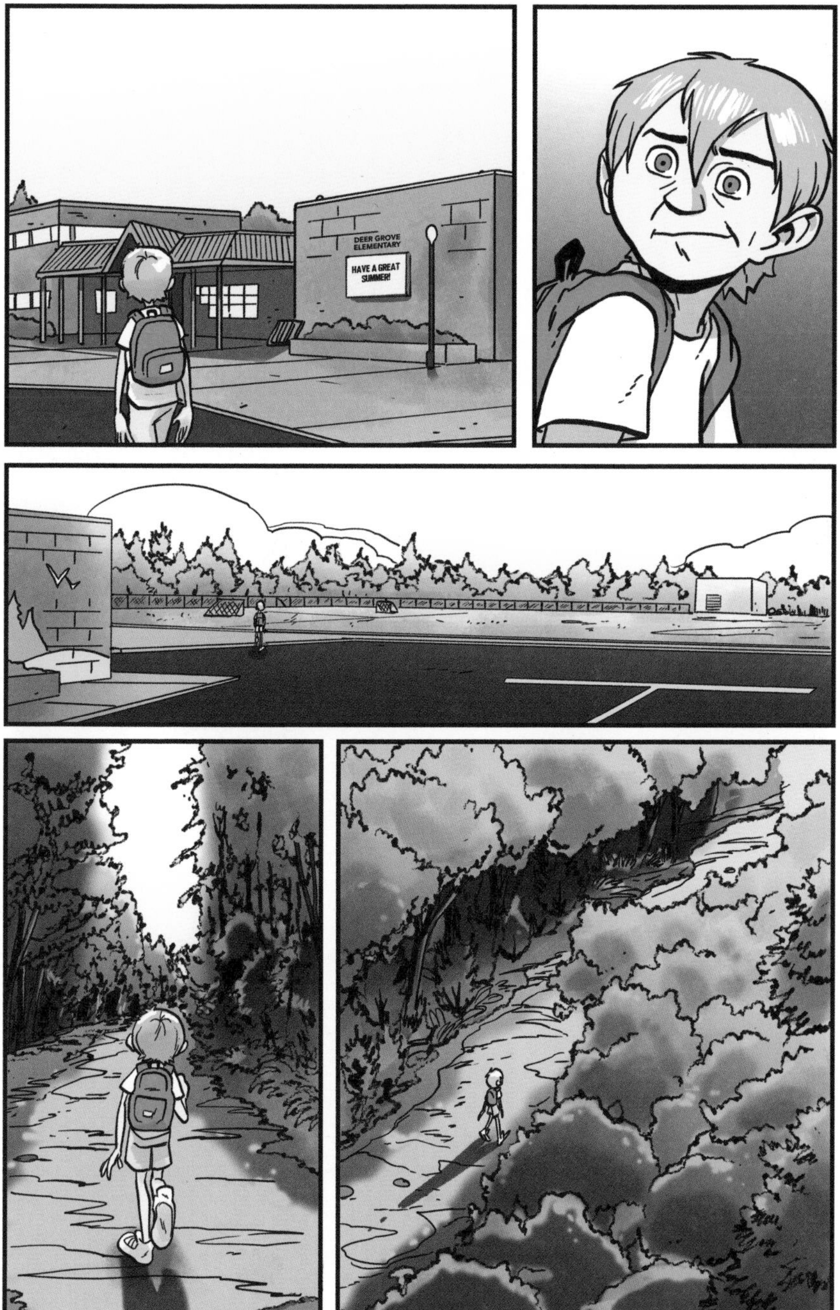
DEER GROVE ELEMENTARY
HAVE A GREAT SUMMER!

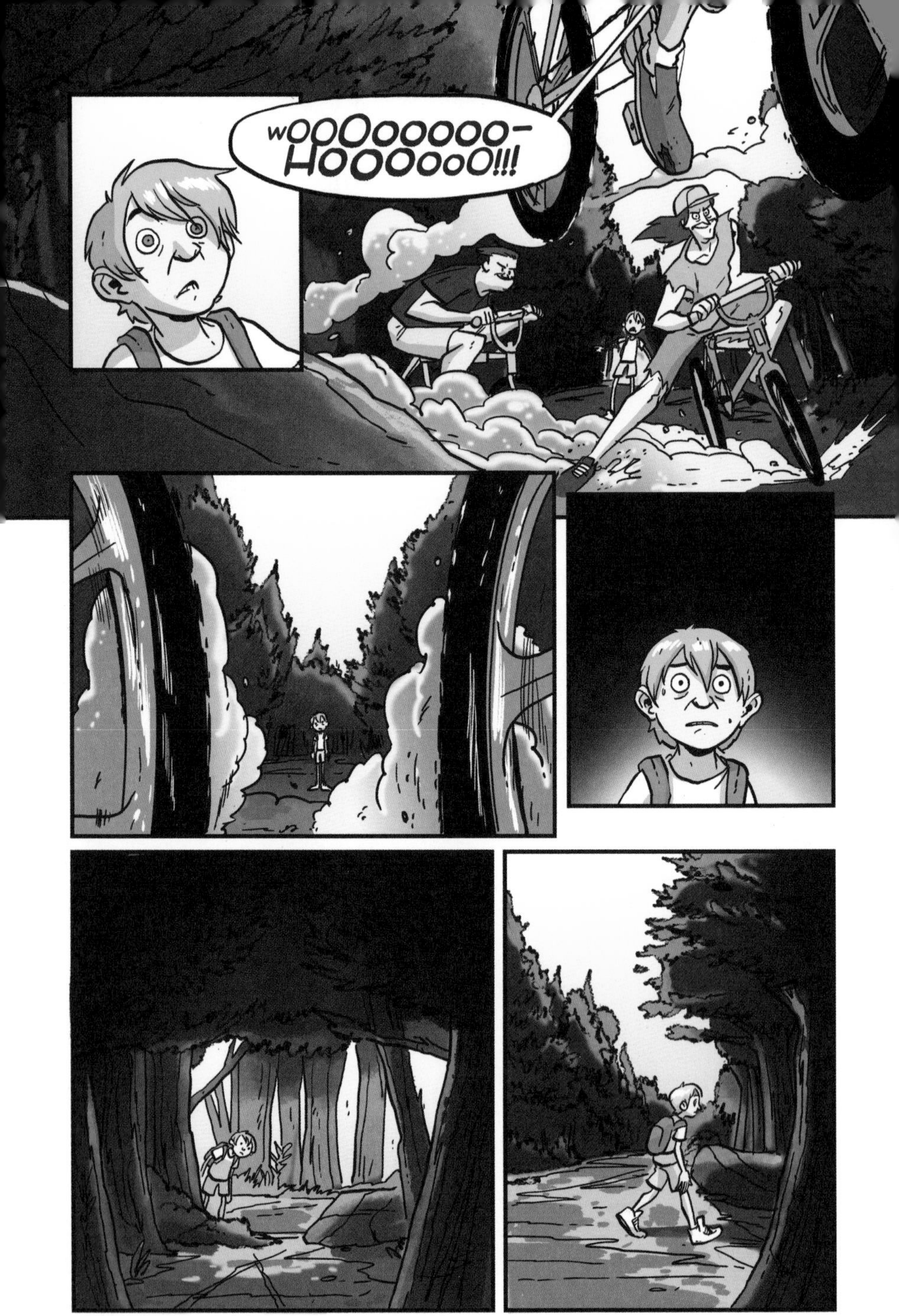
wOOOoooooo-HOOOooO!!!

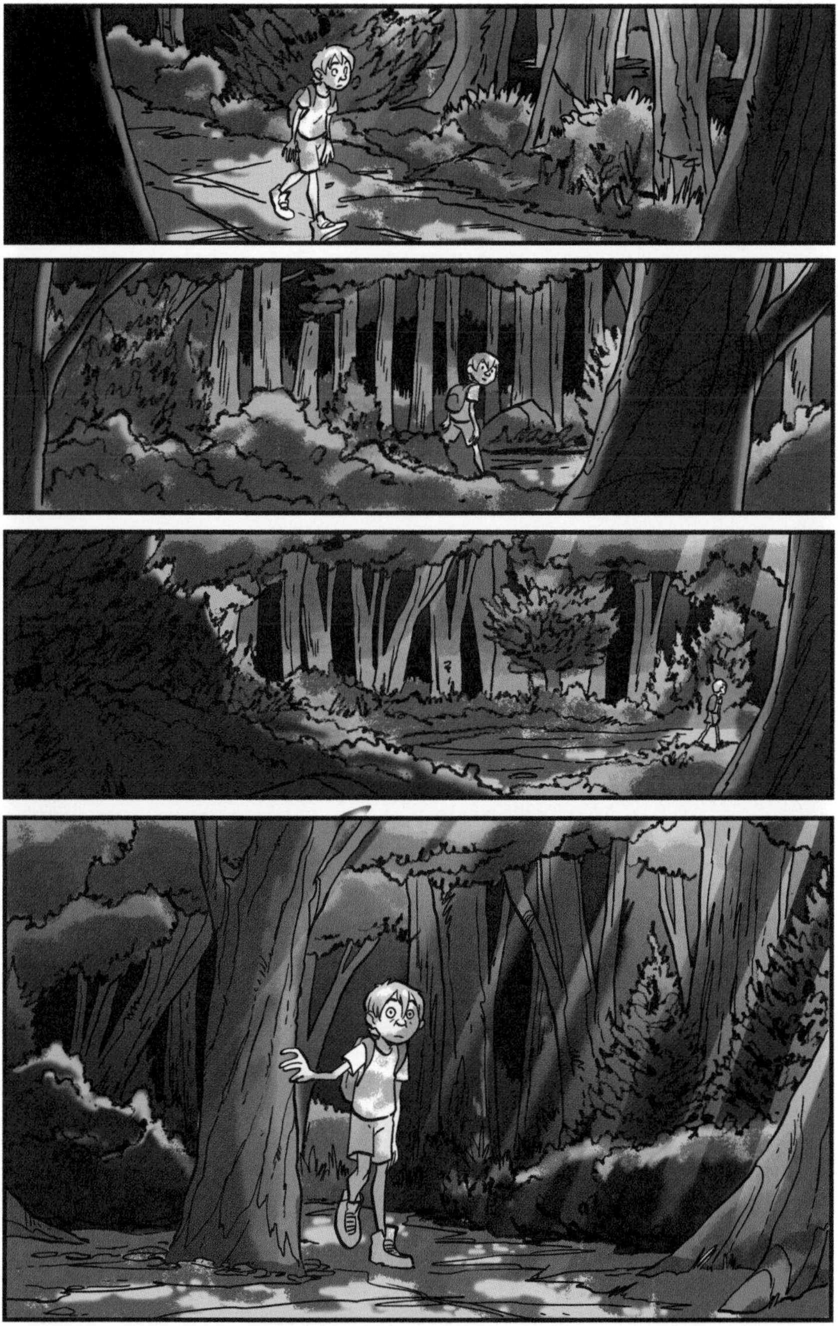

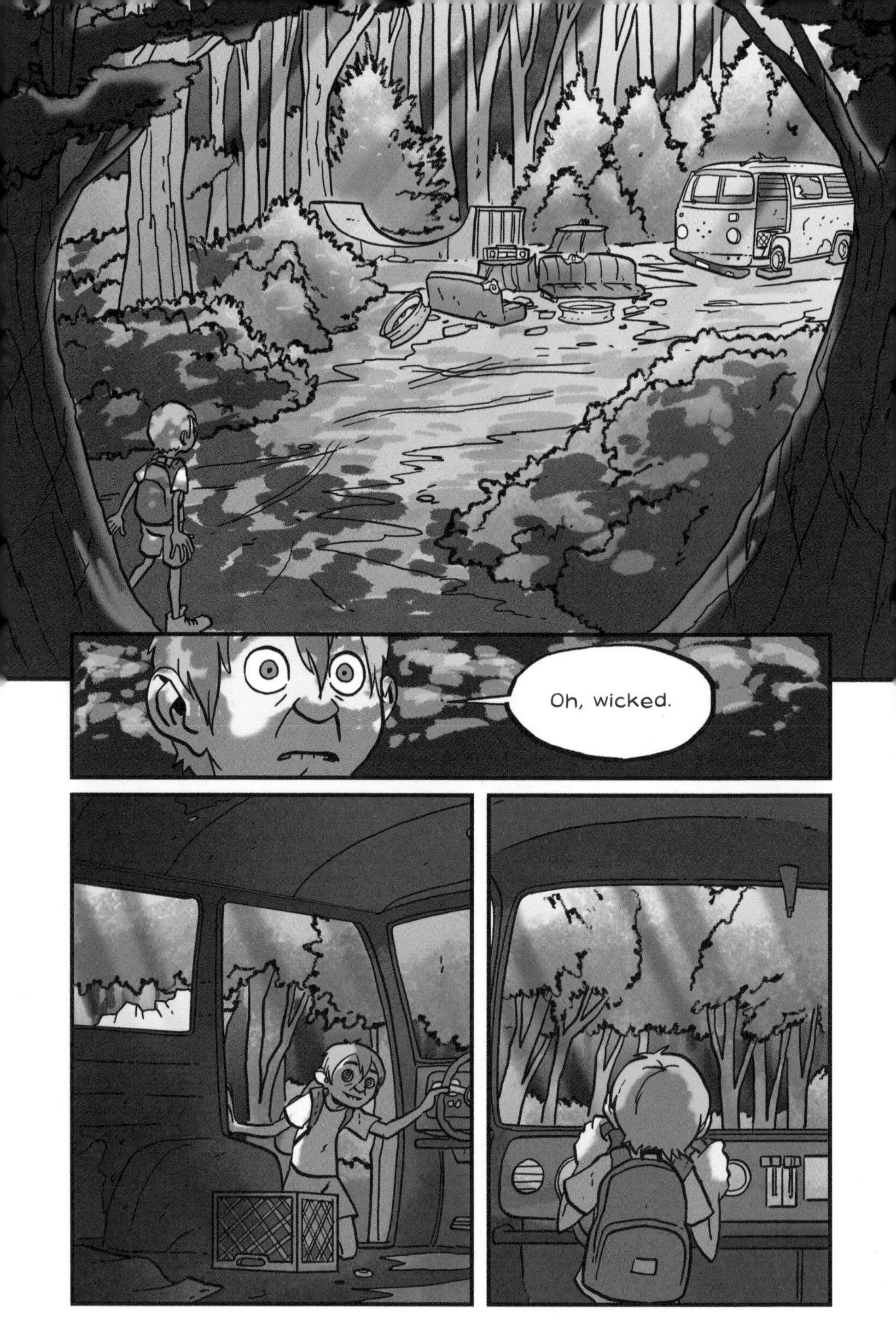
Oh, wicked.

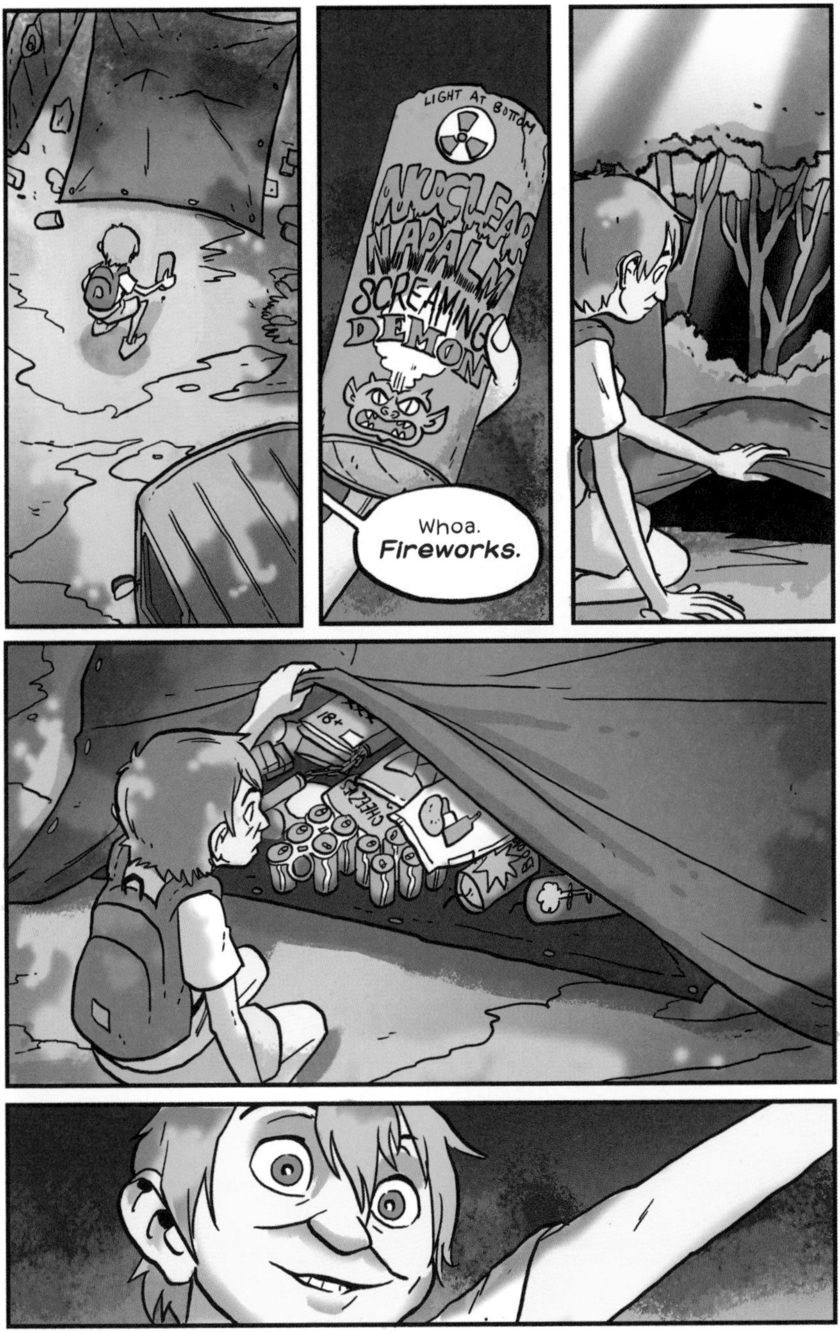
LIGHT AT BOTTOM
NUCLEAR NAPALM SCREAMING DEMON
Whoa. Fireworks.
XXX
18+

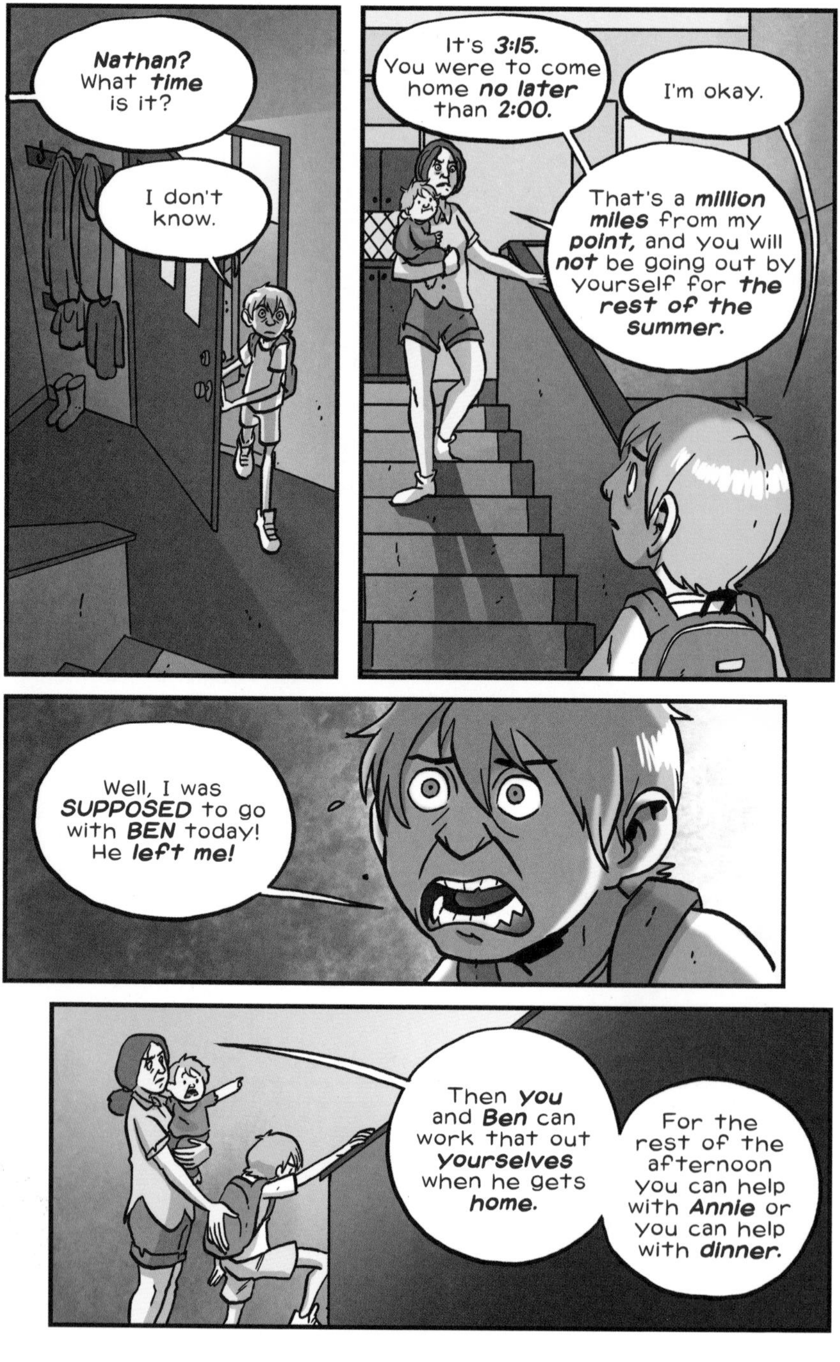
Nathan? What *time* is it?
I don't know.
It's *3:15.* You were to come home *no later* than *2:00.*
I'm okay.
That's a *million miles* from my *point,* and you will *not* be going out by yourself for *the rest of the summer.*
Well, I was *SUPPOSED* to go with *BEN* today! He *left me!*
Then *you* and *Ben* can work that out *yourselves* when he gets *home.*
For the rest of the afternoon you can help with *Annie* or you can help with *dinner.*

We're back, we're back.

How's our **guy?**

Good as can be expected. Bit of **blood work—**

Oh, honey...

We'll find out by the end of the week. For now, he's just got to eat as normally as he can.

Nathan, set the **table,** please. Bowls and spoons.

I'm already **helping.**

Table.

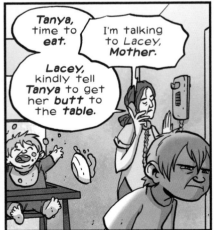

Tanya, time to **eat.**

I'm talking to **Lacey, Mother.**

Lacey, kindly tell **Tanya** to get her **butt** to the **table.**

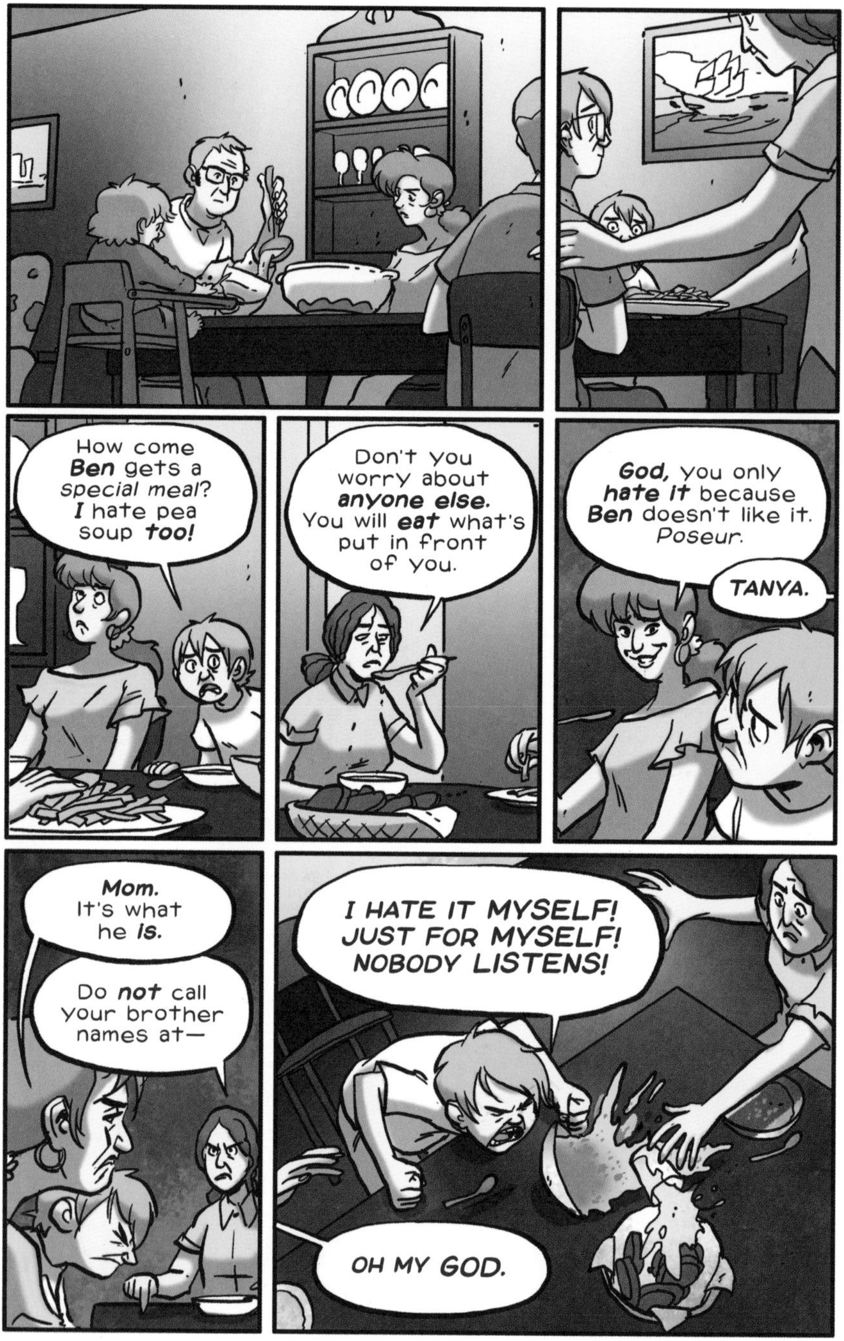
How come **Ben** gets a *special meal*? ***I*** hate pea soup ***too!***
Don't you worry about ***anyone else.*** You will ***eat*** what's put in front of you.
God, you only ***hate it*** because **Ben** doesn't like it. *Poseur.*
TANYA.
Mom. It's what he ***is.***
Do ***not*** call your brother names at—
I HATE IT MYSELF! JUST FOR MYSELF! NOBODY LISTENS!
OH MY GOD.

WHAT?! He **said that?** Shut **UP,** you're such a liar!

HAHAHA

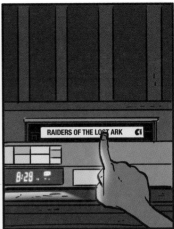

RAIDERS OF THE LOST ARK

8:29

Gimme the **whip!**

Throw me the idol!

No time to **argue!**

Throw me the **idol,** I'll throw you the **whip!**

Gimme the whip!

Adiós, señor.

Mom and Dad are next door at **Carlos and Corrina's. Lacey's** coming here and we're using the TV.

43

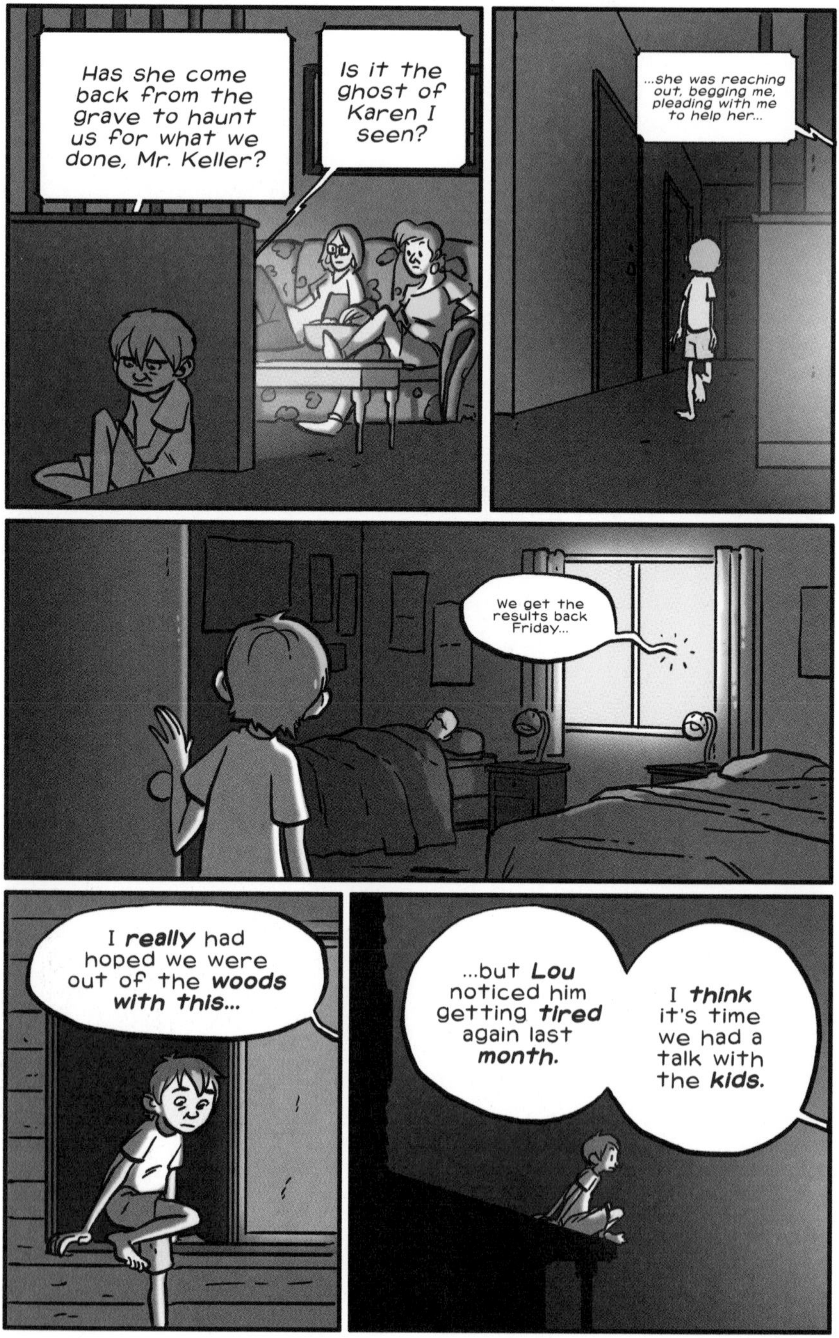
Has she come back from the grave to haunt us for what we done, Mr. Keller?
Is it the ghost of Karen I seen?
...she was reaching out, begging me, pleading with me to help her...
We get the results back Friday...
I really had hoped we were out of the woods with this...
...but Lou noticed him getting tired again last month.
I think it's time we had a talk with the kids.

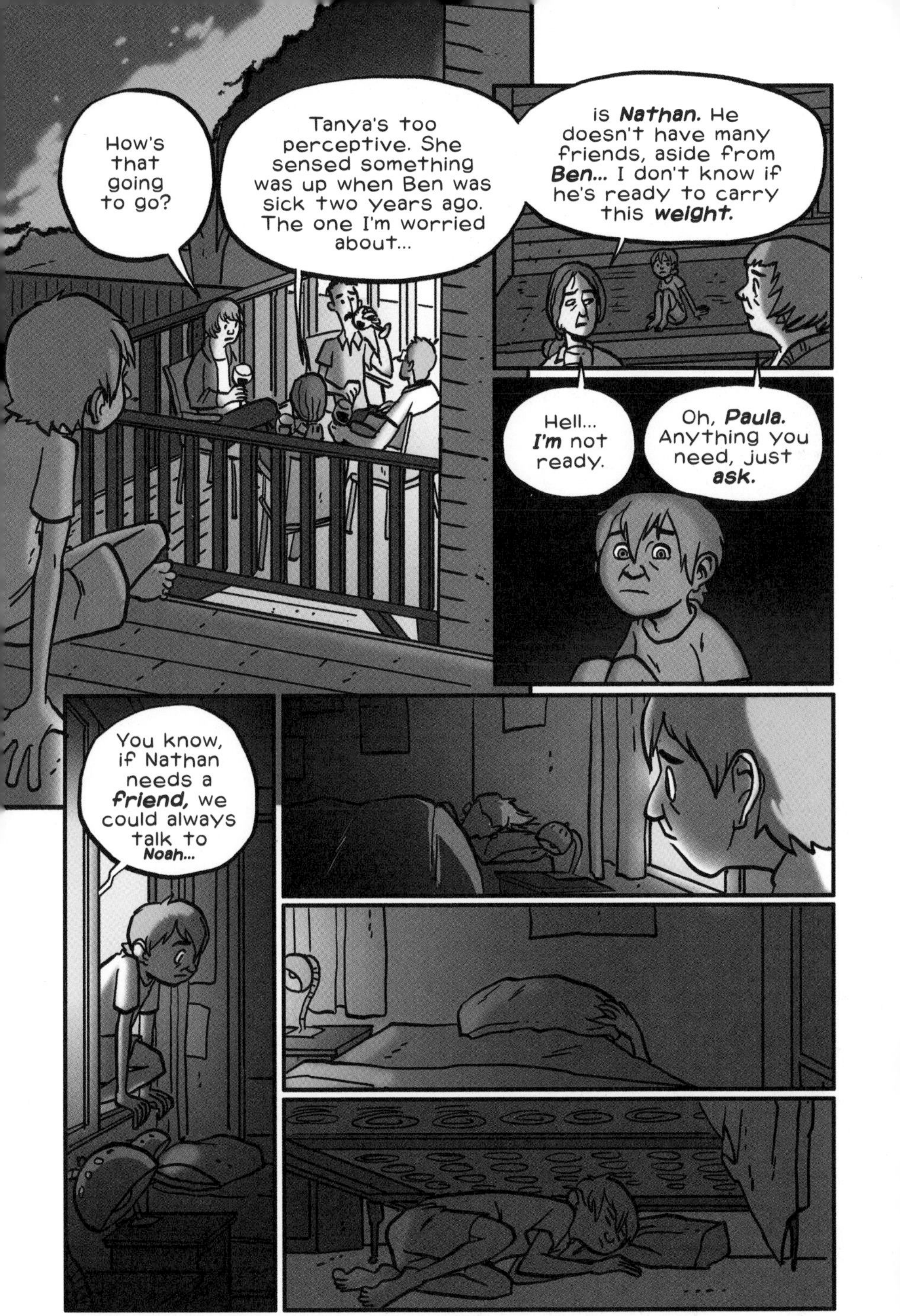
How's that going to go?
Tanya's too perceptive. She sensed something was up when Ben was sick two years ago. The one I'm worried about...
is **Nathan.** He doesn't have many friends, aside from **Ben...** I don't know if he's ready to carry this **weight.**
Hell... ***I'm*** not ready.
Oh, **Paula.** Anything you need, just **ask.**
You know, if Nathan needs a ***friend,*** we could always talk to ***Noah...***
...

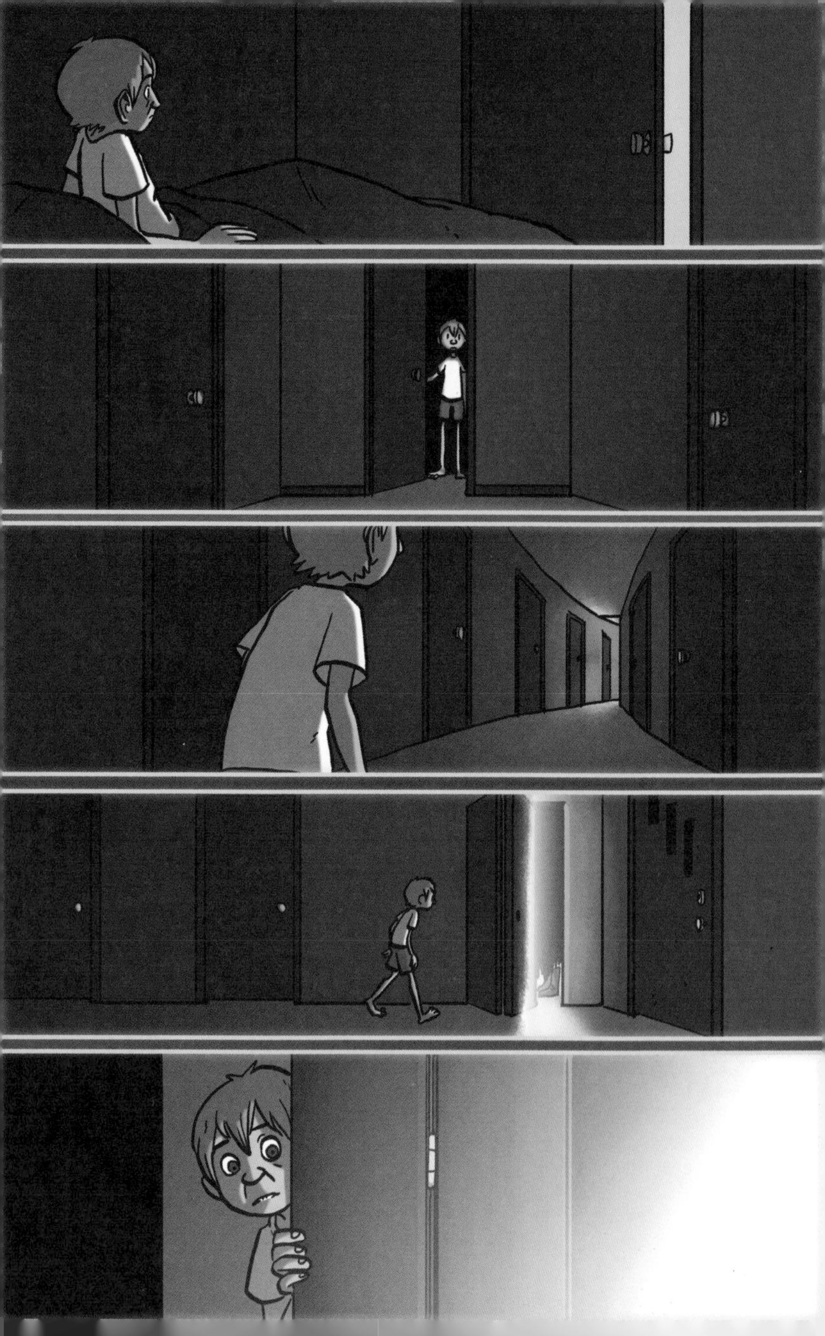

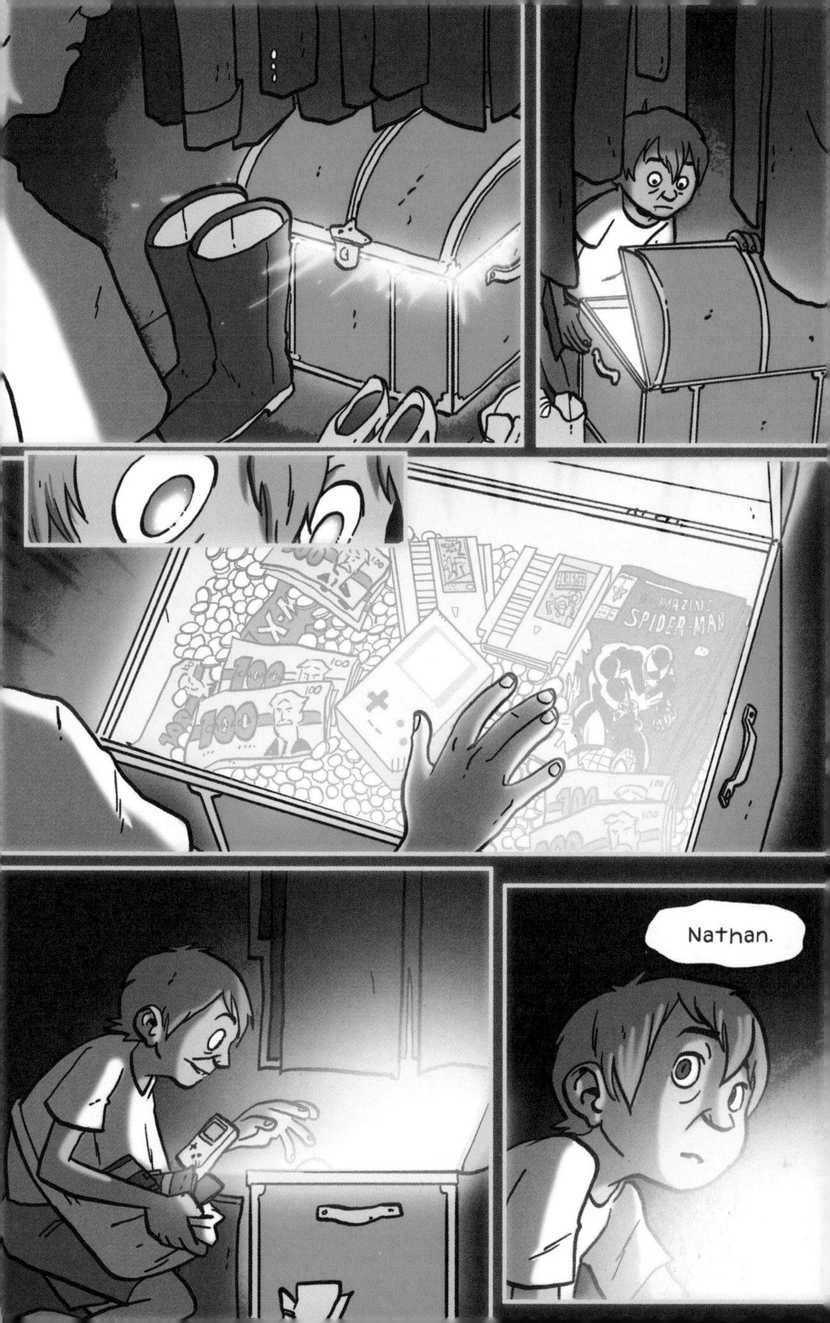
SPIDER-MAN
Nathan.

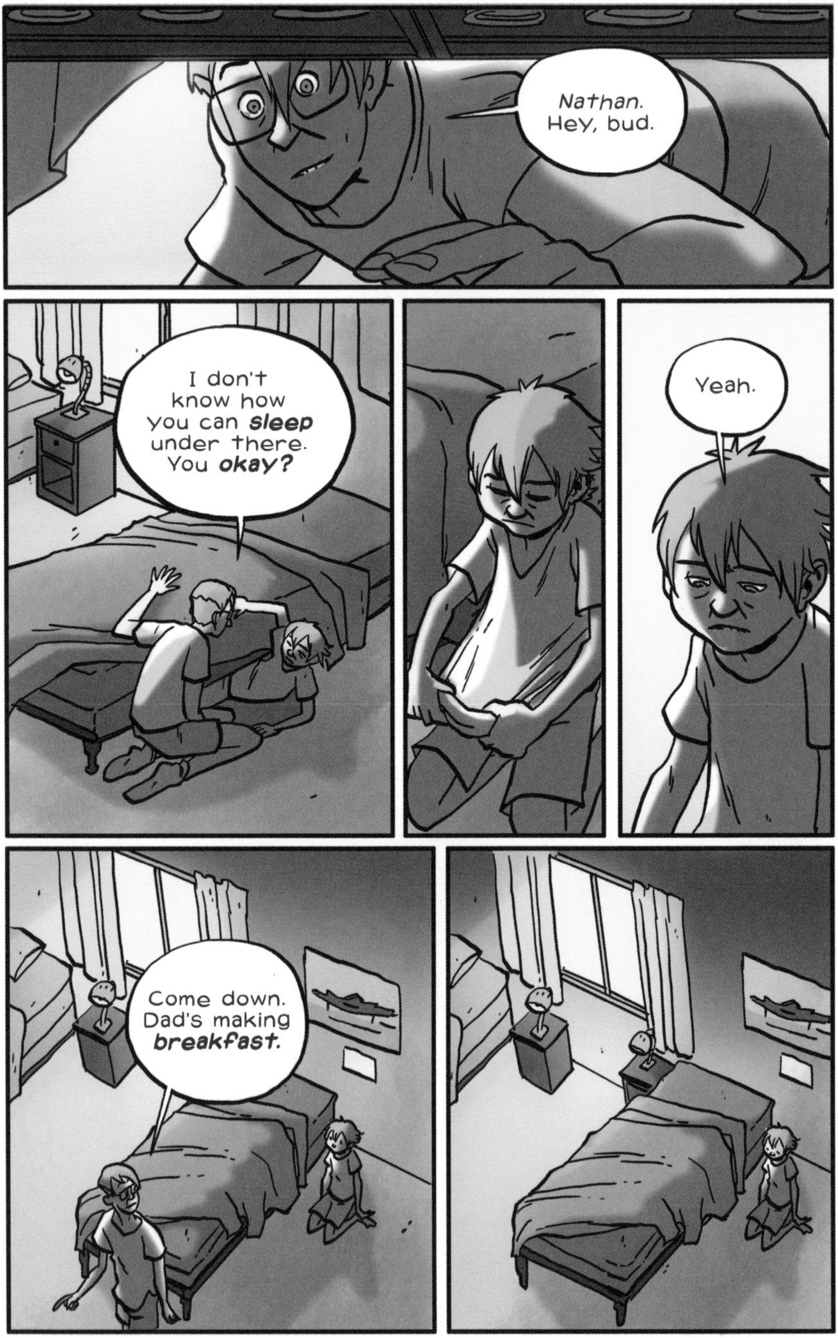
Nathan. Hey, bud.
I don't know how you can sleep under there. You okay?
Yeah.
Come down. Dad's making breakfast.

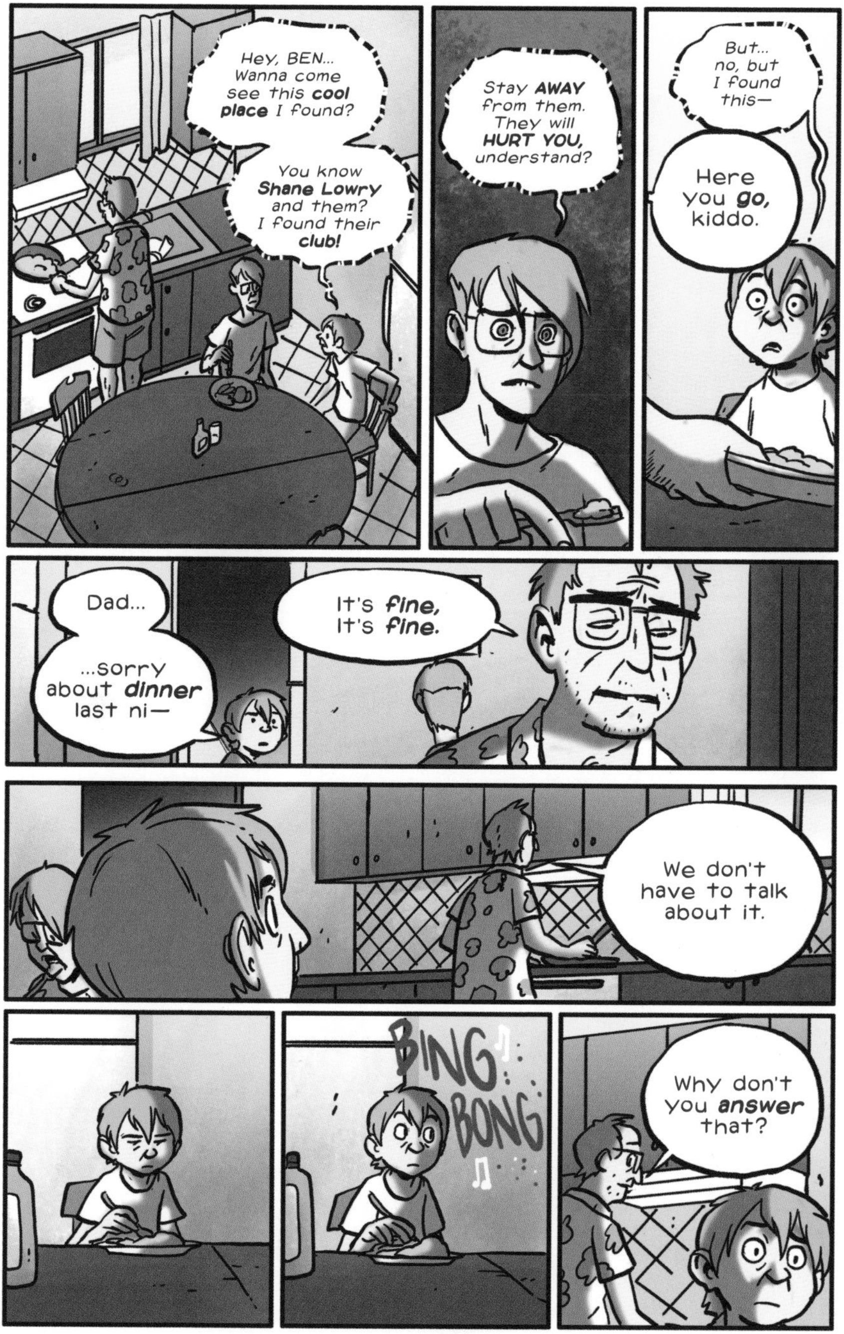

Hey, BEN... Wanna come see this **cool place** I found?
You know **Shane Lowry** and them? I found their **club!**
Stay **AWAY** from them. They will **HURT YOU,** understand?
But... no, but I found this—
Here you **go,** kiddo.
Dad...
...sorry about **dinner** last ni—
It's **fine,** It's **fine.**
We don't have to talk about it.
BING BONG
Why don't you **answer** that?

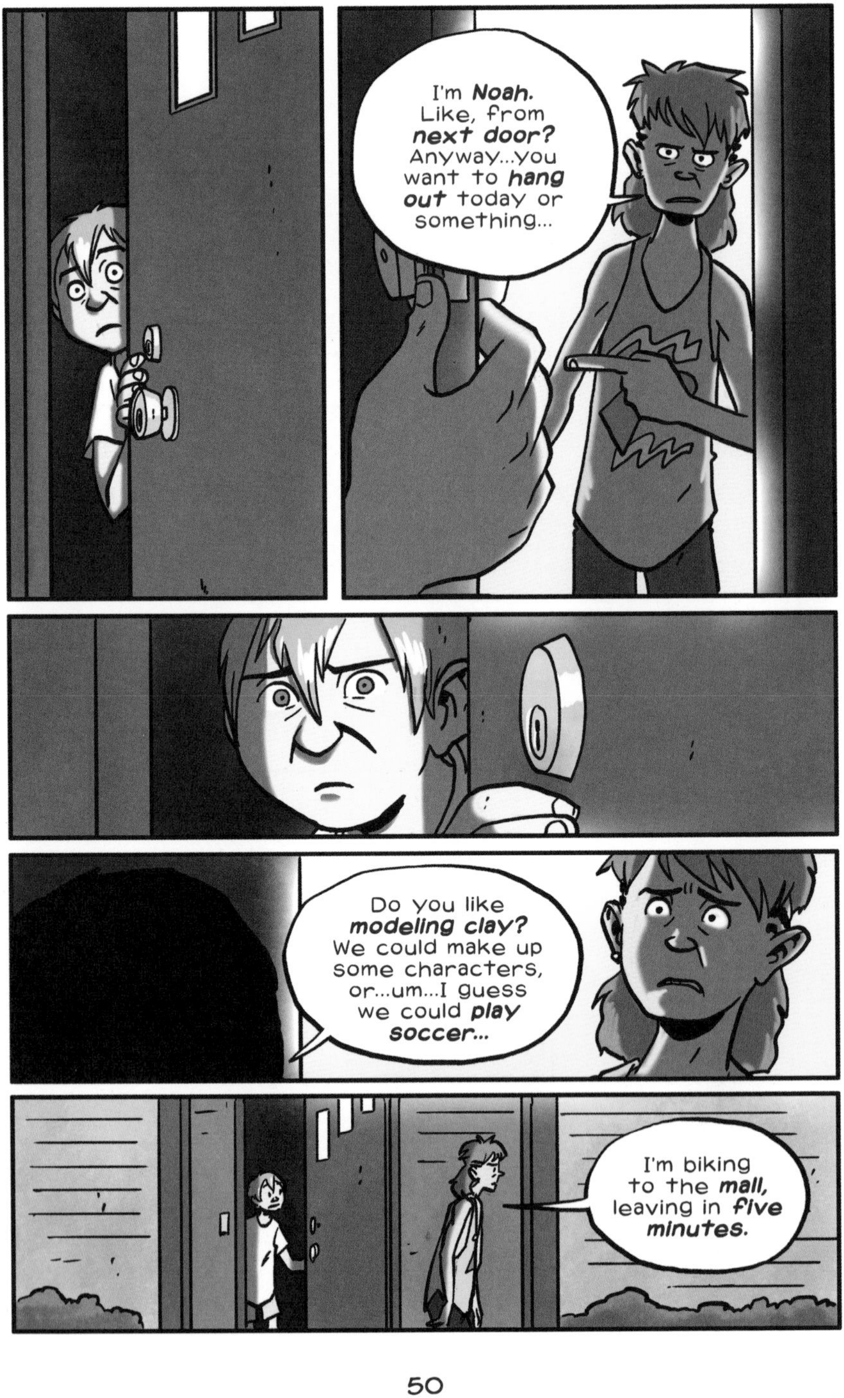
I'm **Noah.** Like, from ***next door?*** Anyway...you want to ***hang out*** today or something...
Do you like ***modeling clay?*** We could make up some characters, or...um...I guess we could ***play soccer...***
I'm biking to the ***mall,*** leaving in ***five minutes.***

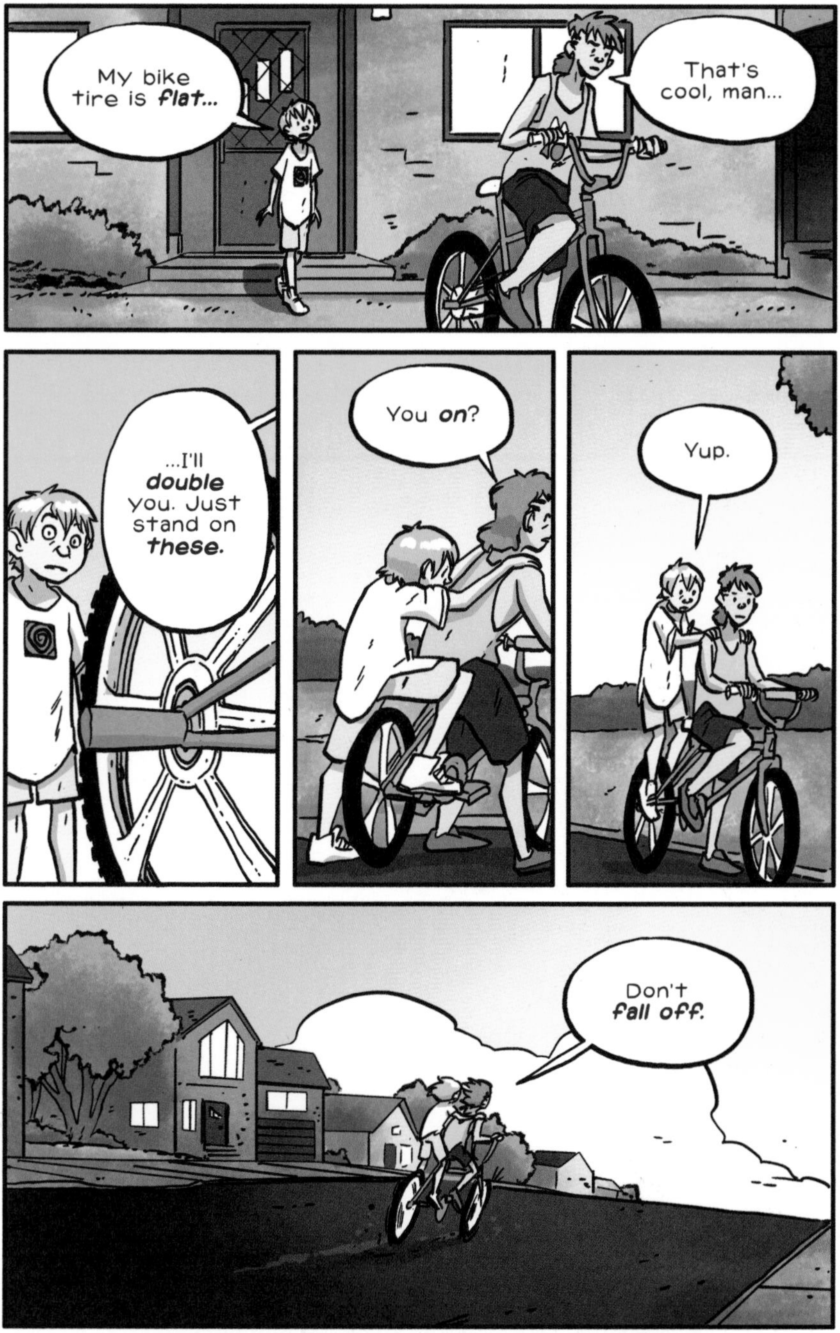
My bike tire is *flat...*
That's cool, man...
...I'll **double** you. Just stand on ***these.***
You **on**?
Yup.
Don't ***fall off.***

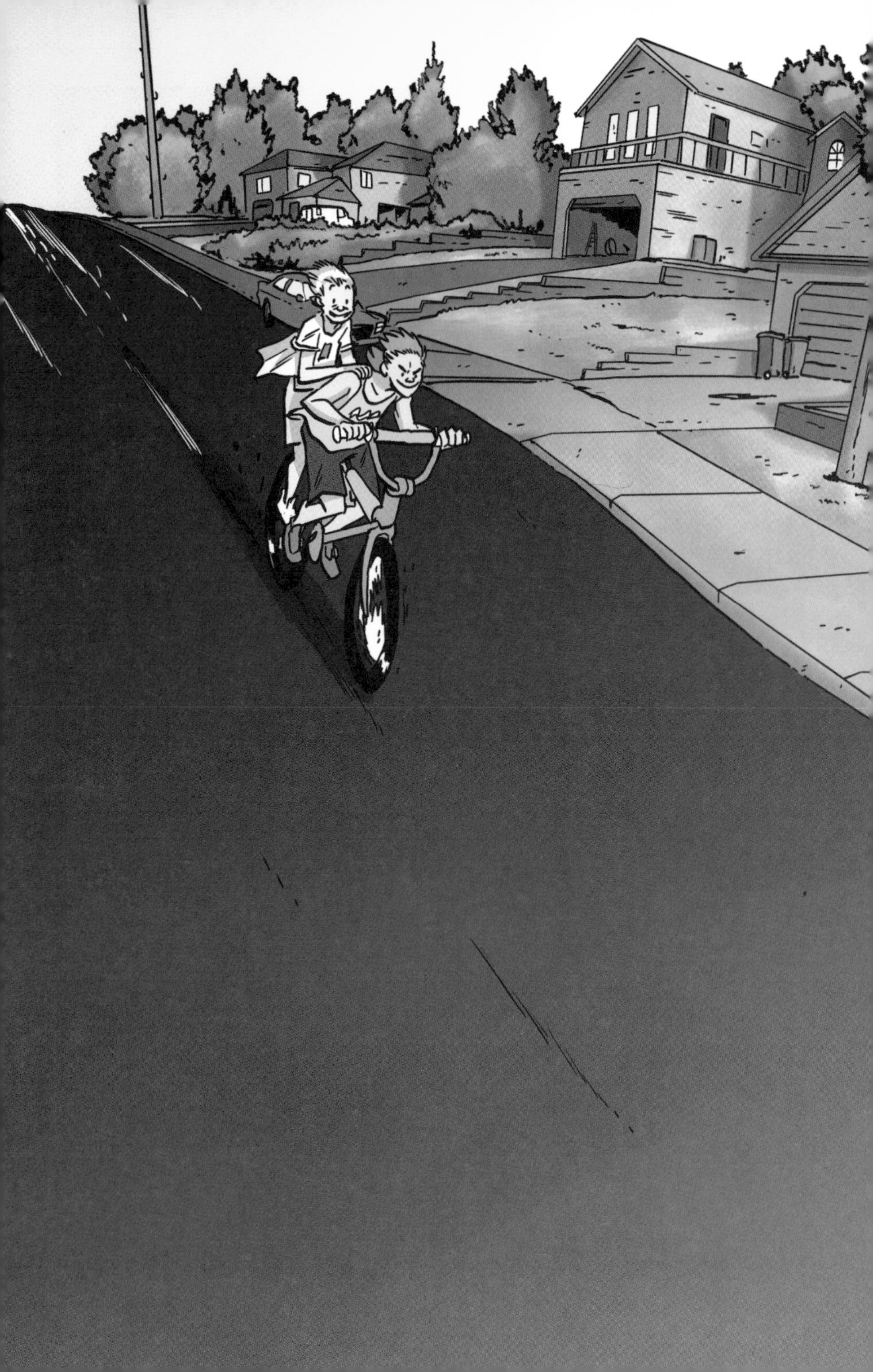

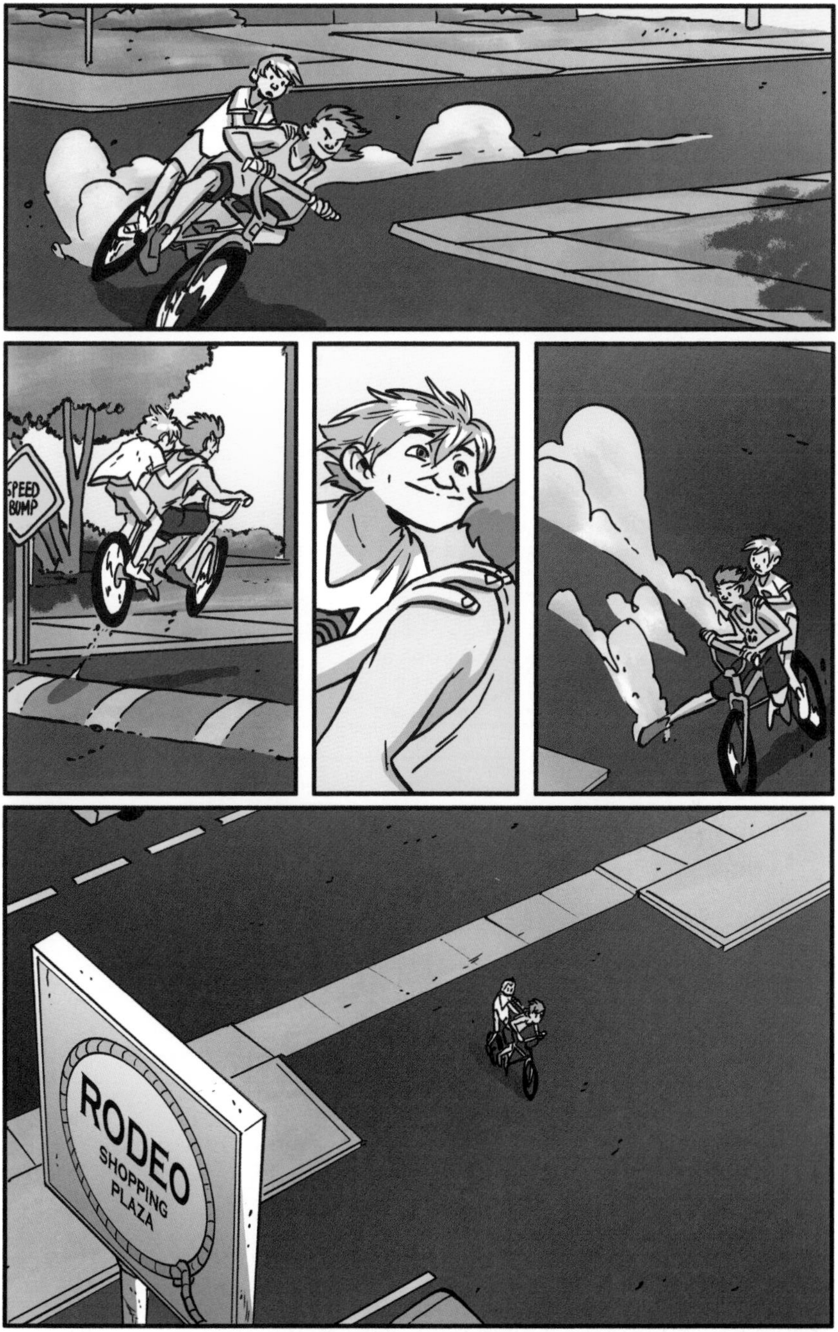
SPEED BUMP
RODEO SHOPPING PLAZA

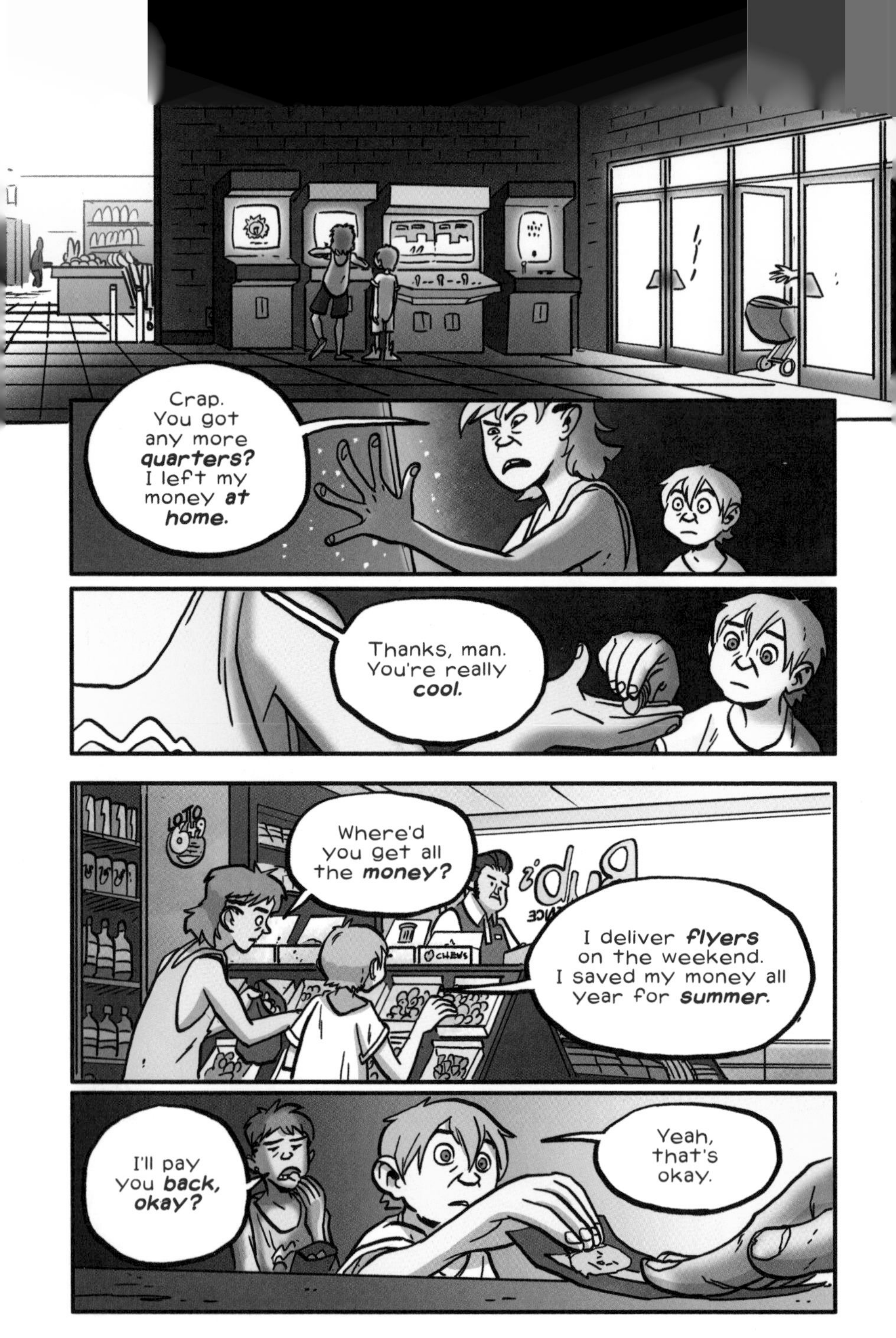
Crap. You got any more **quarters?** I left my money **at home.**
Thanks, man. You're really **cool.**
LOTTO 6/49
CHEWS
Where'd you get all the **money?**
I deliver **flyers** on the weekend. I saved my money all year for **summer.**
I'll pay you **back, okay?**
Yeah, that's okay.

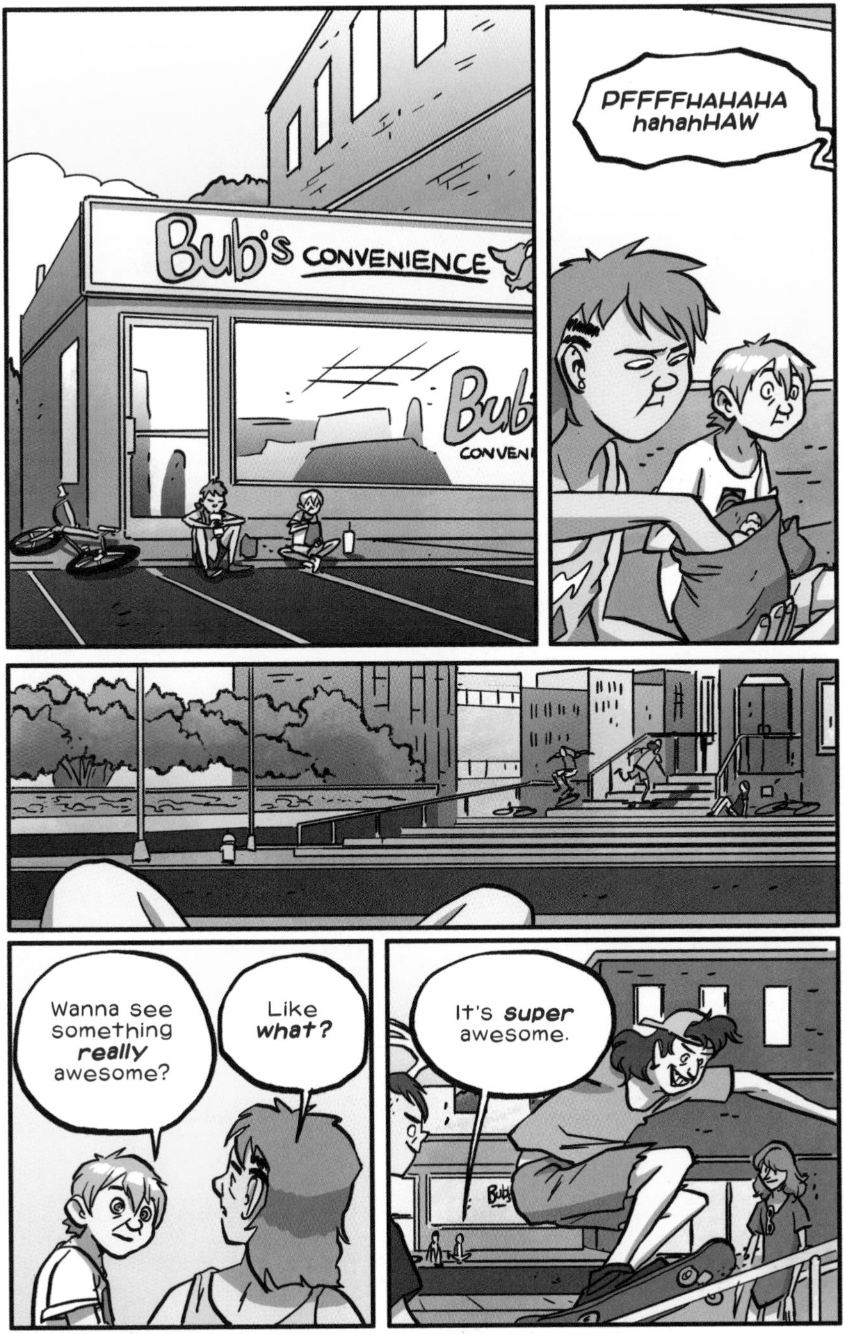
Bub's CONVENIENCE
Bub's CONVENI
PFFFFHAHAHA hahahHAW
Wanna see something **really** awesome?
Like **what?**
It's **super** awesome.

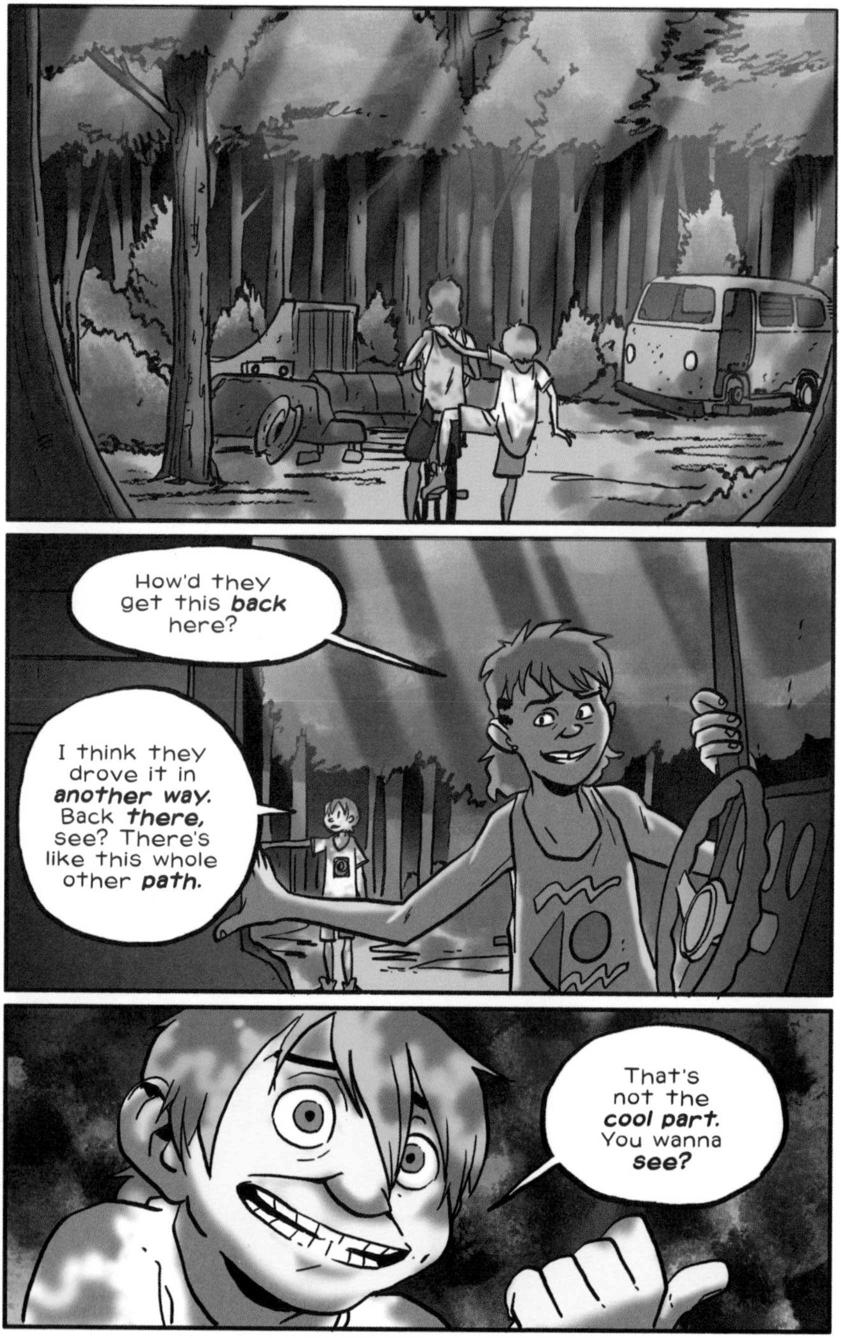
How'd they get this **back** here?
I think they drove it in **another way.** Back **there,** see? There's like this whole other **path.**
That's not the **cool part.** You wanna **see?**

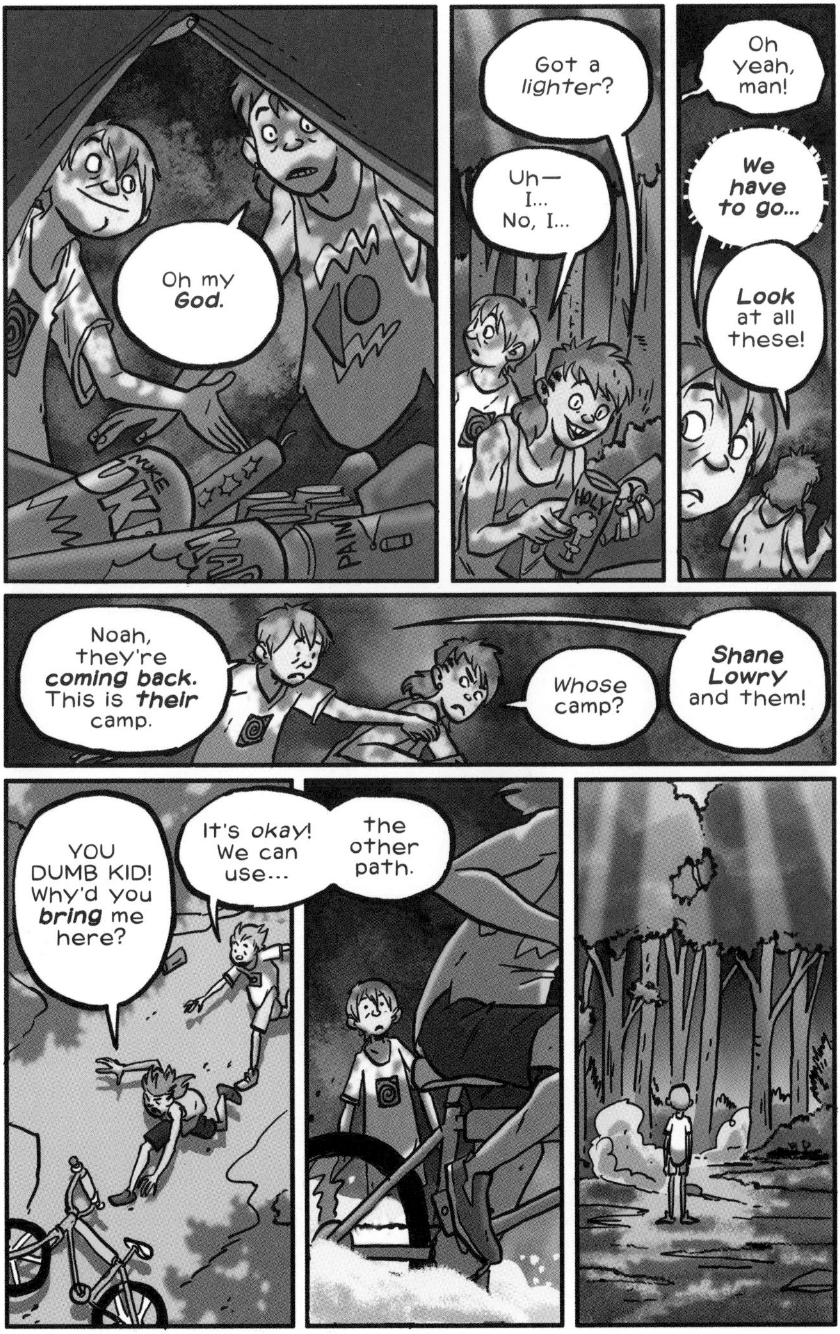
Oh my *God.*
Got a *lighter*?
Uh— I... No, I...
Oh yeah, man!
We have to go...
Look at all these!
Noah, they're ***coming back.*** This is ***their*** camp.
Whose camp?
Shane Lowry and them!
YOU DUMB KID! Why'd you ***bring*** me here?
It's *okay*! We can use...
the other path.

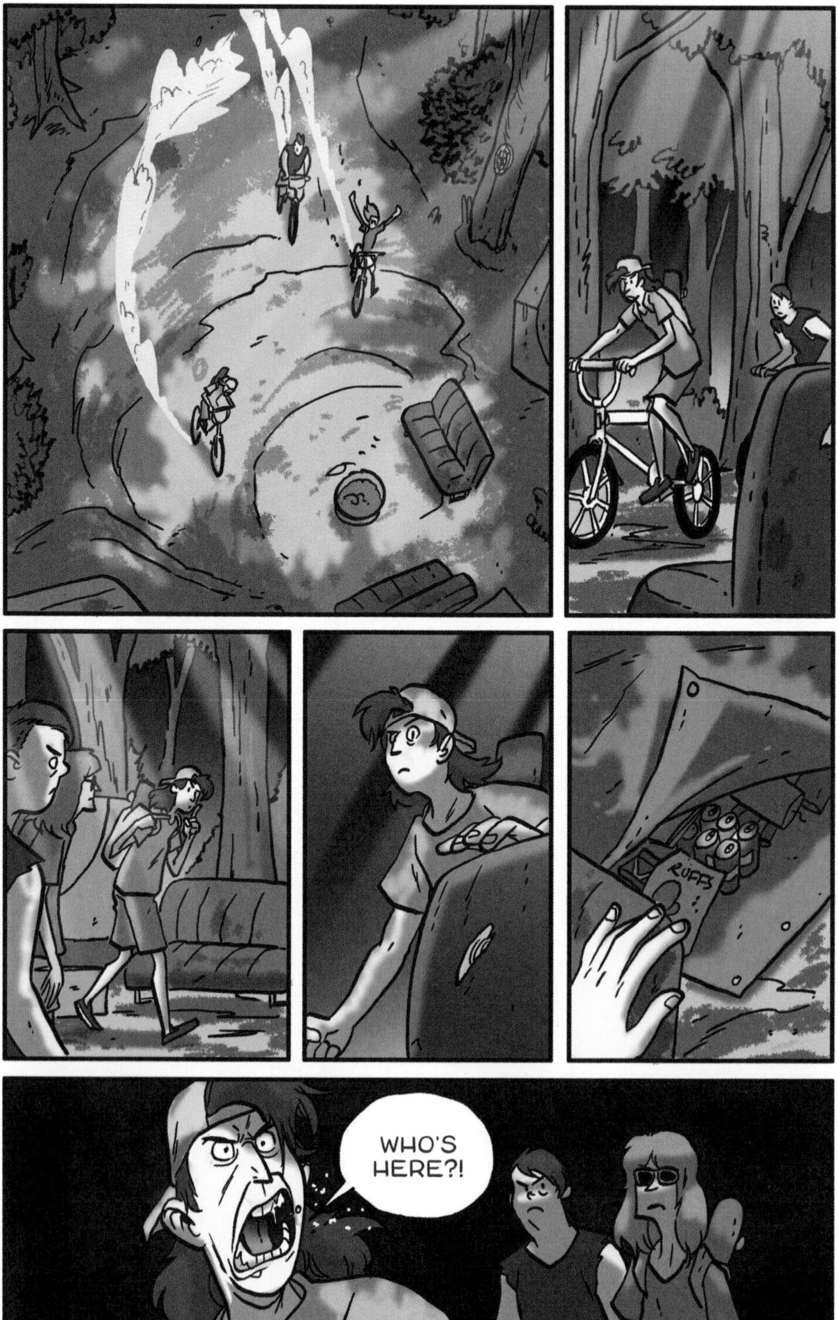
RUFFS
WHO'S HERE?!

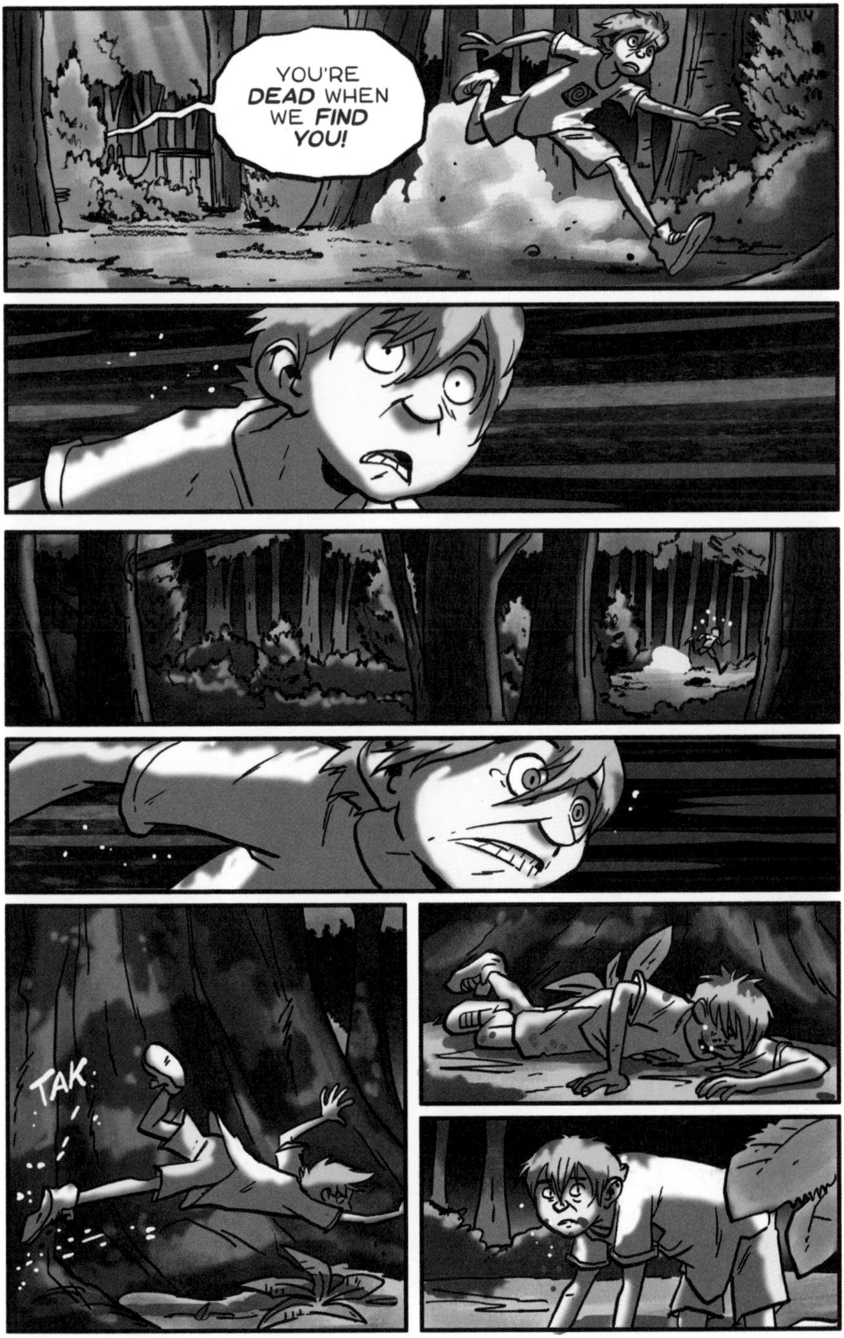
YOU'RE **DEAD** WHEN WE **FIND YOU!**
TAK

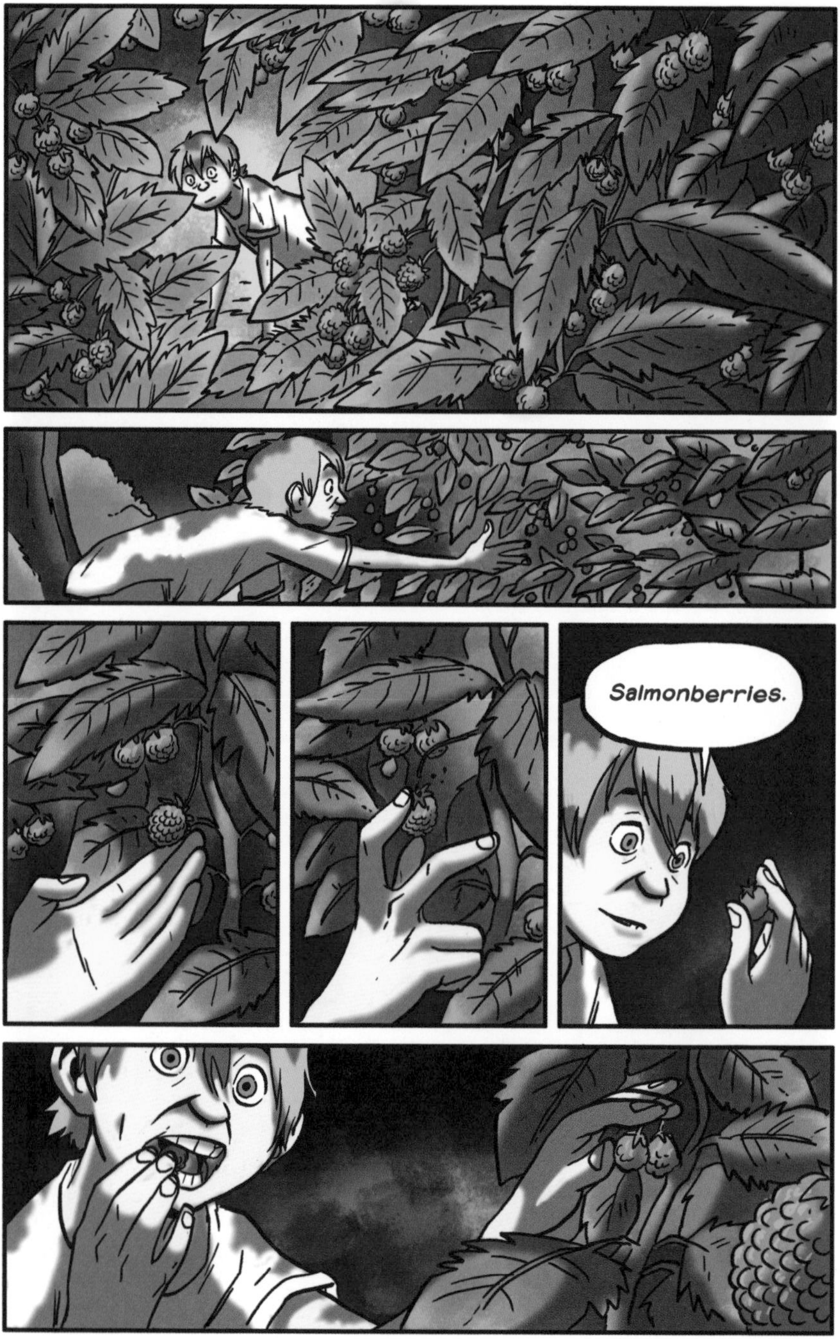
Salmonberries.

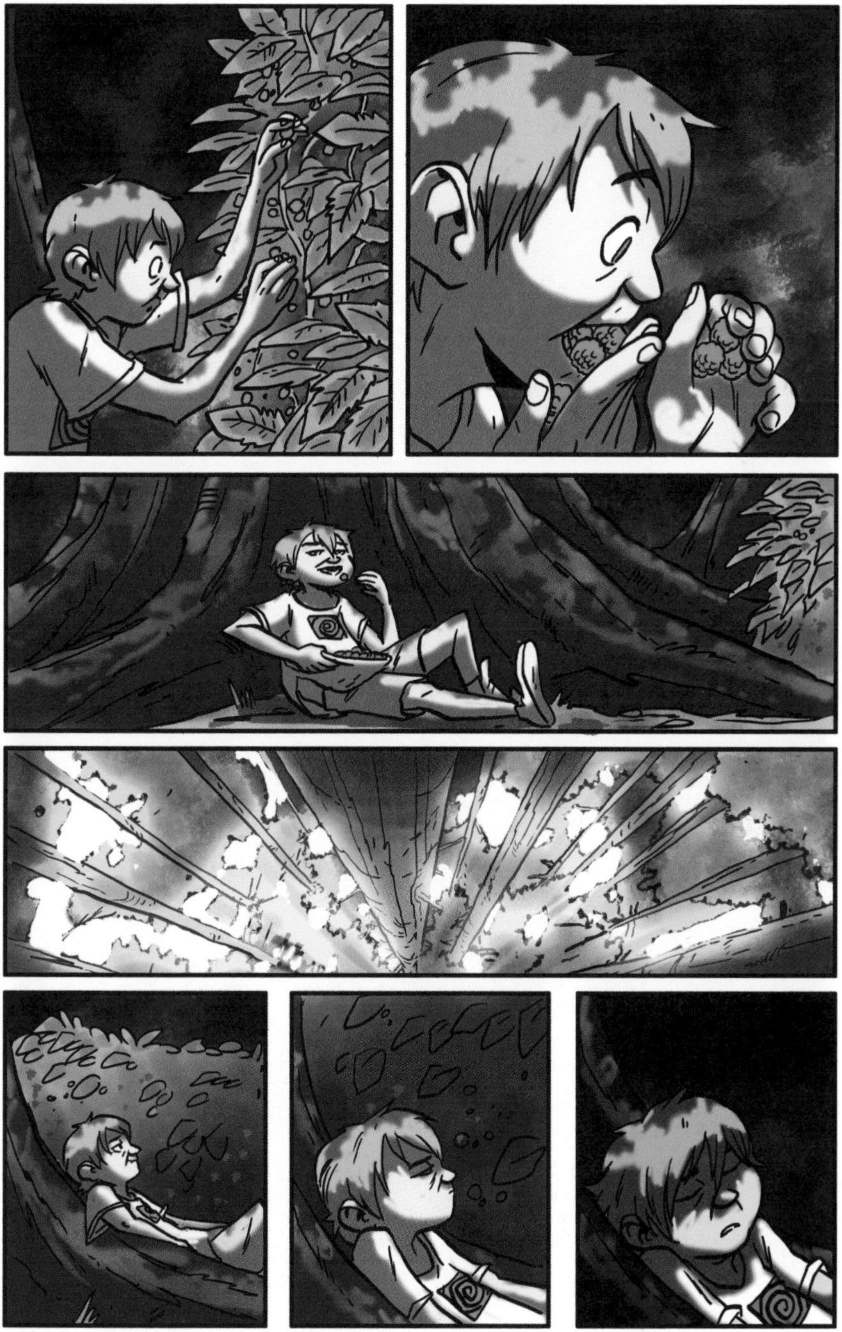

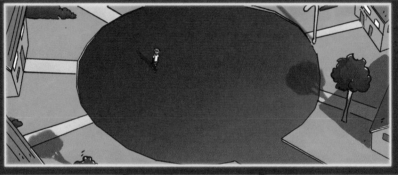

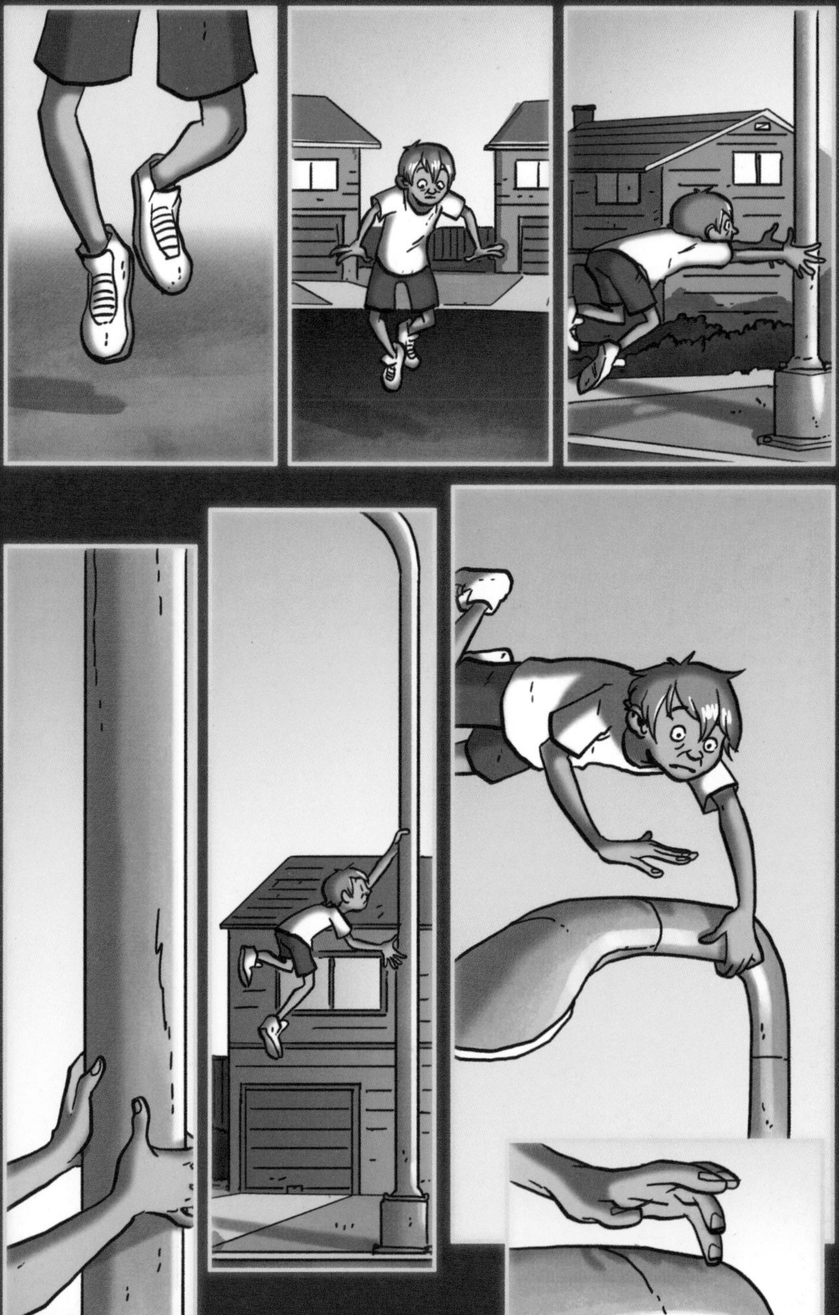

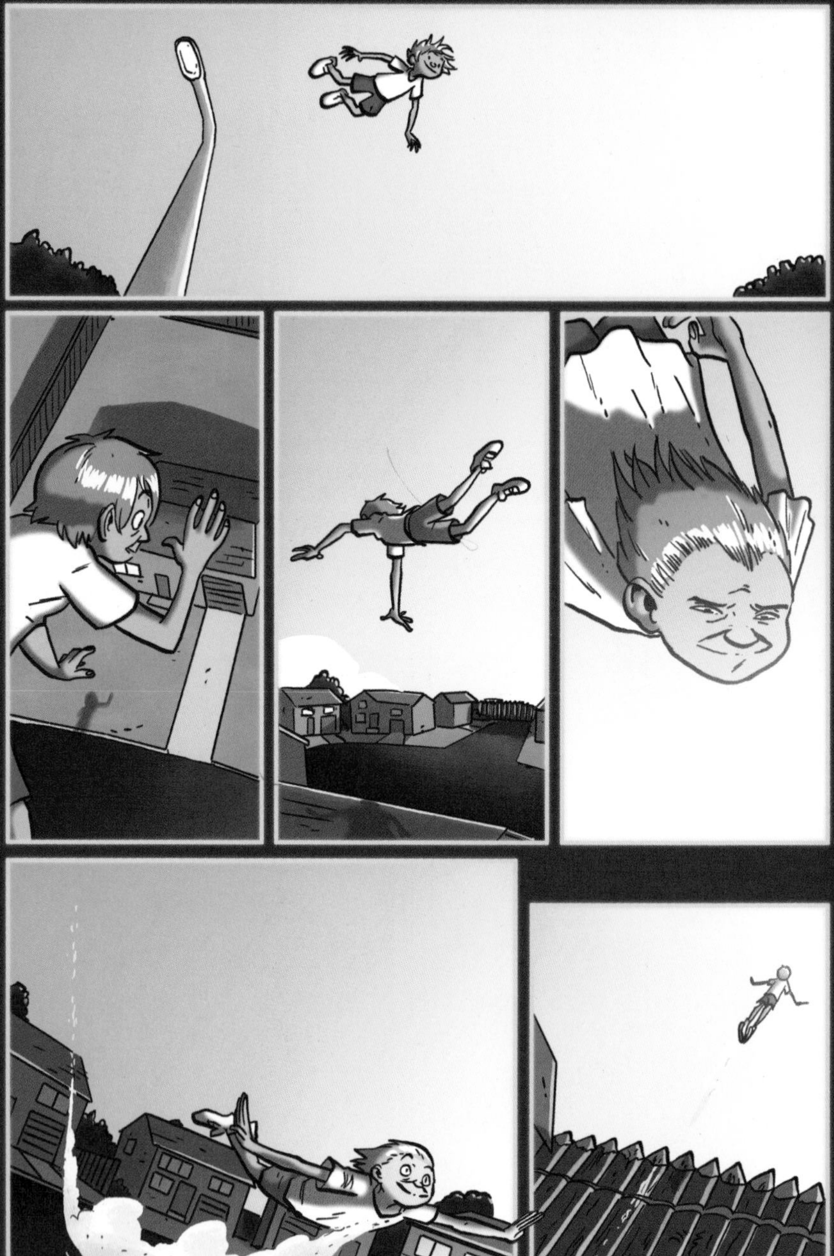

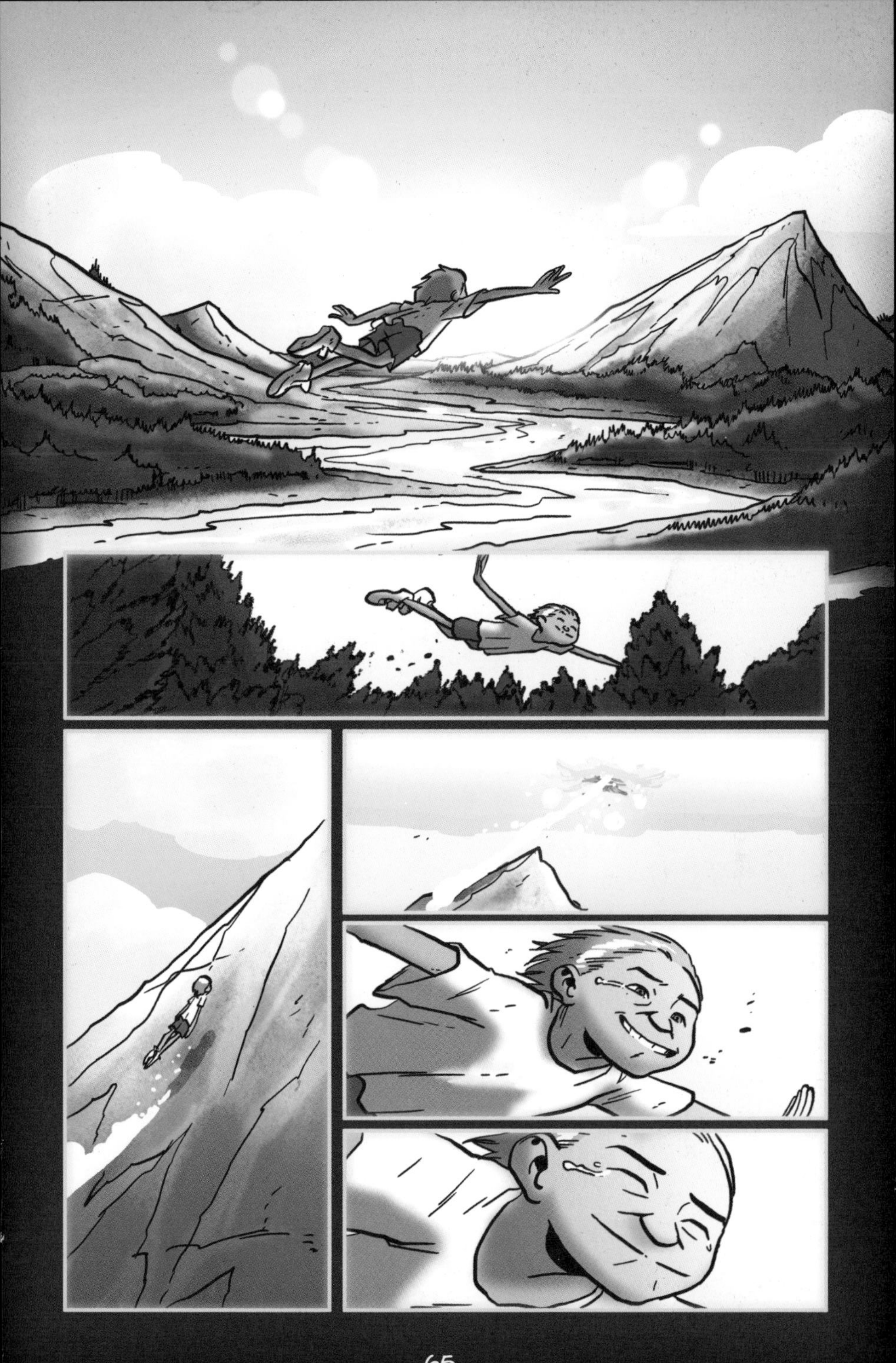

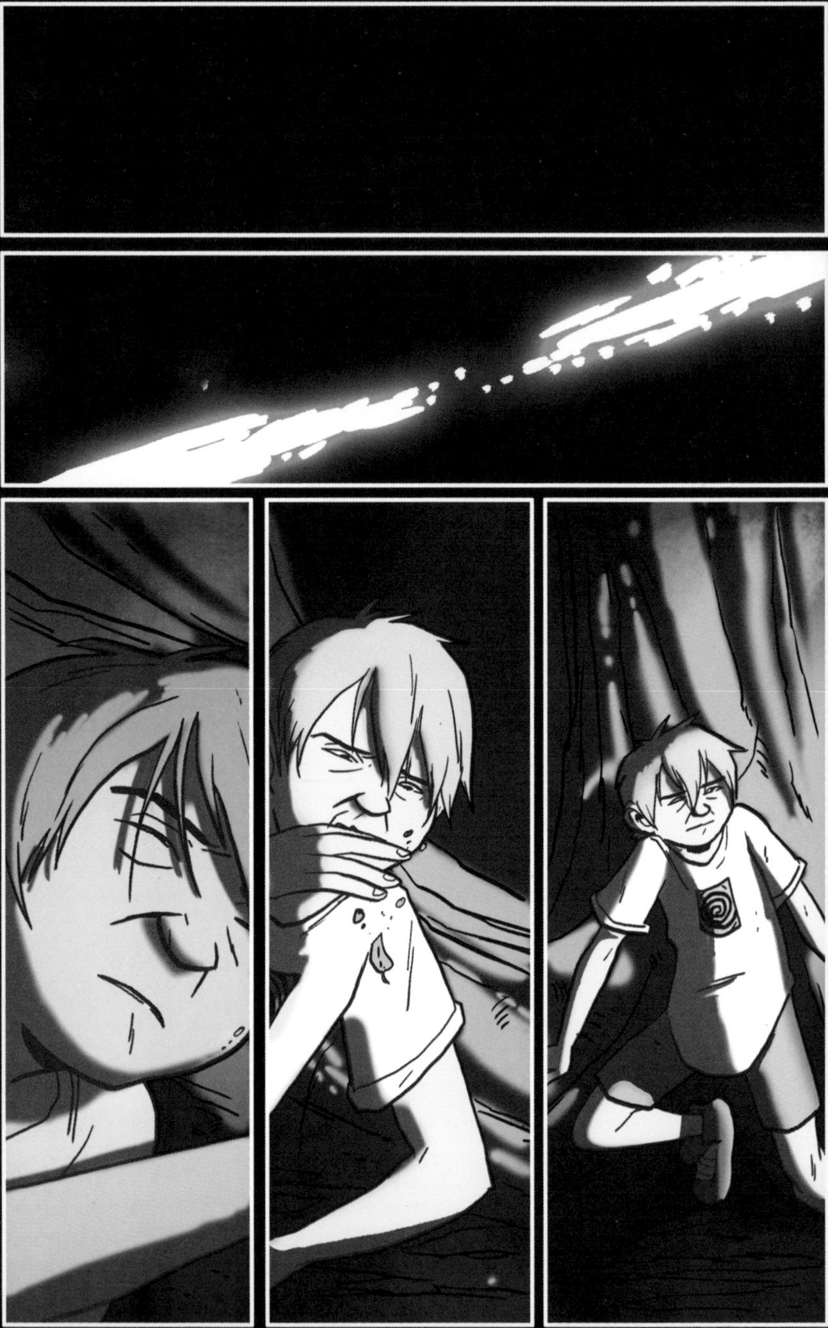

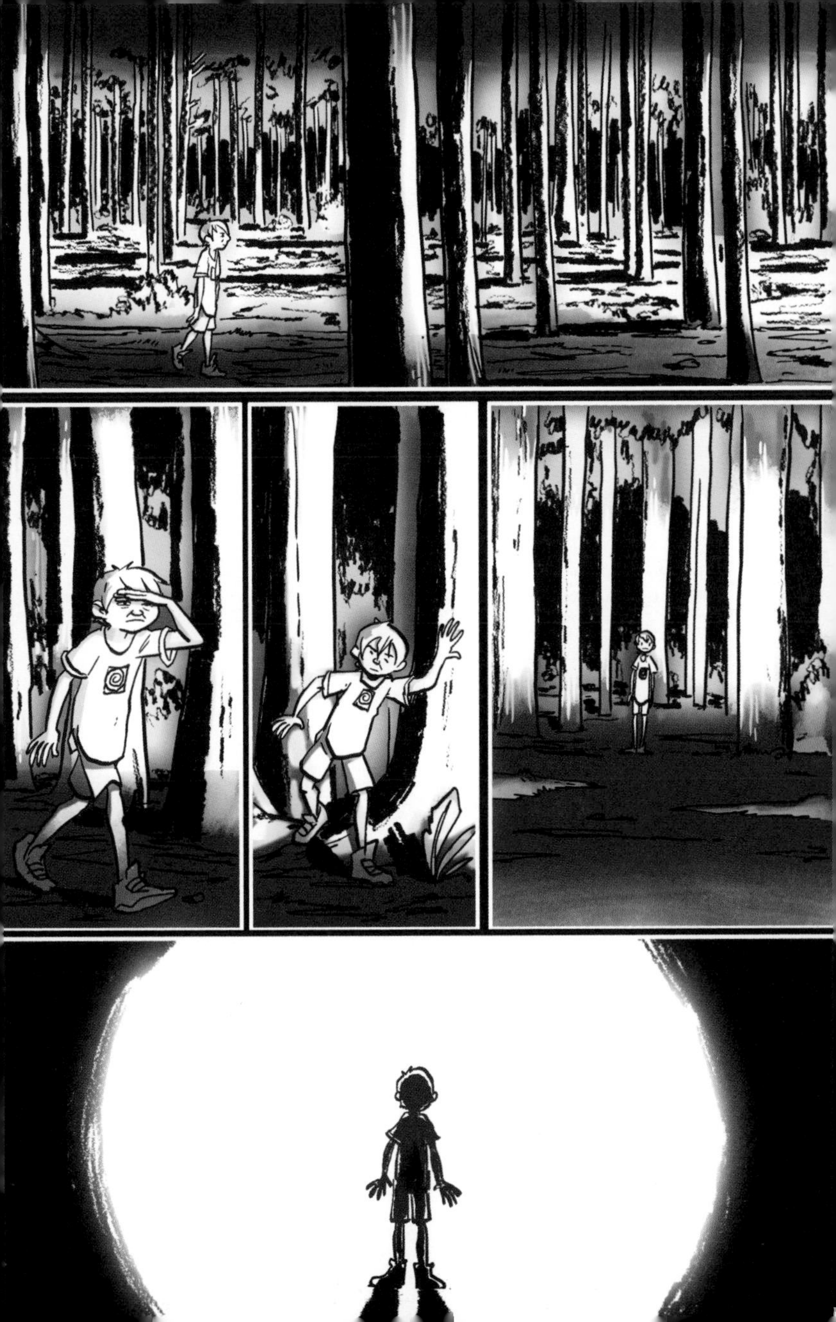

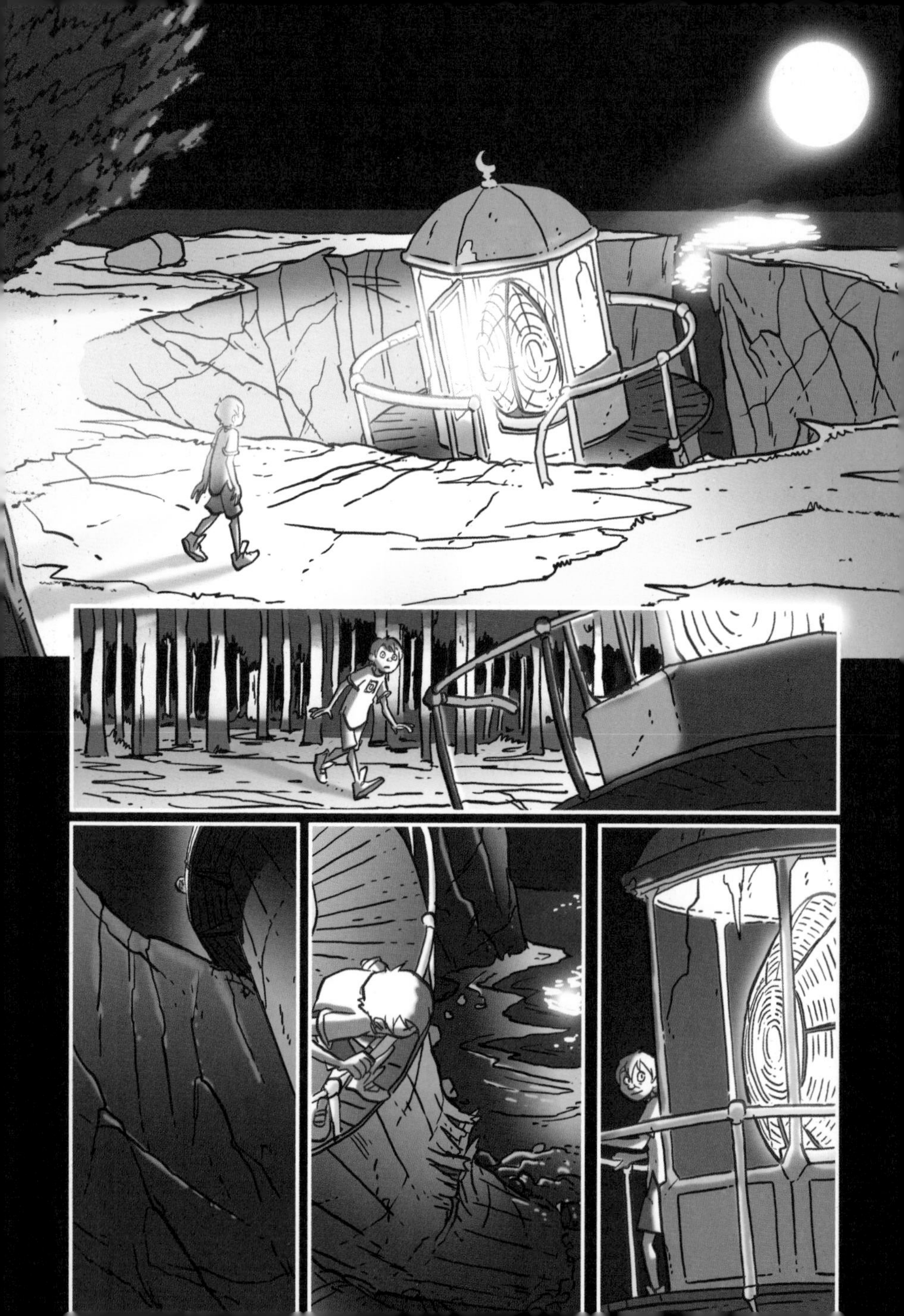

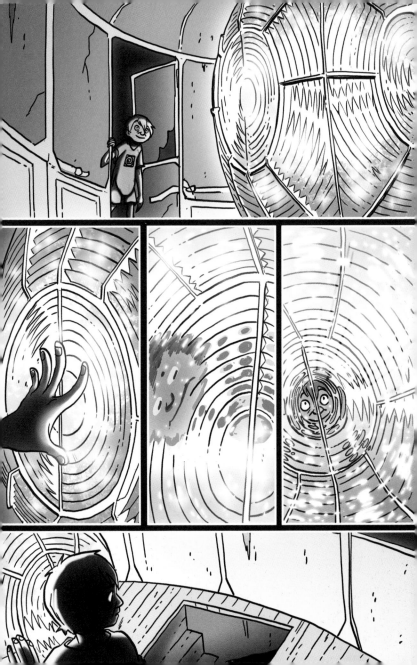

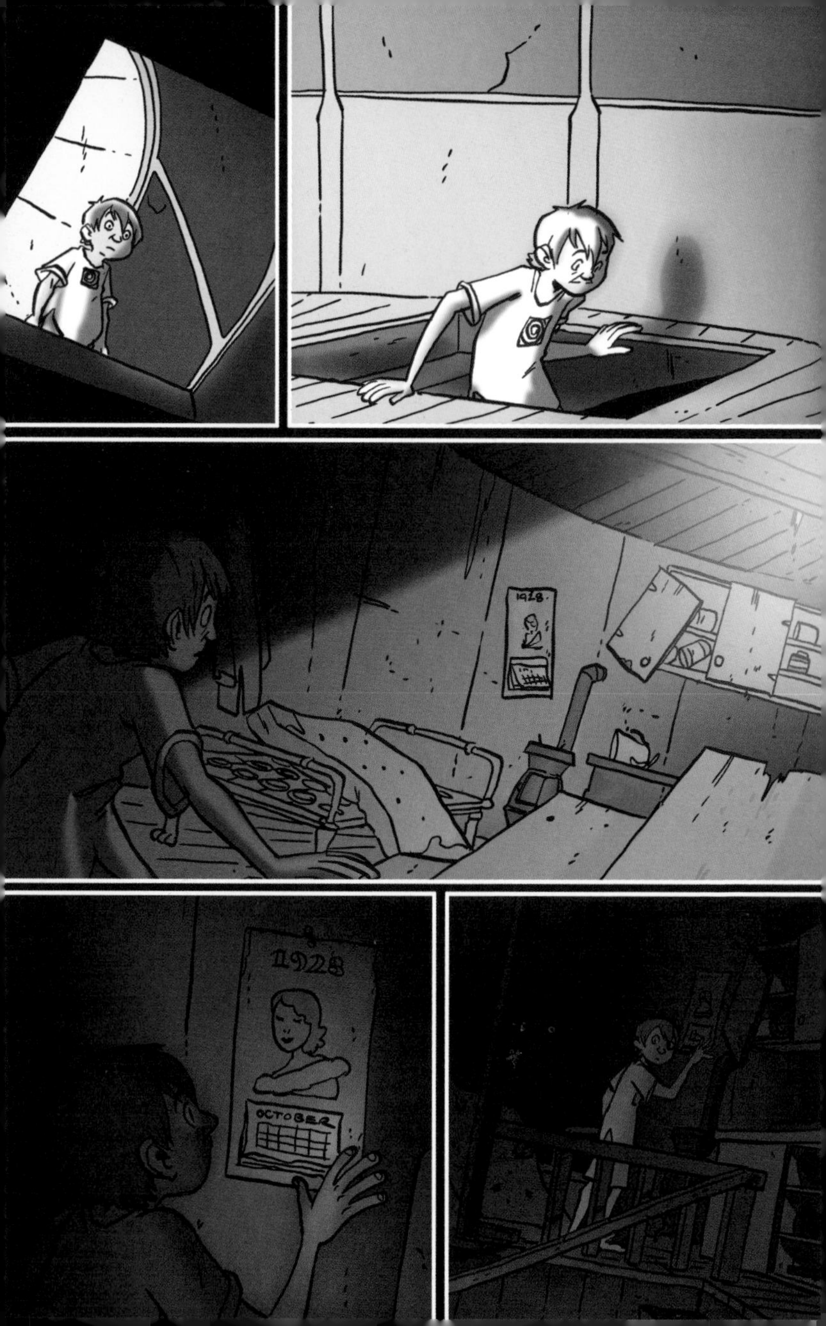
1928
1928
OCTOBER

Wow.

RUMMBLE

RRUMMBLLE

AAAHH!

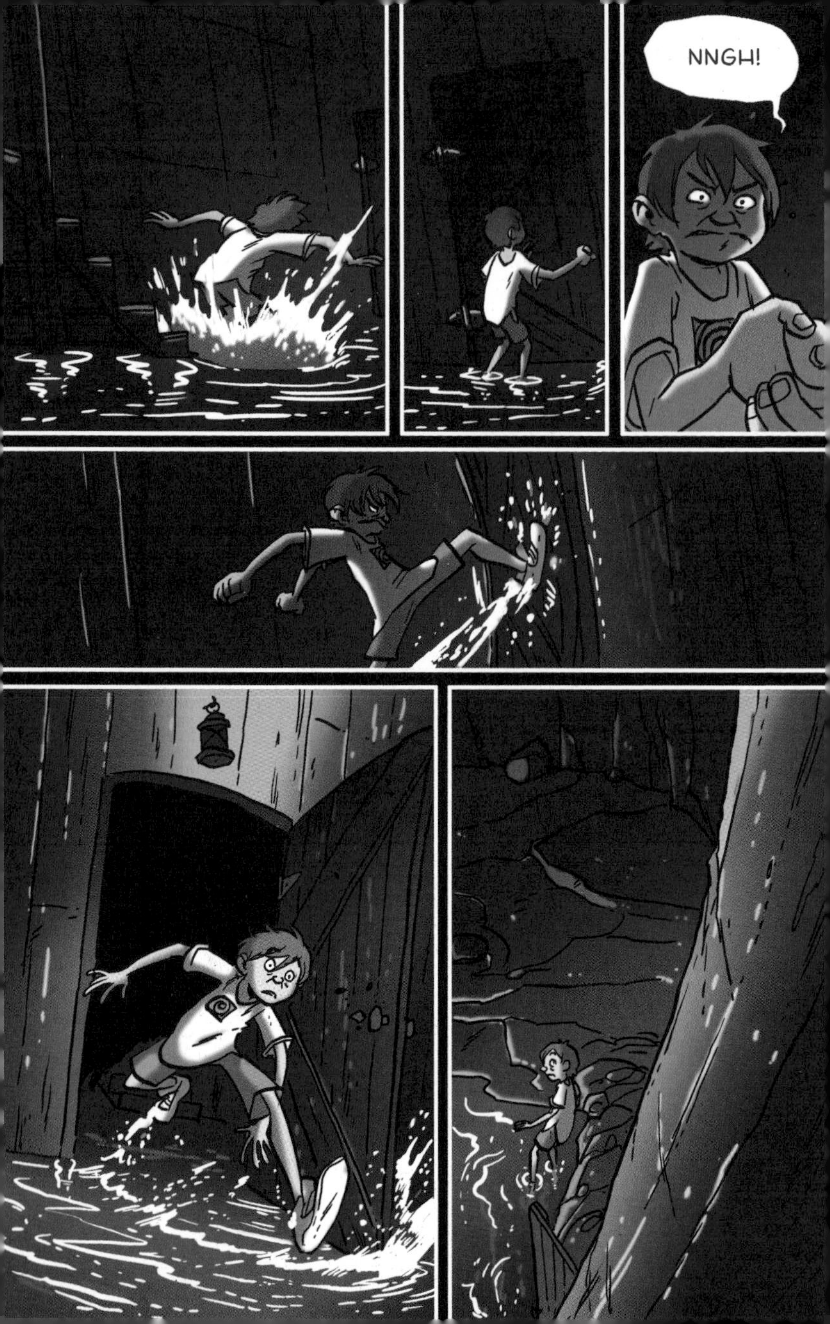
NNGH!

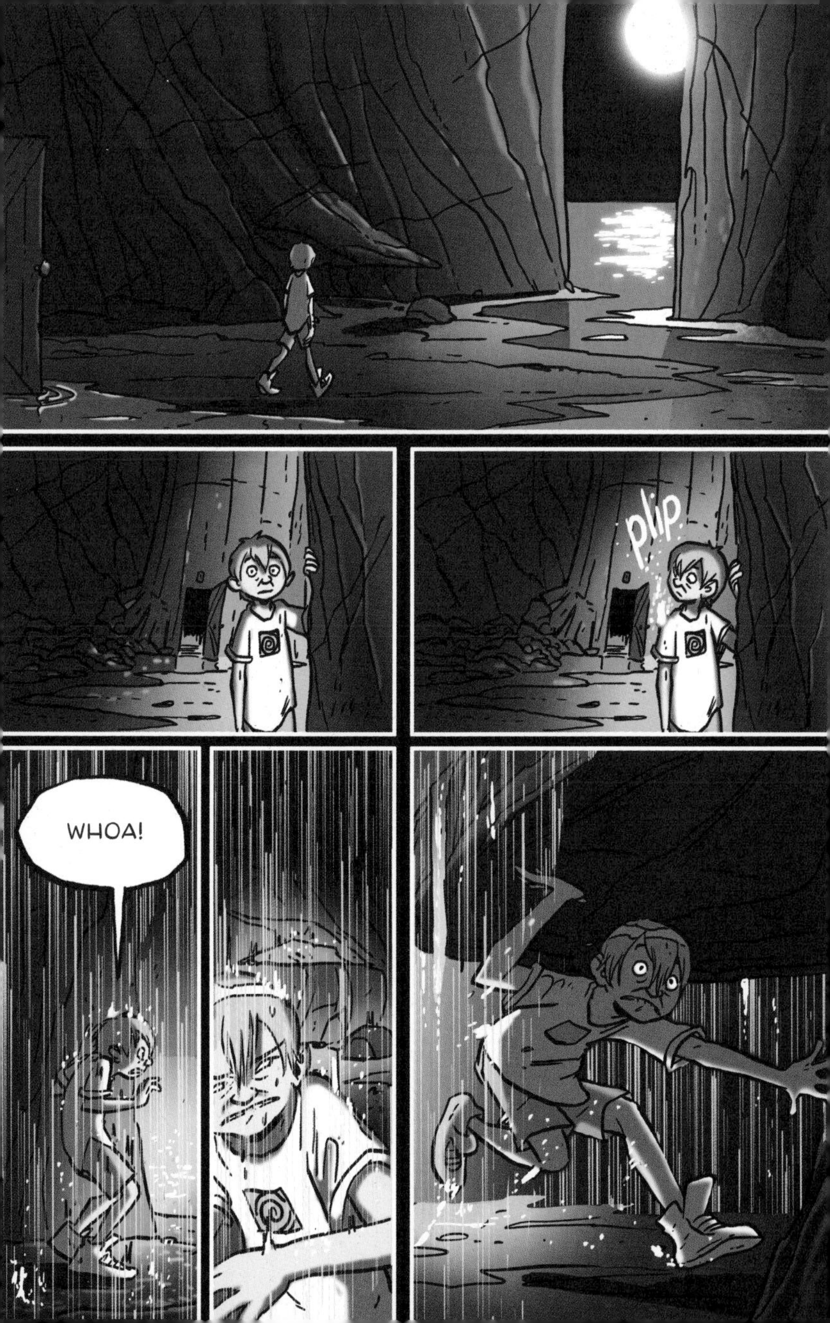
plip
WHOA!

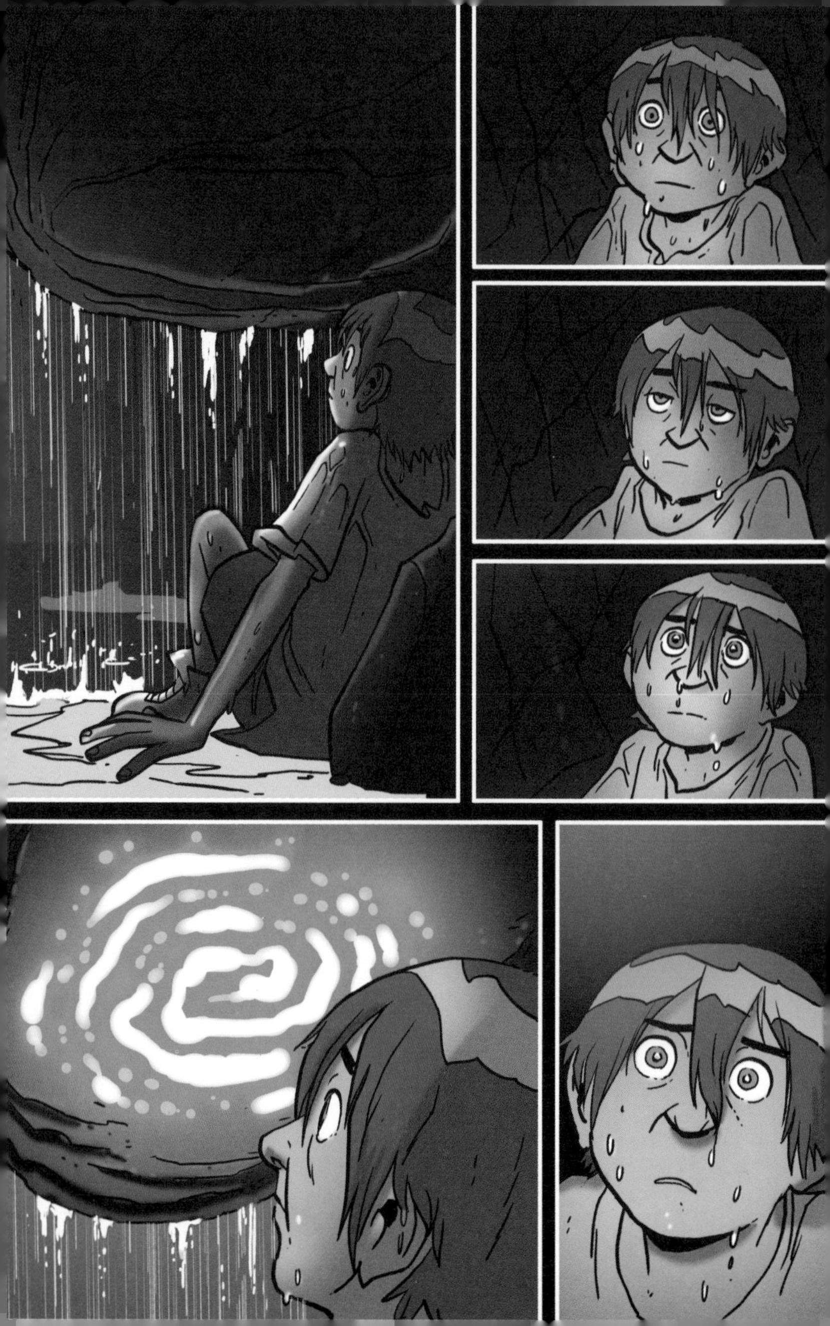

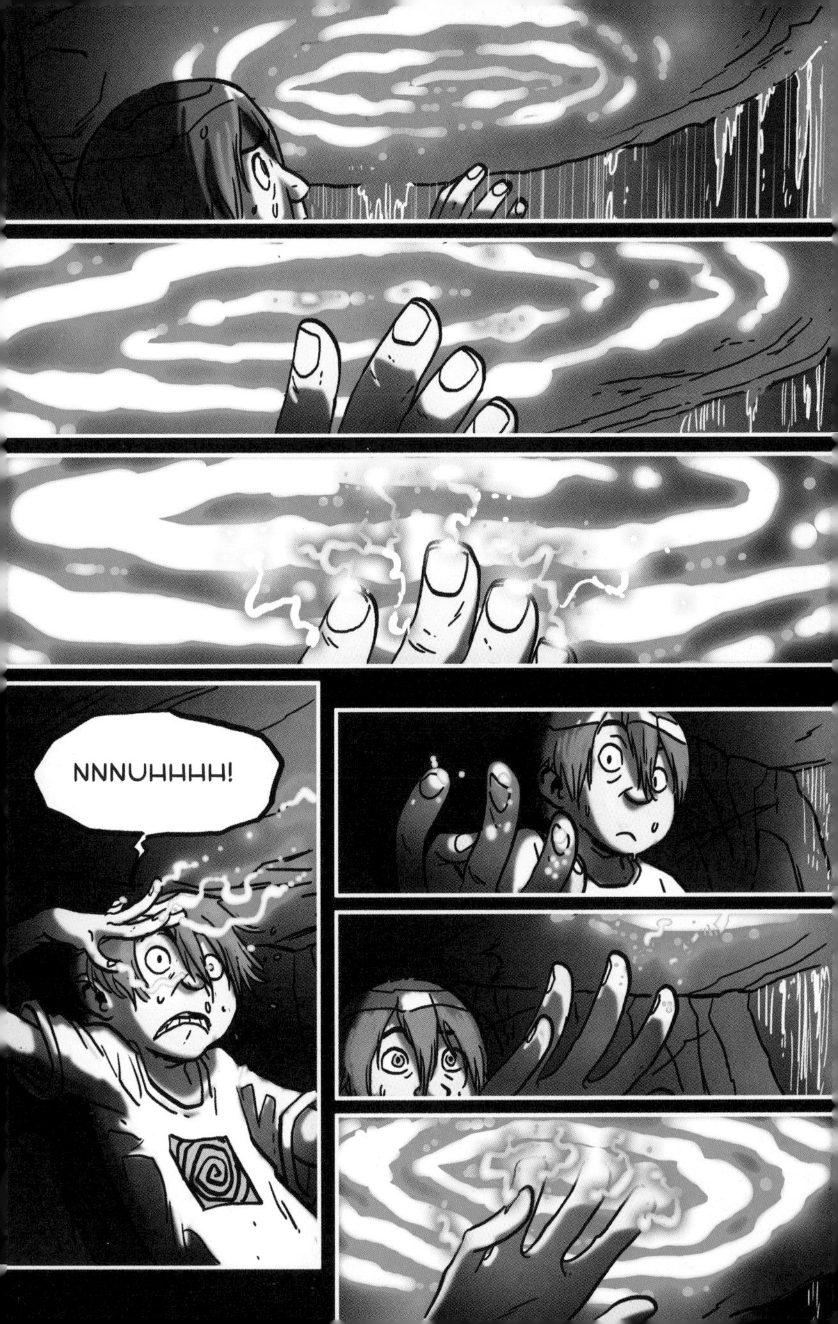
NNNUHHHH!

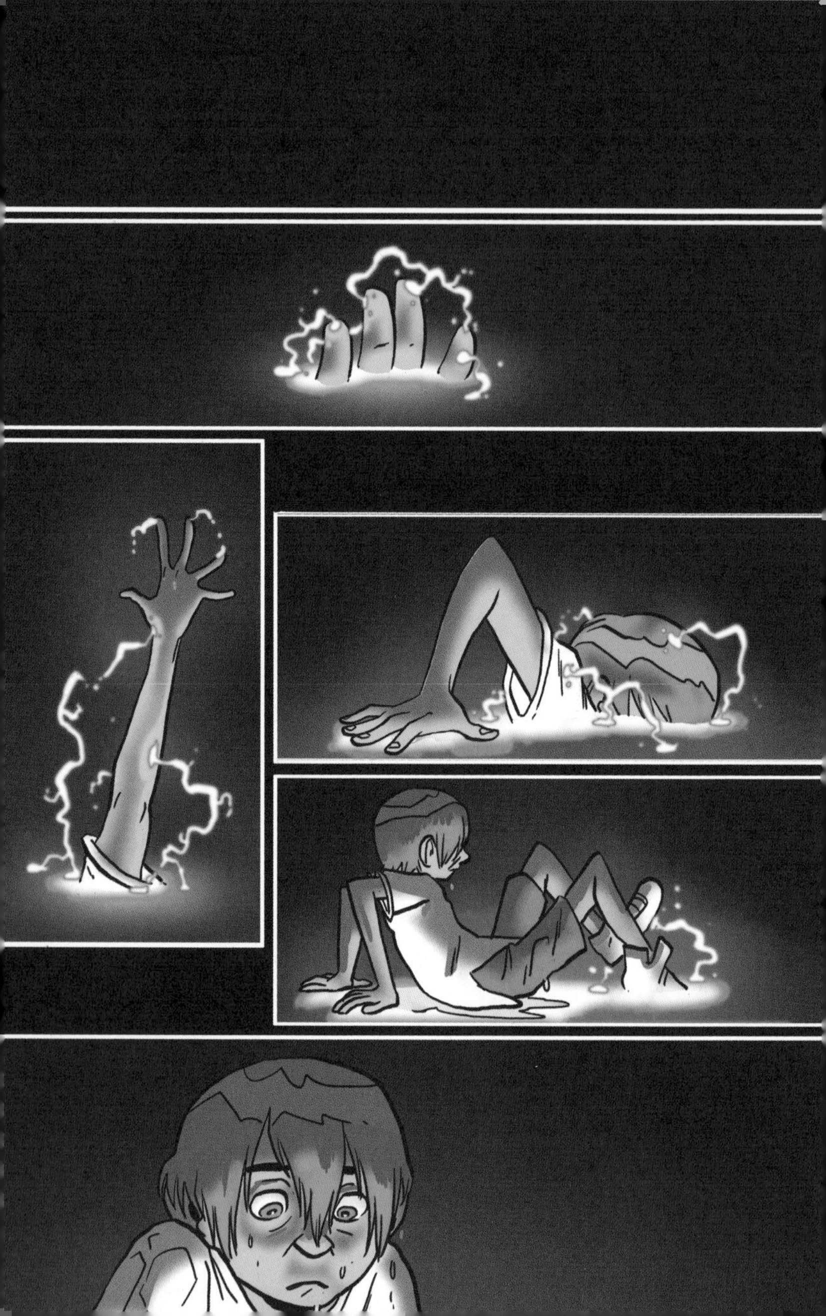

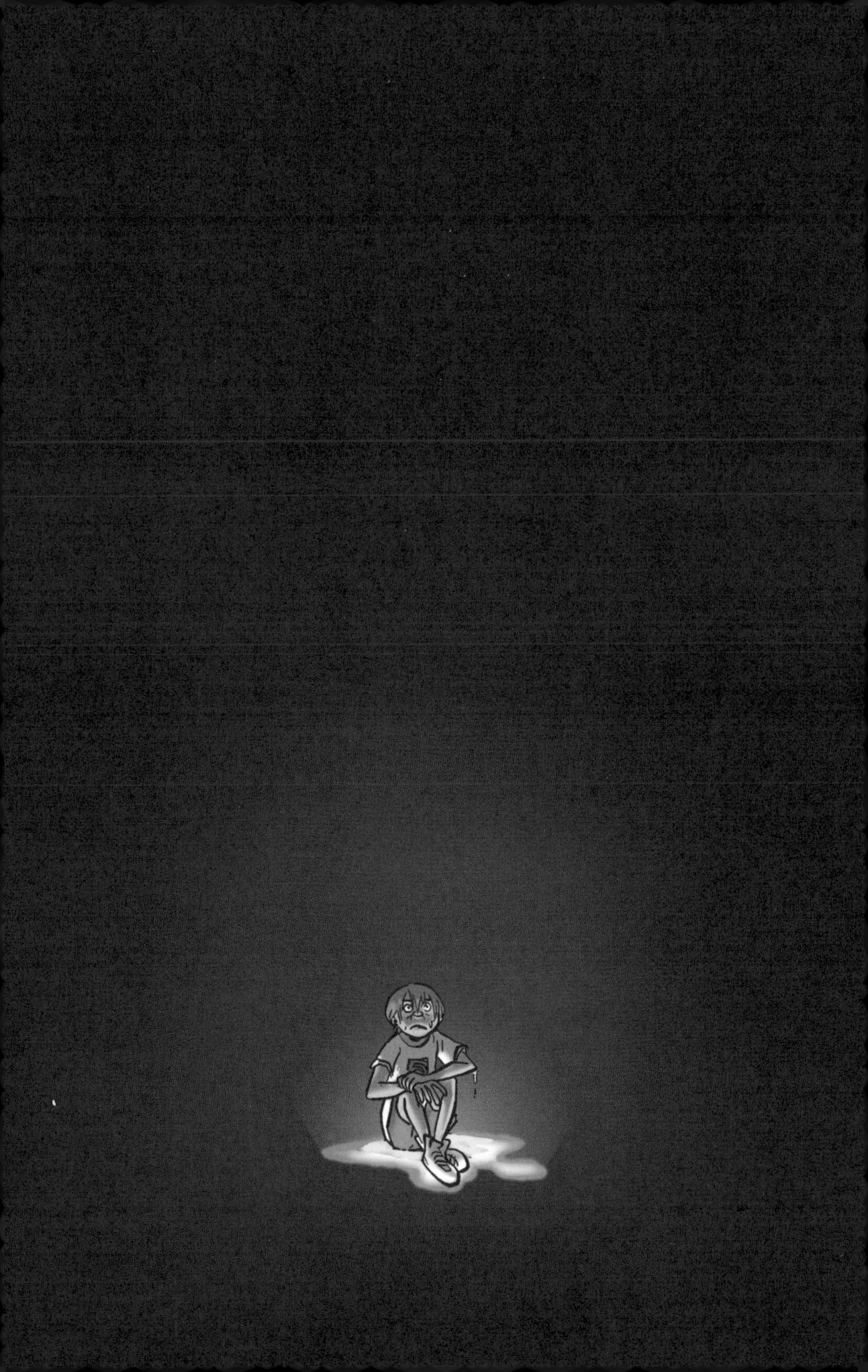

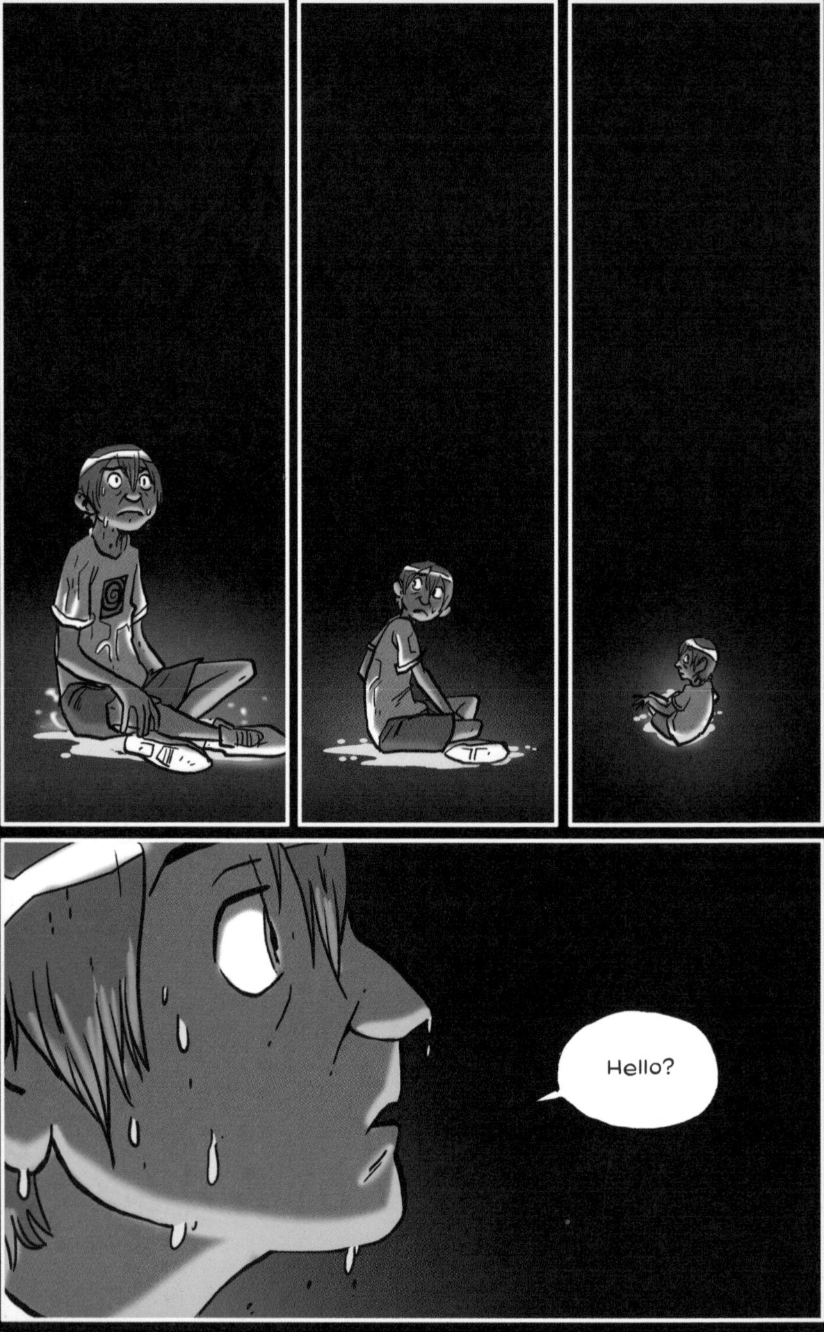
Hello?

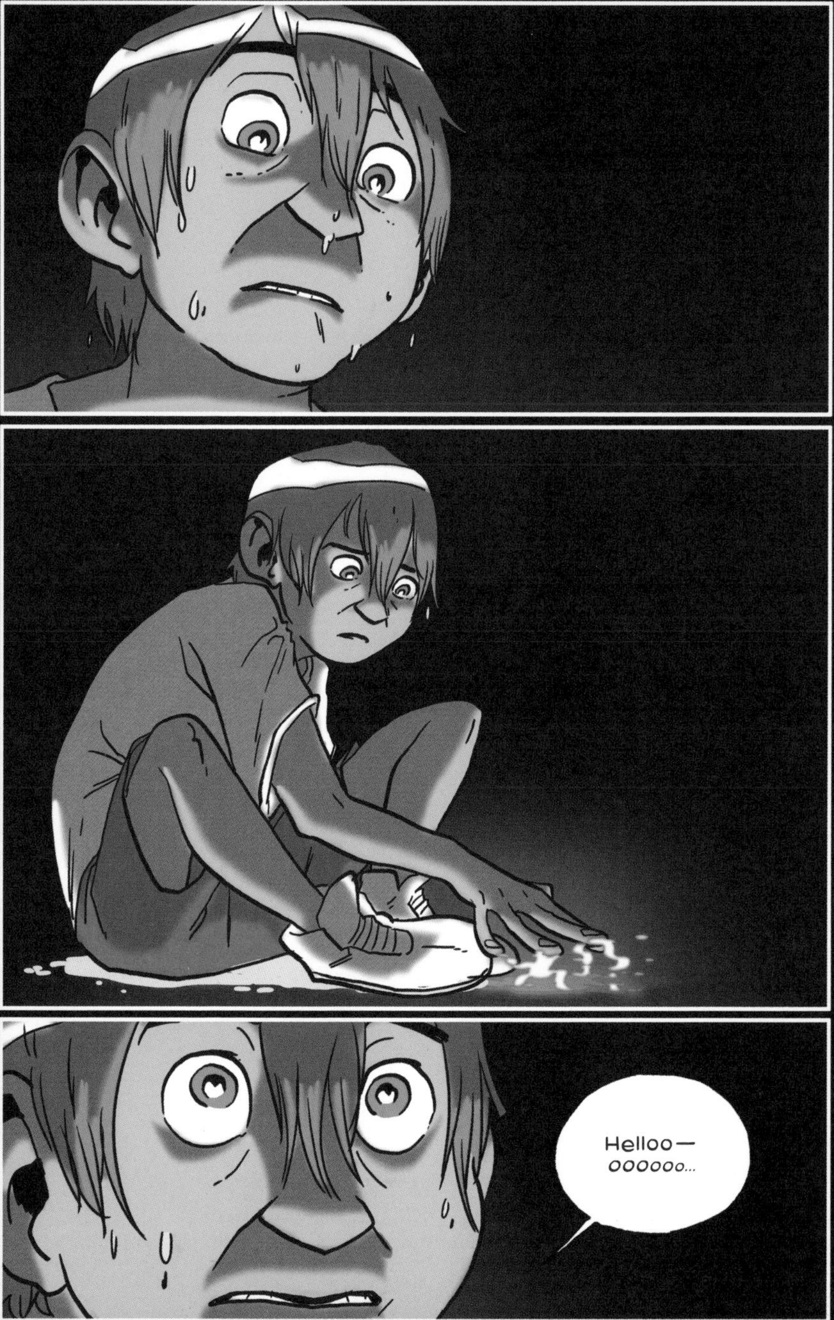
Helloo—
oooooo...

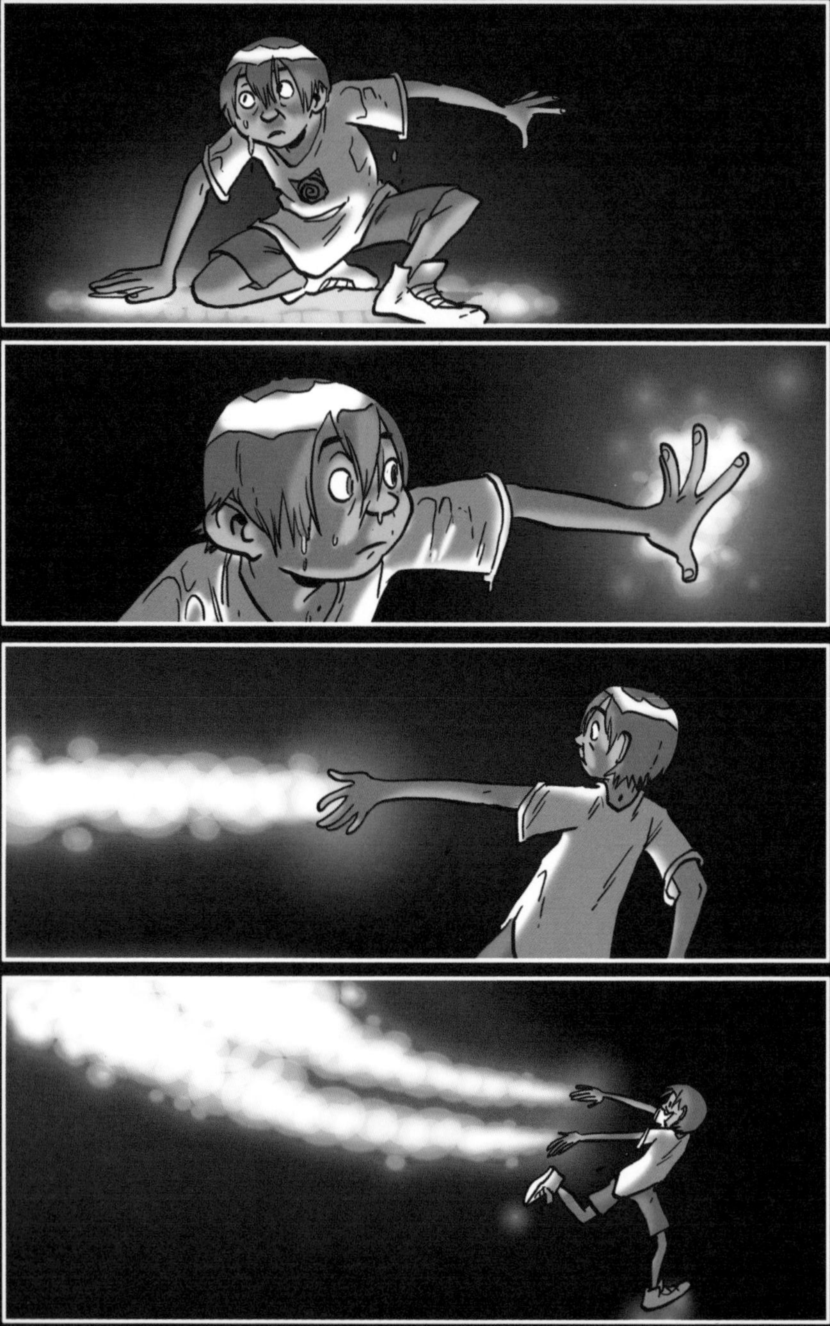

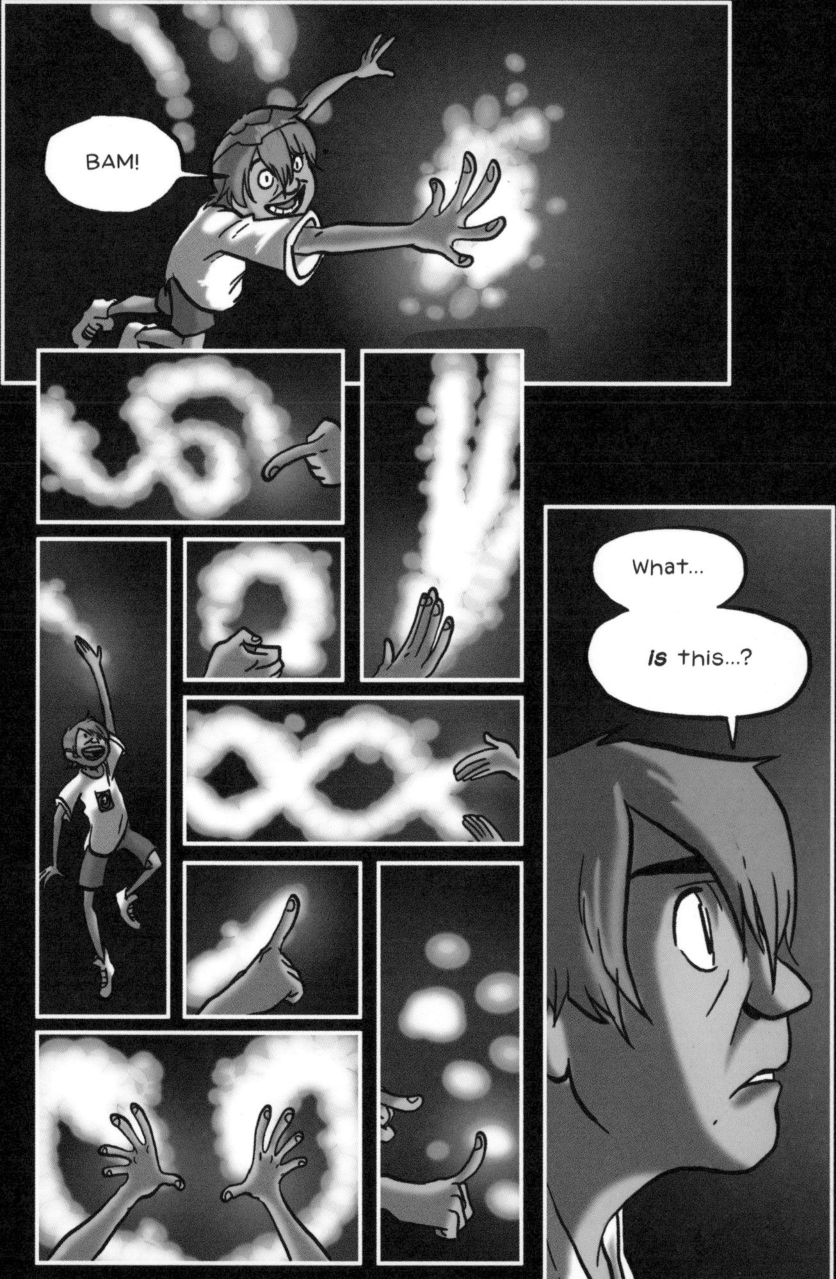
BAM!
What...
is this...?

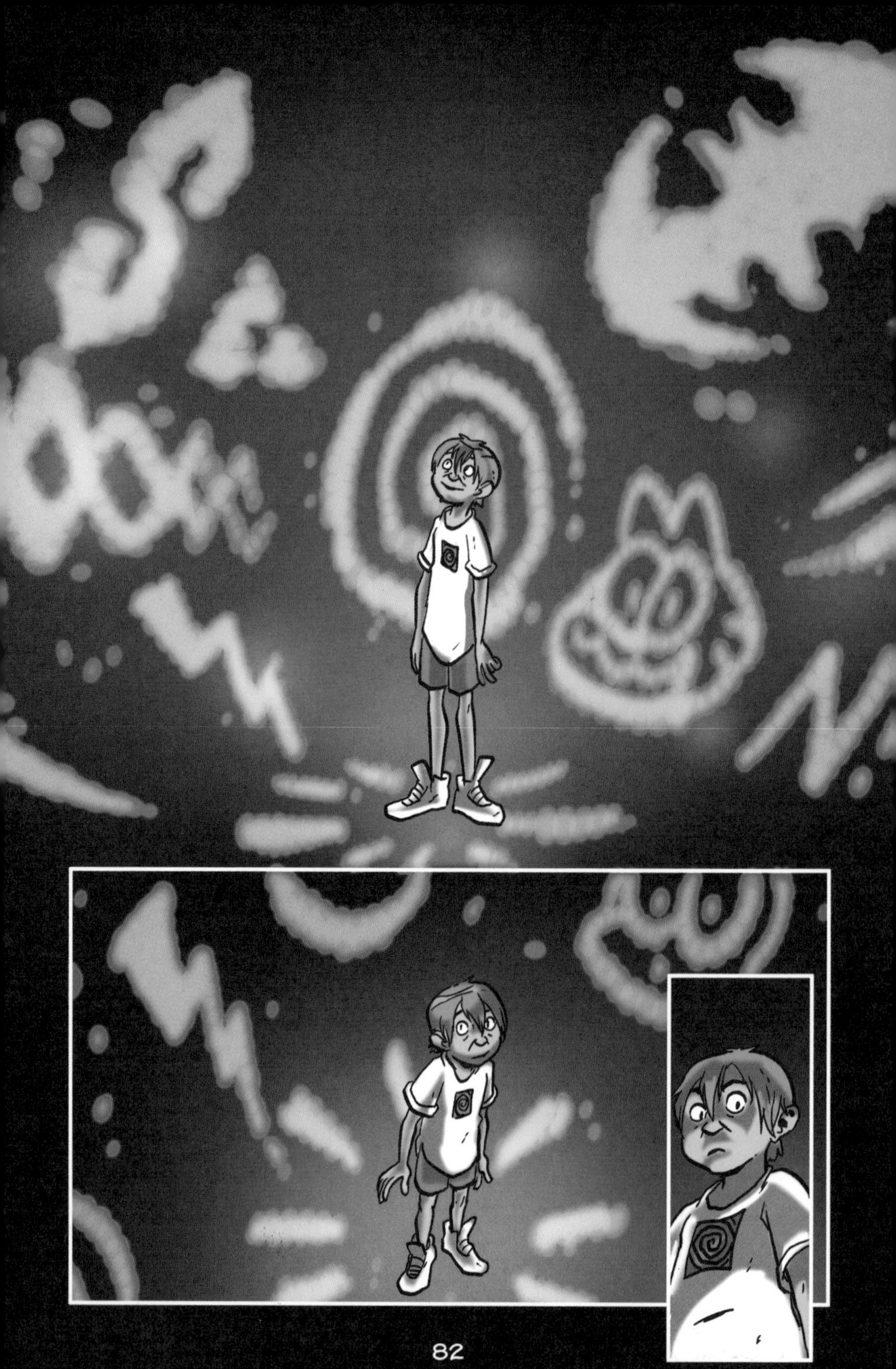

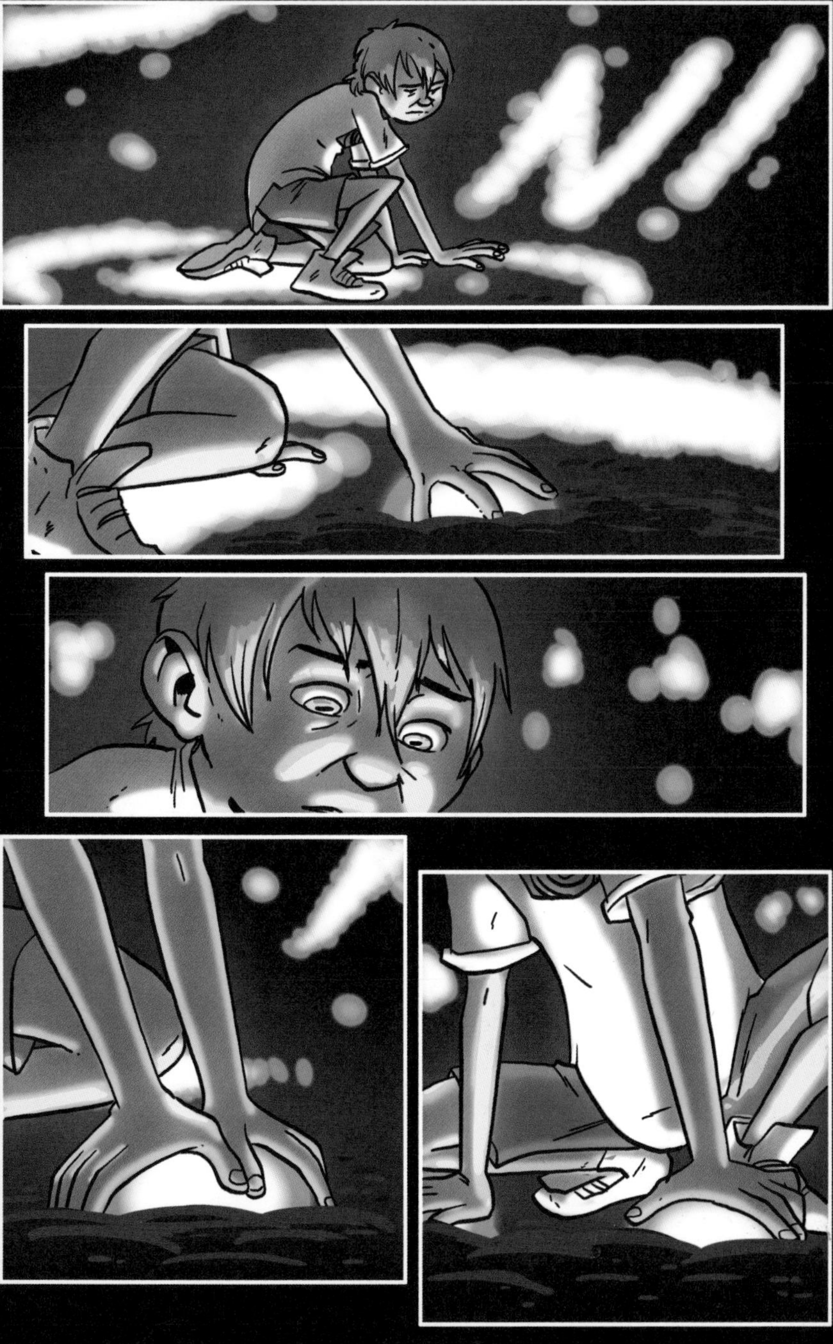

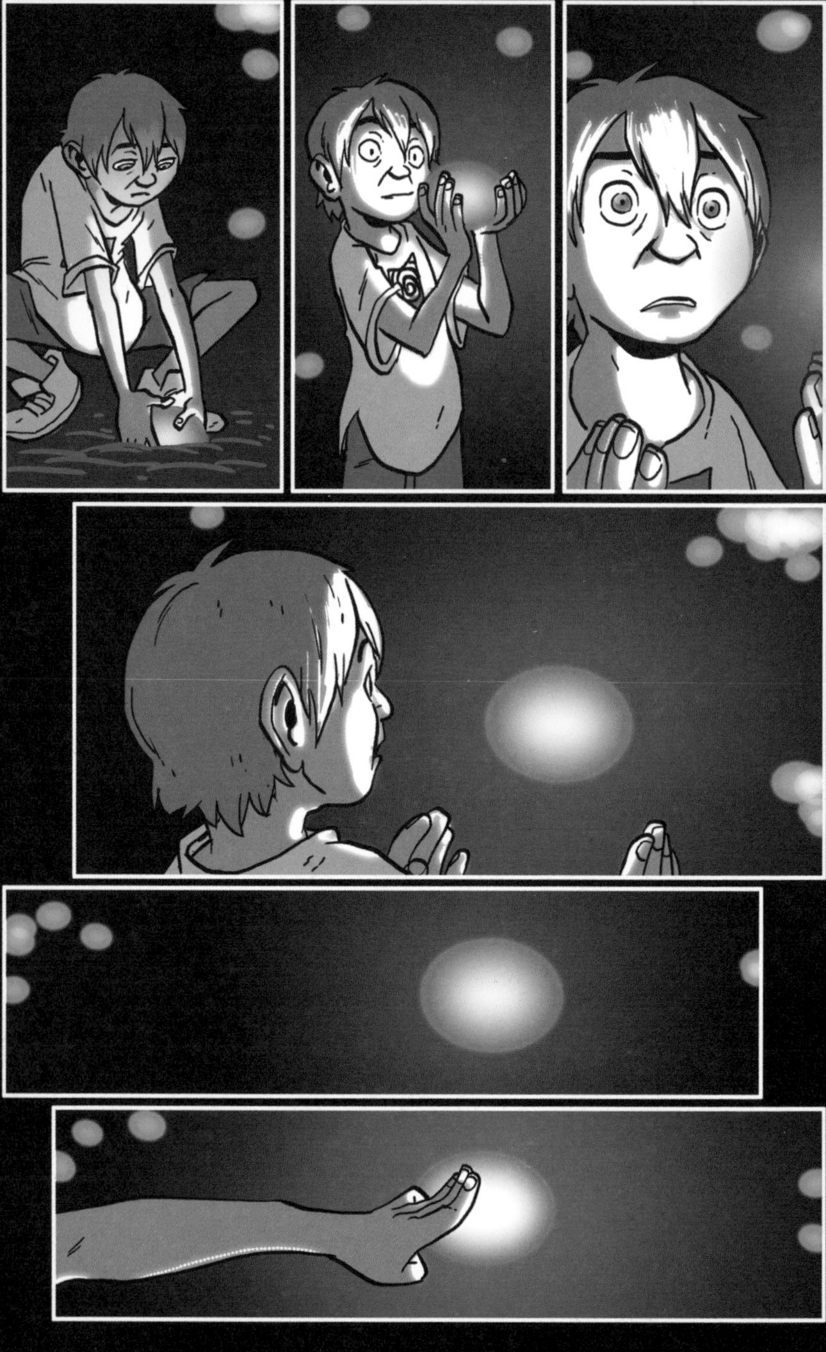

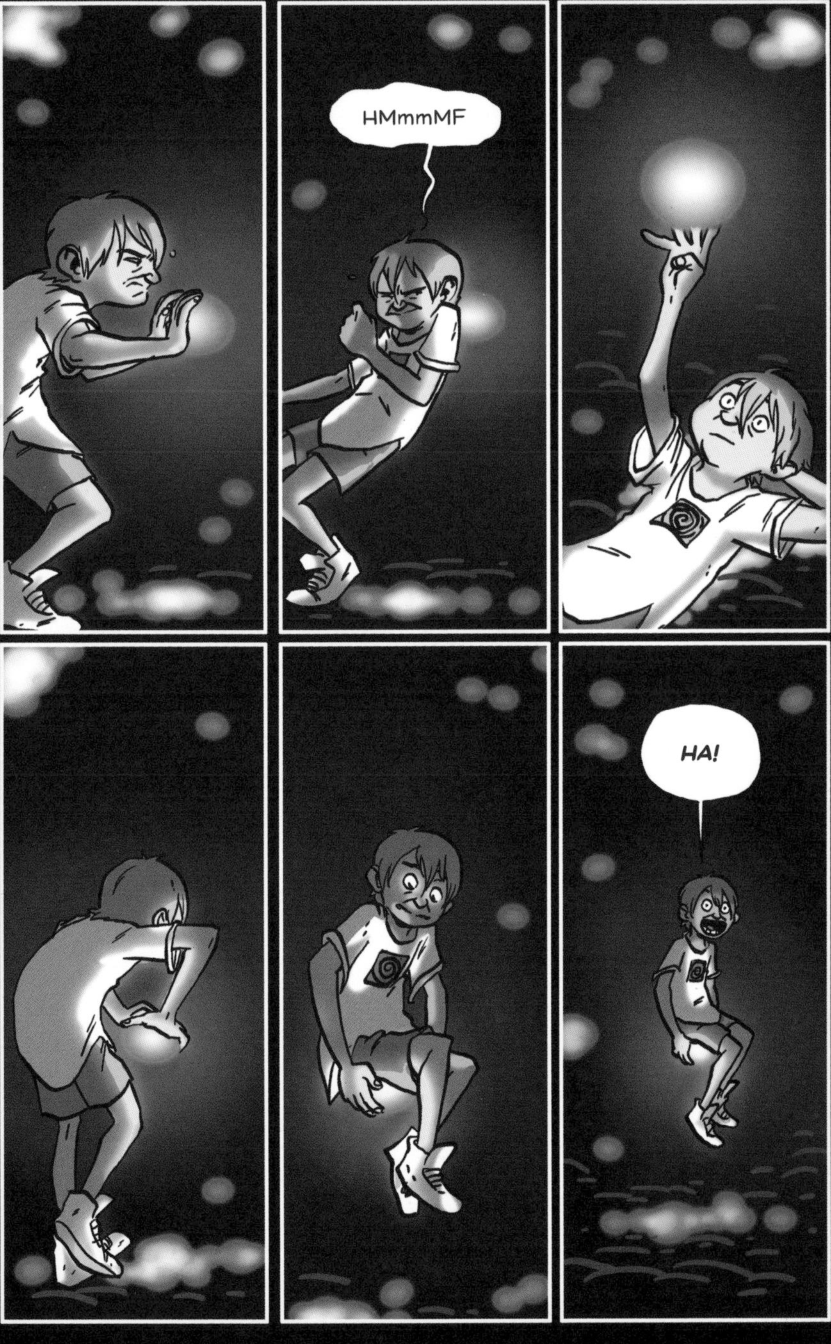
HMmmMF
HA!

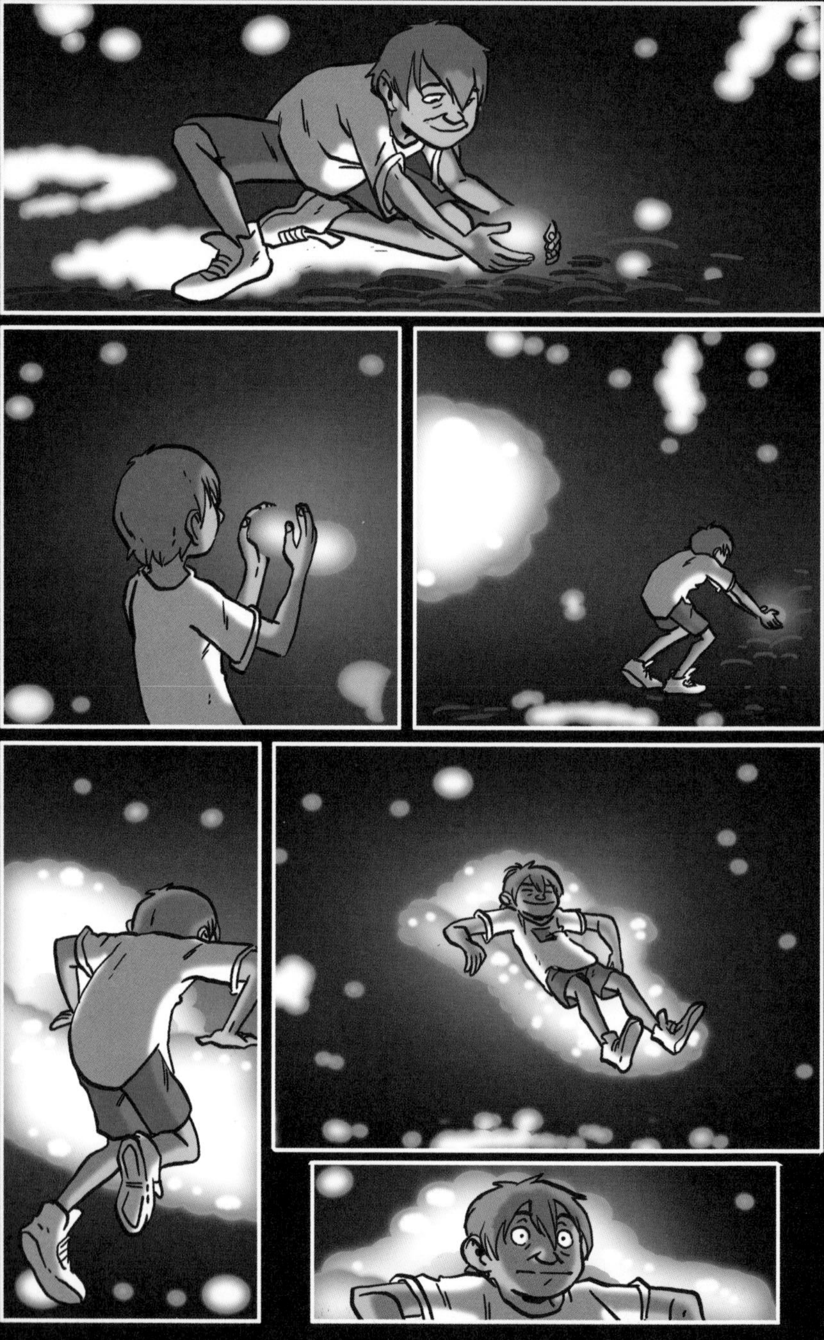

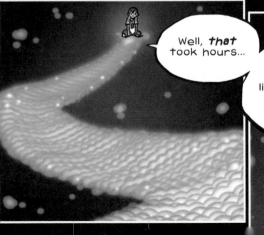

Well, **that** took hours...

but I **feeeel** like this is gonna be **worth it.**

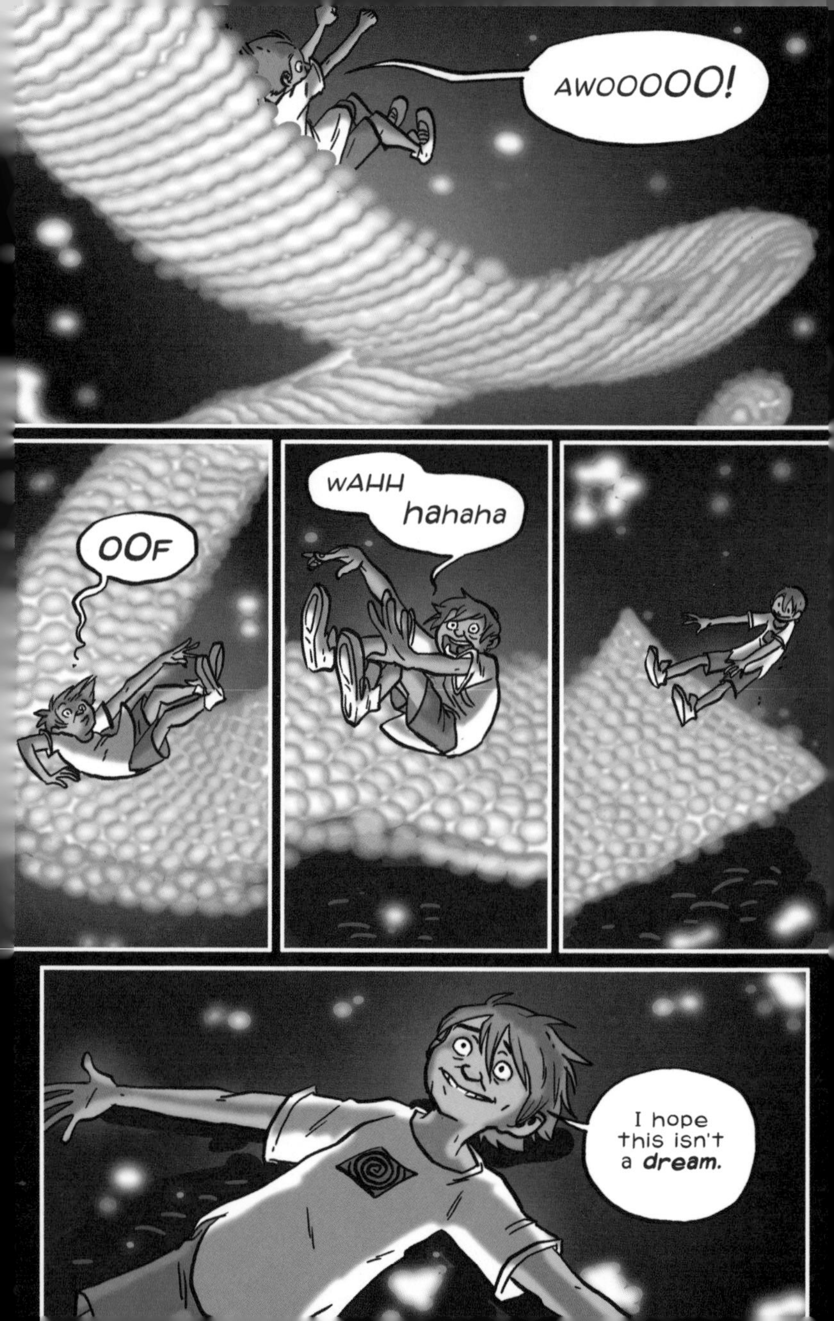
AWOOOOOO!
OOF
WAHH hahaha
I hope this isn't a **dream.**

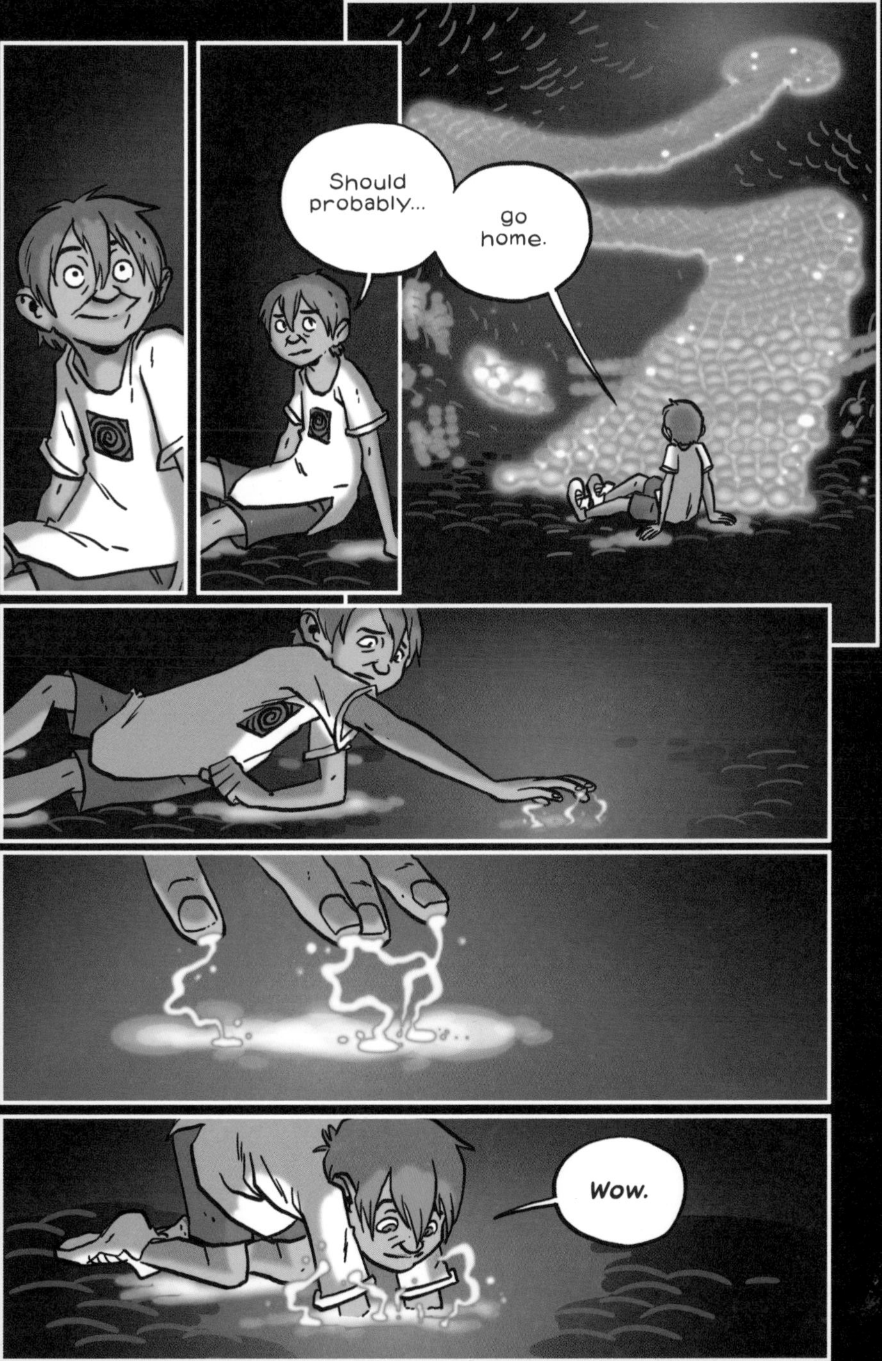
Should probably...
go home.
Wow.

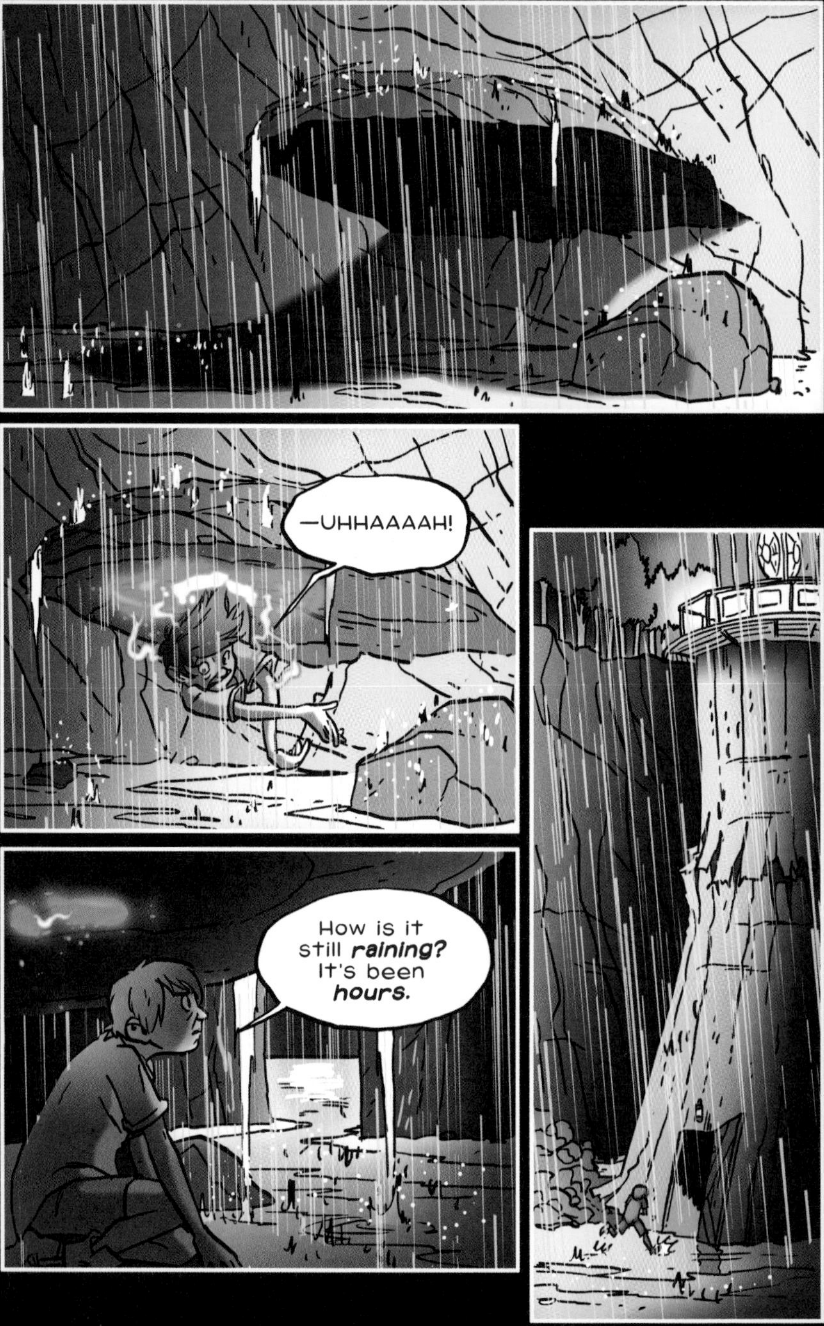
—UHHAAAAH!
How is it still *raining?* It's been *hours.*

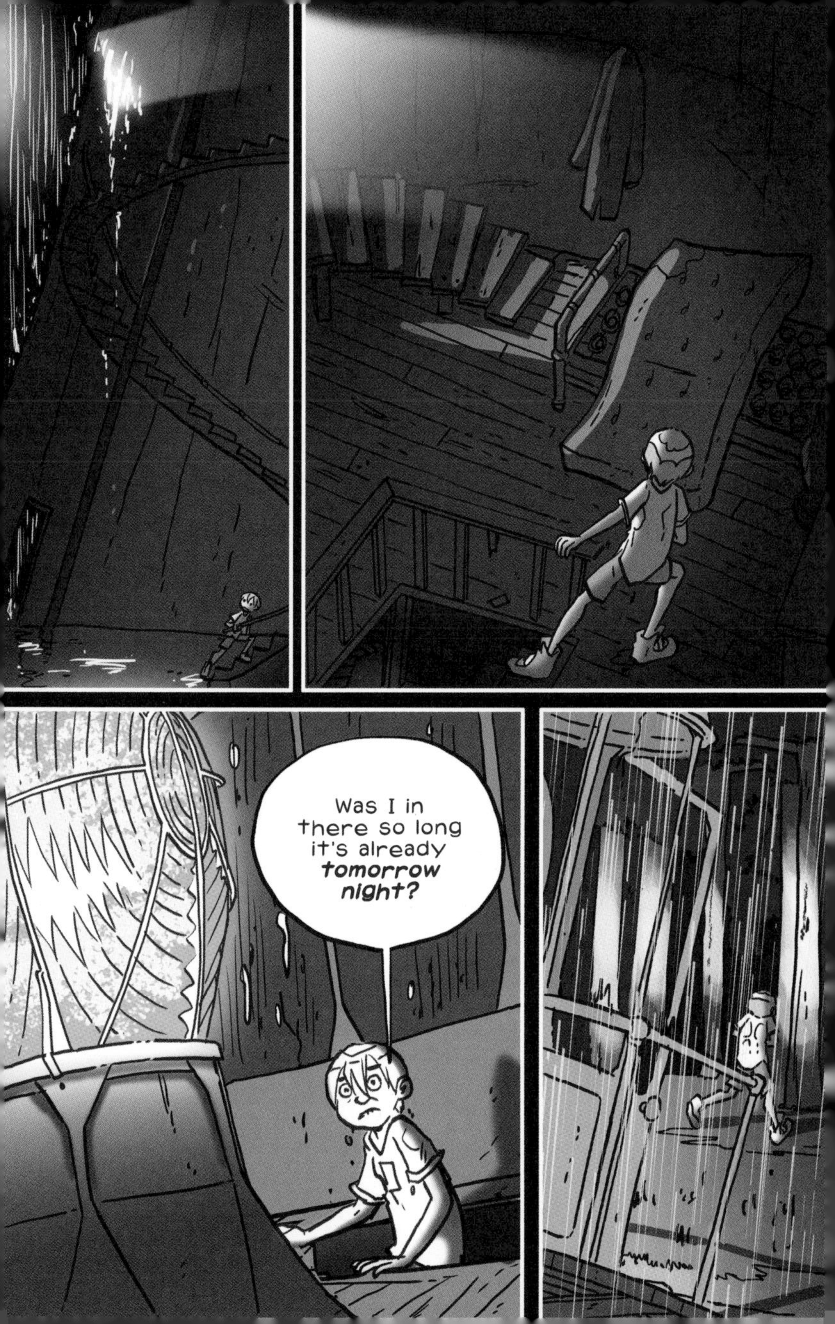
Was I in there so long it's already **tomorrow night?**

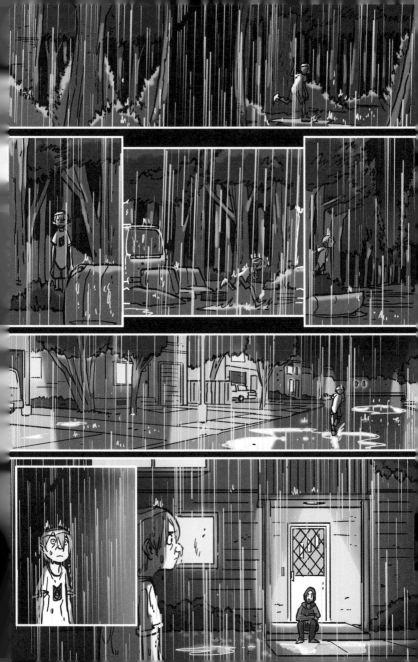

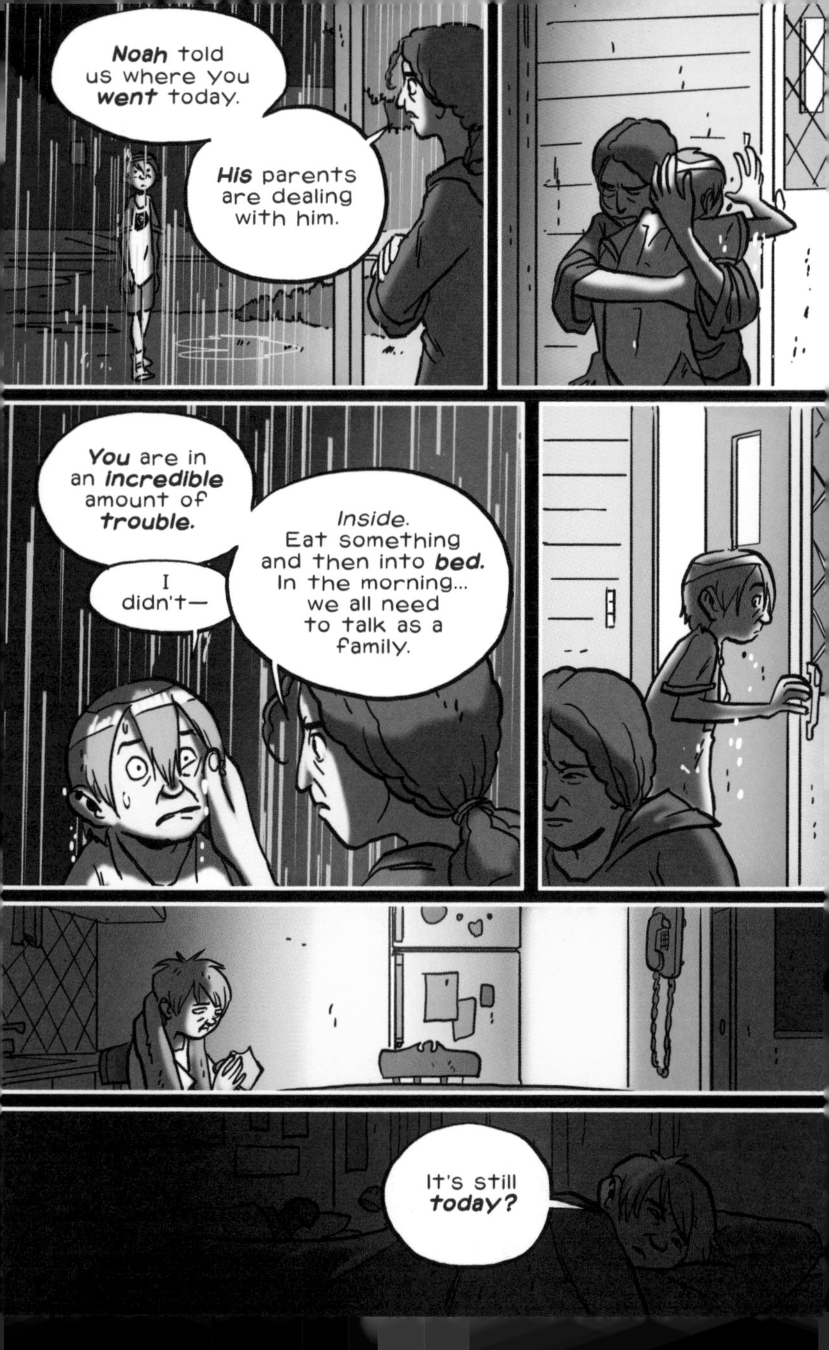

Noah told us where you went today.
His parents are dealing with him.
You are in an incredible amount of trouble.
I didn't—
Inside. Eat something and then into bed. In the morning... we all need to talk as a family.
It's still today?

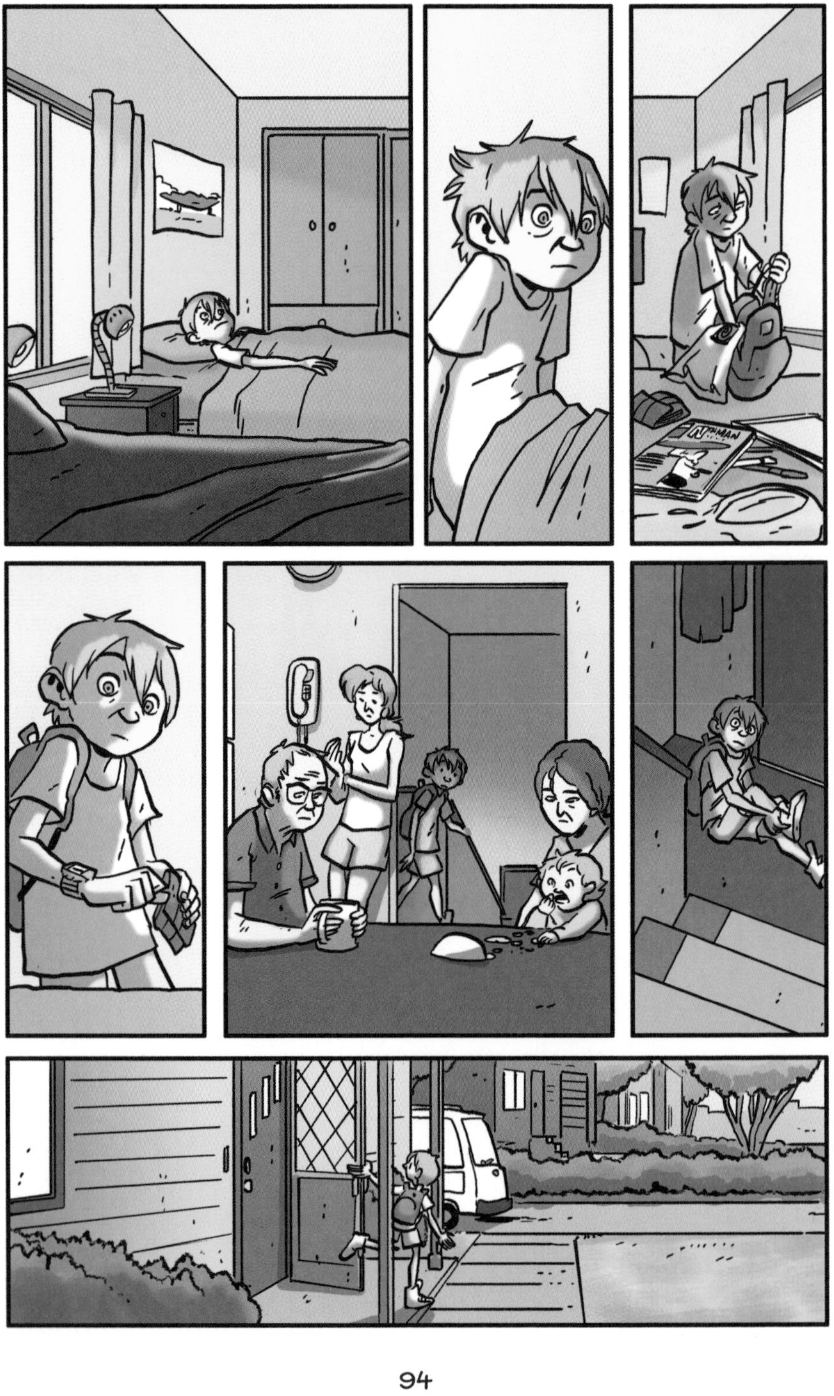

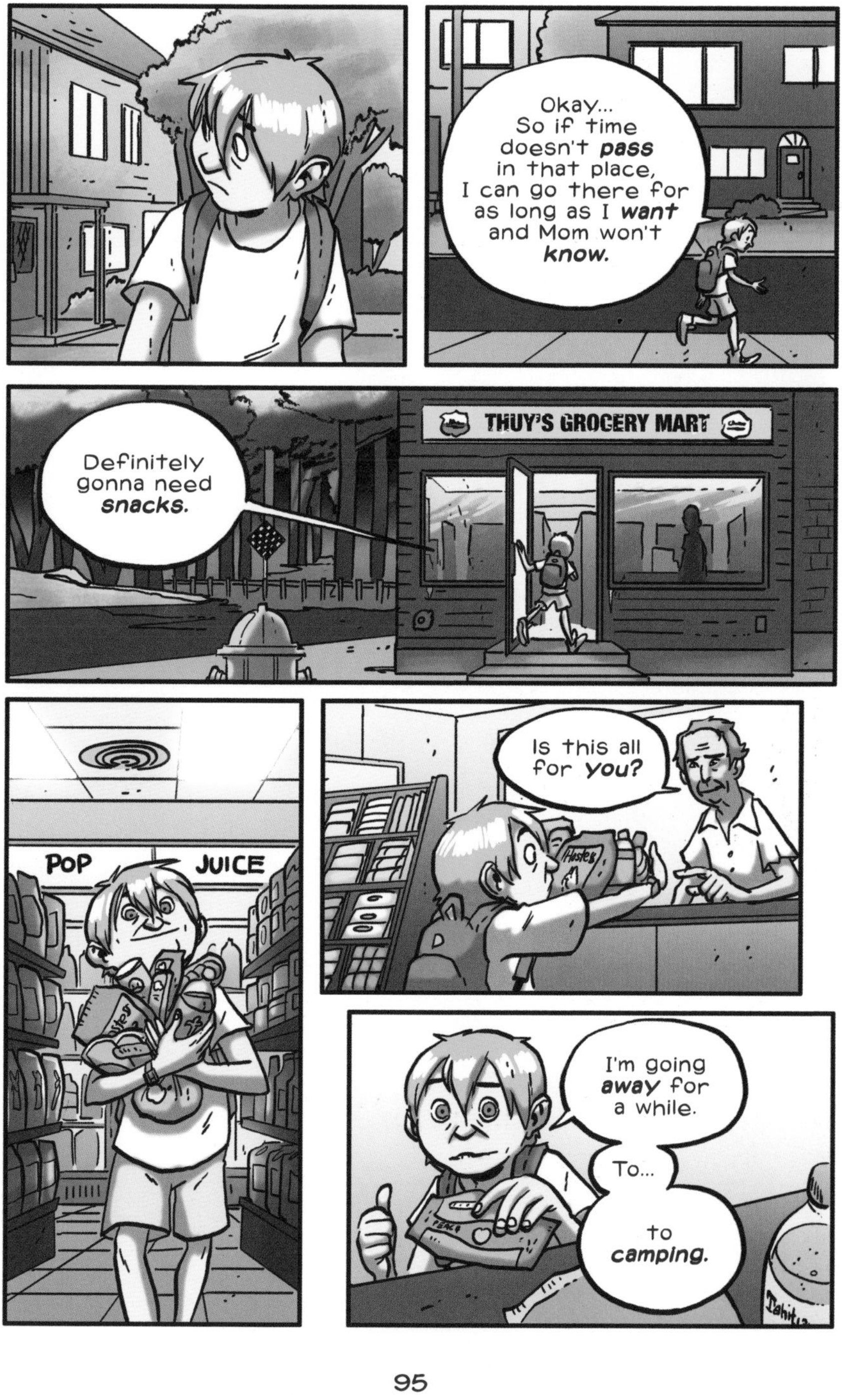
Okay... So if time doesn't **pass** in that place, I can go there for as long as I **want** and Mom won't **know.**
THUY'S GROCERY MART
Definitely gonna need **snacks.**
POP
JUICE
Is this all for **you?**
I'm going **away** for a while.
To...
to **camping.**

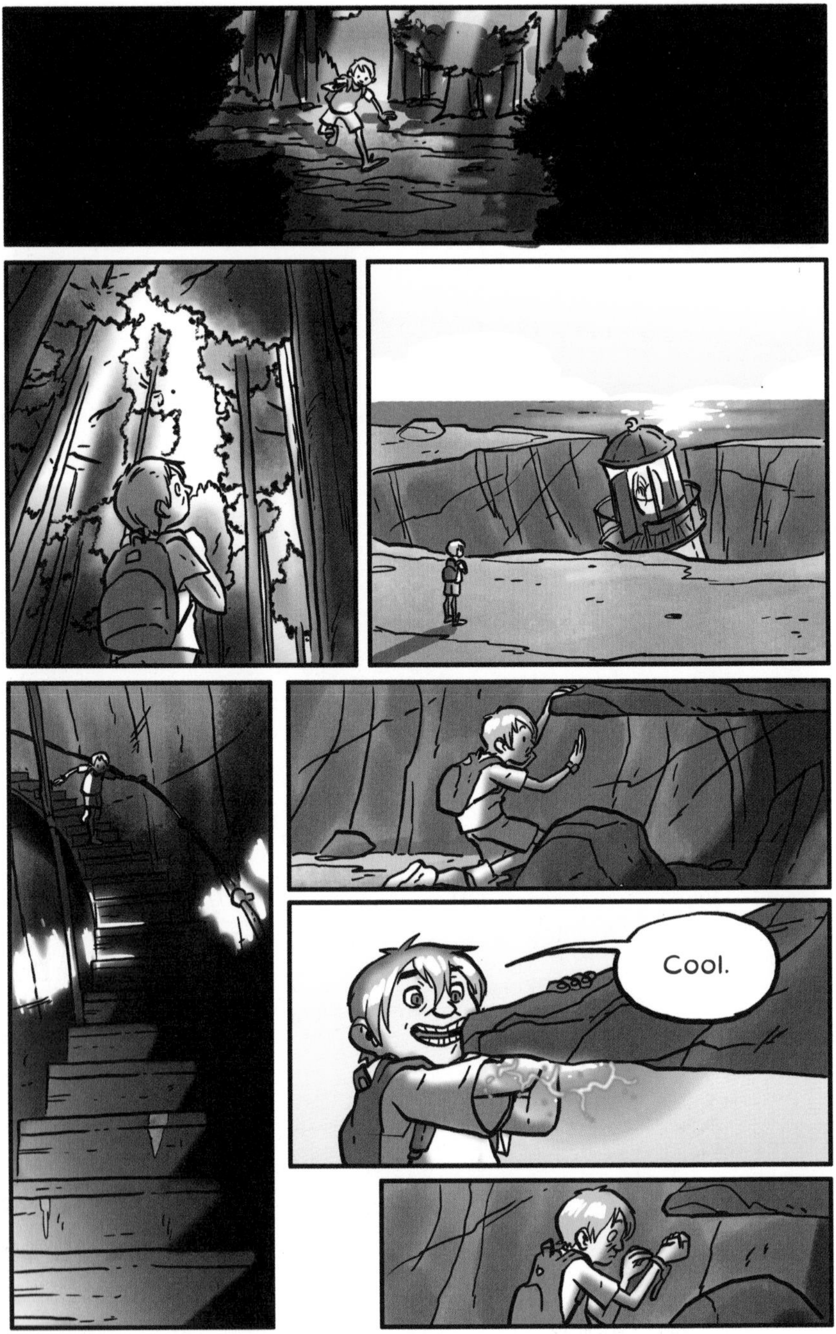
Cool.

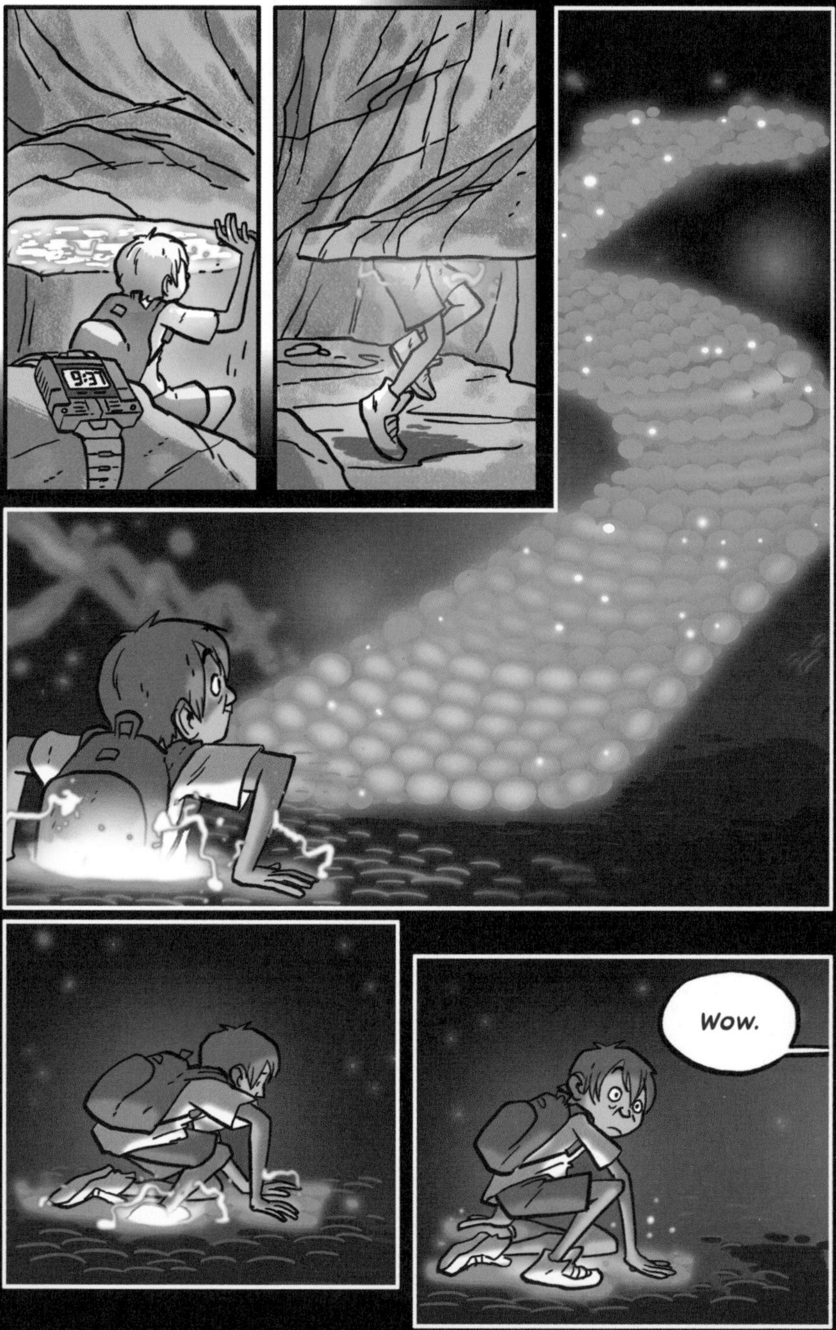
Wow.

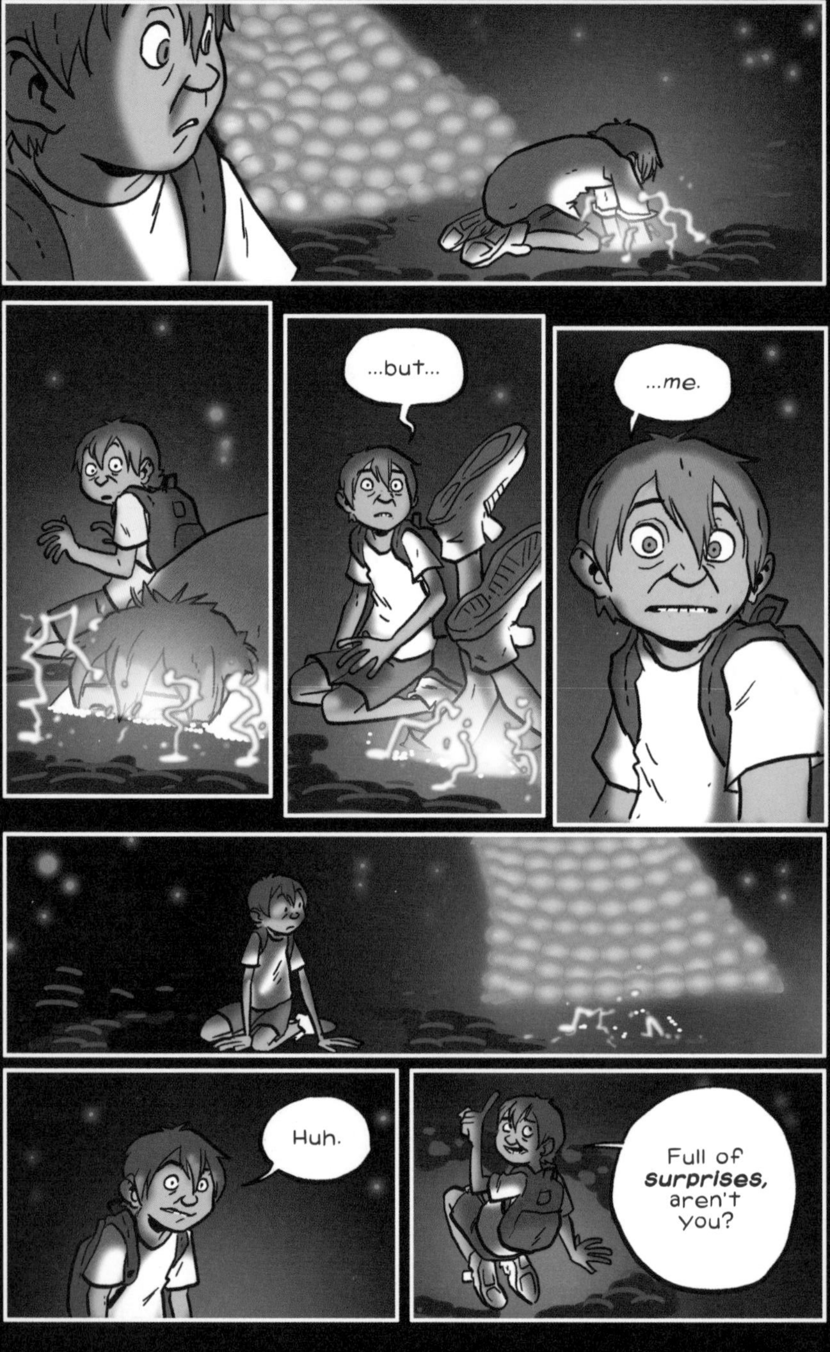
...but...
...me.
Huh.
Full of
surprises,
aren't
you?

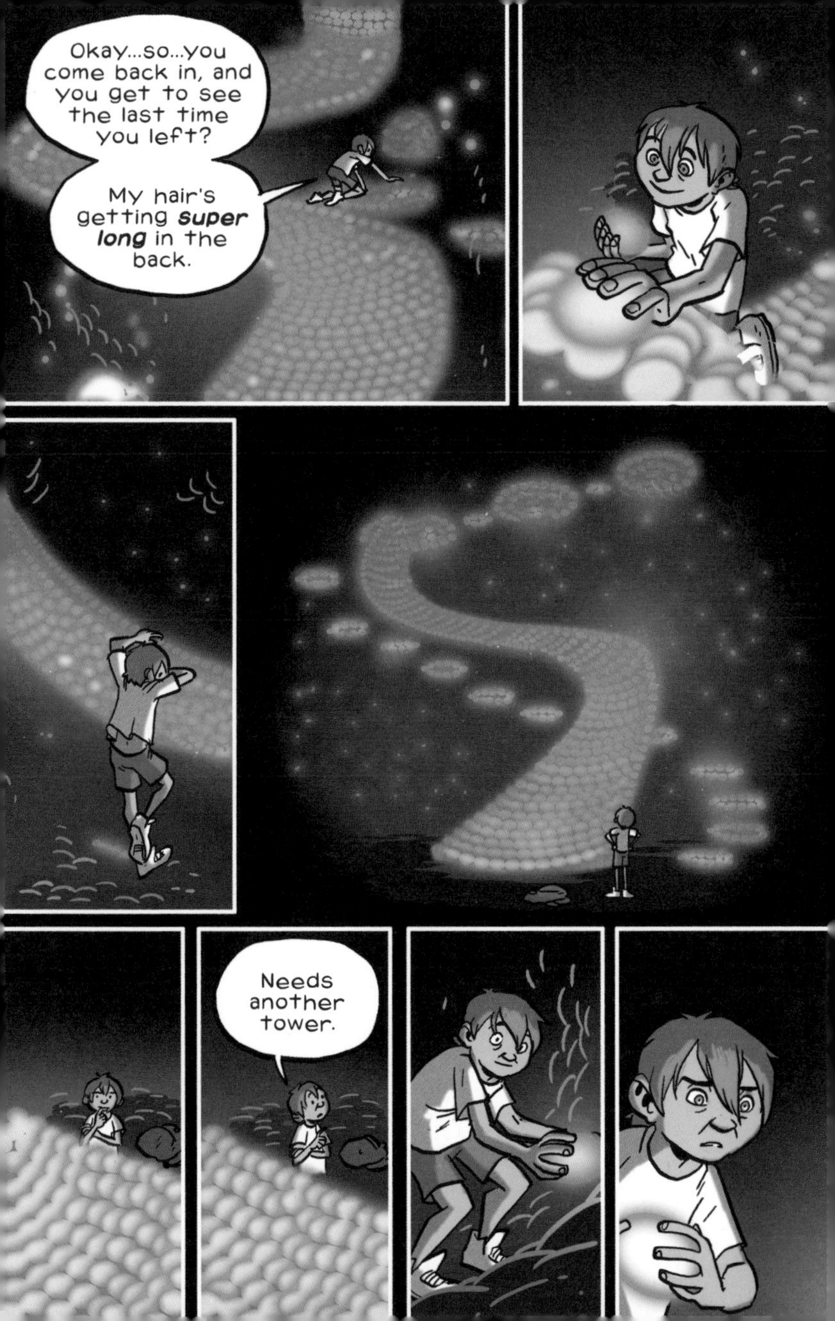
Okay...so...you come back in, and you get to see the last time you left?
My hair's getting **super long** in the back.
Needs another tower.

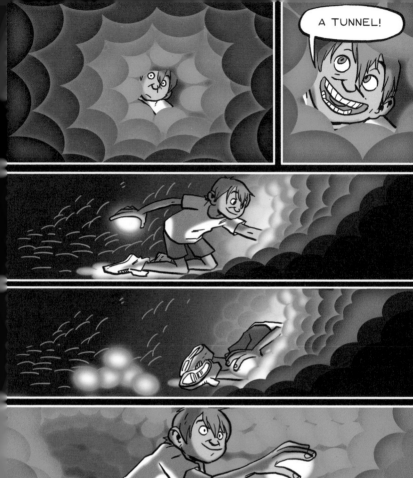

A TUNNEL!

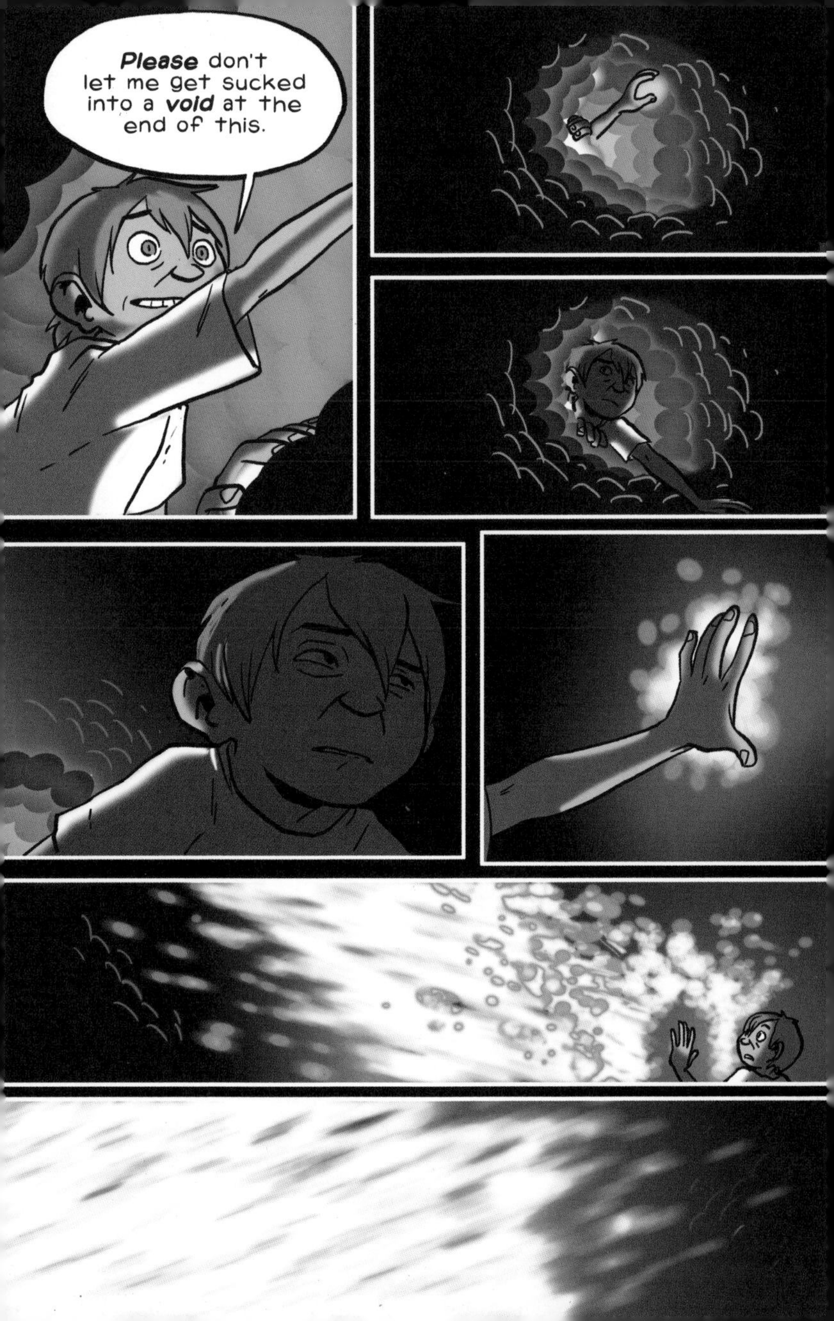
Please don't let me get sucked into a *void* at the end of this.

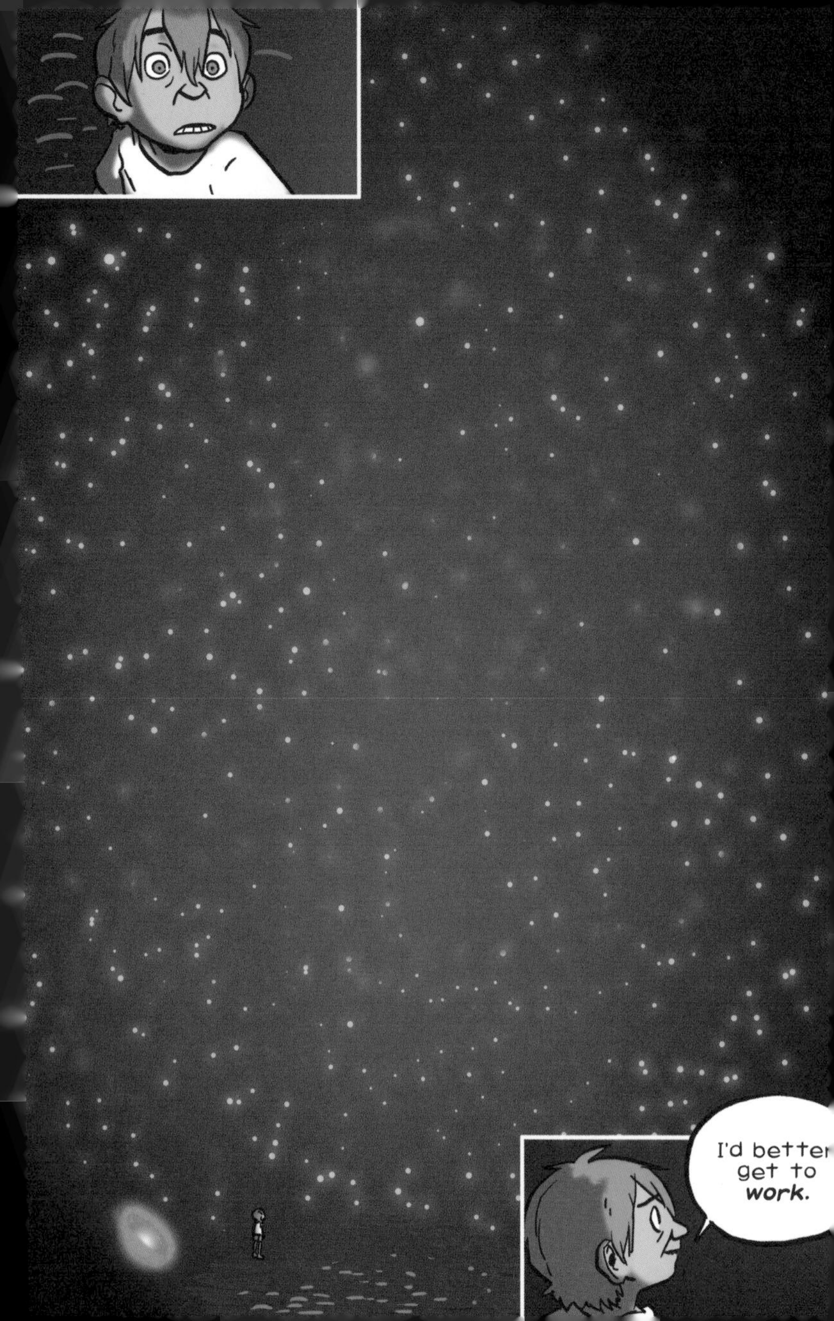
I'd better get to *work.*

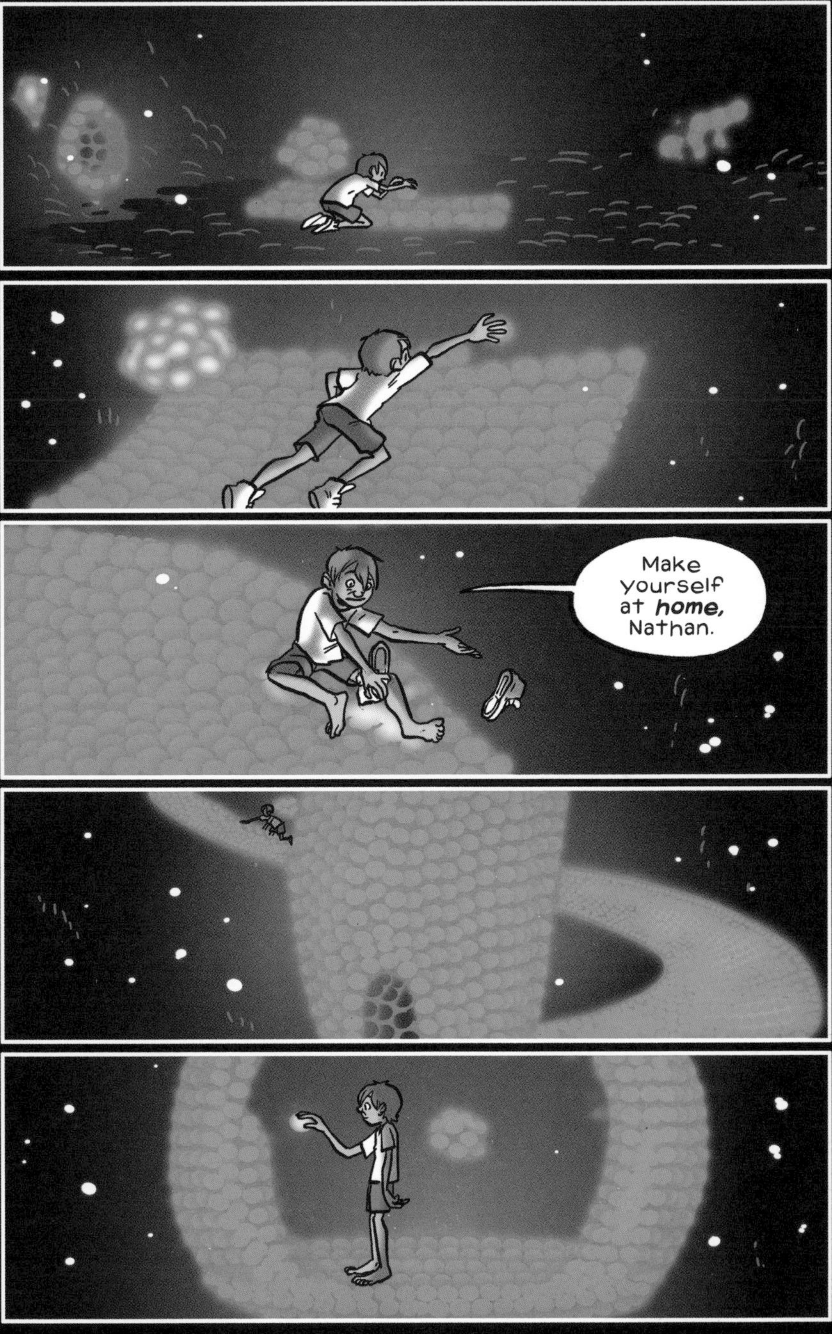
Make yourself at **home,** Nathan.

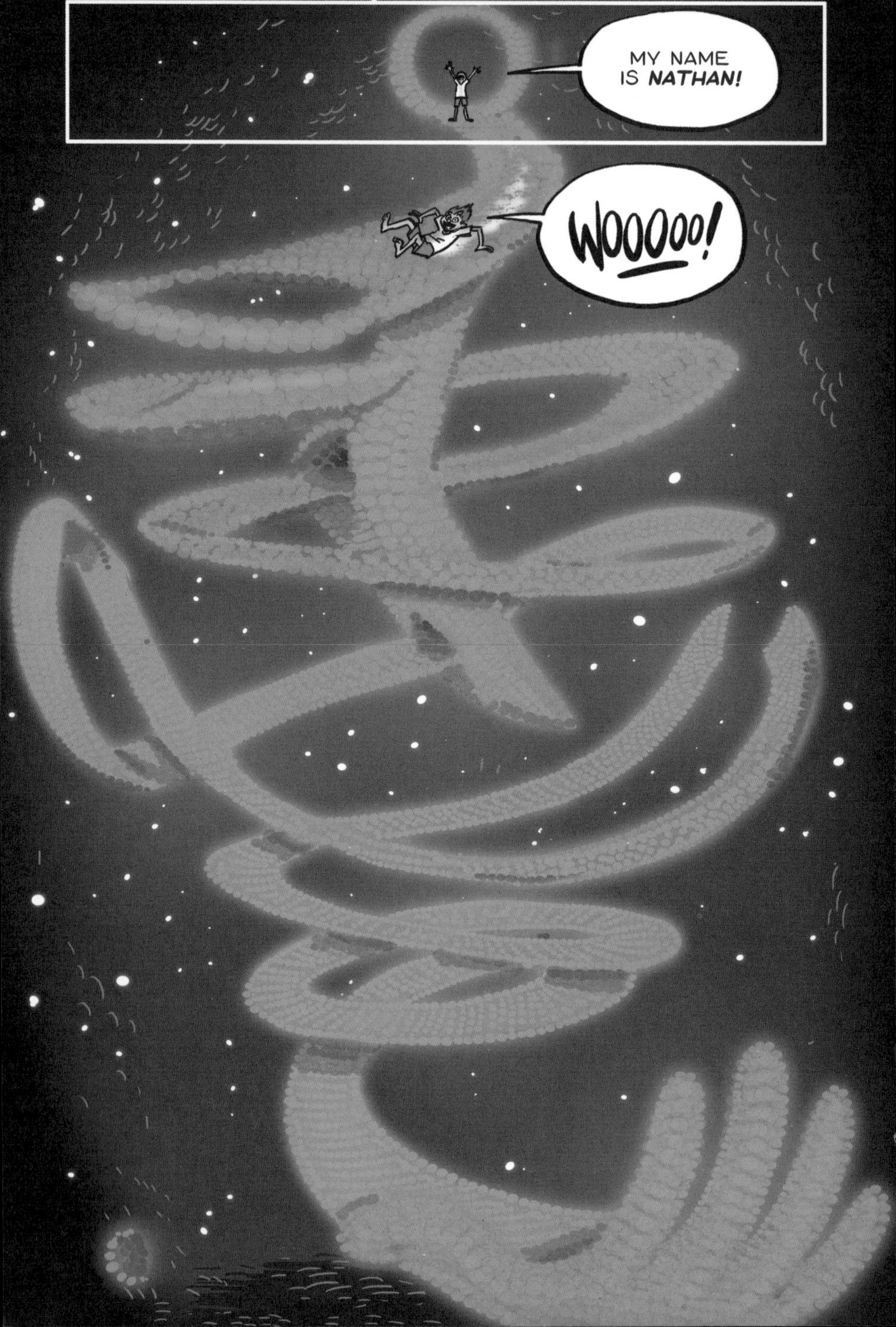
MY NAME IS NATHAN!
WOOOOO!

WHAAAAAAAAAAAAAAHAHAHAHAAAA

AHHHHHWOOP
HAHA HA
AHAHA

·whoa·

WUHOOOAA—

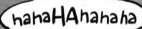

hahaHAhahaha

I'm doing *that* again.

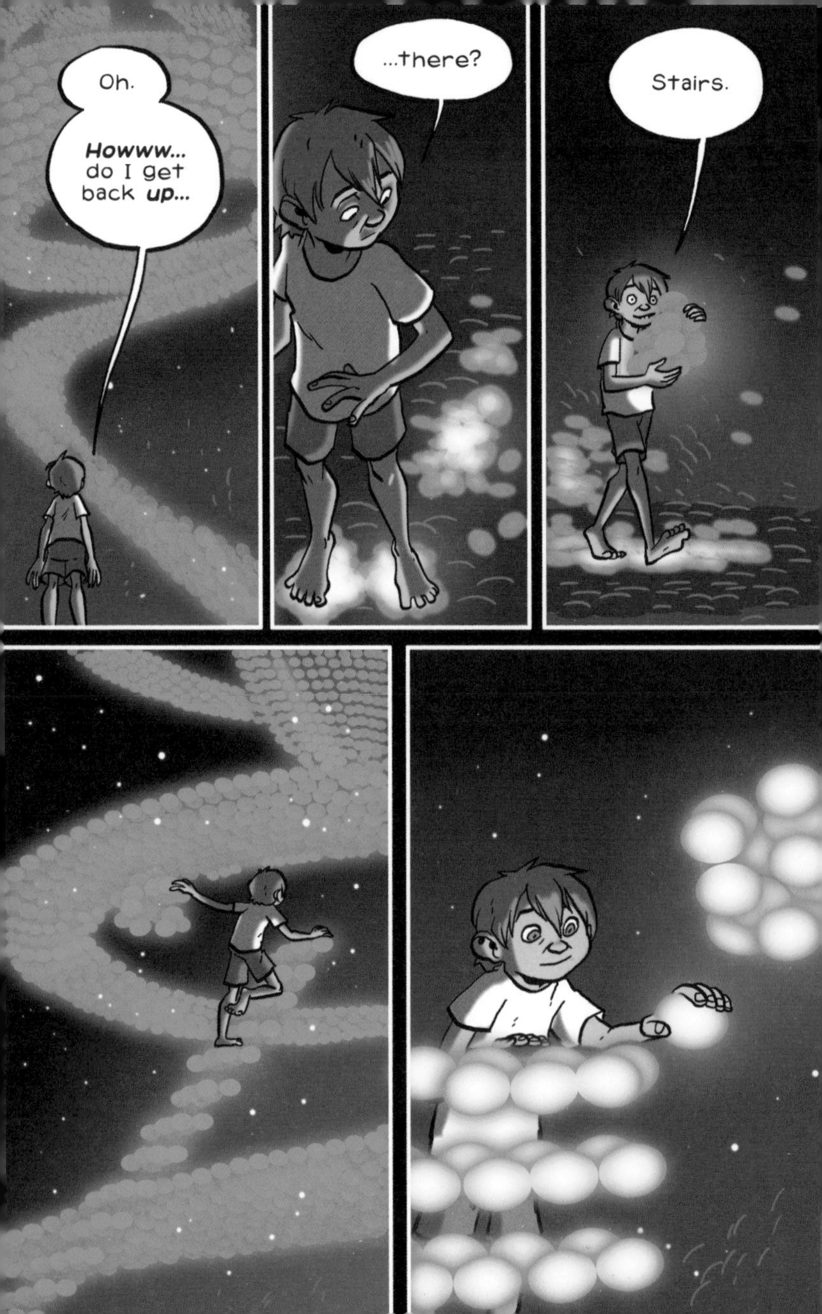
Oh.
Howww... do I get back **up...**
...there?
Stairs.

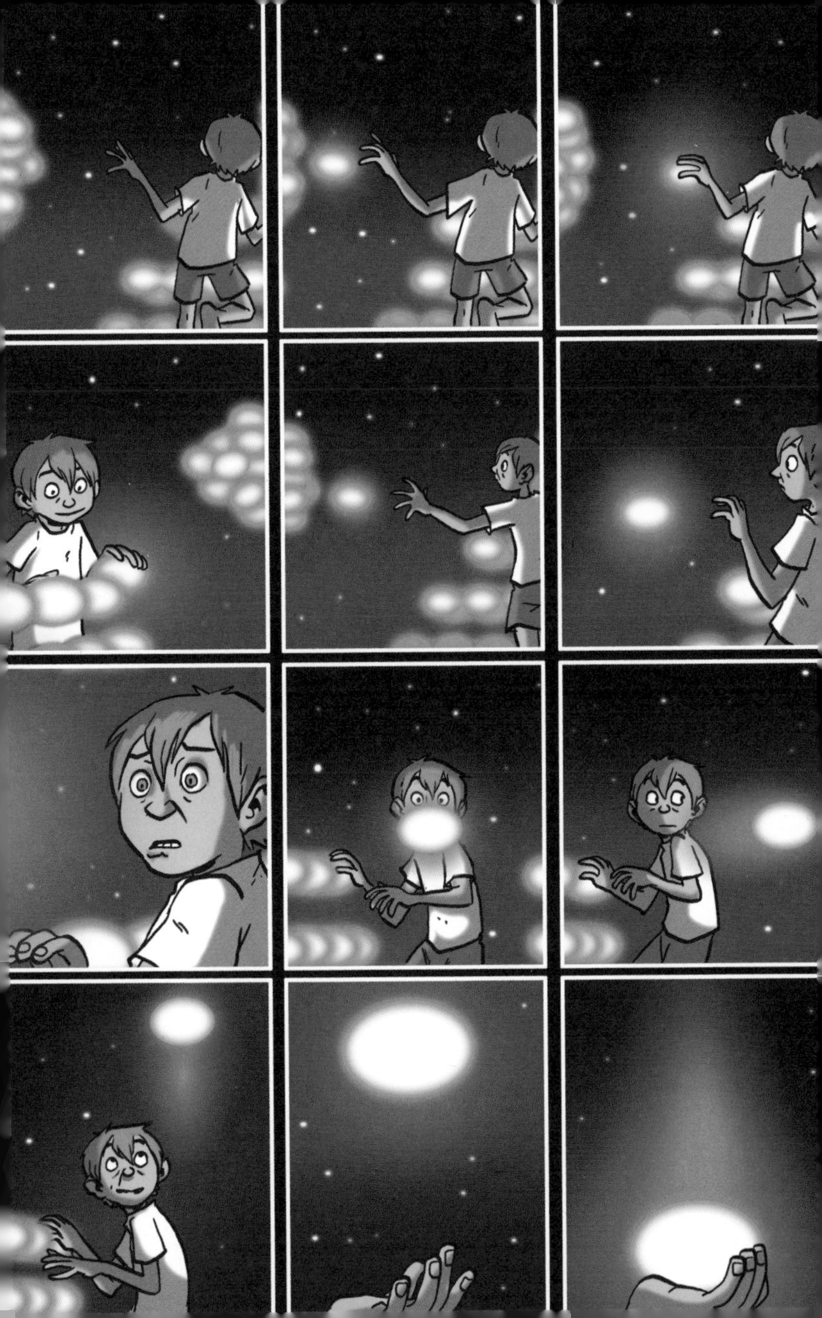

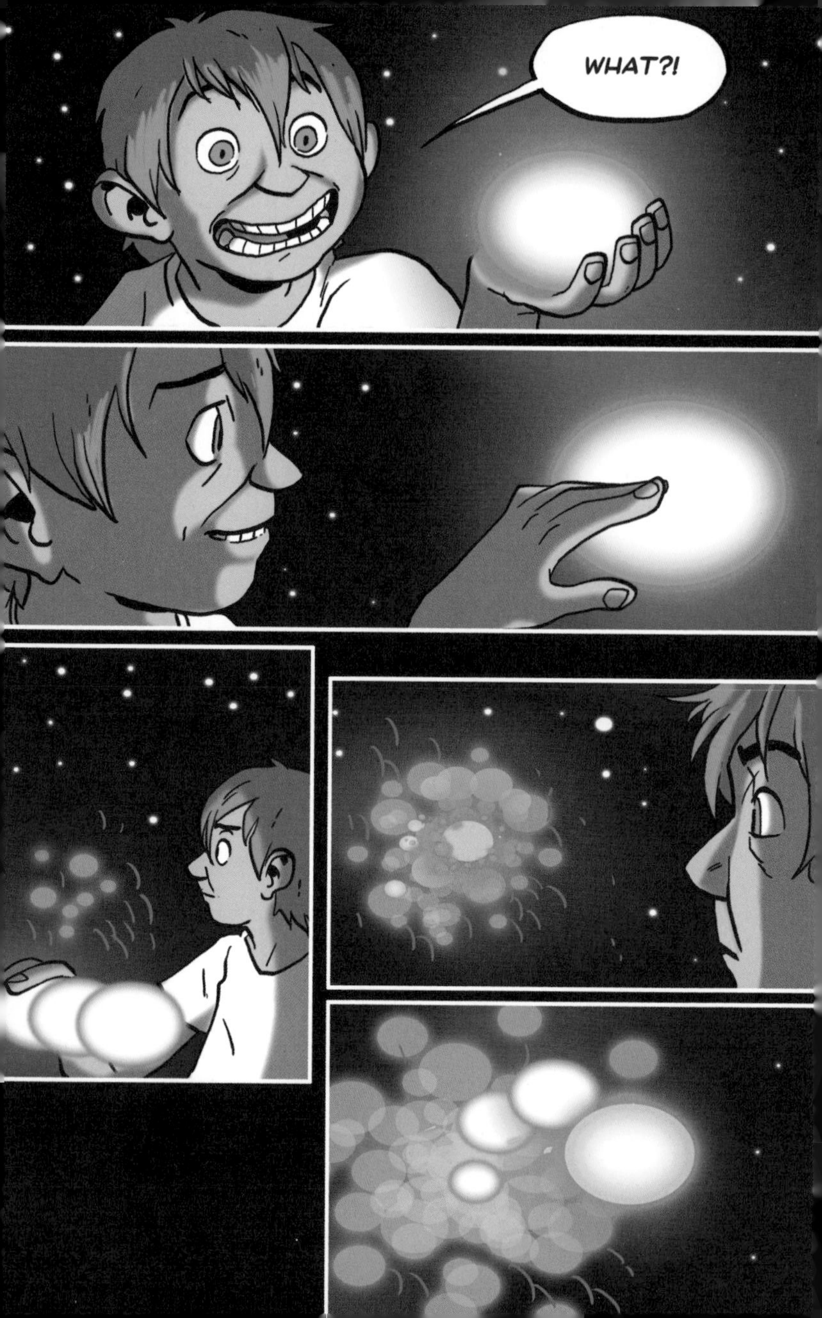
WHAT?!

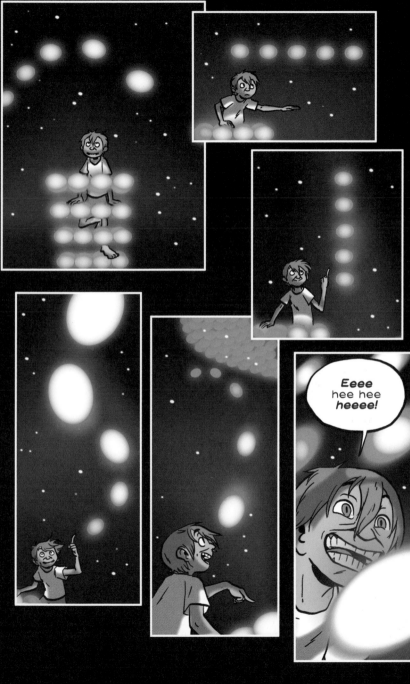

Eeee hee hee *heeee!*

109

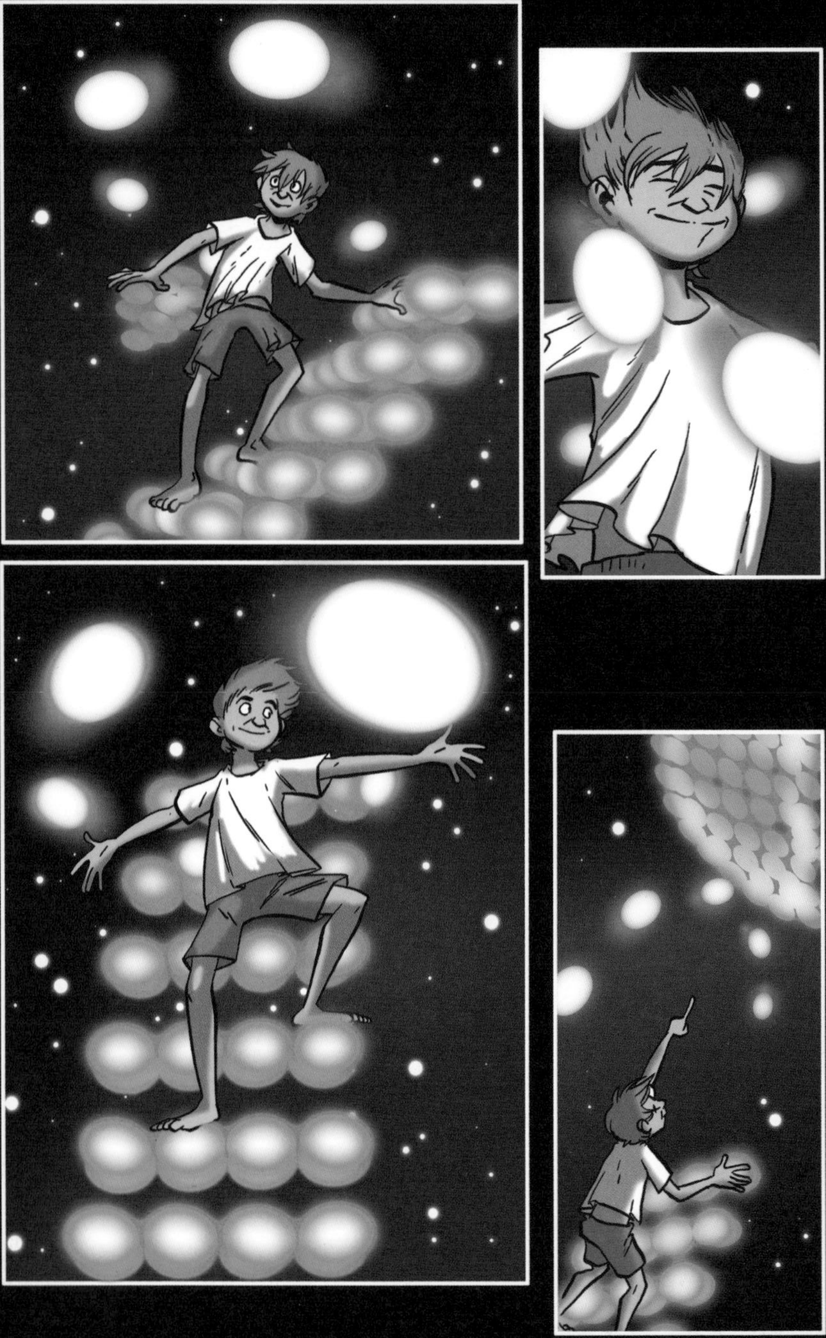

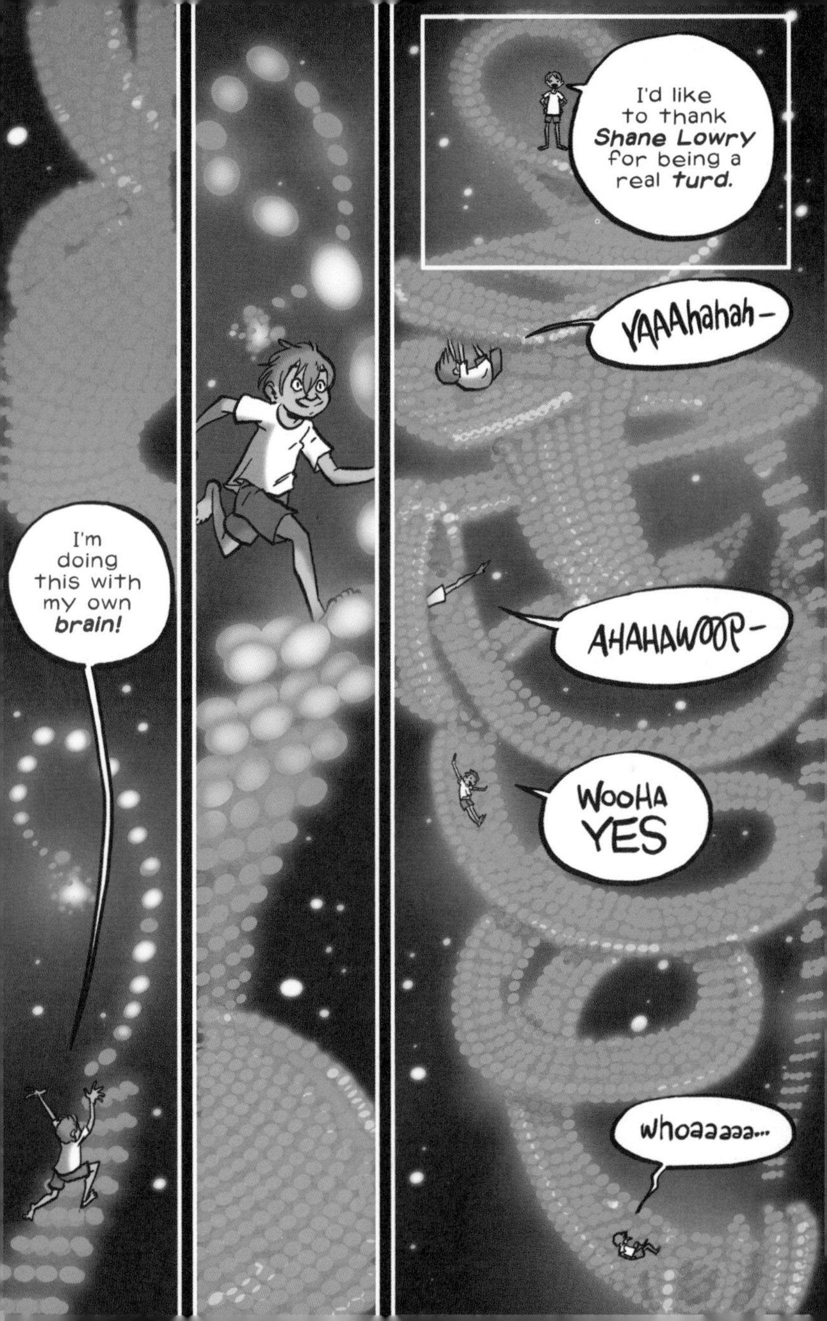
I'm doing this with my own brain!
I'd like to thank Shane Lowry for being a real turd.
YAAAhahah-
AHAHAWOOP-
WOOHA YES
whoaaaaa...

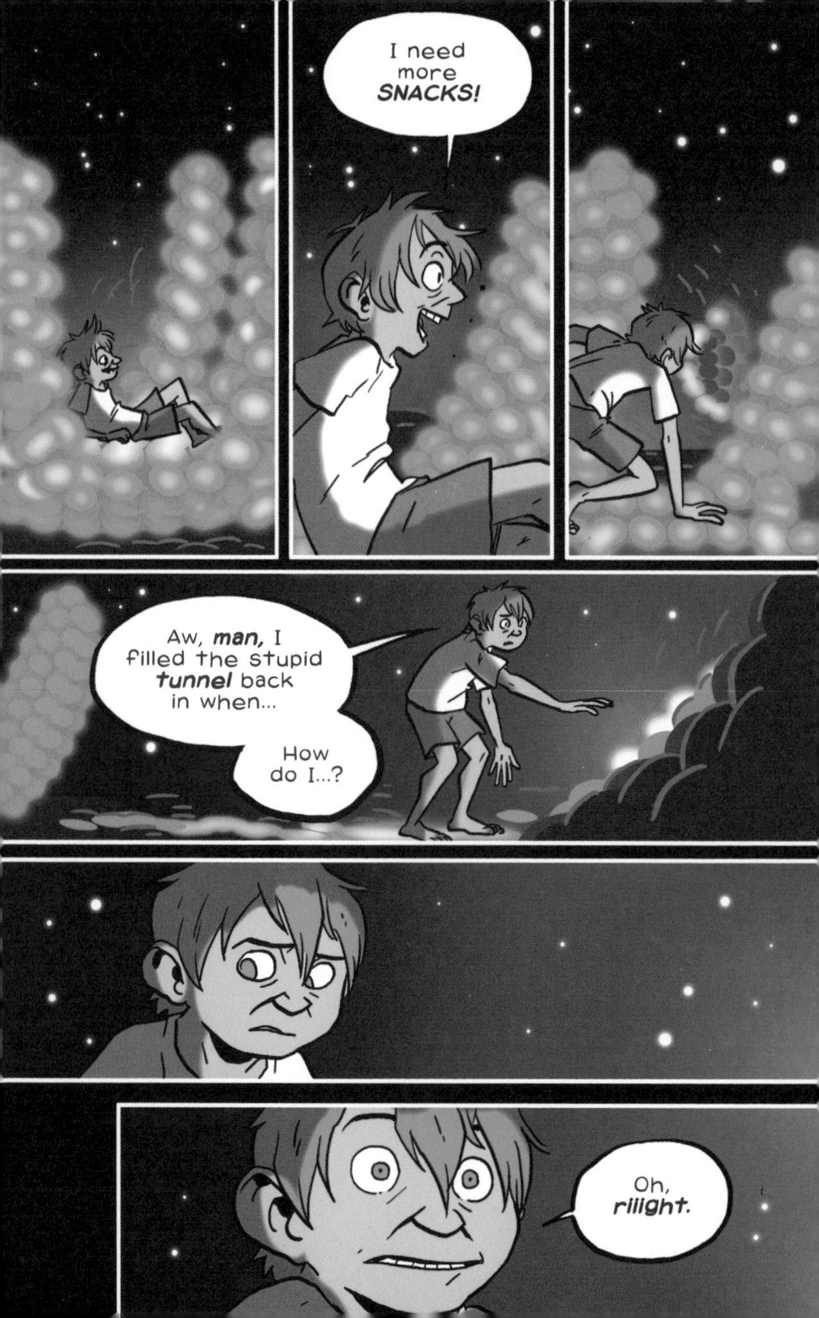
I need more SNACKS!
Aw, man, I filled the stupid tunnel back in when...
How do I...?
Oh, riiight.

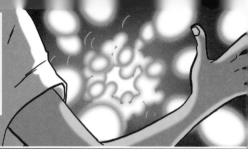

This isn't a *dream...*

It's like... *magic* or *science* or something.

It's *real.* That's the most amazing thing about it.

Still starving... Gumballs... a *pencil*...

I need more *food.*

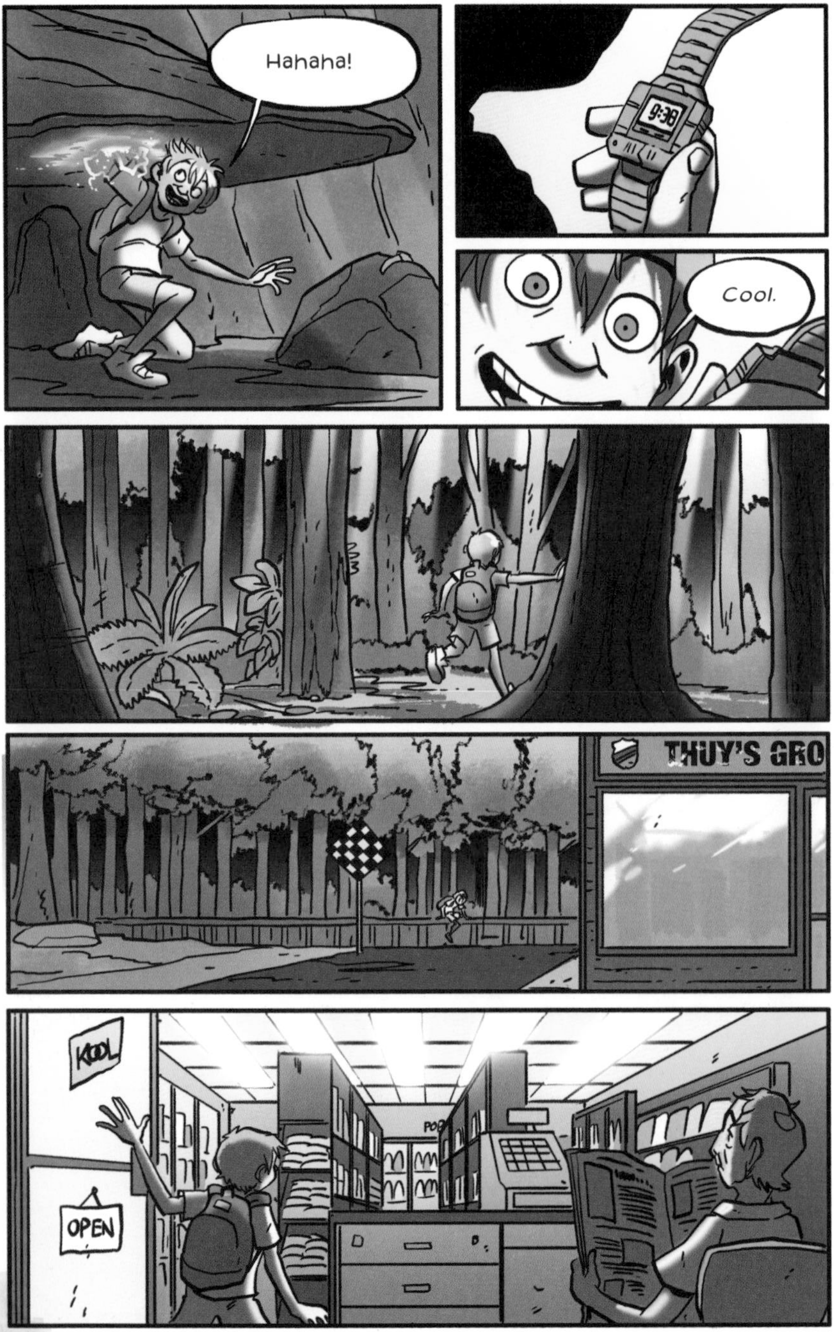
Hahaha!
9:38
Cool.
THUY'S GRO
KOOL
OPEN

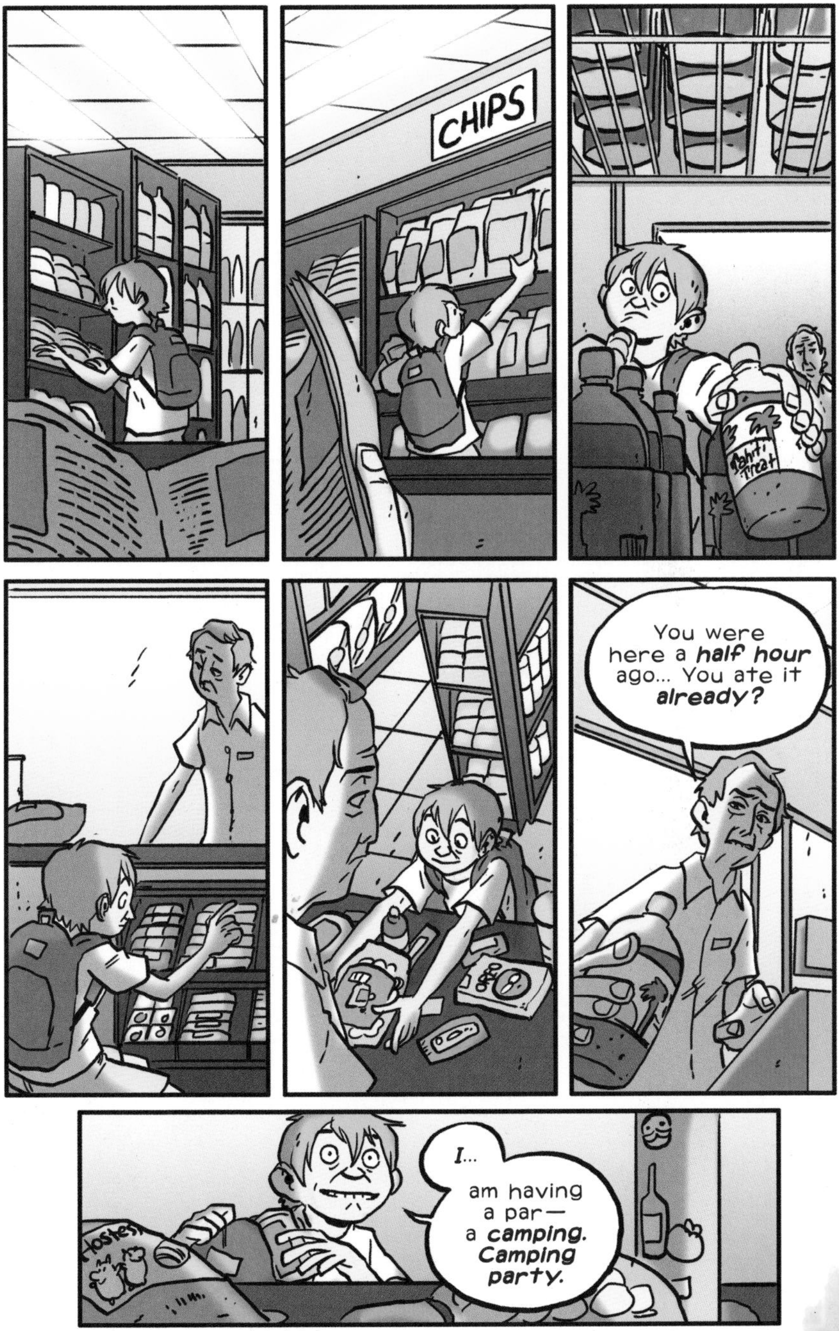
CHIPS
Tahiti Treat
You were here a half hour ago... You ate it already?
I...
am having a par— a camping. Camping party.
Hostess

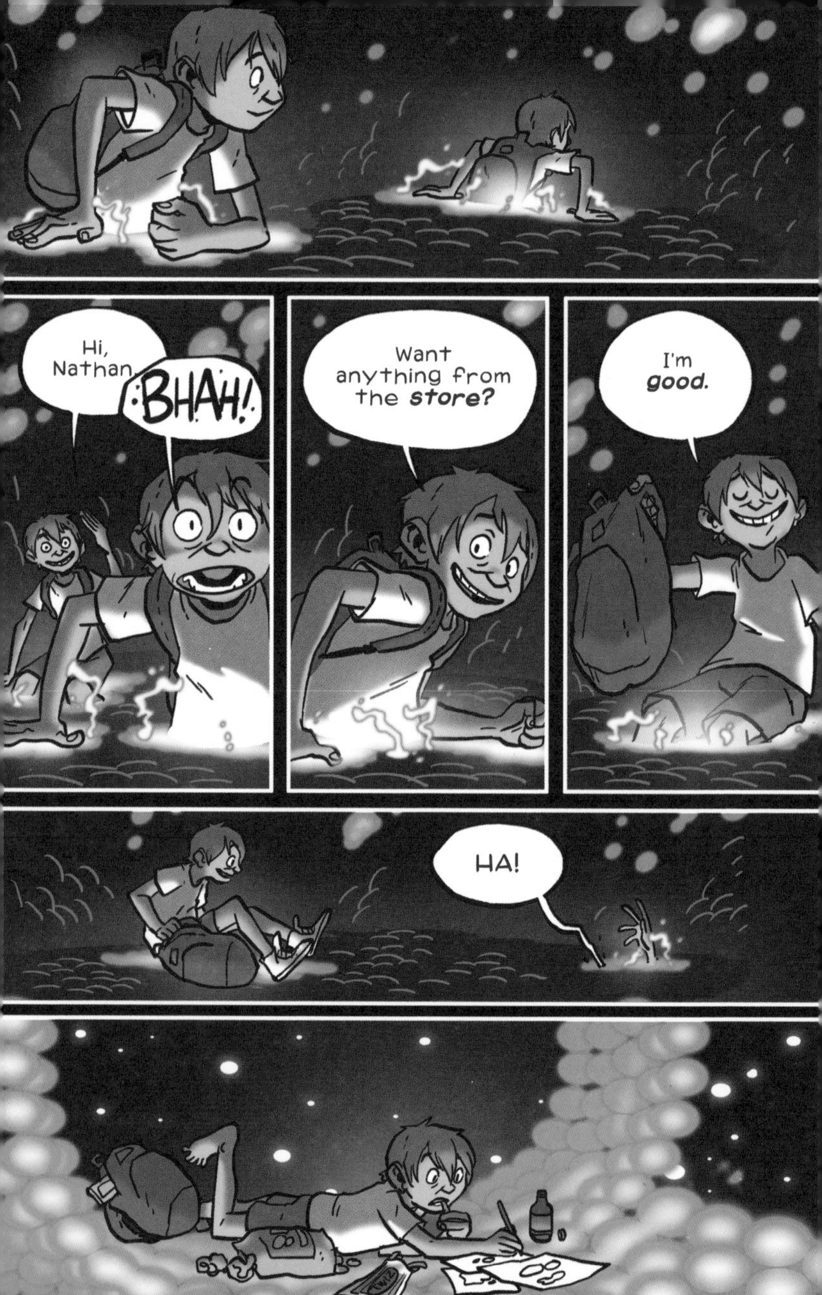
Hi, Nathan.
BHAH!
Want anything from the store?
I'm good.
HA!

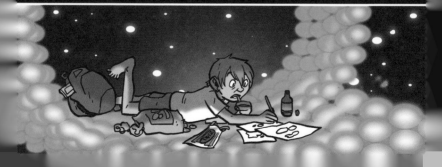

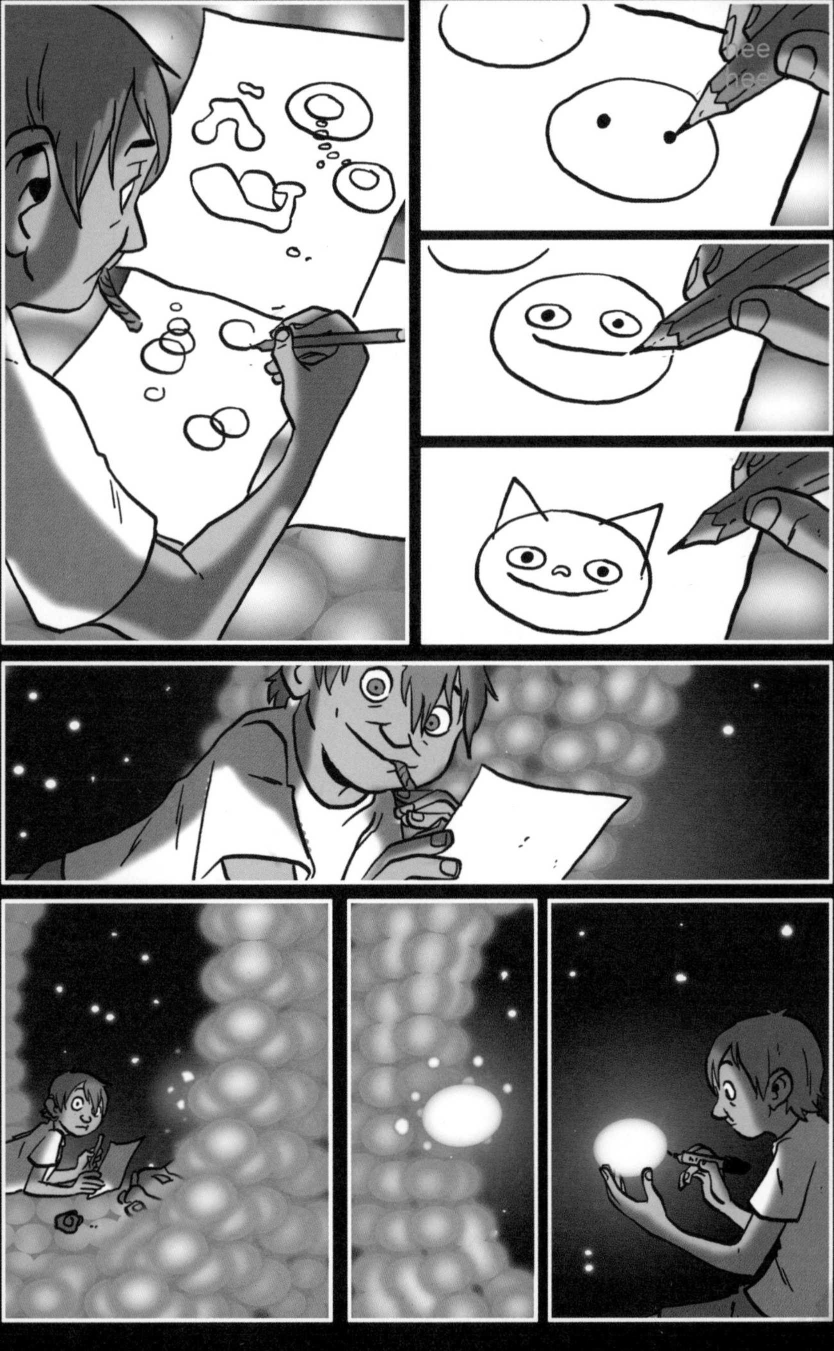
hee
hee

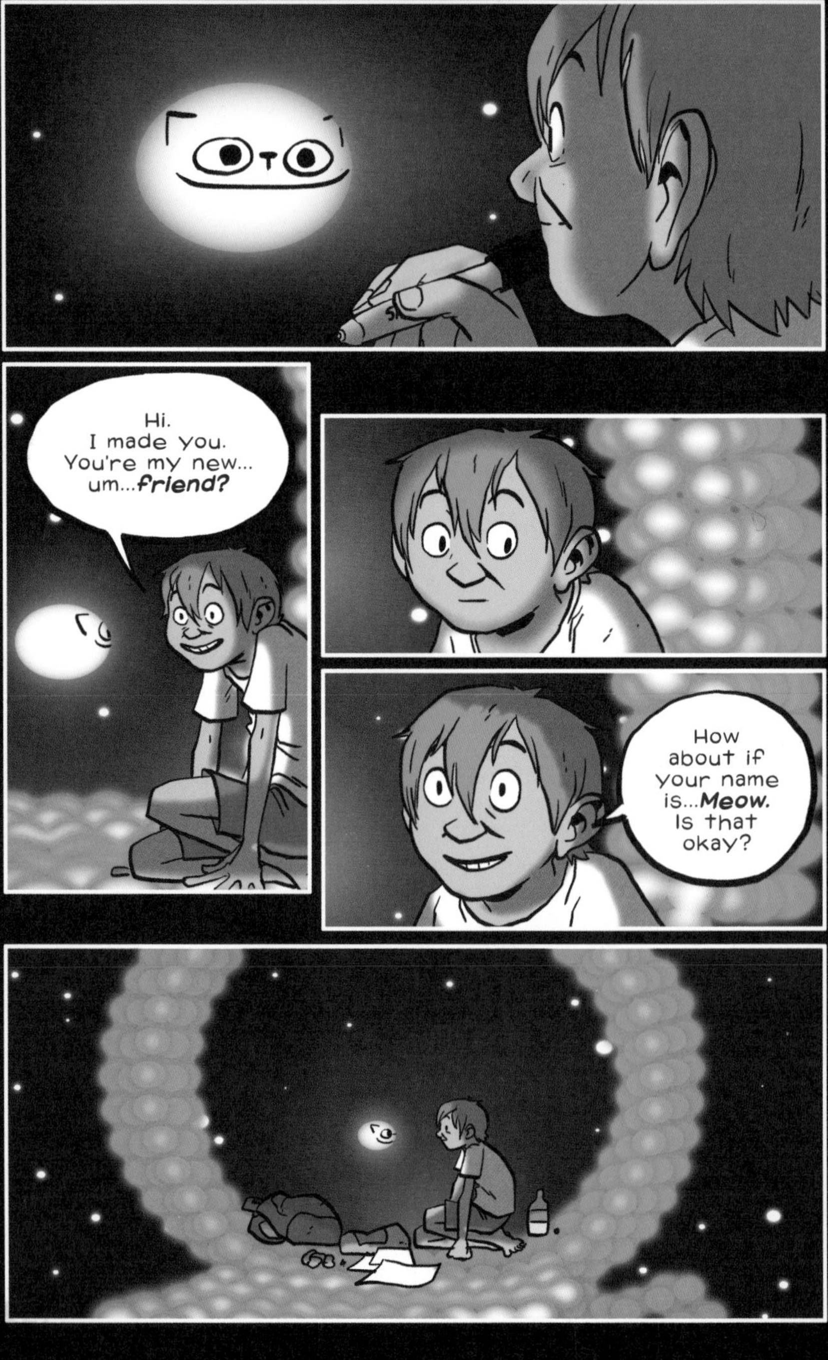
Hi. I made you. You're my new... um...*friend?*
How about if your name is...**Meow.** Is that okay?

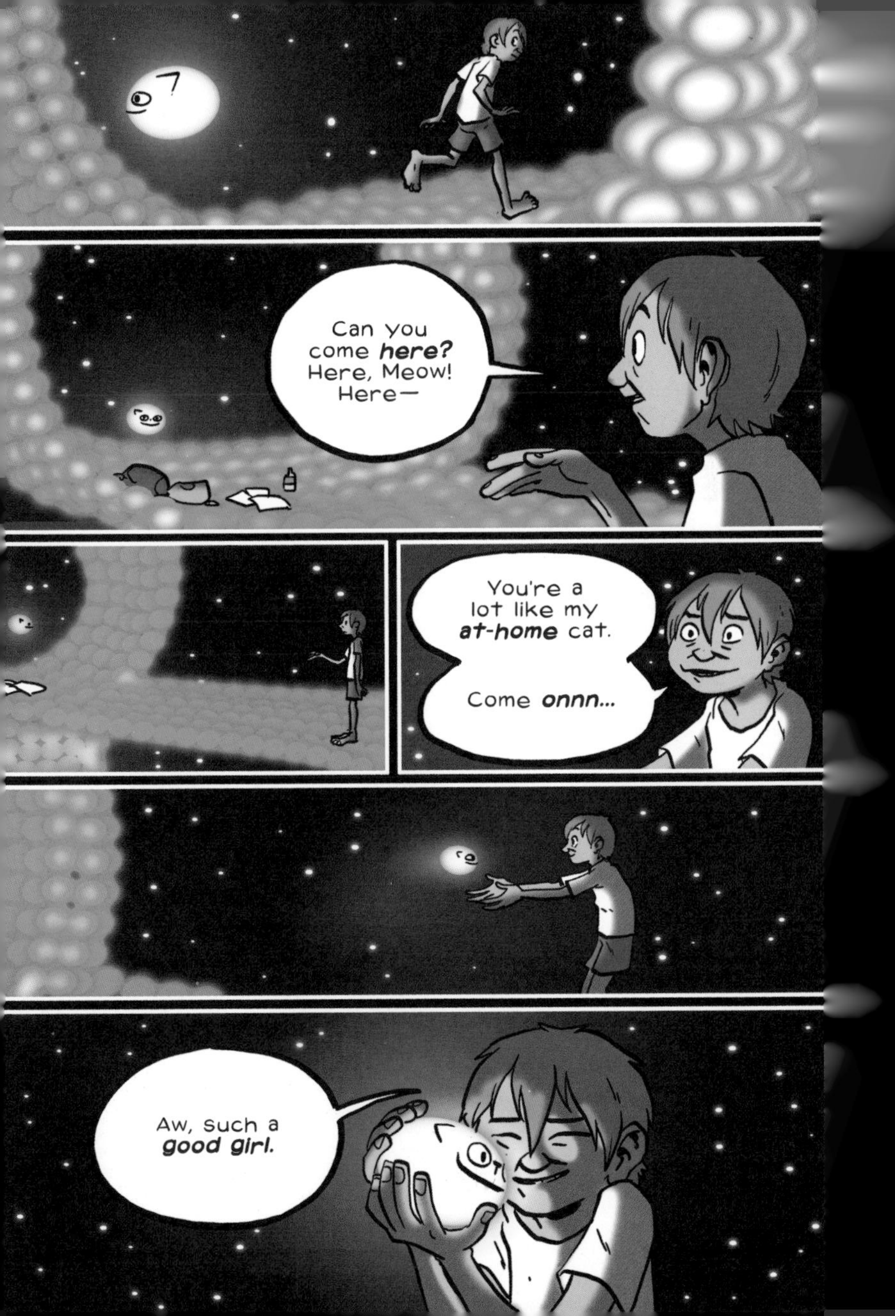
Can you come *here?* Here, Meow! Here—
You're a lot like my ***at-home*** cat.
Come ***onnn...***
Aw, such a ***good girl.***

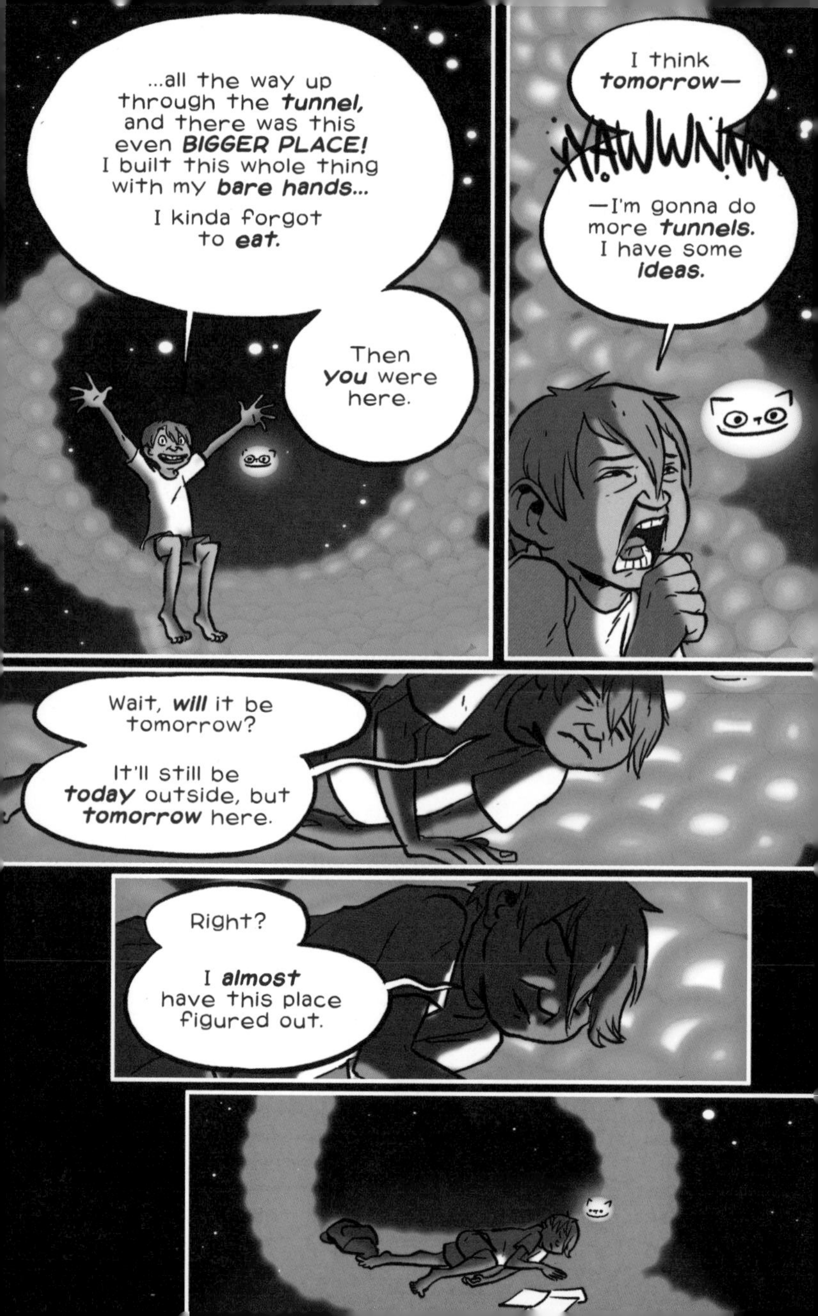
...all the way up through the *tunnel,* and there was this even *BIGGER PLACE!* I built this whole thing with my *bare hands...*
I kinda forgot to *eat.*
Then *you* were here.
I think *tomorrow—*
YAWWNNN
—I'm gonna do more *tunnels.* I have some *ideas.*
Wait, *will* it be tomorrow?
It'll still be *today* outside, but *tomorrow* here.
Right?
I *almost* have this place figured out.

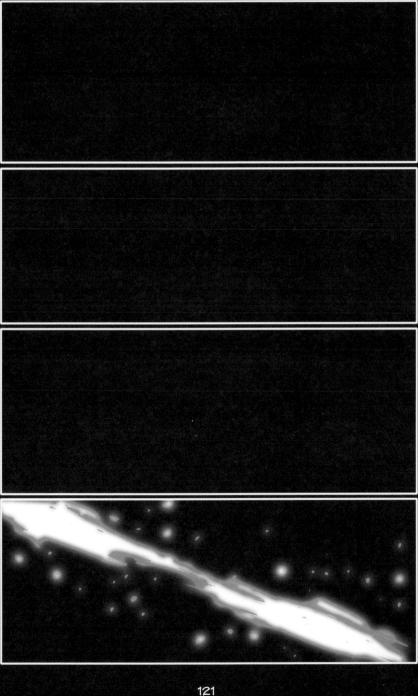

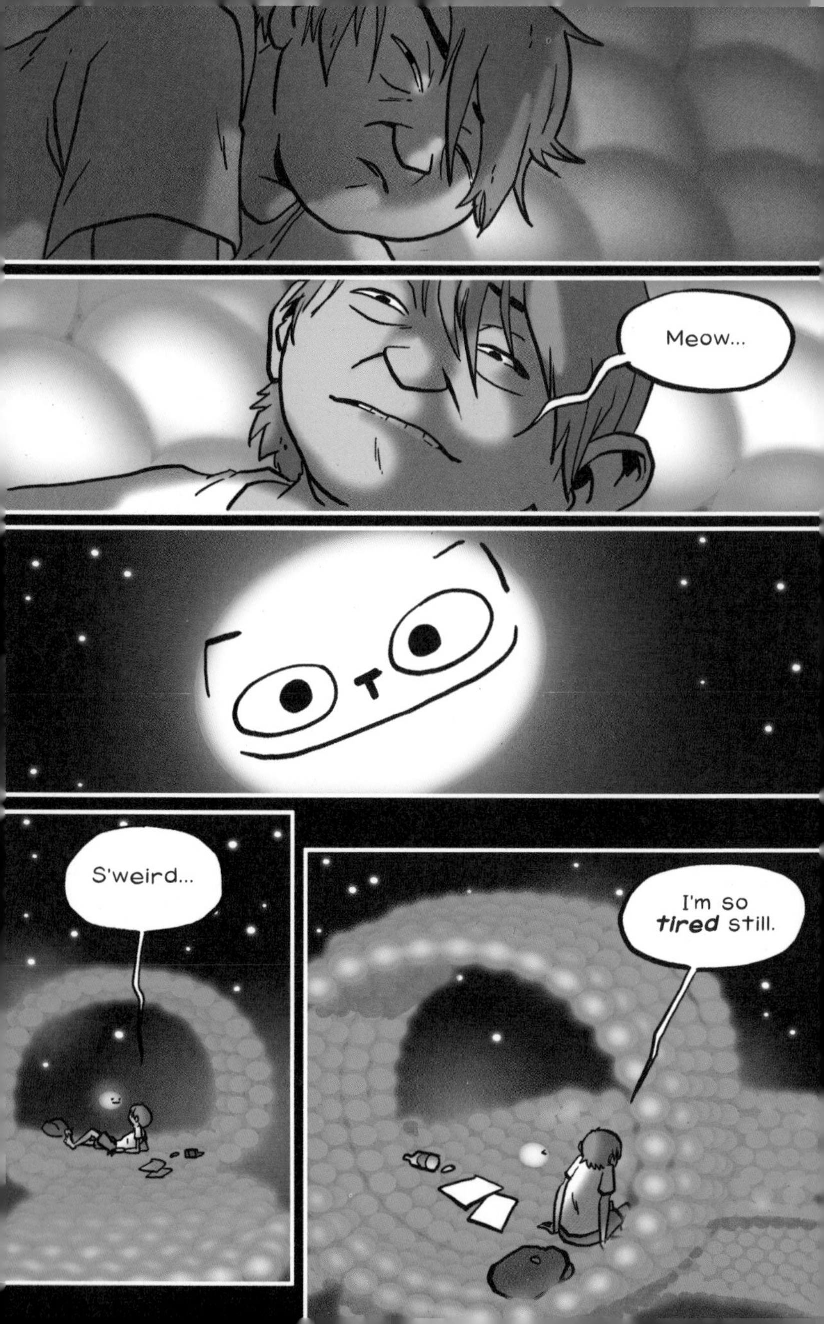
Meow...
S'weird...
I'm so *tired* still.

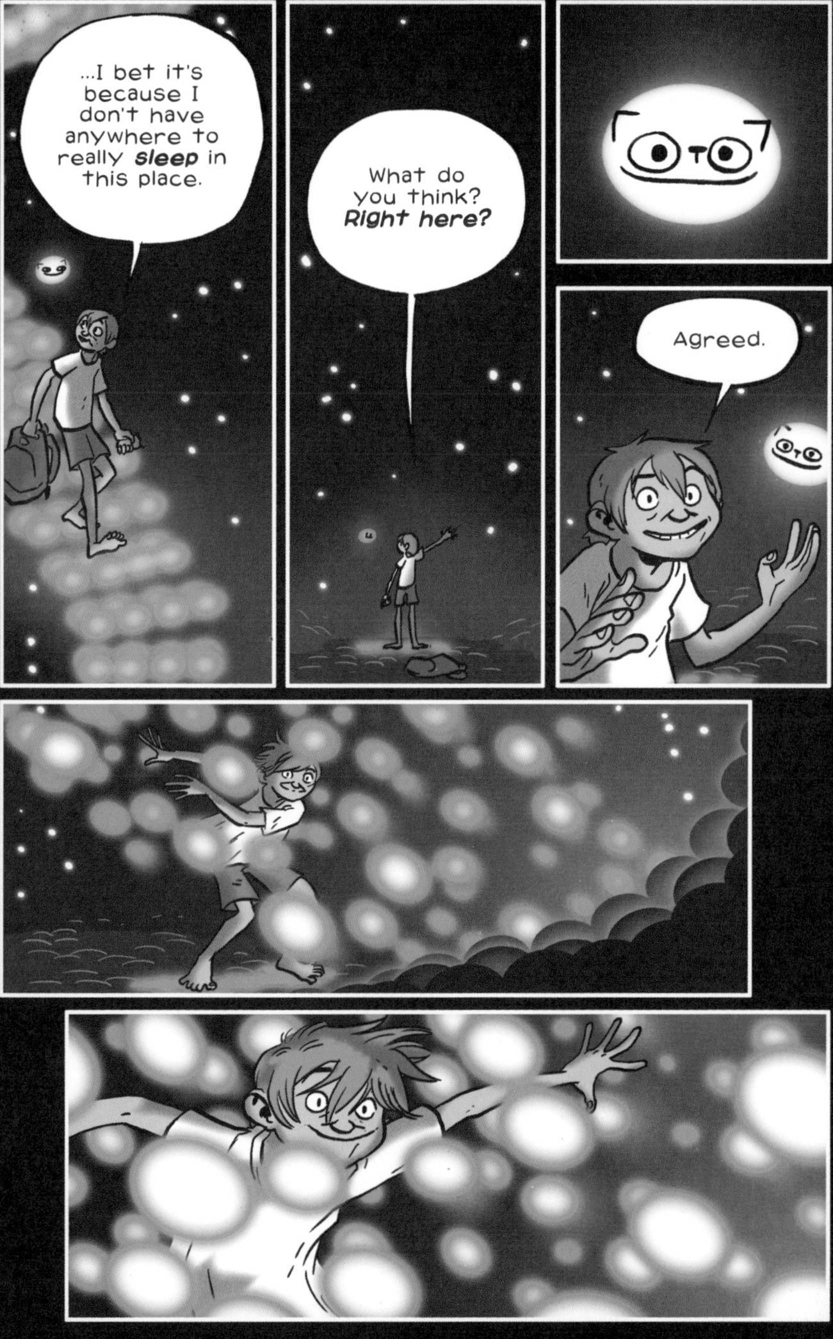
...I bet it's because I don't have anywhere to really *sleep* in this place.
What do you think? **Right here?**
Agreed.

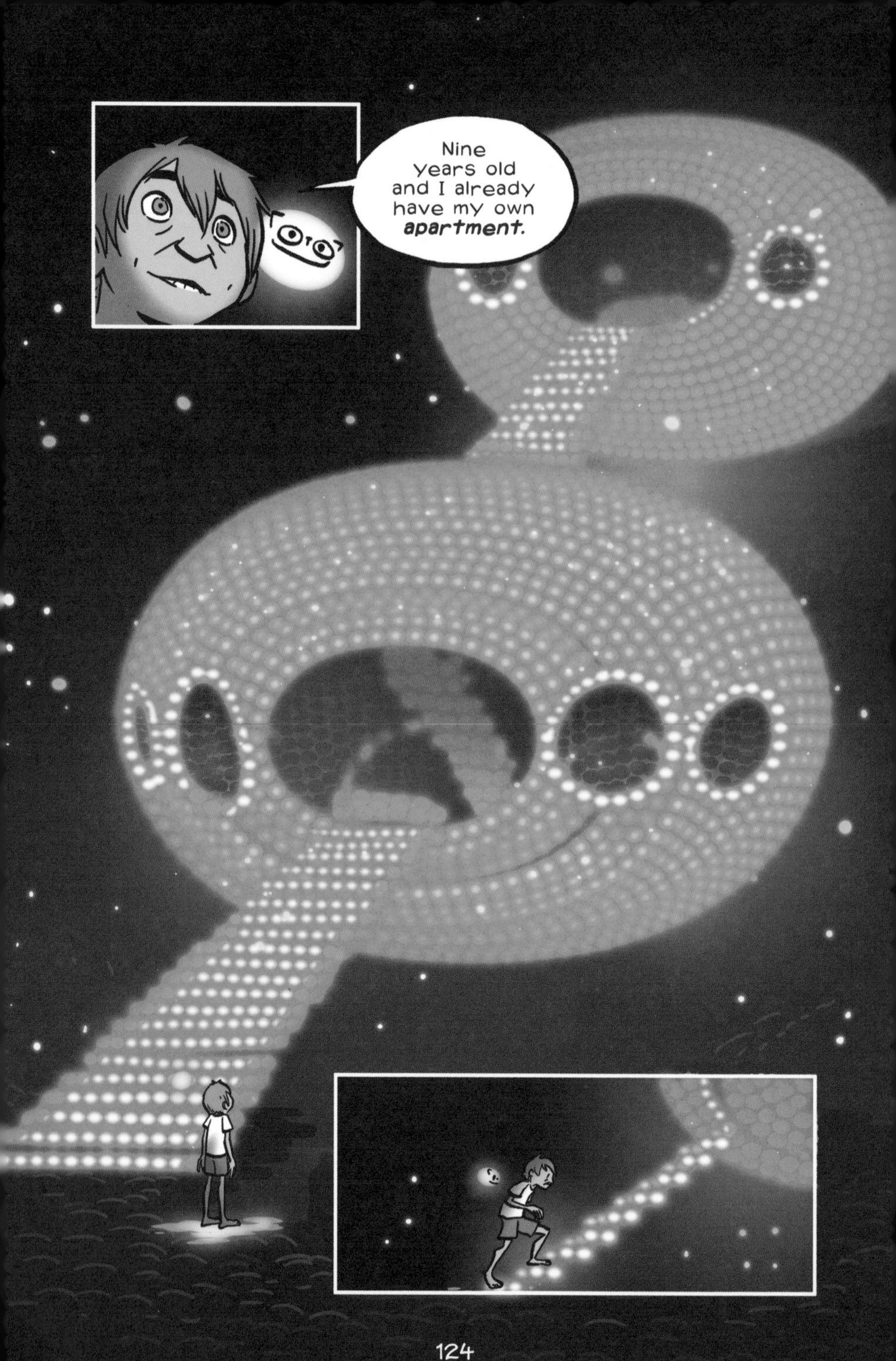
Nine years old and I already have my own **apartment**.

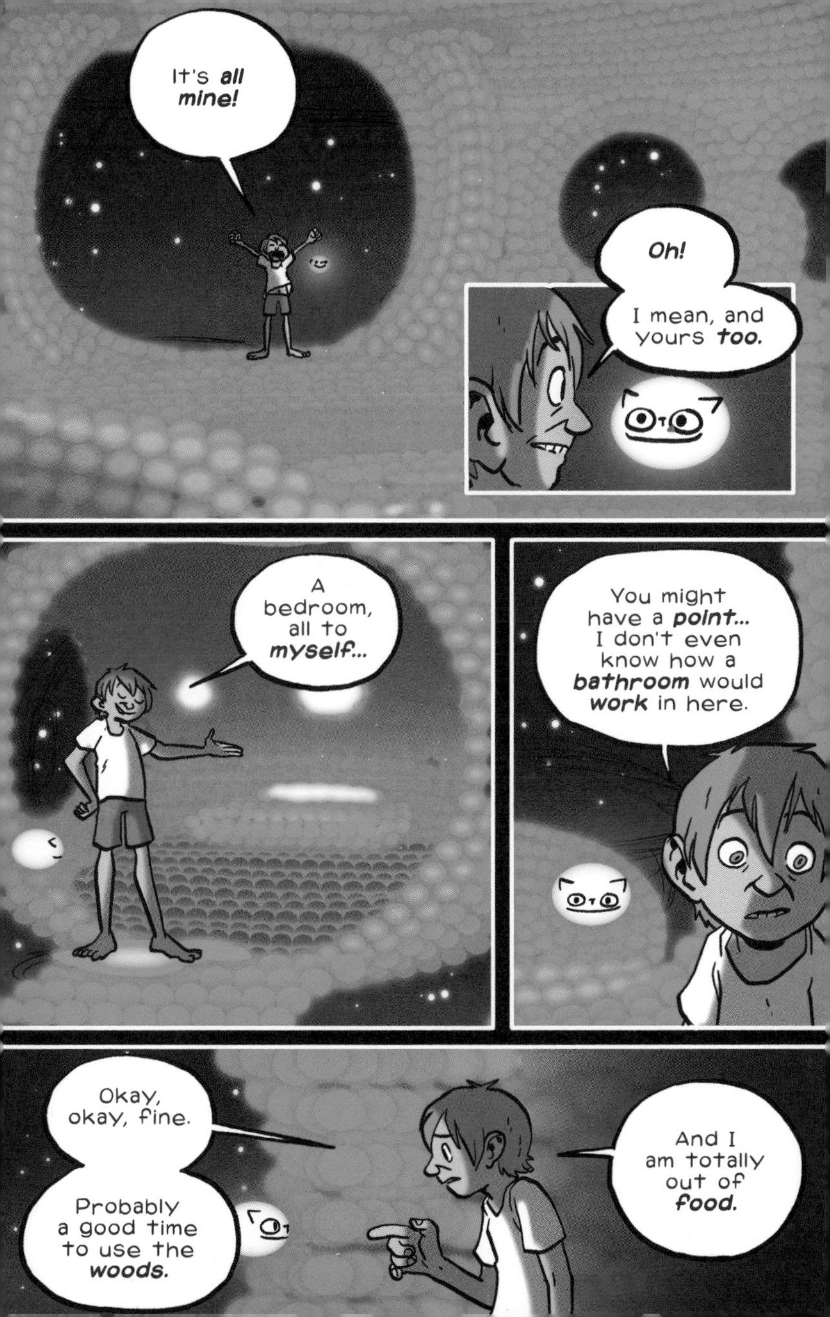

It's **all** **mine!**
Oh!
I mean, and yours **too.**
A bedroom, all to **myself...**
You might have a **point...** I don't even know how a **bathroom** would **work** in here.
Okay, okay, fine.
Probably a good time to use the **woods.**
And I am totally out of **food.**

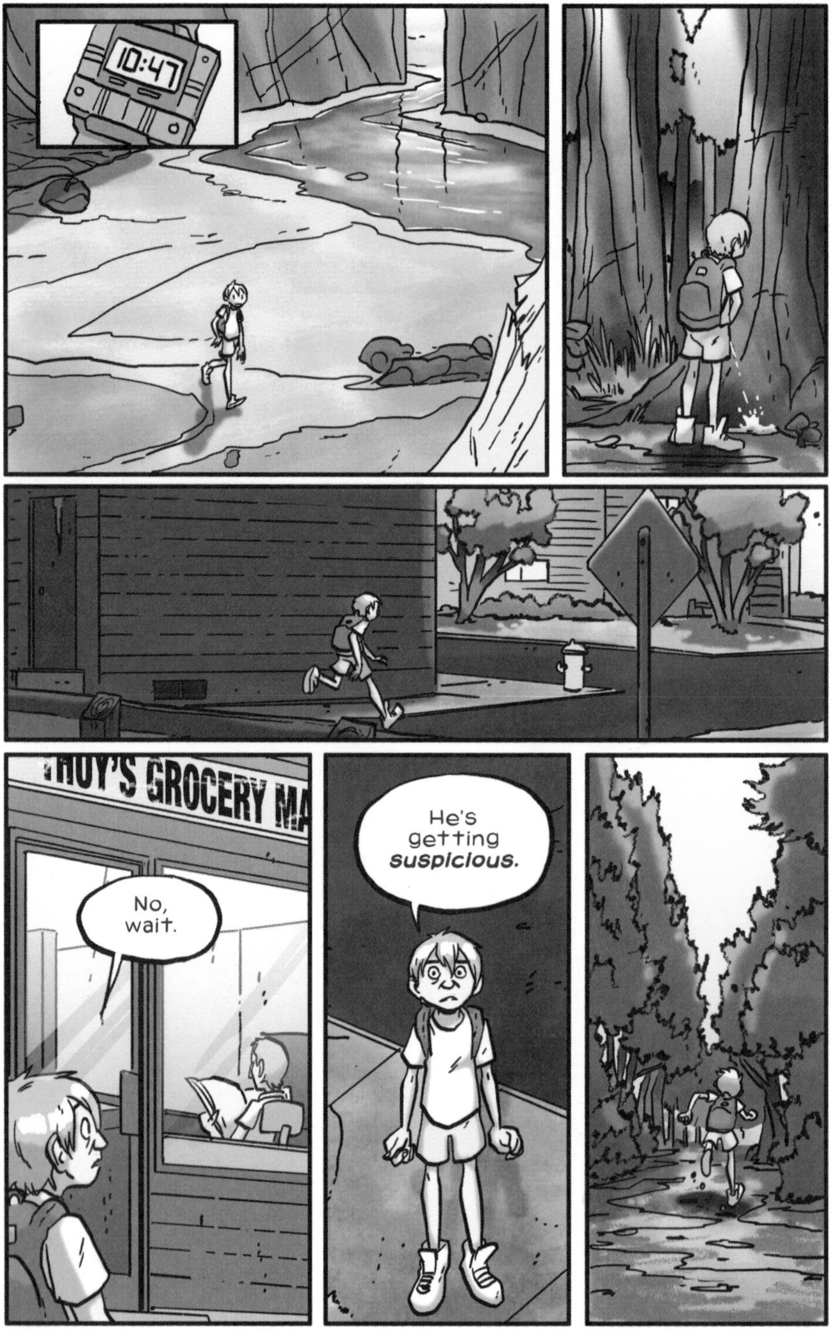
10:47
HOY'S GROCERY MA
No, wait.
He's getting ***suspicious.***

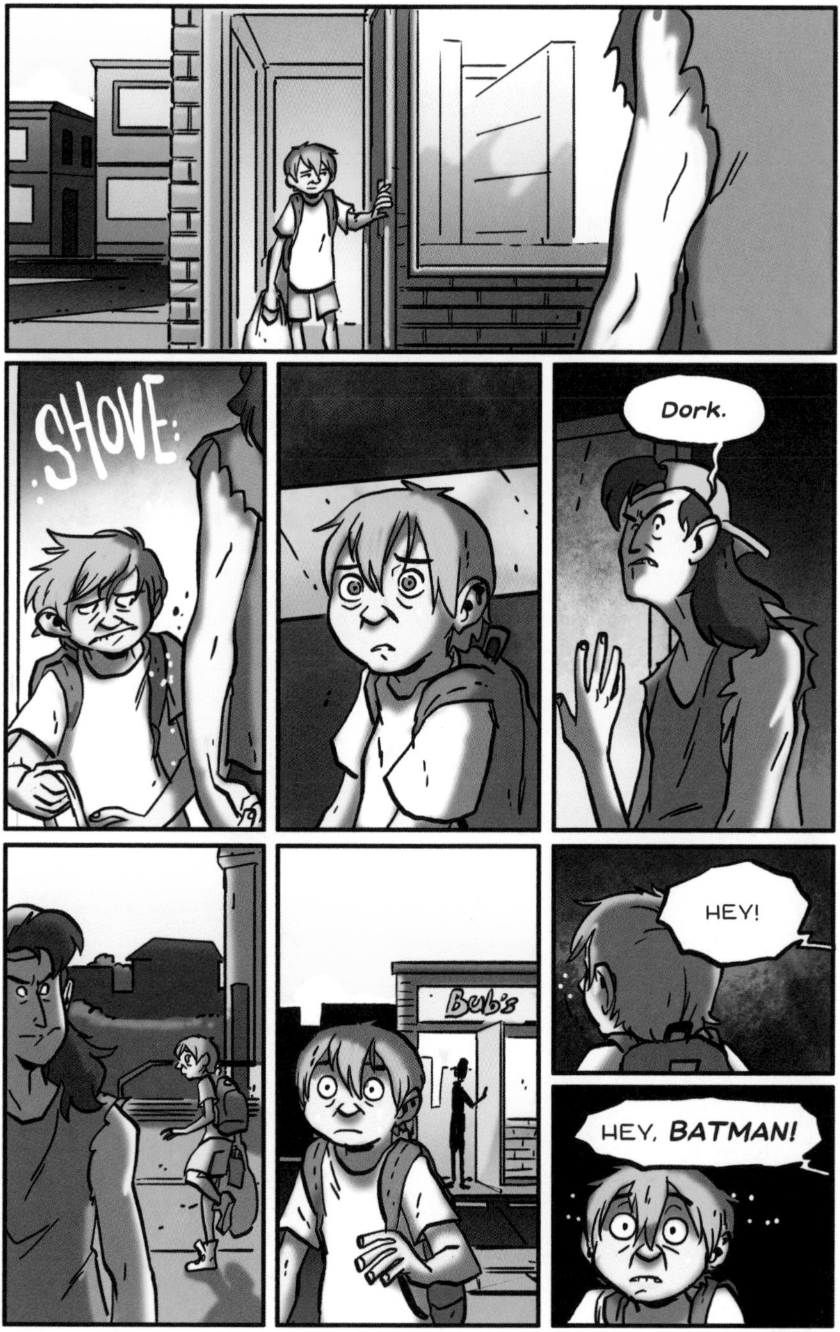
SHOVE
Dork.
HEY!
HEY, BATMAN!
Bub's

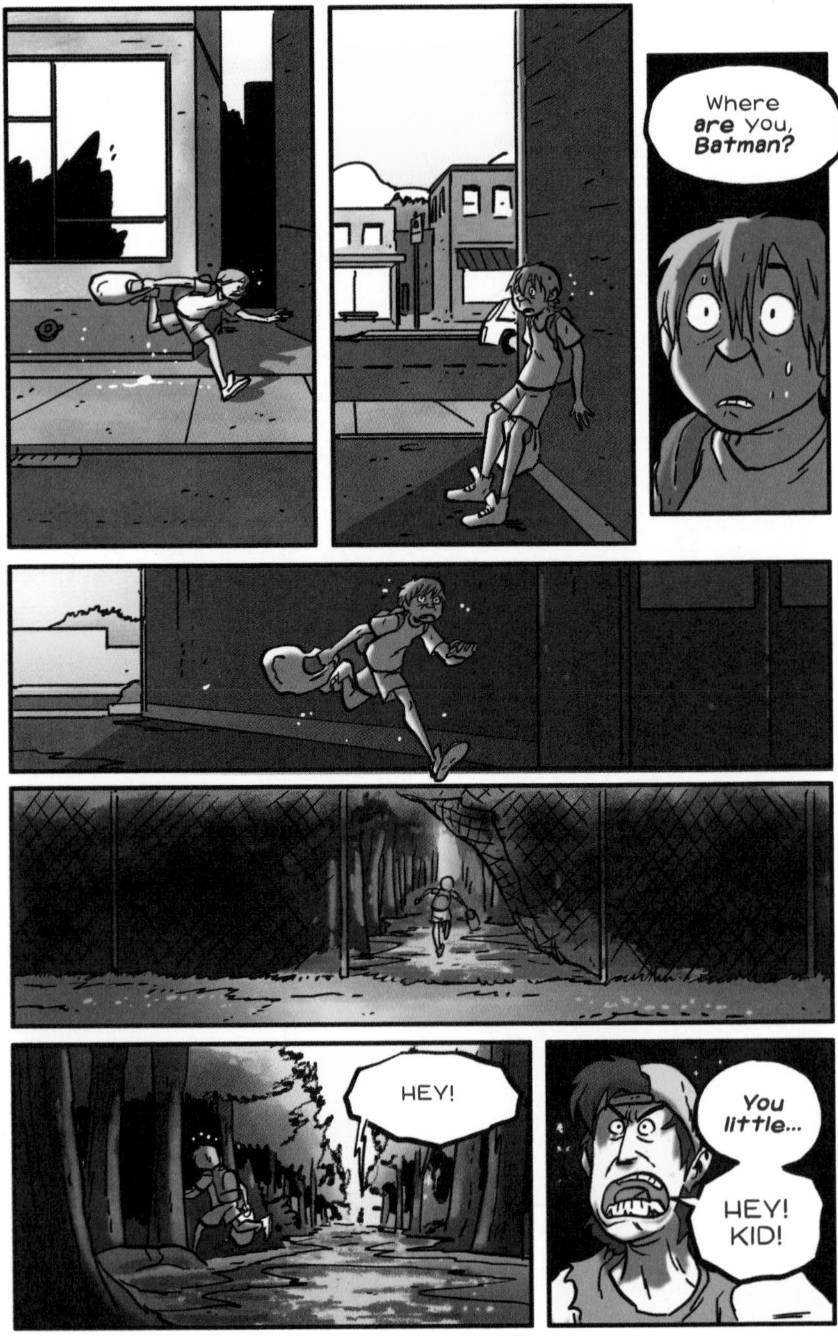
Where are you, Batman?
HEY!
You little...
HEY! KID!

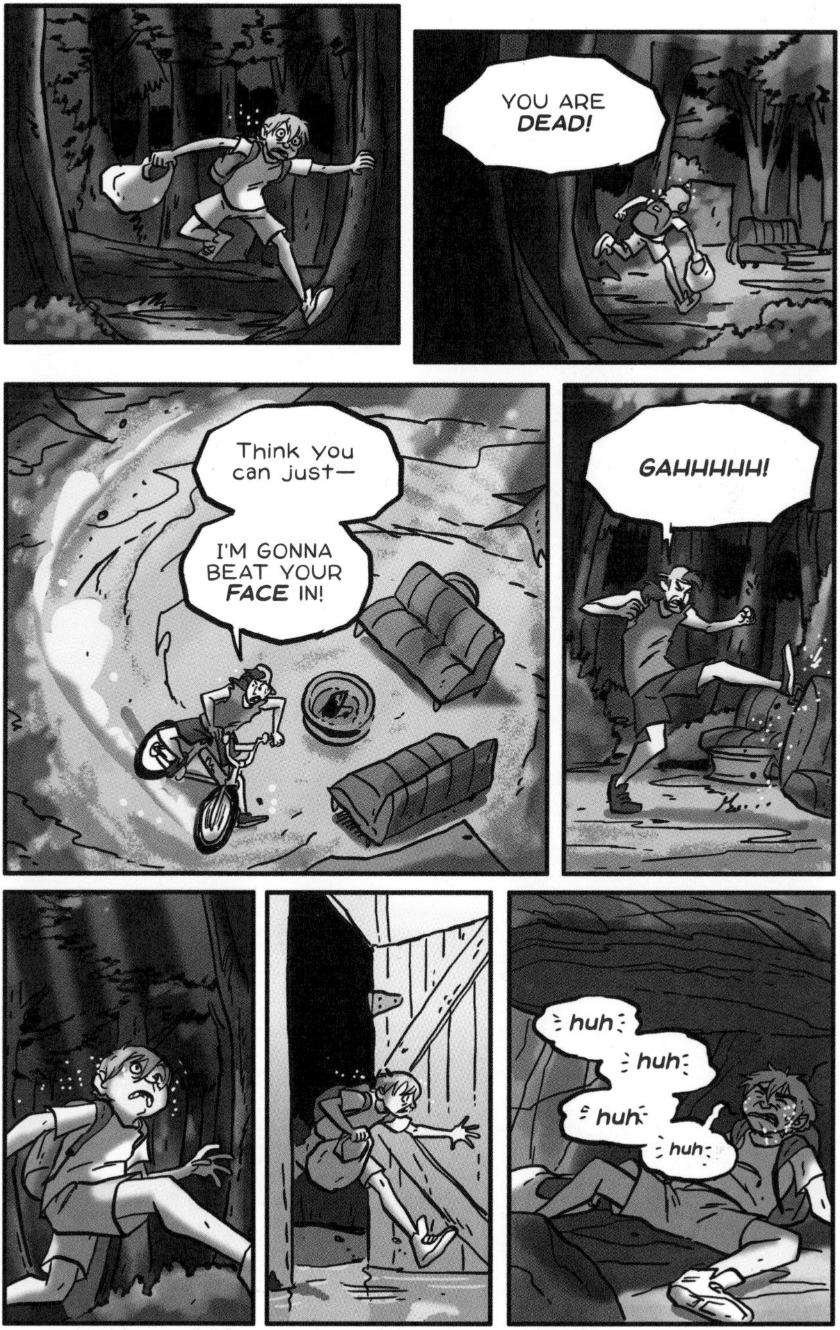
YOU ARE DEAD!
Think you can just—
I'M GONNA BEAT YOUR FACE IN!
GAHHHHH!
huh
huh
huh
huh

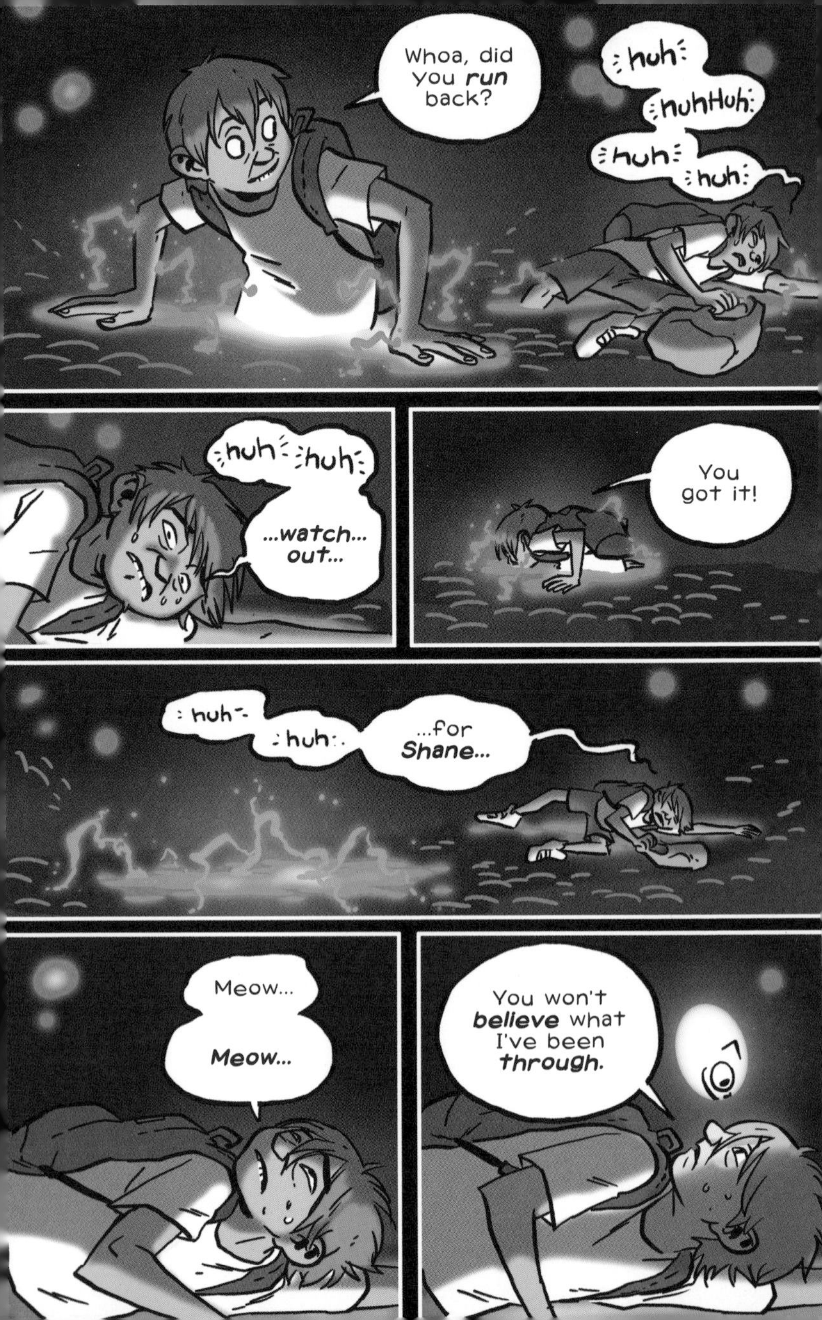
Whoa, did you *run* back?
huh
huhHuh
huh
huh
huh huh
...watch... out...
You got it!
huh
huh
...for Shane...
Meow...
Meow...
You won't *believe* what I've been *through*.

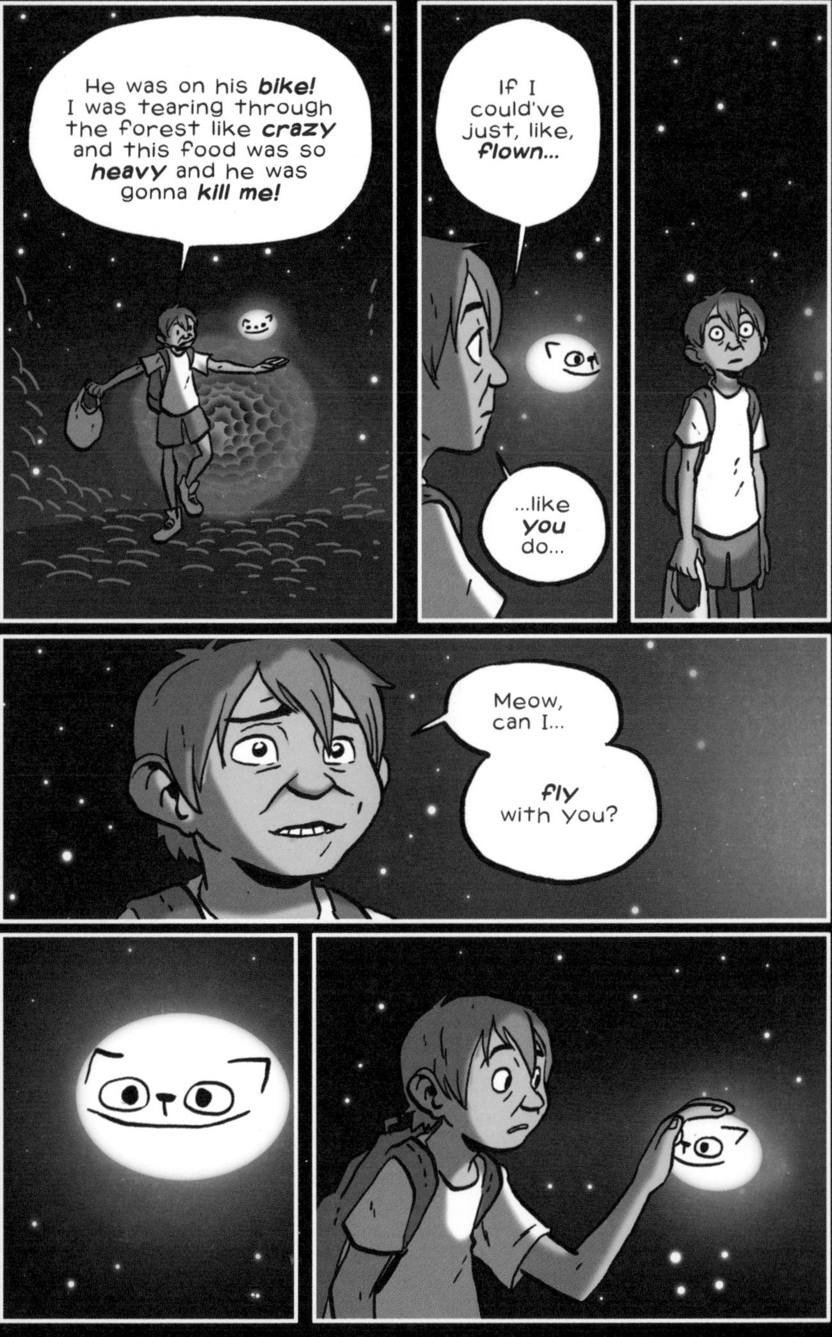
He was on his bike! I was tearing through the forest like crazy and this food was so heavy and he was gonna kill me!
If I could've just, like, flown...
...like you do...
Meow, can I...
fly with you?

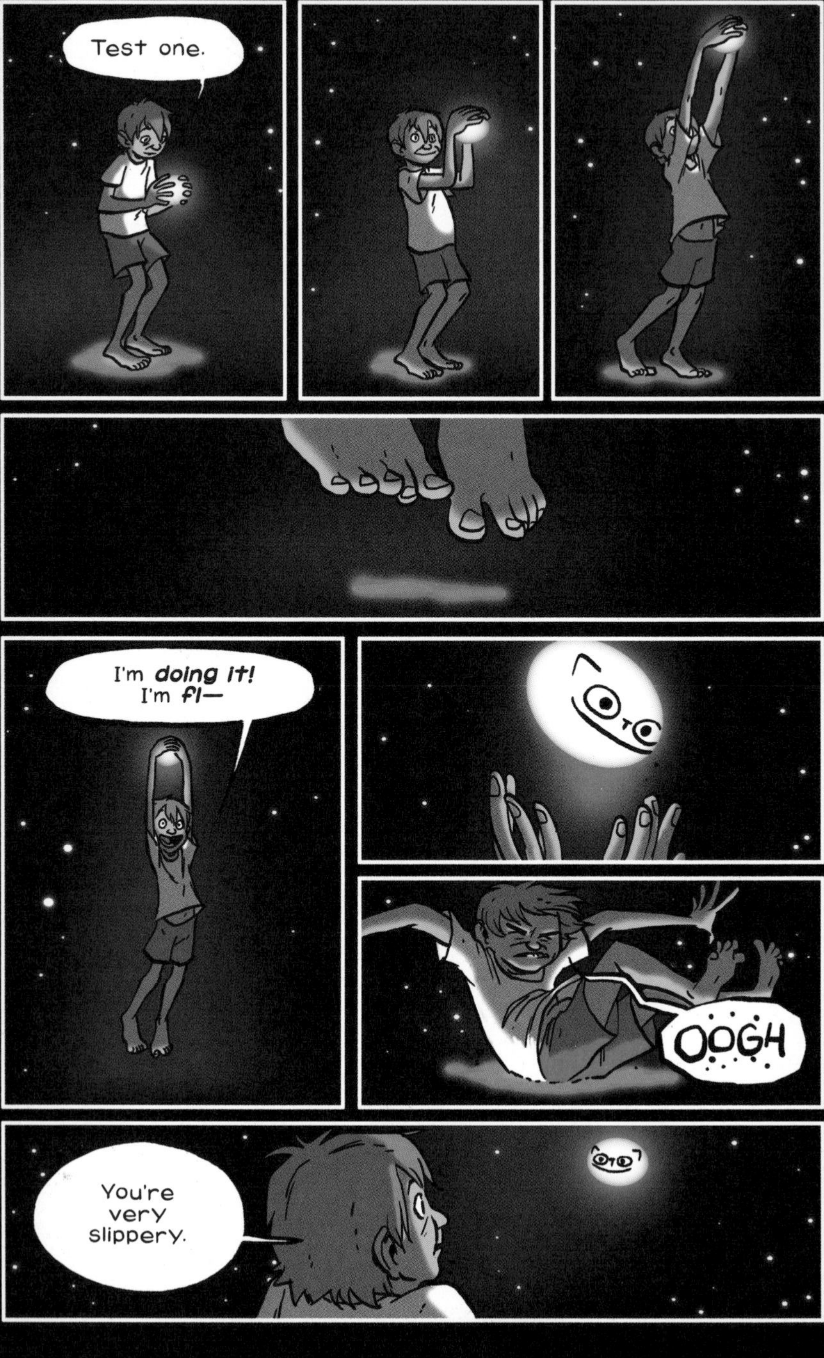
Test one.
I'm doing it! I'm fl—
OOGH
You're very slippery.

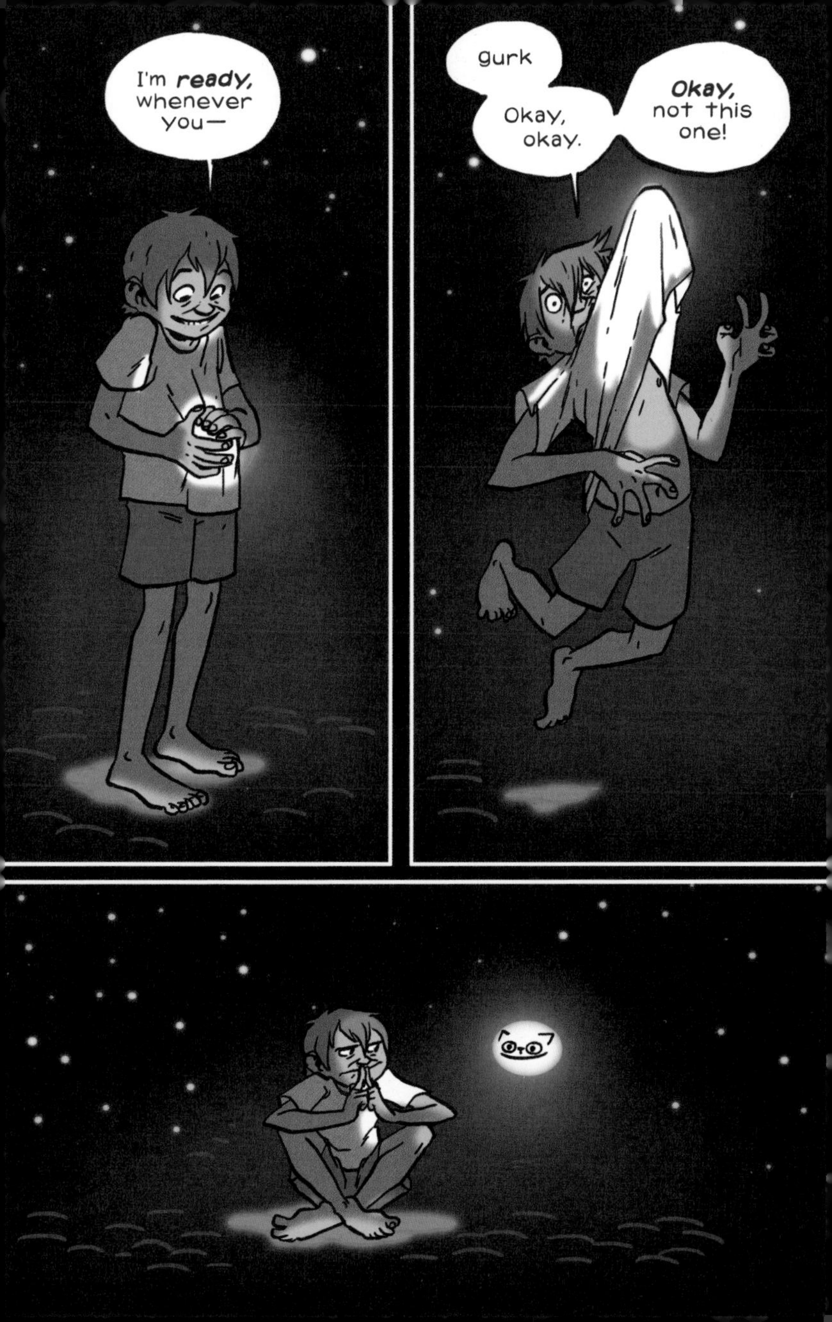

I'm *ready,* whenever you—
gurk
Okay, okay.
Okay, not this one!

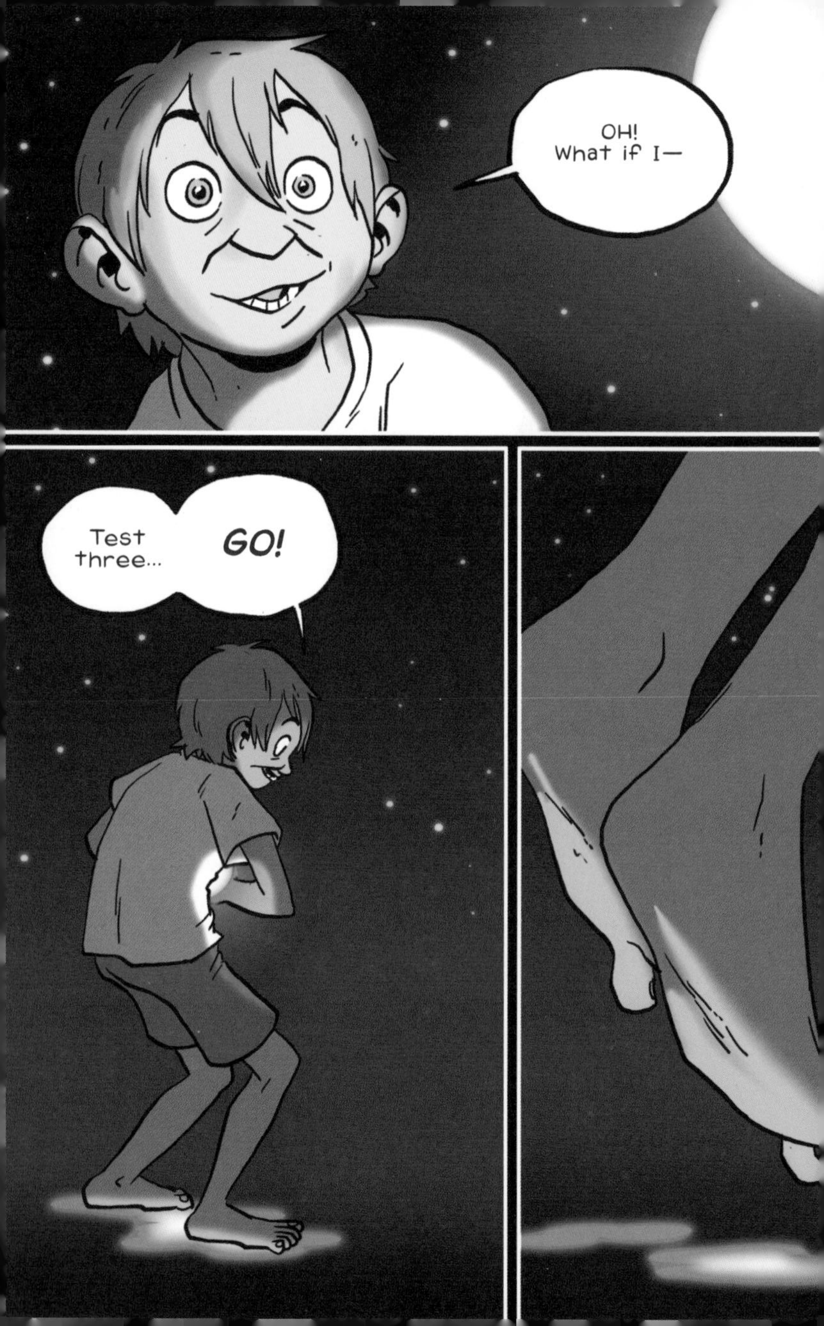
OH! What if I—
Test three...
GO!

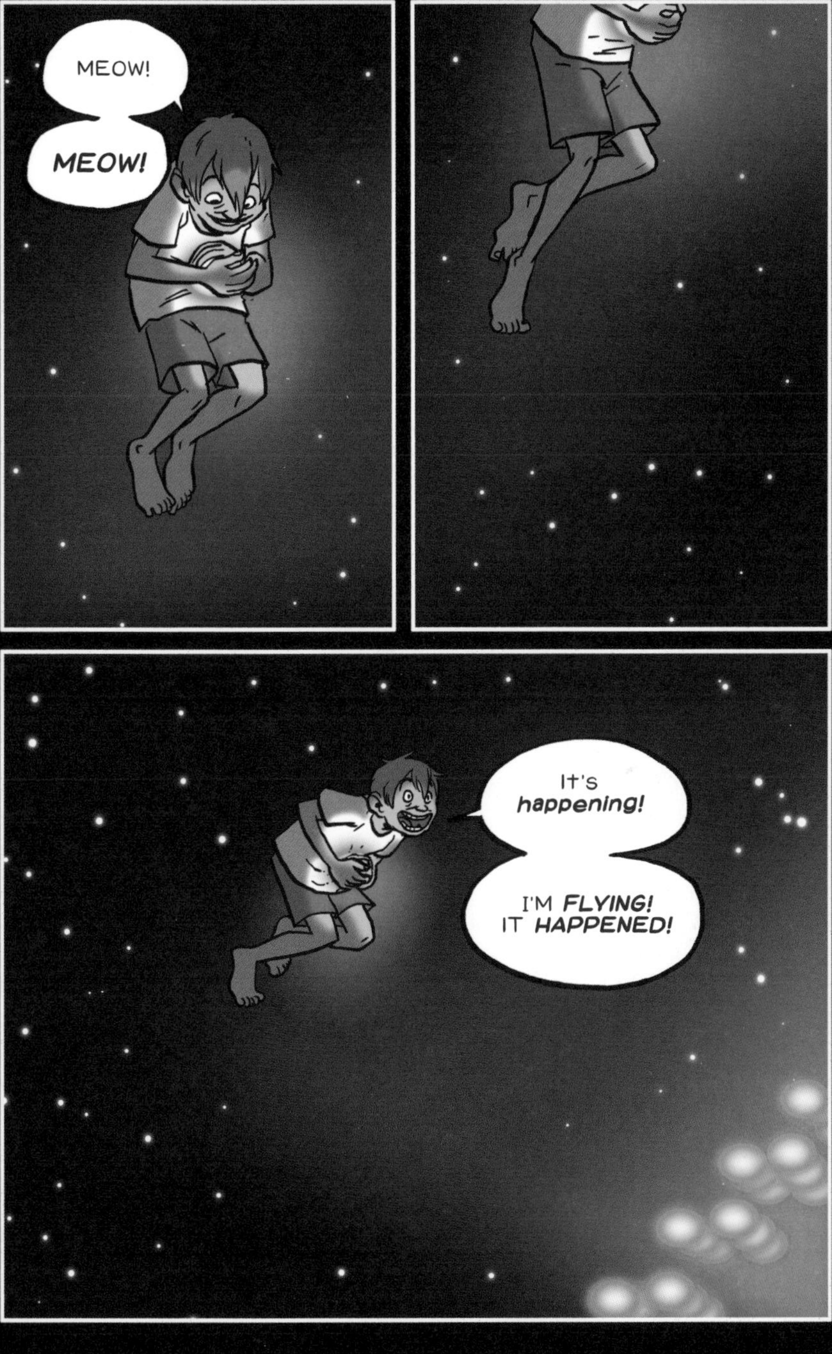
MEOW!
MEOW!
It's happening!
I'M FLYING! IT HAPPENED!

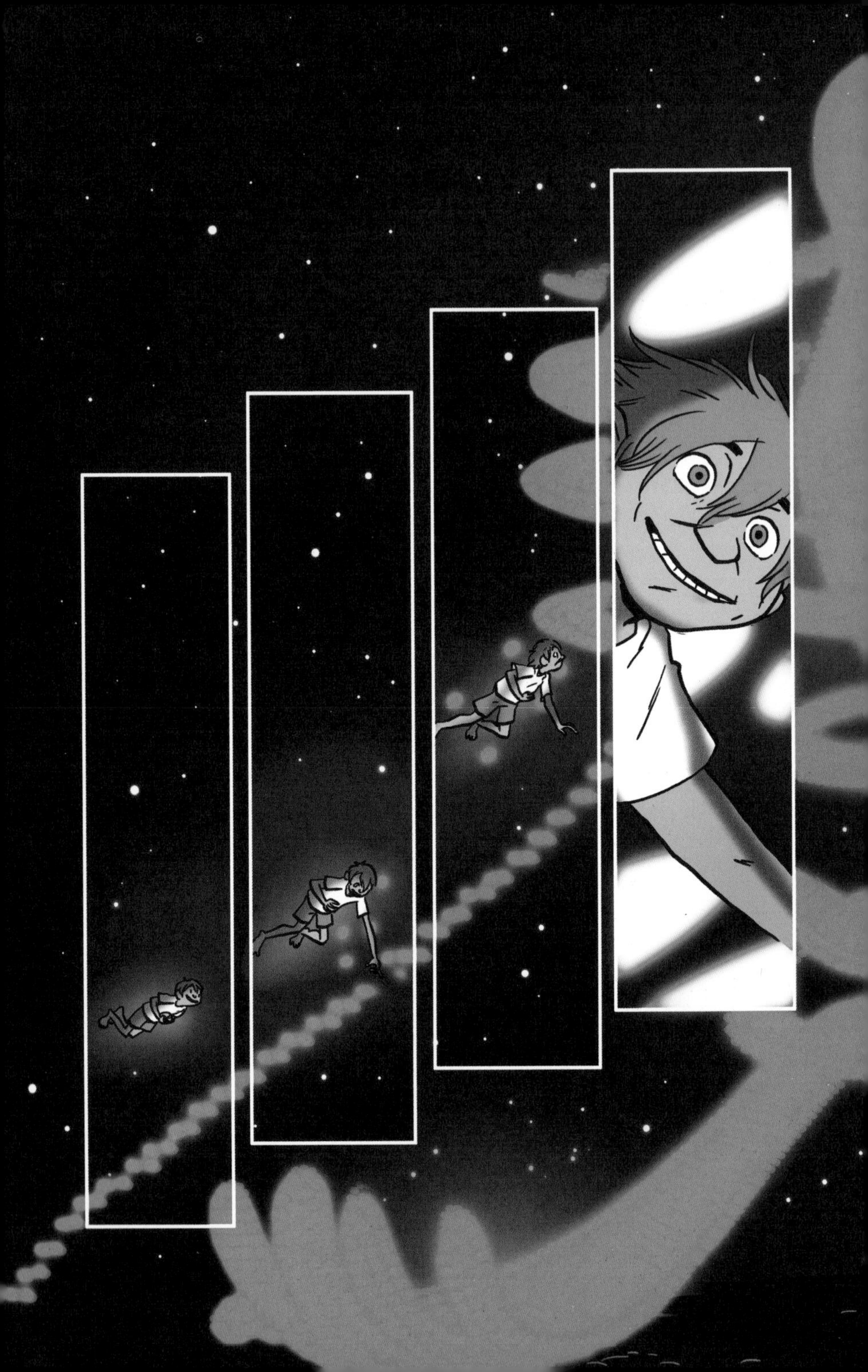

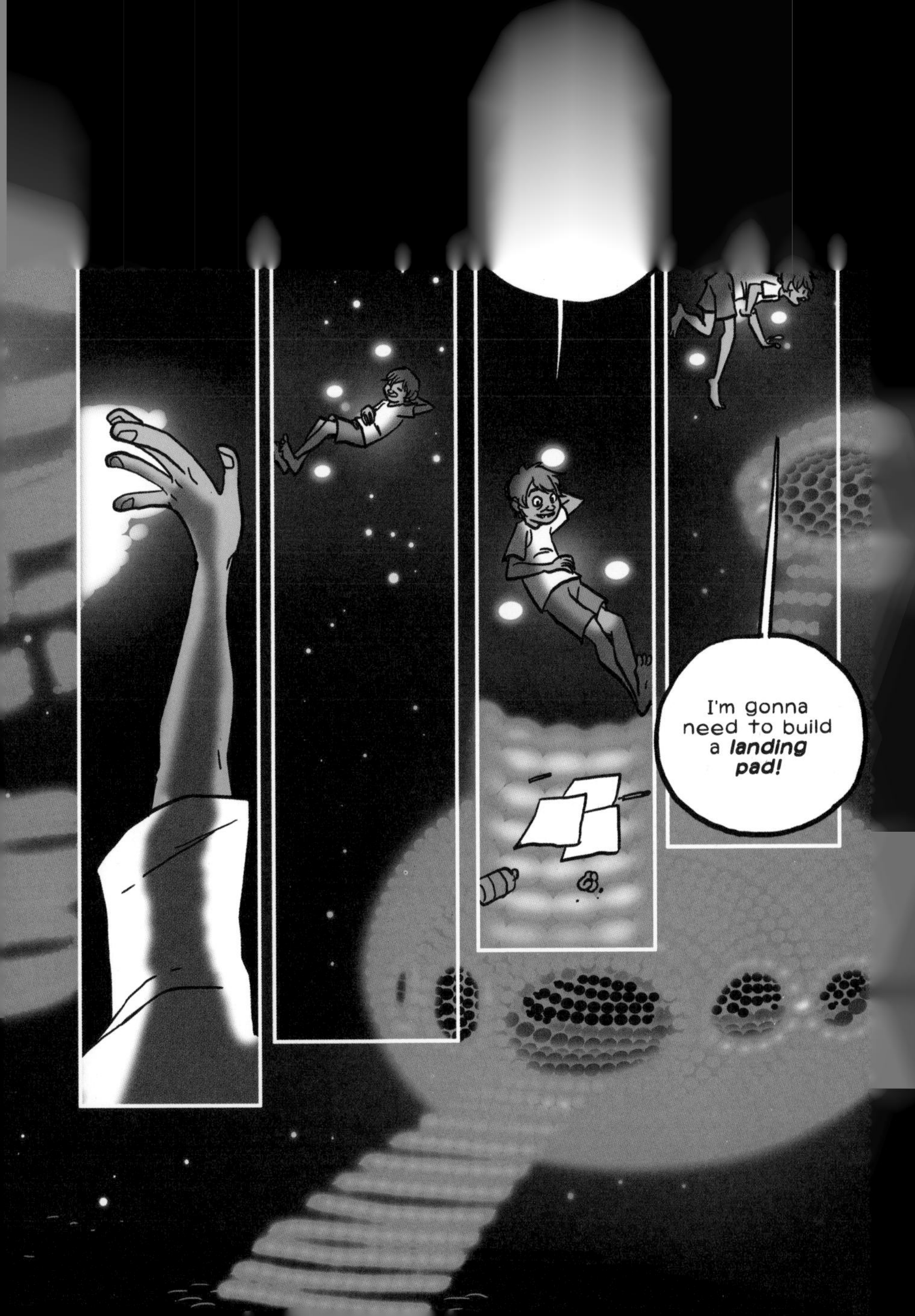
I'm gonna need to build a *landing pad!*

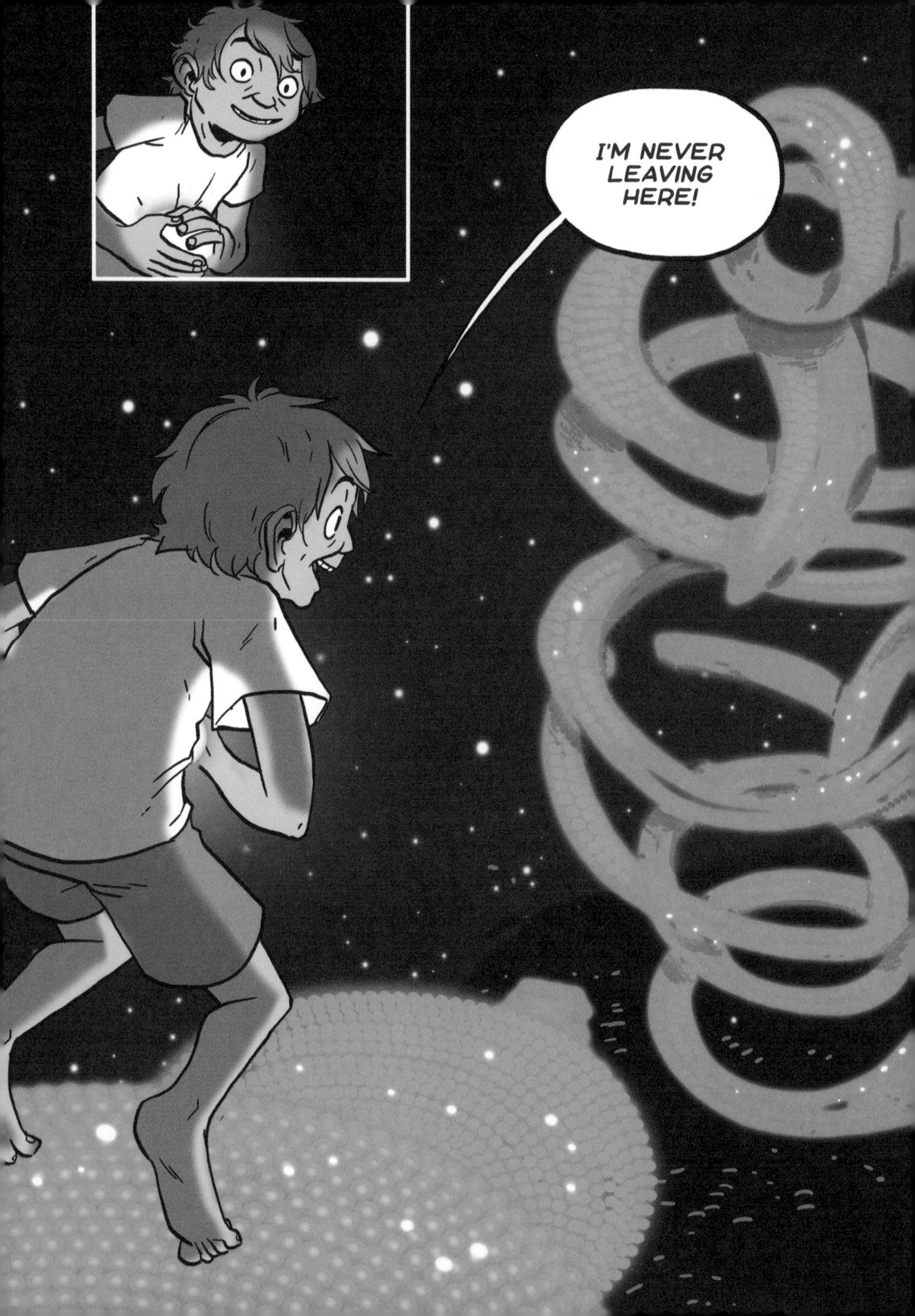
I'M NEVER LEAVING HERE!

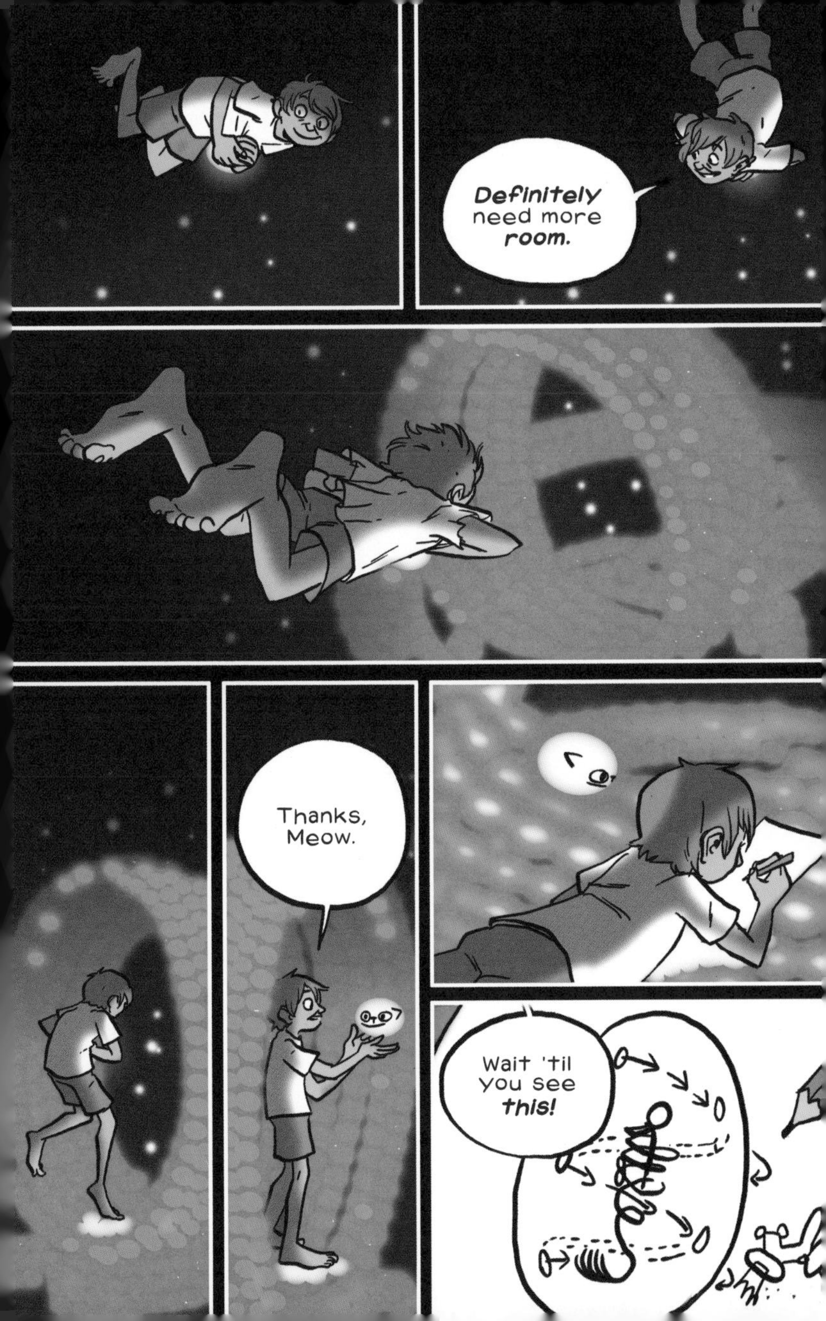
Definitely need more room.
Thanks, Meow.
Wait 'til you see this!

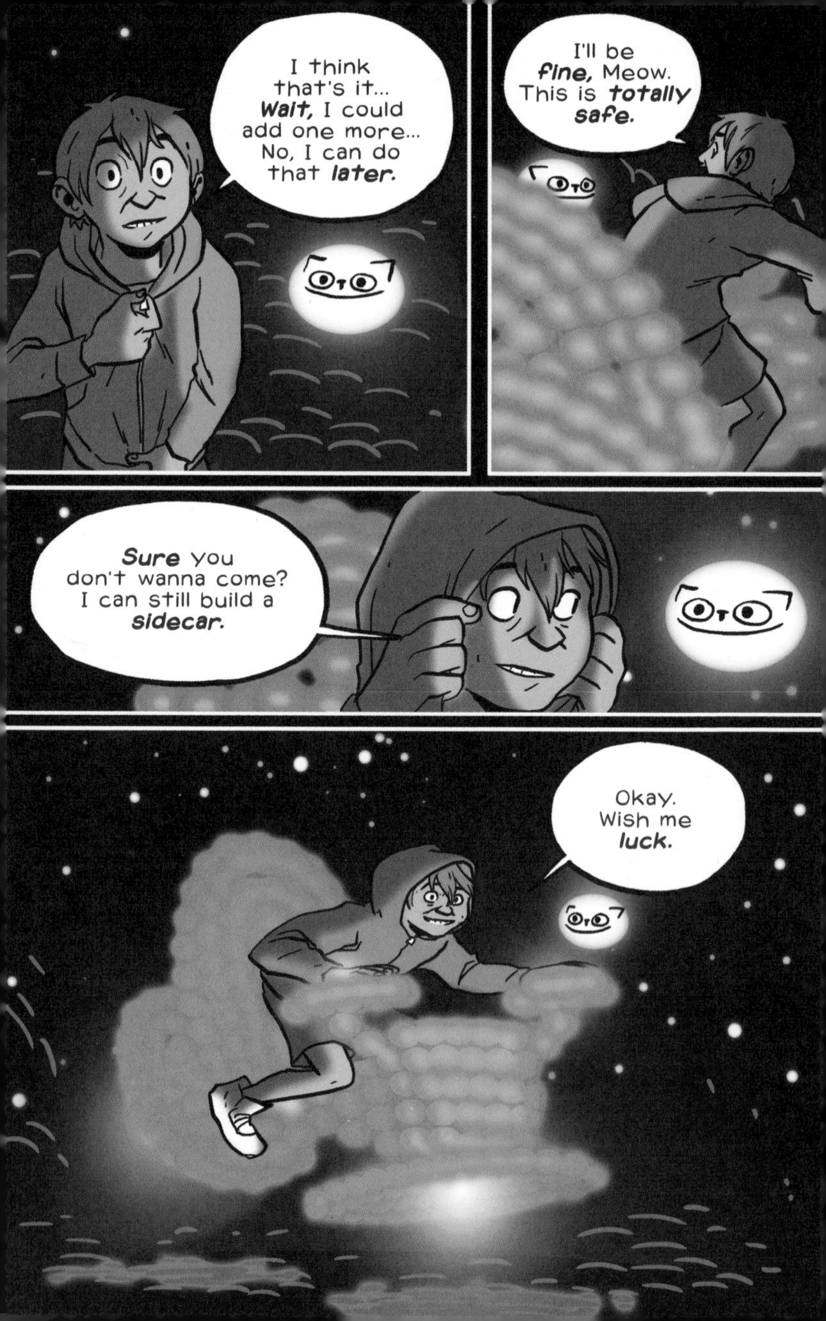
I think that's it... **Wait,** I could add one more... No, I can do that **later.**
I'll be **fine,** Meow. This is **totally safe.**
Sure you don't wanna come? I can still build a **sidecar.**
Okay. Wish me **luck.**

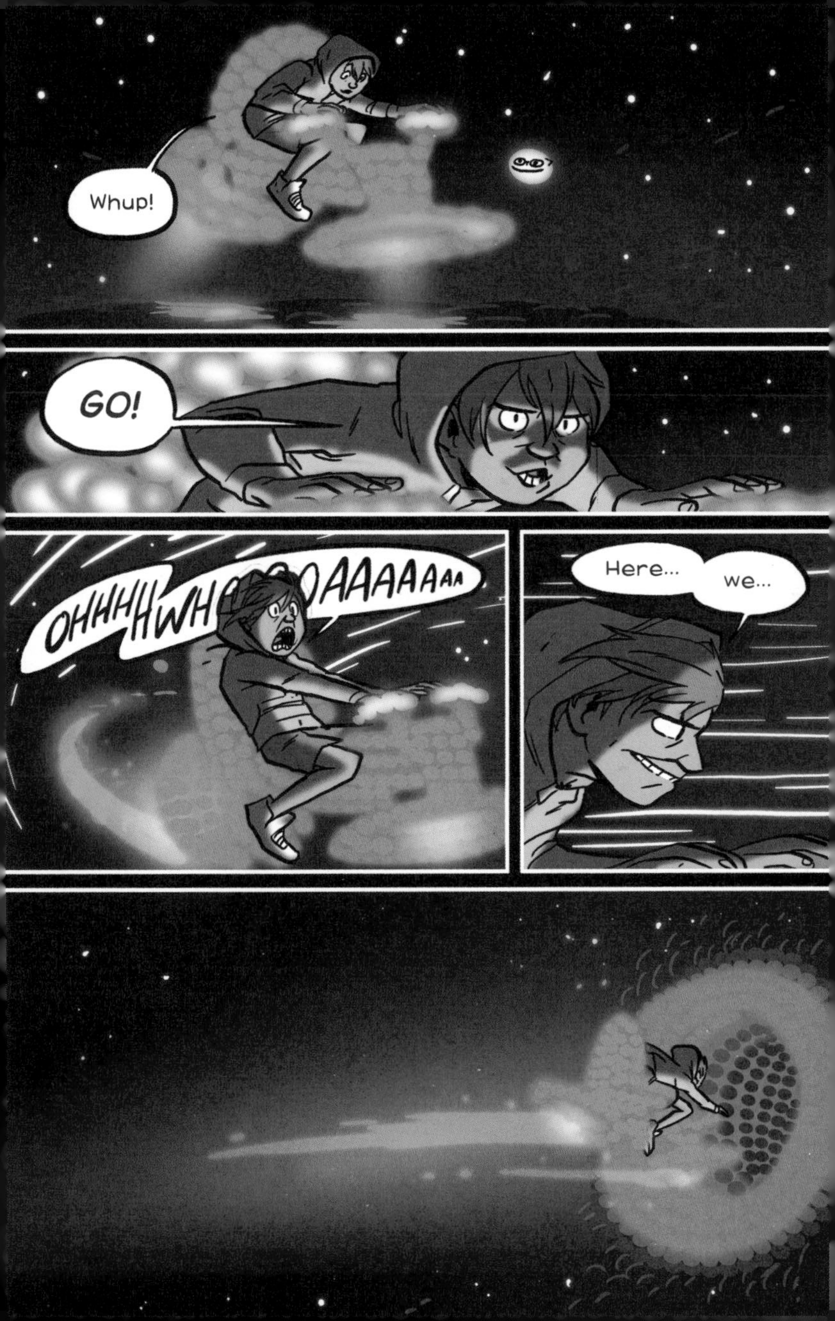

Whup!
GO!
OHHHHHWHOOOOAAAAAAA
Here...
we...

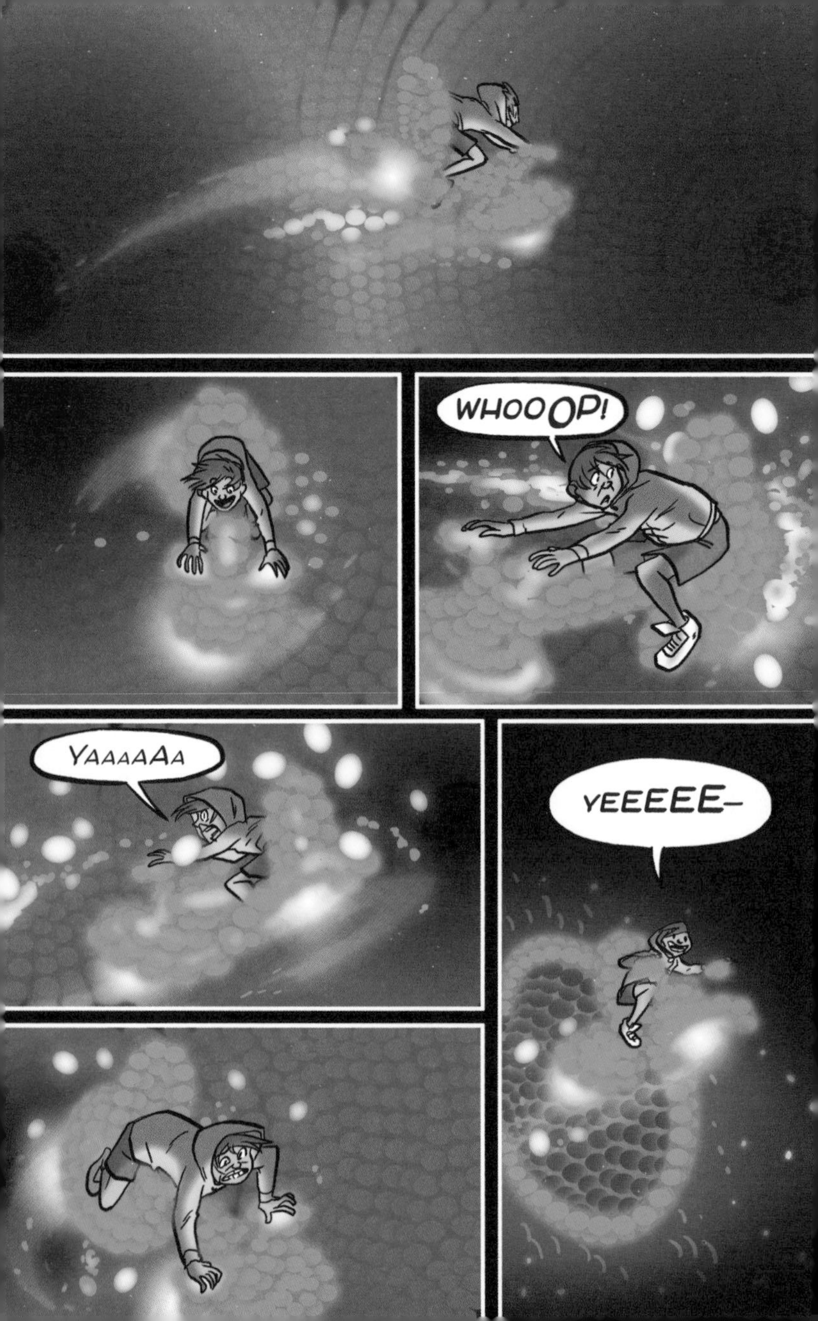
WHOOOP!
YAAAAAA
YEEEEE-

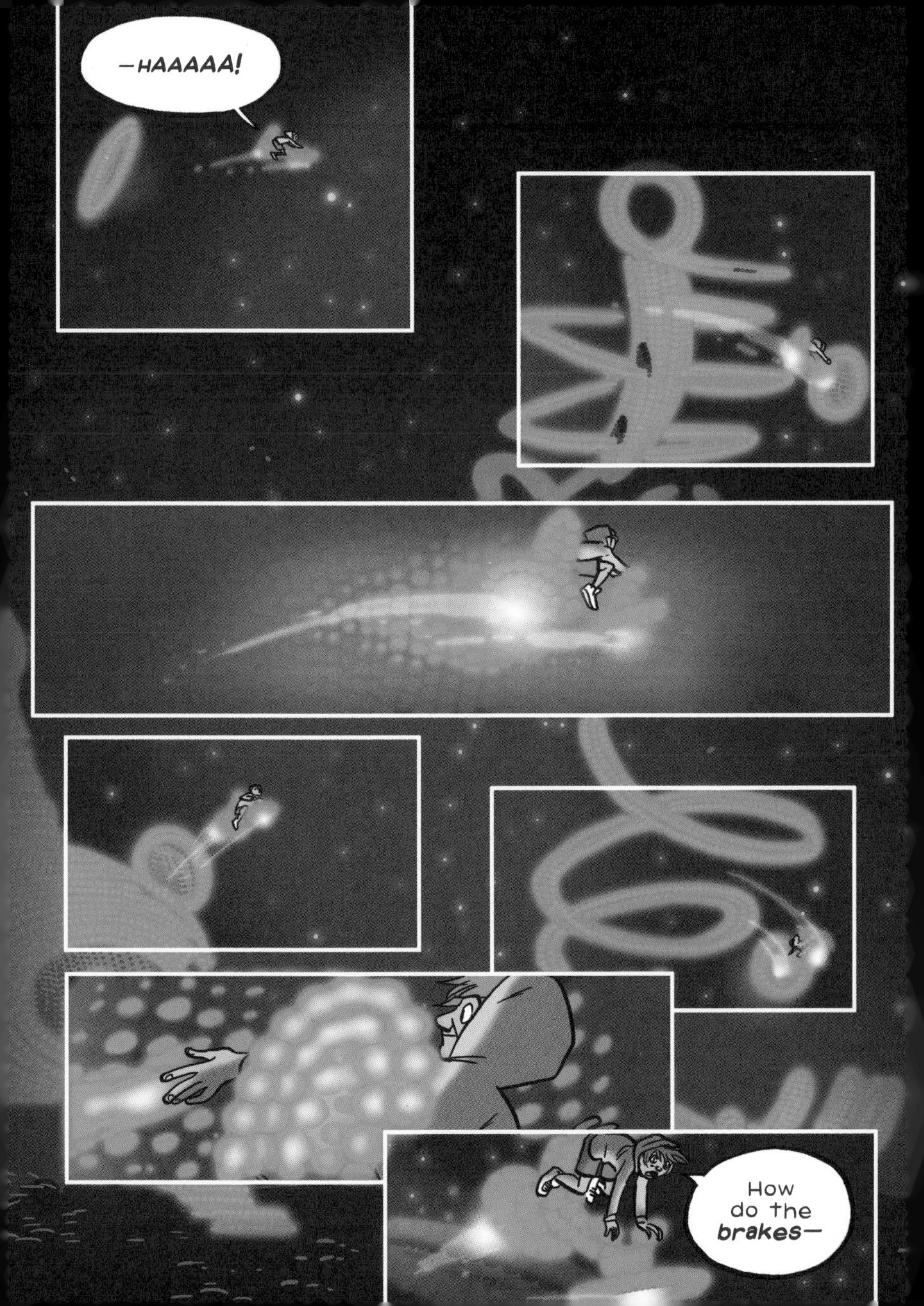
—HAAAAA!
How do the *brakes*—

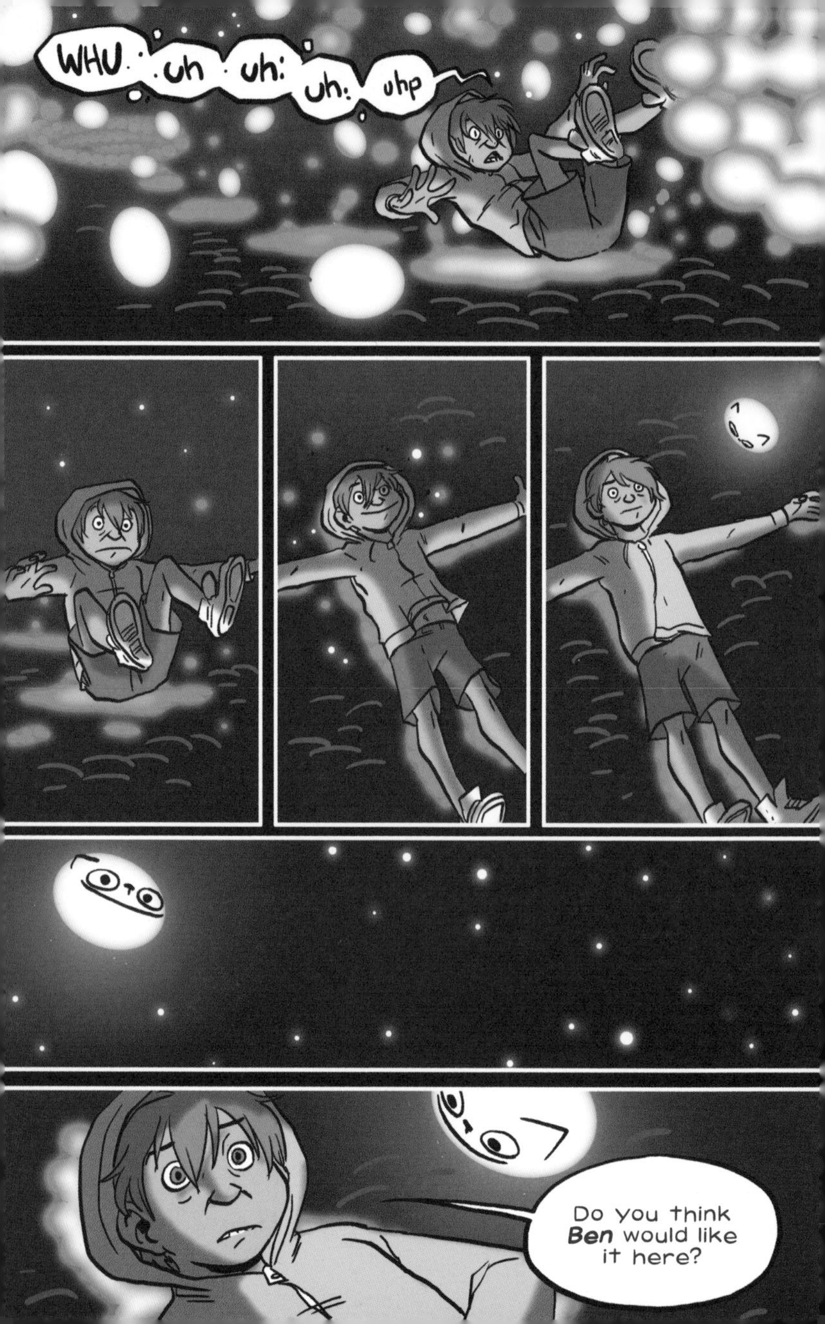
WHU. uh uh: uh! uhp
Do you think **Ben** would like it here?

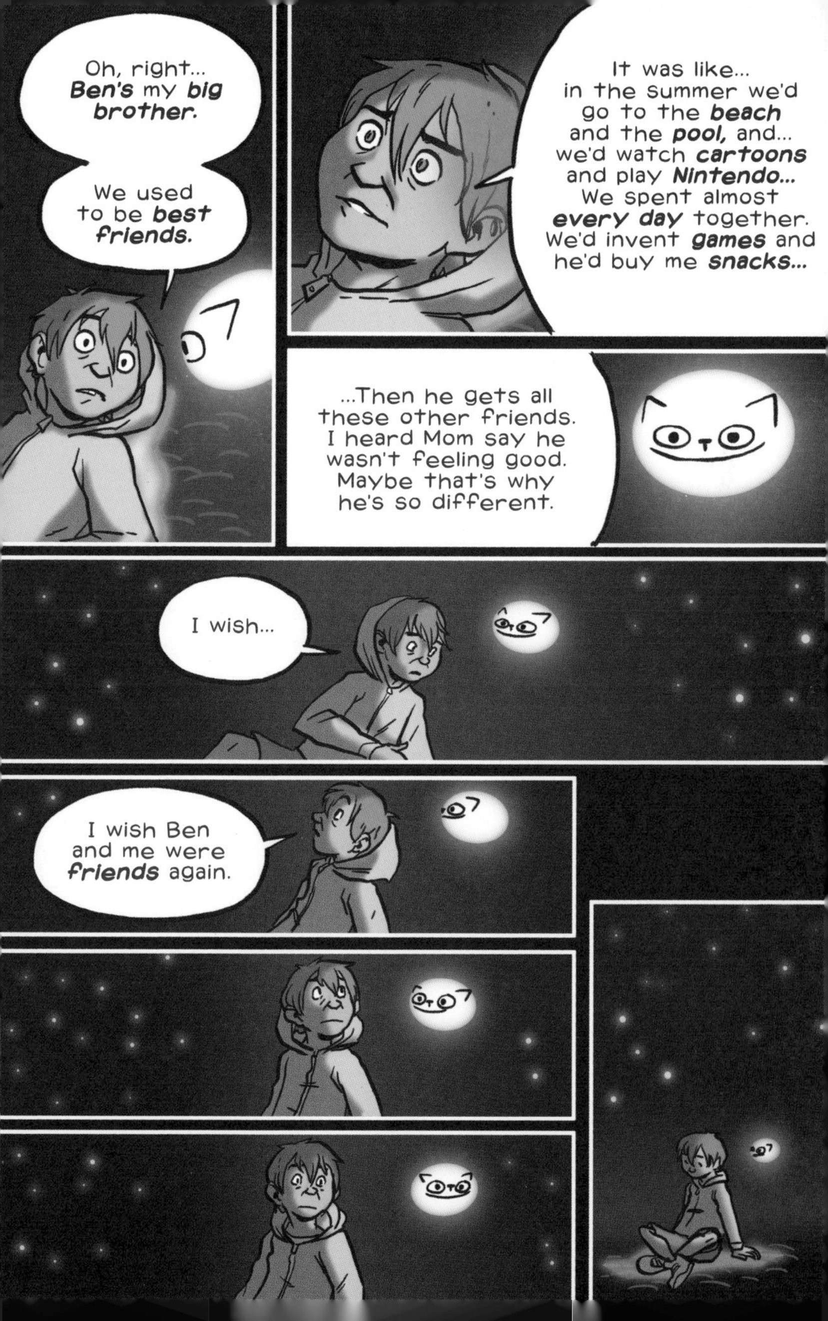
Oh, right... Ben's my big brother.
We used to be best friends.
It was like... in the summer we'd go to the beach and the pool, and... we'd watch cartoons and play Nintendo... We spent almost every day together. We'd invent games and he'd buy me snacks...
...Then he gets all these other friends. I heard Mom say he wasn't feeling good. Maybe that's why he's so different.
I wish...
I wish Ben and me were friends again.

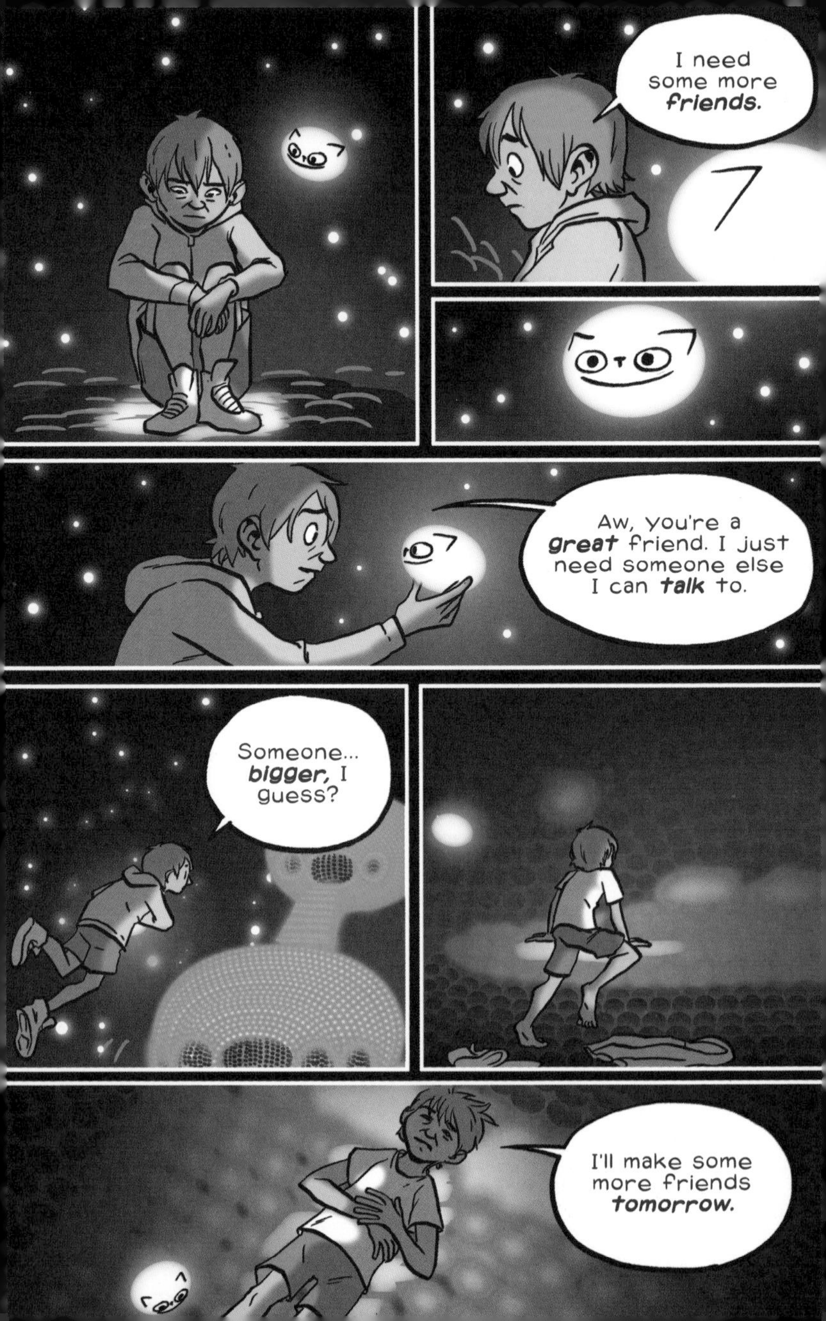

I need some more friends.
Aw, you're a great friend. I just need someone else I can talk to.
Someone... bigger, I guess?
I'll make some more friends tomorrow.

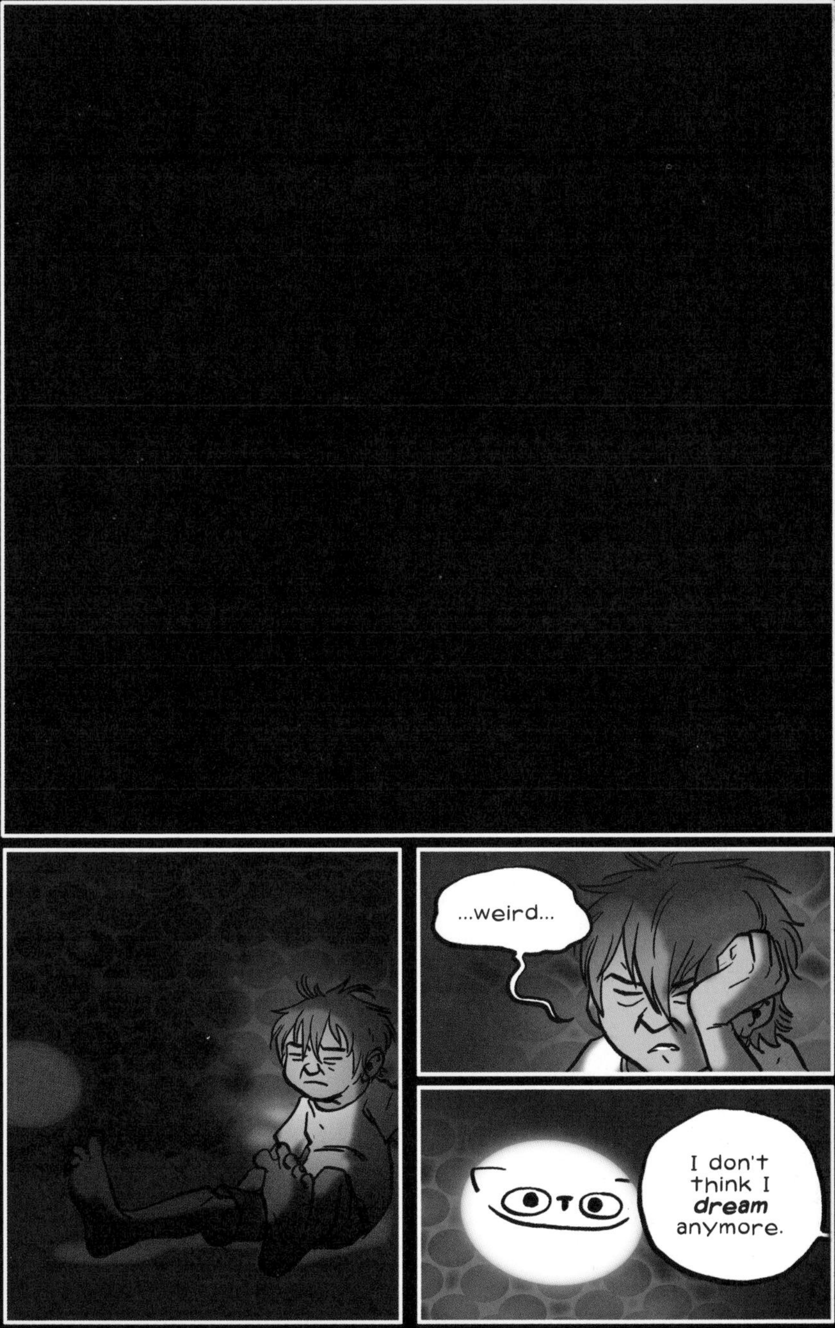
...weird...
I don't think I *dream* anymore.

DONUTS
CINNAMON
How many friends, you think? Three?
Free's goob.
I like you. You agree with me on a lot of issues.

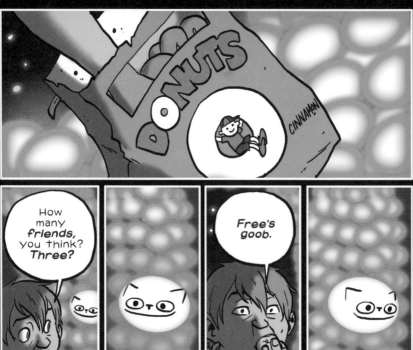

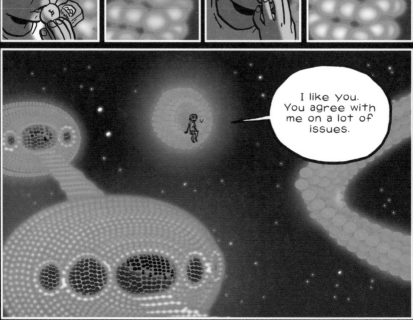

Okay... let's try *this*...

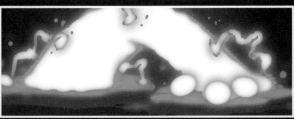

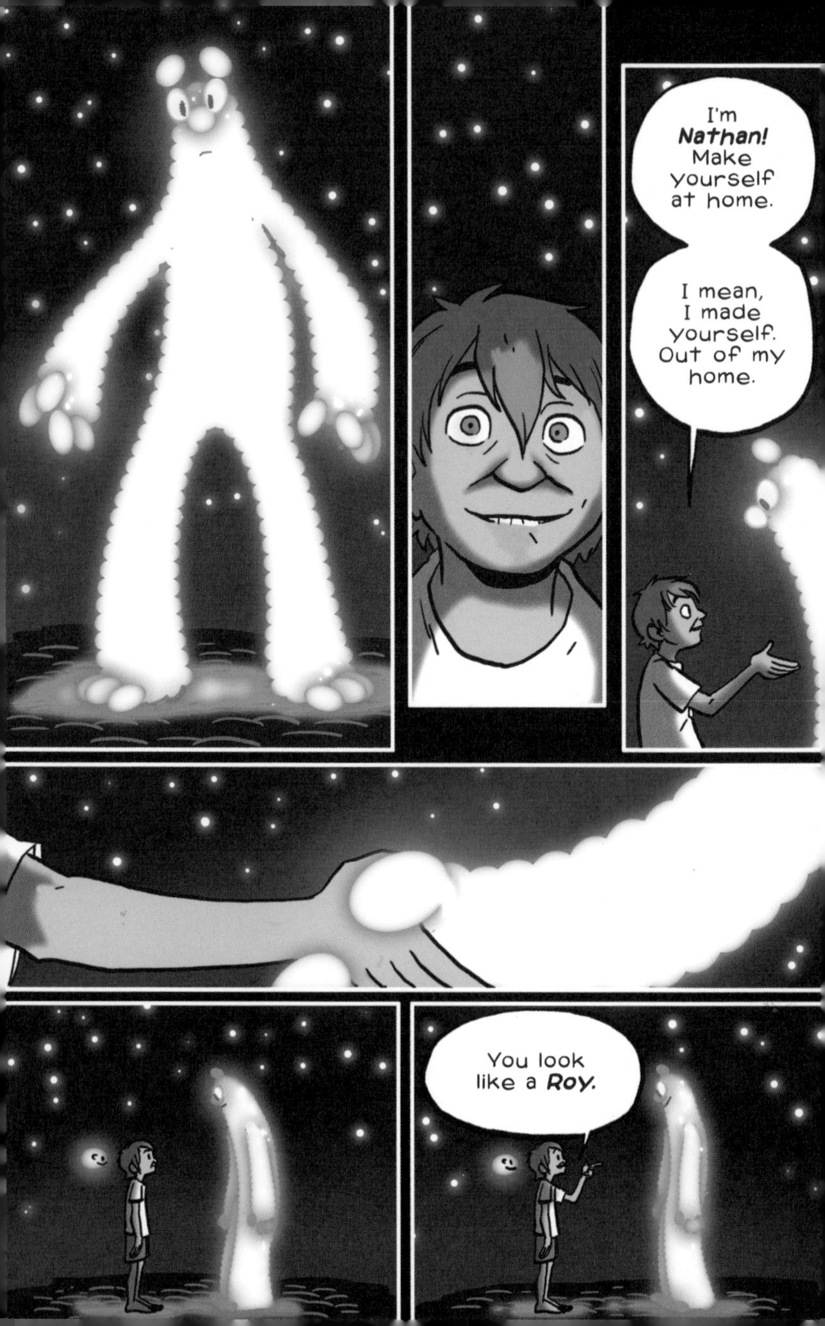

I'm **Nathan!** Make yourself at home.
I mean, I made yourself. Out of my home.
You look like a **Roy.**

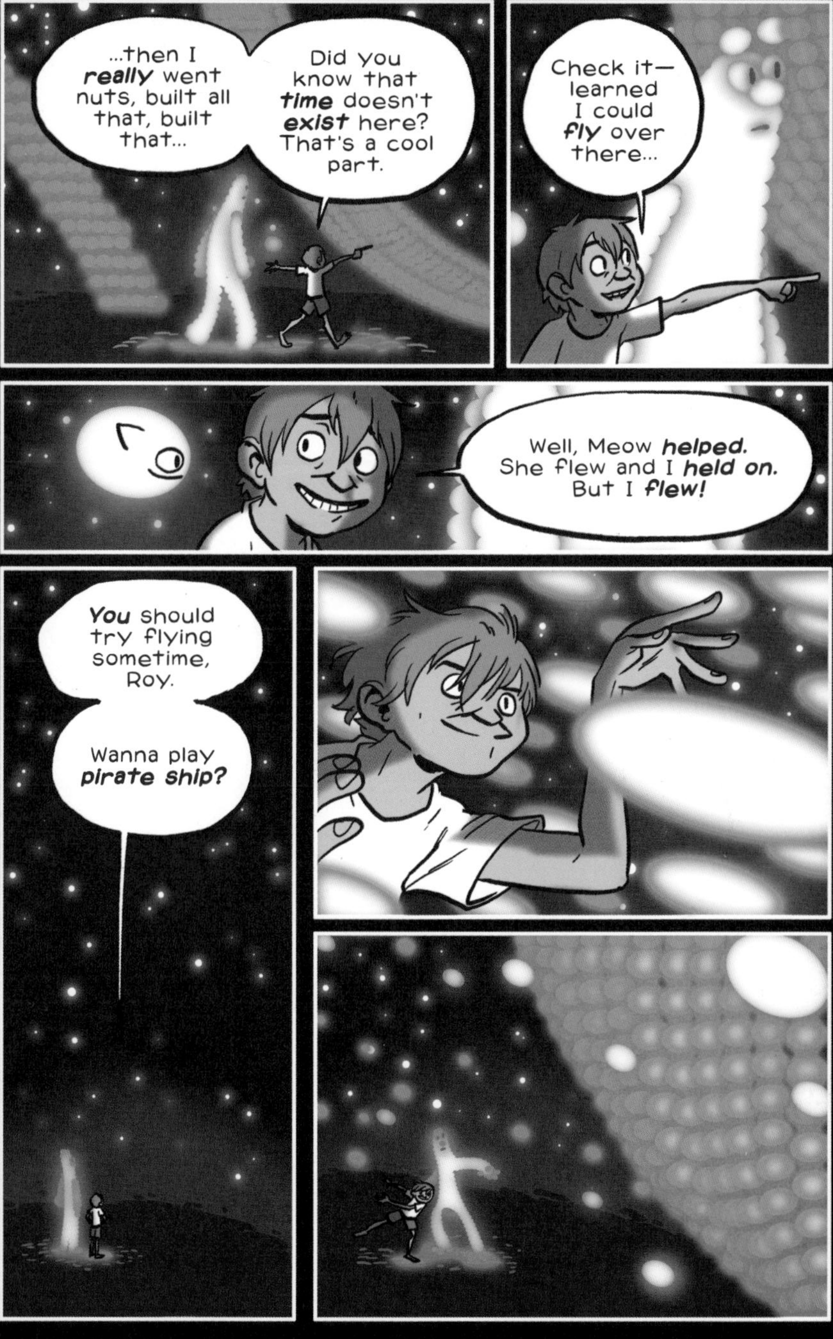
...then I **really** went nuts, built all that, built that...
Did you know that **time** doesn't **exist** here? That's a cool part.
Check it— learned I could **fly** over there...
Well, Meow **helped.** She flew and I **held on.** But I **flew!**
You should try flying sometime, Roy.
Wanna play **pirate ship?**

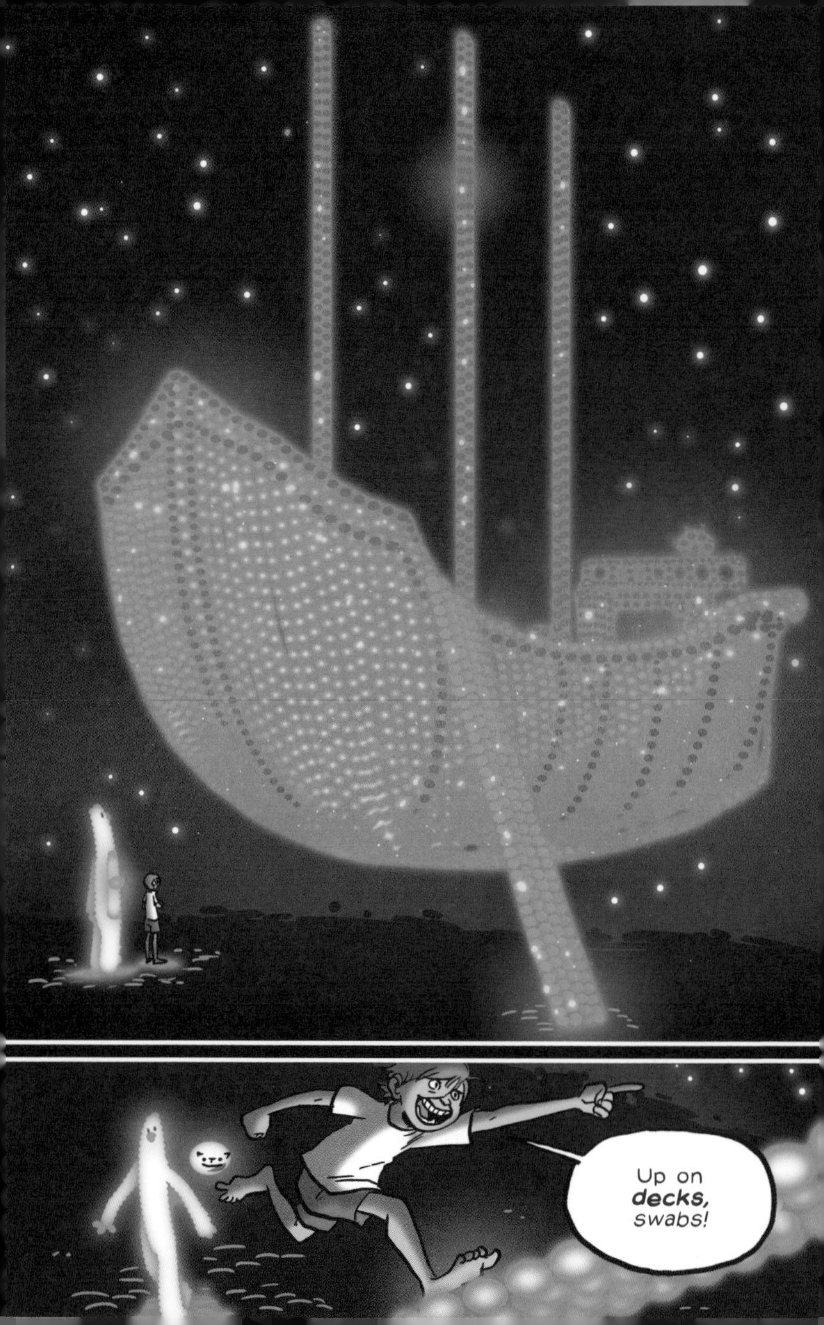
Up on **decks,** swabs!

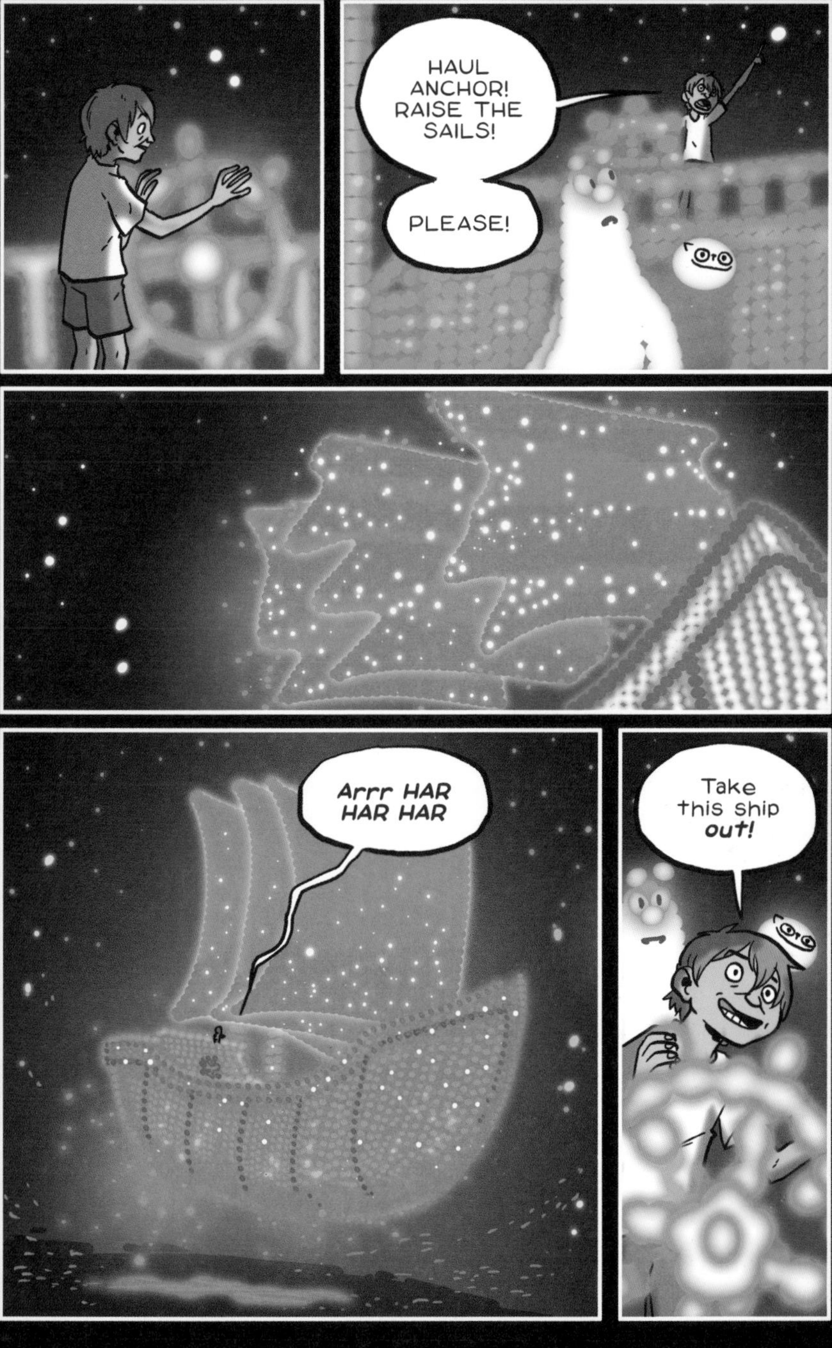
HAUL ANCHOR! RAISE THE SAILS!
PLEASE!
Arrr HAR HAR HAR
Take this ship **out!**

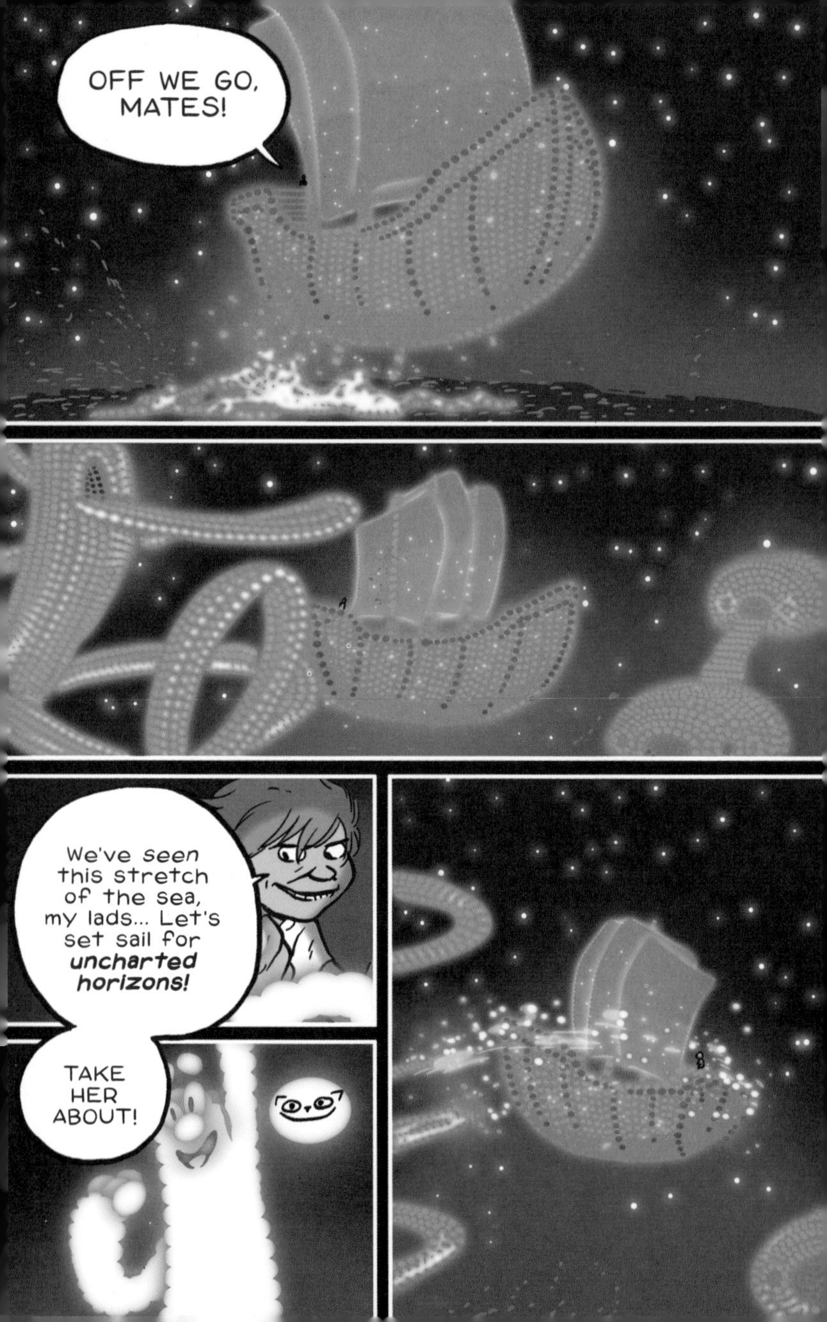
OFF WE GO, MATES!
We've *seen* this stretch of the sea, my lads... Let's set sail for ***uncharted horizons!***
TAKE HER ABOUT!

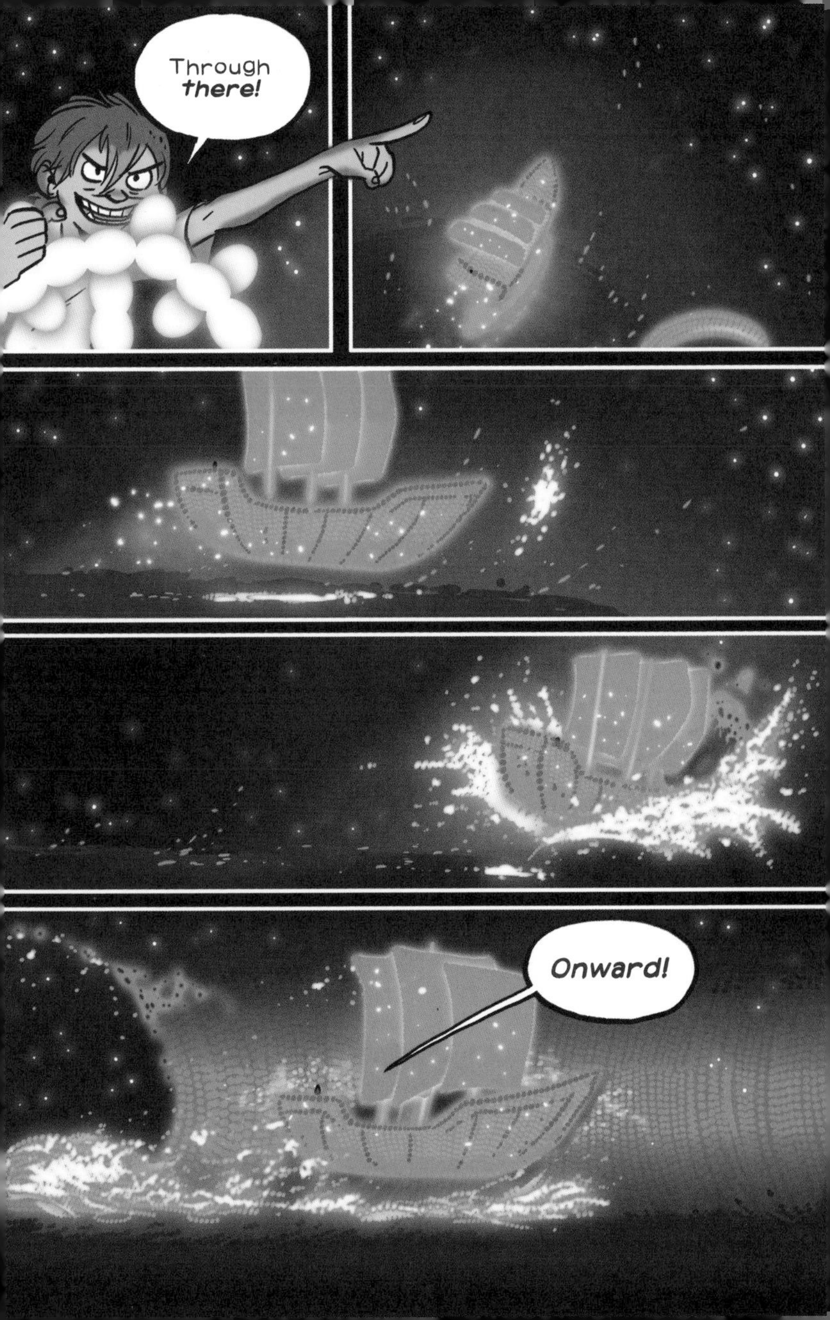
Through *there!*
Onward!

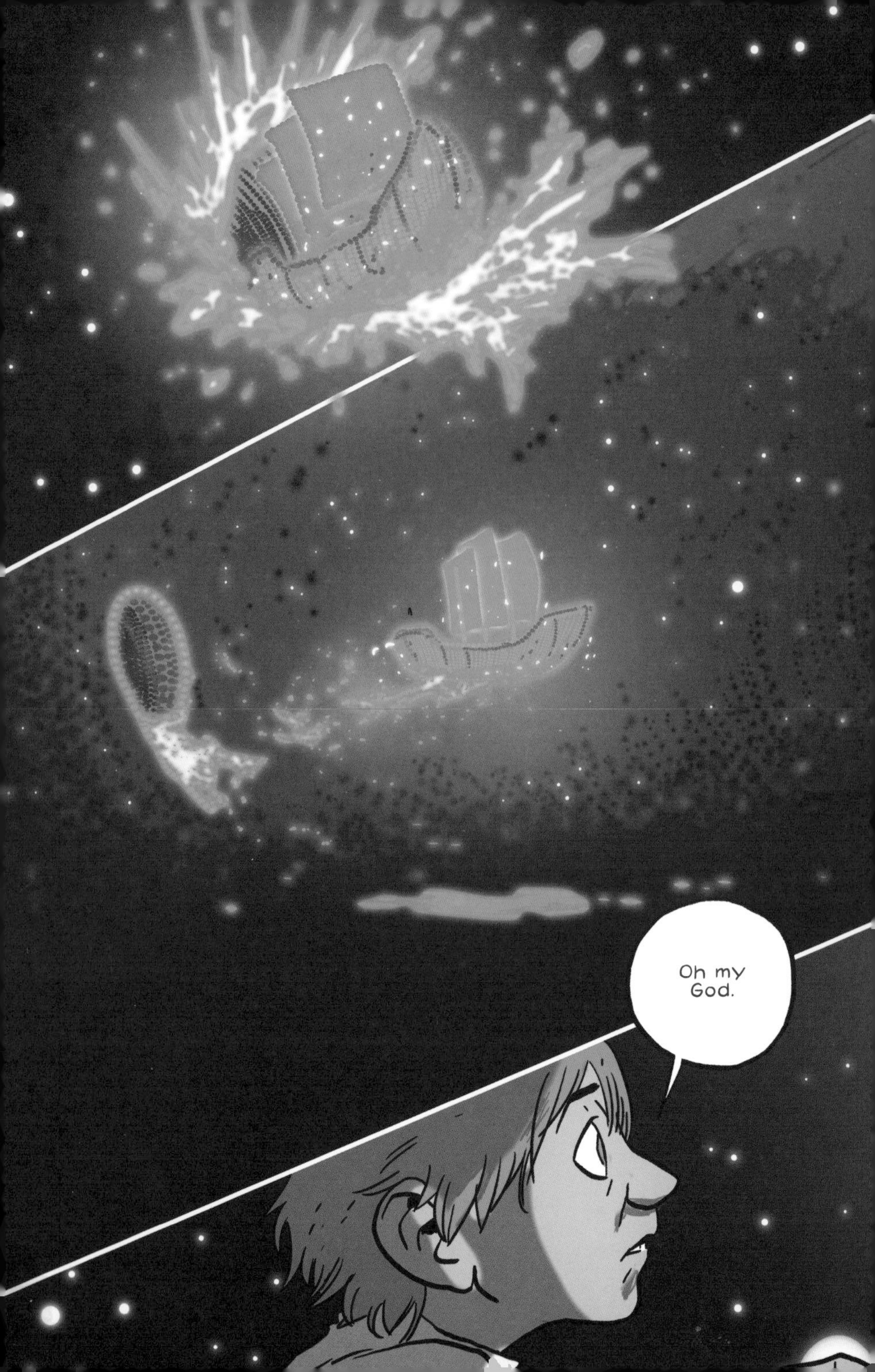
Oh my God.

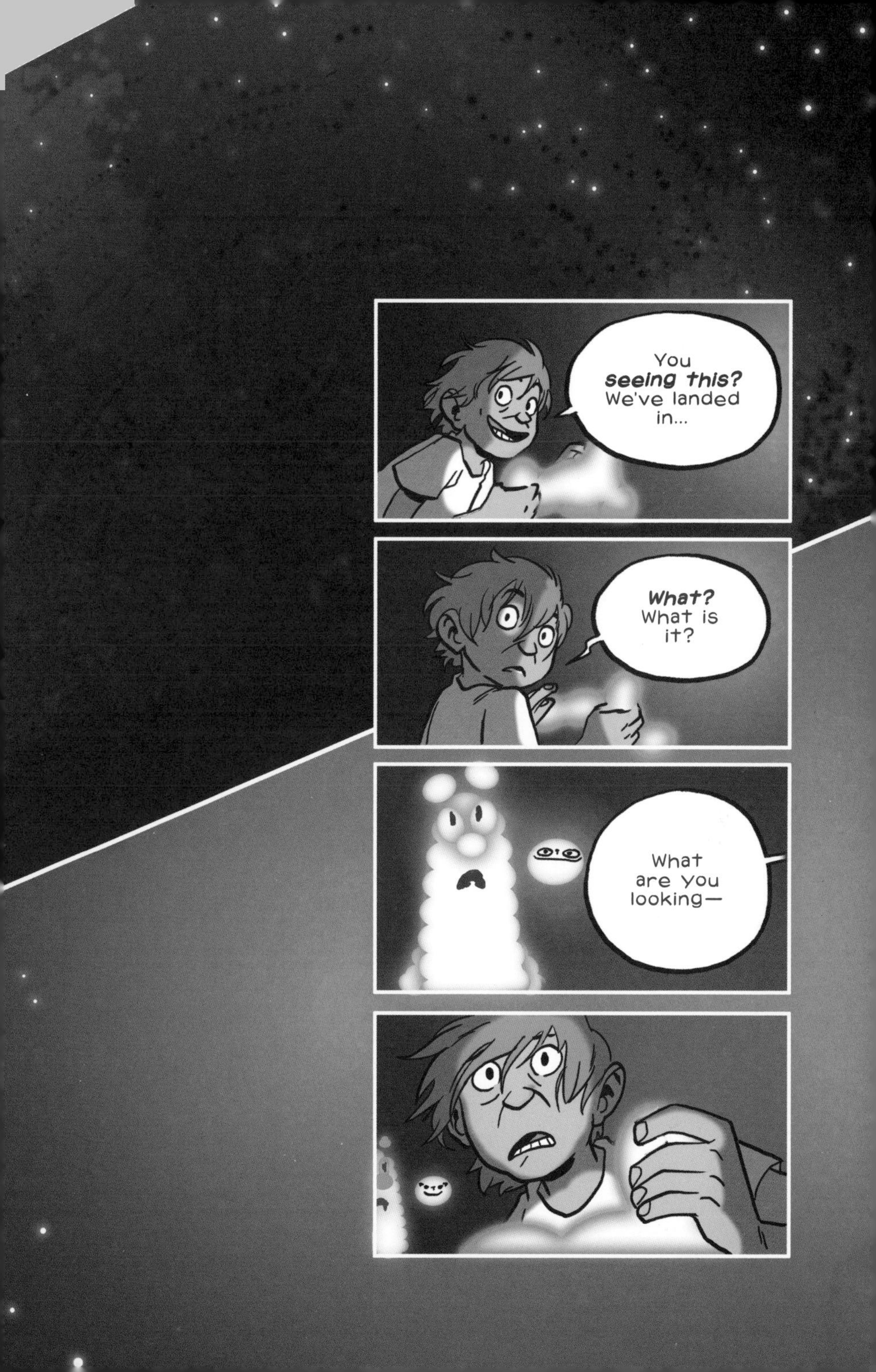
You **seeing this?** We've landed in...
What? What is it?
What are you looking—

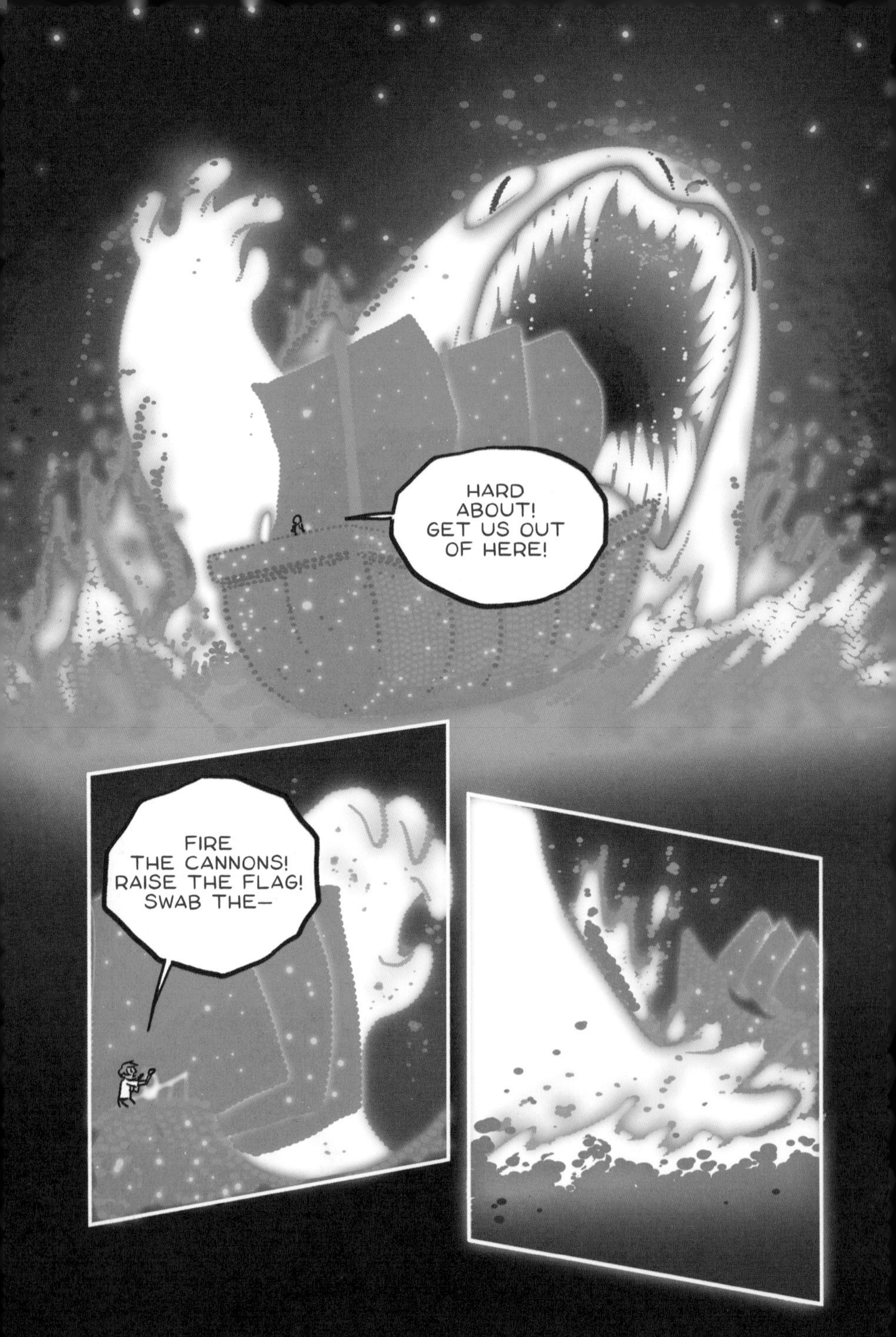
HARD ABOUT! GET US OUT OF HERE!
FIRE THE CANNONS! RAISE THE FLAG! SWAB THE—

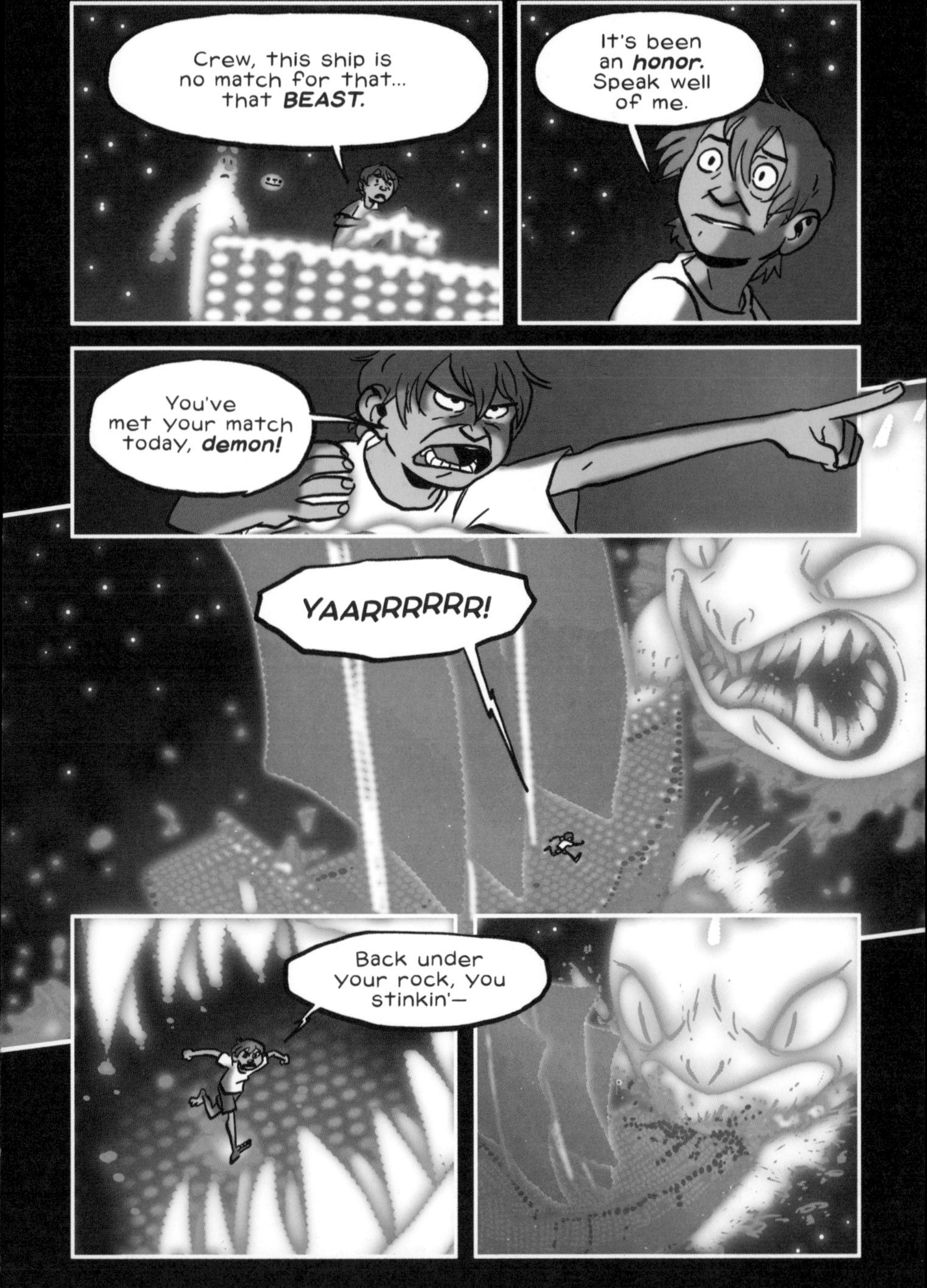
Crew, this ship is no match for that... that **BEAST.**
It's been an ***honor.*** Speak well of me.
You've met your match today, ***demon!***
YAARRRRRR!
Back under your rock, you stinkin'—

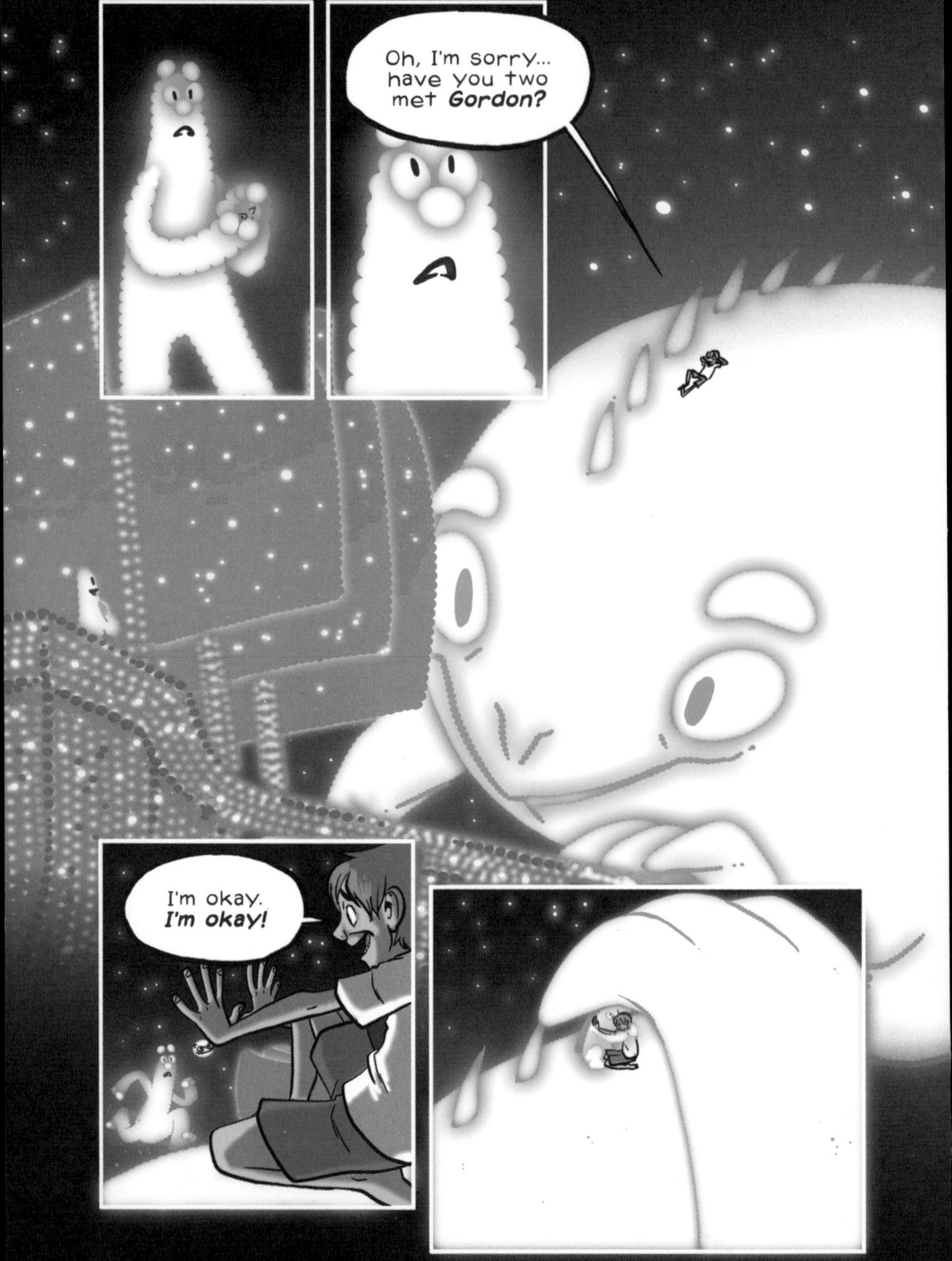
Oh, I'm sorry... have you two met *Gordon?*
I'm okay. ***I'm okay!***

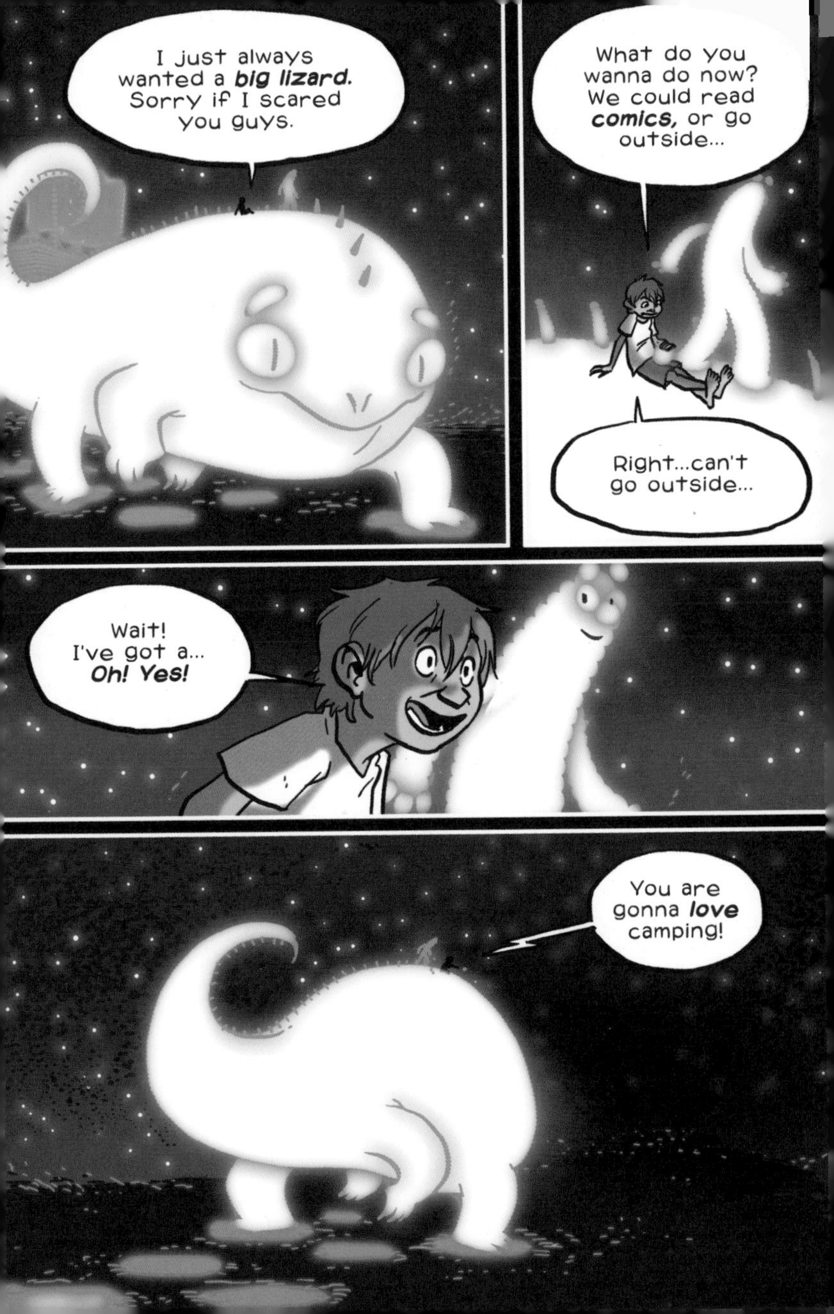
I just always wanted a ***big lizard.*** Sorry if I scared you guys.
What do you wanna do now? We could read ***comics,*** or go outside...
Right...can't go outside...
Wait! I've got a... ***Oh! Yes!***
You are gonna ***love*** camping!

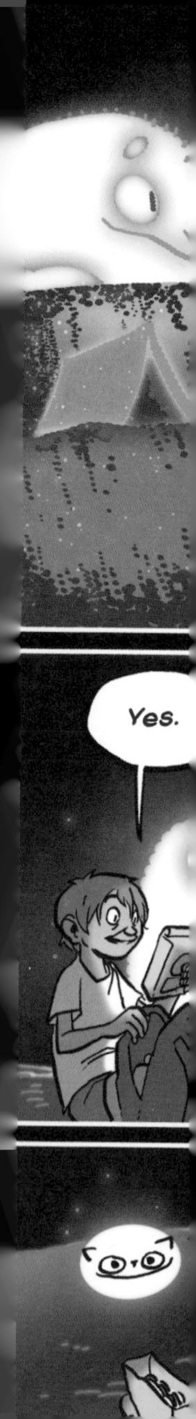
Yes.

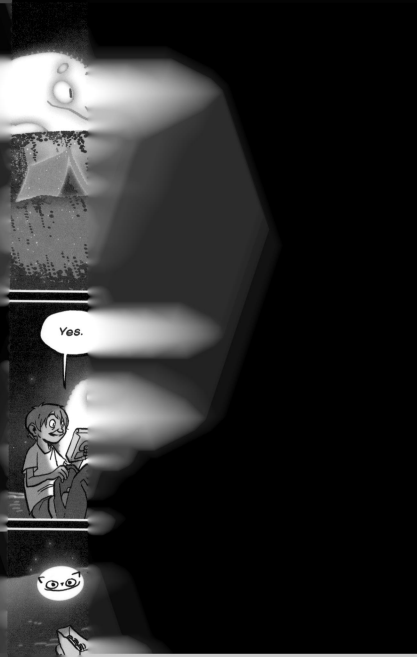

...Is it, like, *weird* if I call you guys my *best friends?*

It's just... I *made* you. You're a *part* of me.

Is that *weird* if we're *friends?*

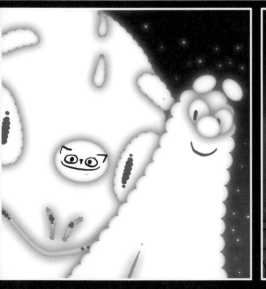

I guess it's probably *okay,* if you're a part of who I am.

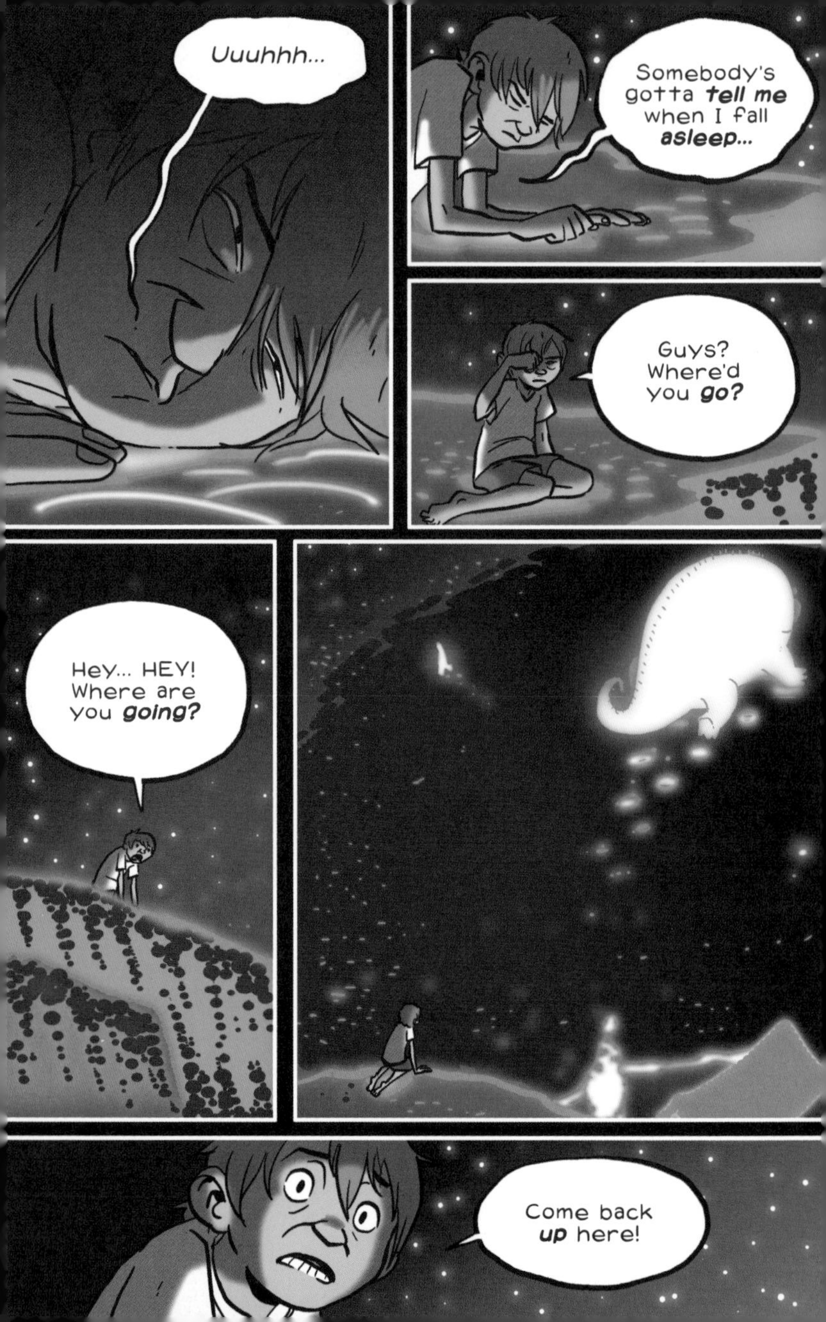
Uuuhhh...
Somebody's gotta **tell me** when I fall **asleep...**
Guys? Where'd you **go?**
Hey... HEY! Where are you **going?**
Come back **up** here!

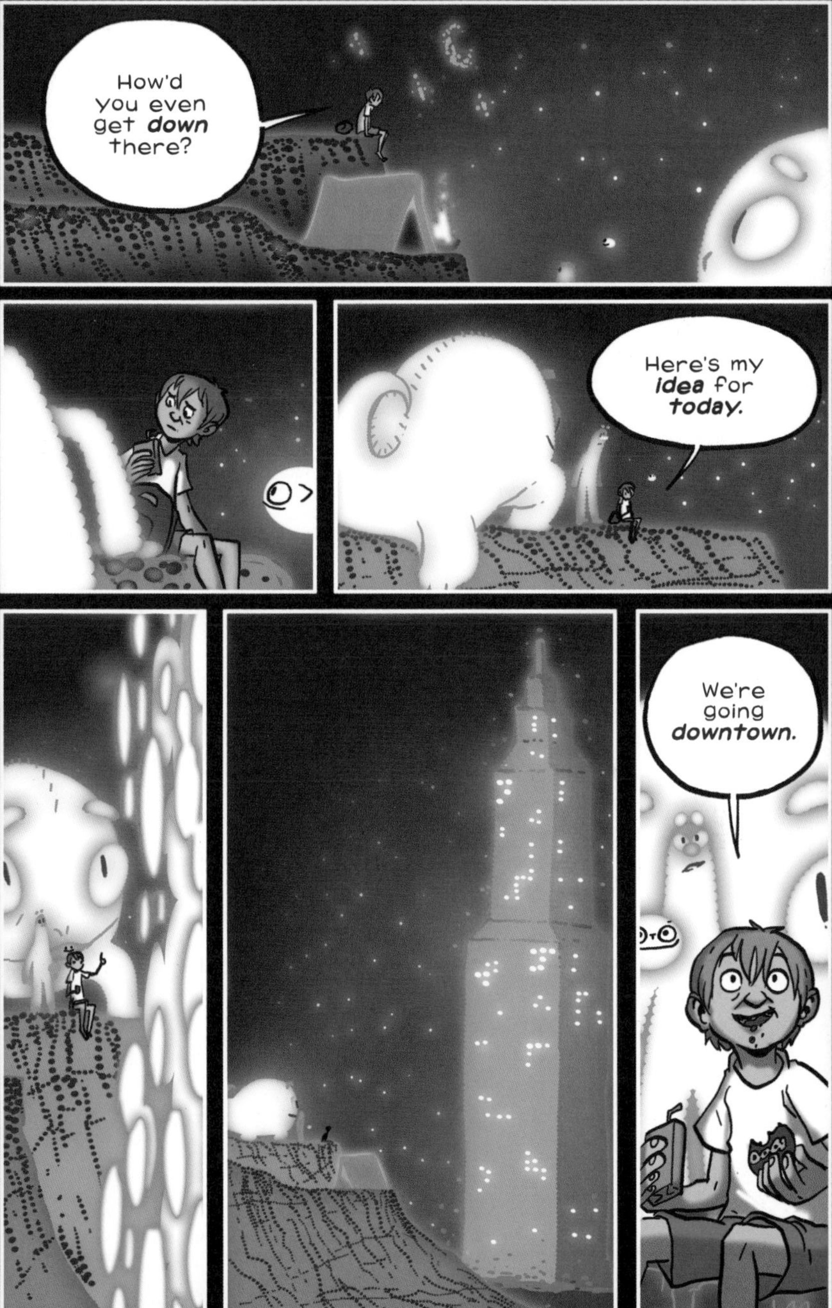
How'd you even get *down* there?
Here's my *idea* for *today.*
We're going *downtown.*

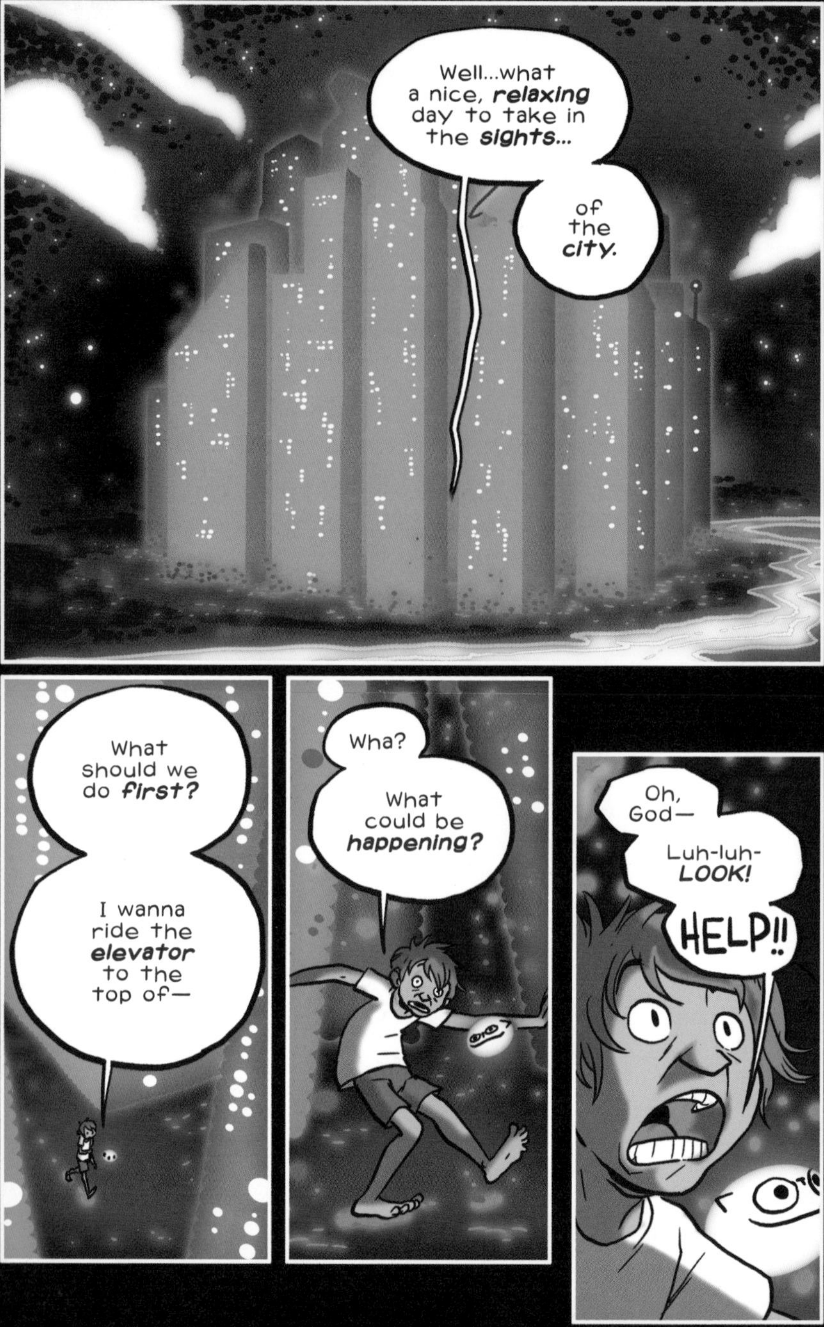
Well...what a nice, relaxing day to take in the sights...
of the city.
What should we do first?
I wanna ride the elevator to the top of—
Wha?
What could be happening?
Oh, God—
Luh-luh-LOOK!
HELP!!

It's *Roydan* the *Gargantuan!*

WE'RE *DOOMED!*

Wait! The *ancient savior* will *protect us!*

KING GORDO! WE CALL ON YOU IN OUR HOUR OF NEED!

KING GORDO! Roydan is *destroying our beloved city!*

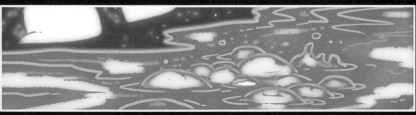

He's out of **control!** Who can stop—

YES!

KING GORDO! *YES!*

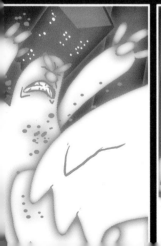

You can't do that to our *city,* Gargantuan! *King Gordo's* here to ruin your *day!*

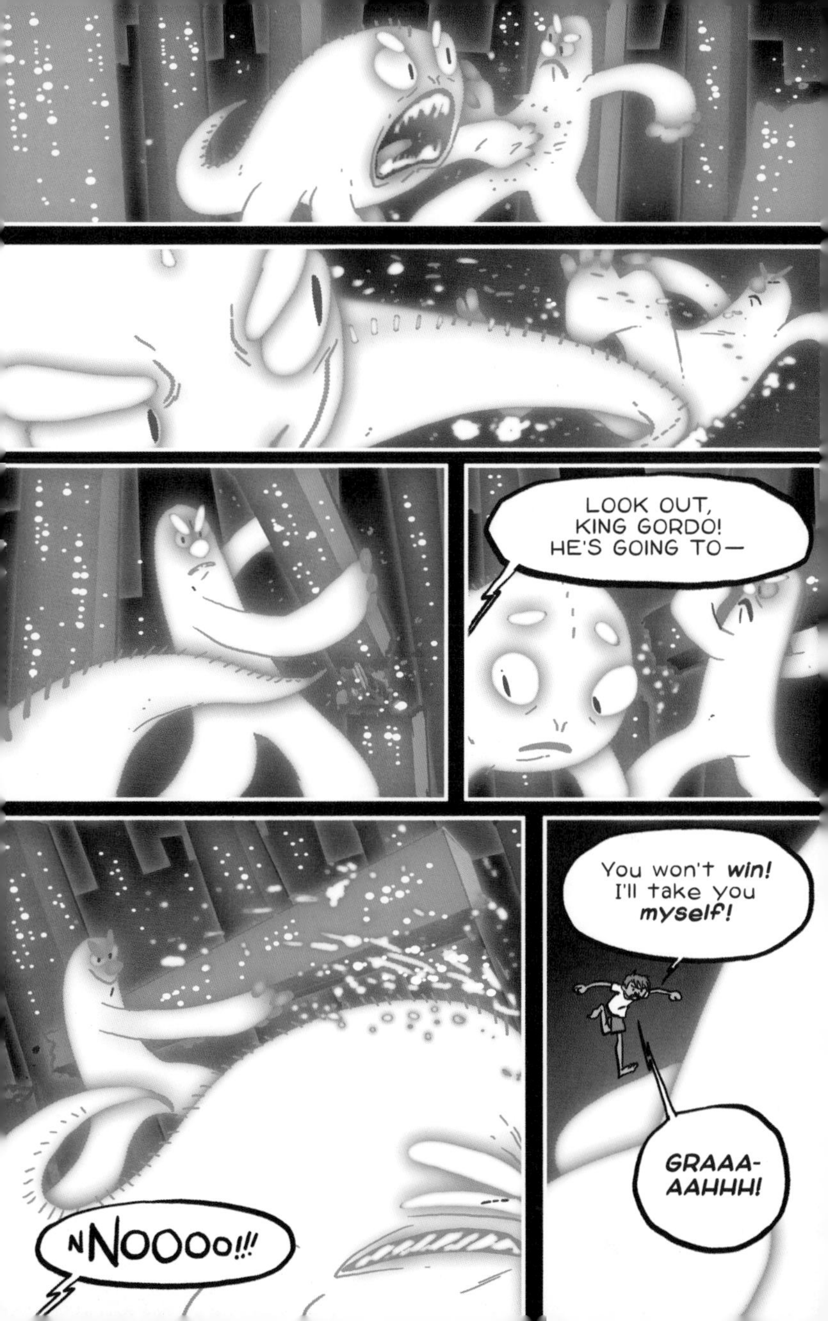
LOOK OUT, KING GORDO! HE'S GOING TO—
You won't *win!* I'll take you *myself!*
GRAAA-AAHHH!
NNOOOO!!!

You're gonna be *spittin' teeth!*
Come on, Meow!
HEY!
Try it, *twerp!* You'll wish you were never—
whup
WHHHHAAAAha—
—aaaaaaaa.

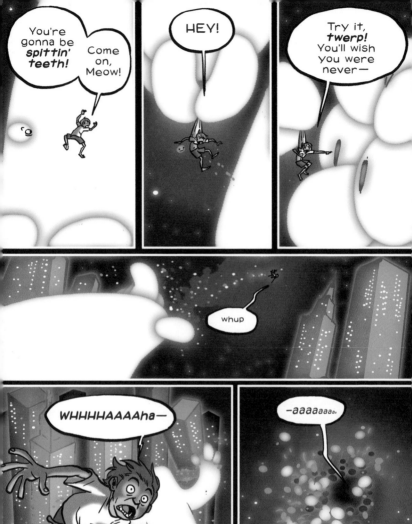

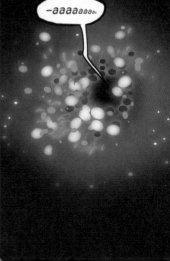

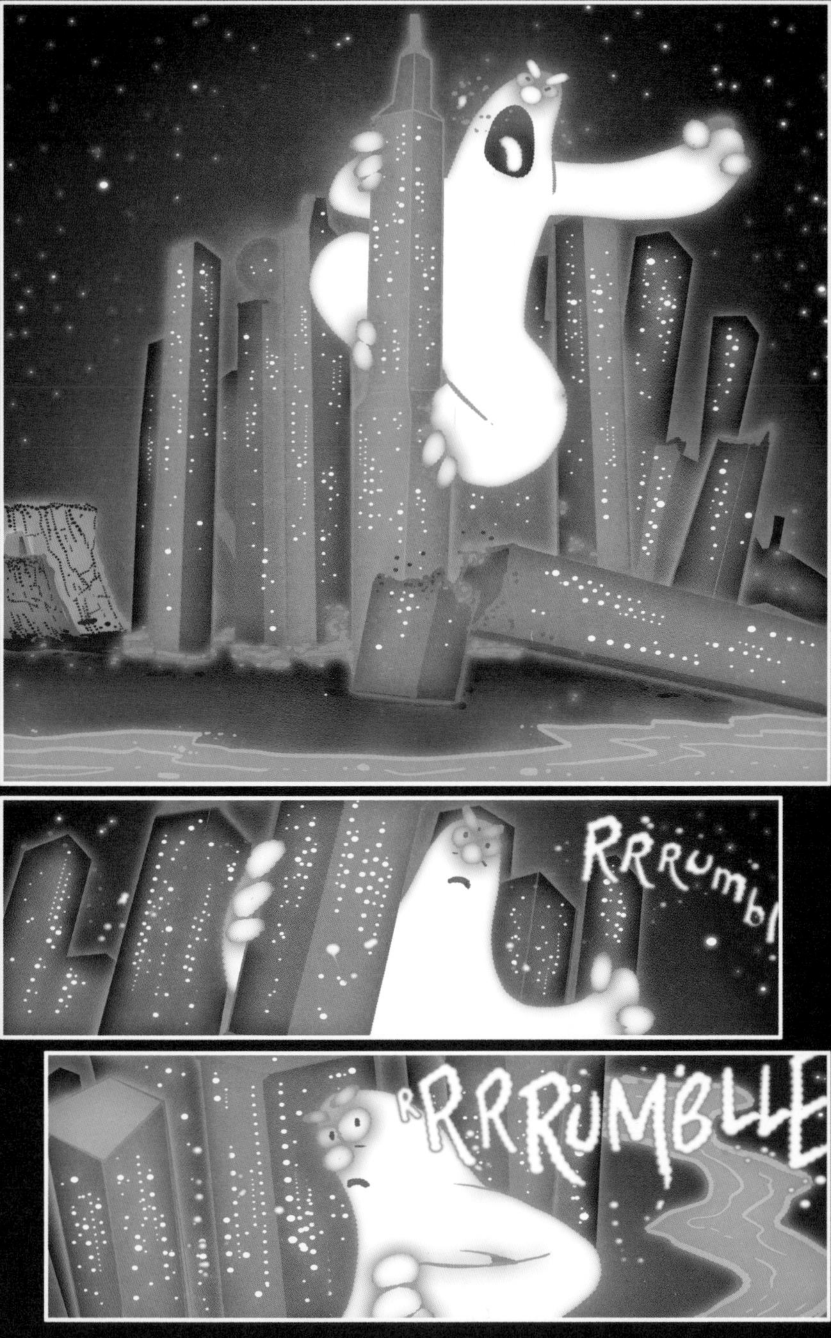
RRRUMBL
RRRRUMBLLE

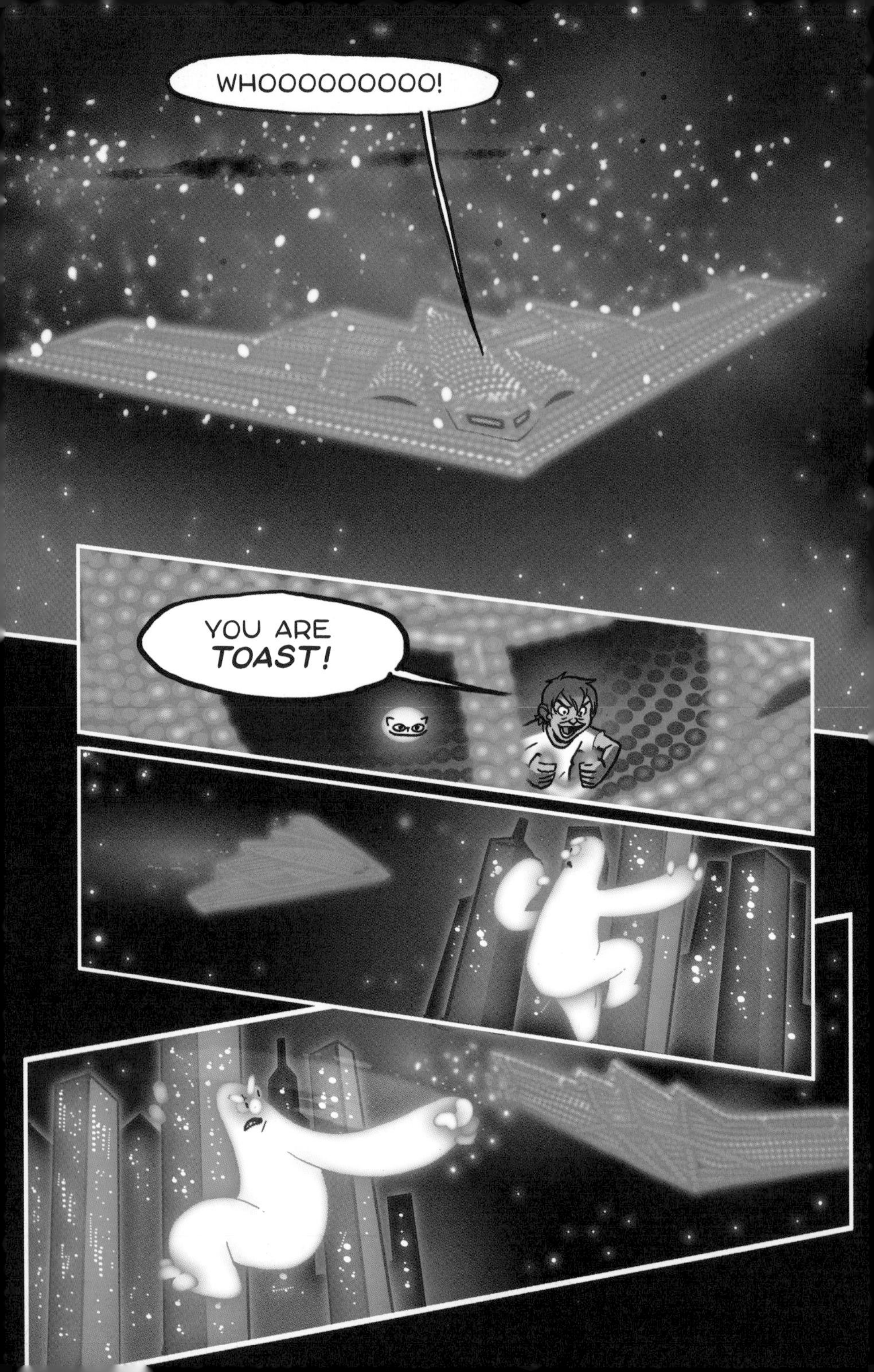
WHOOOOOOOOO!
YOU ARE TOAST!

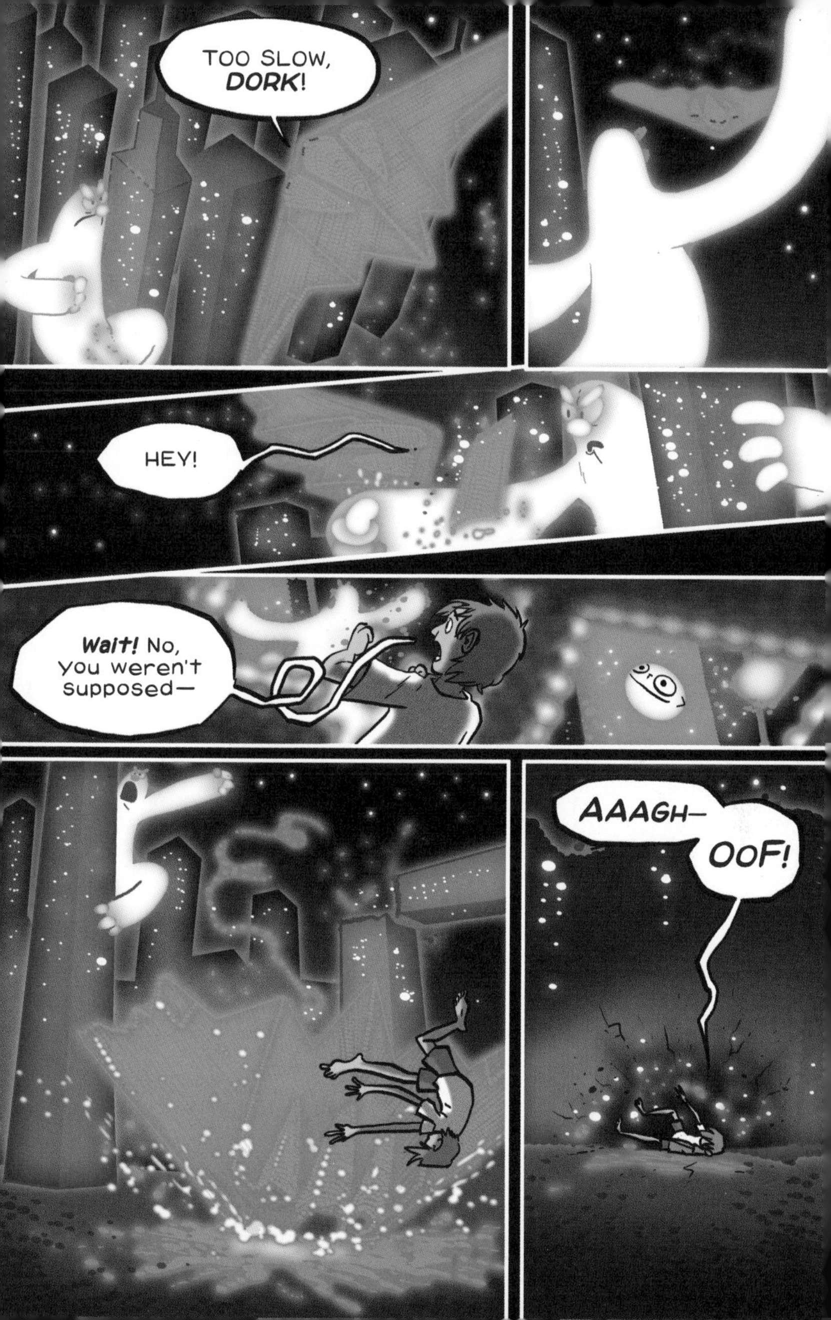
TOO SLOW, **DORK**!
HEY!
Wait! No, you weren't supposed—
AAAGH—
OOF!

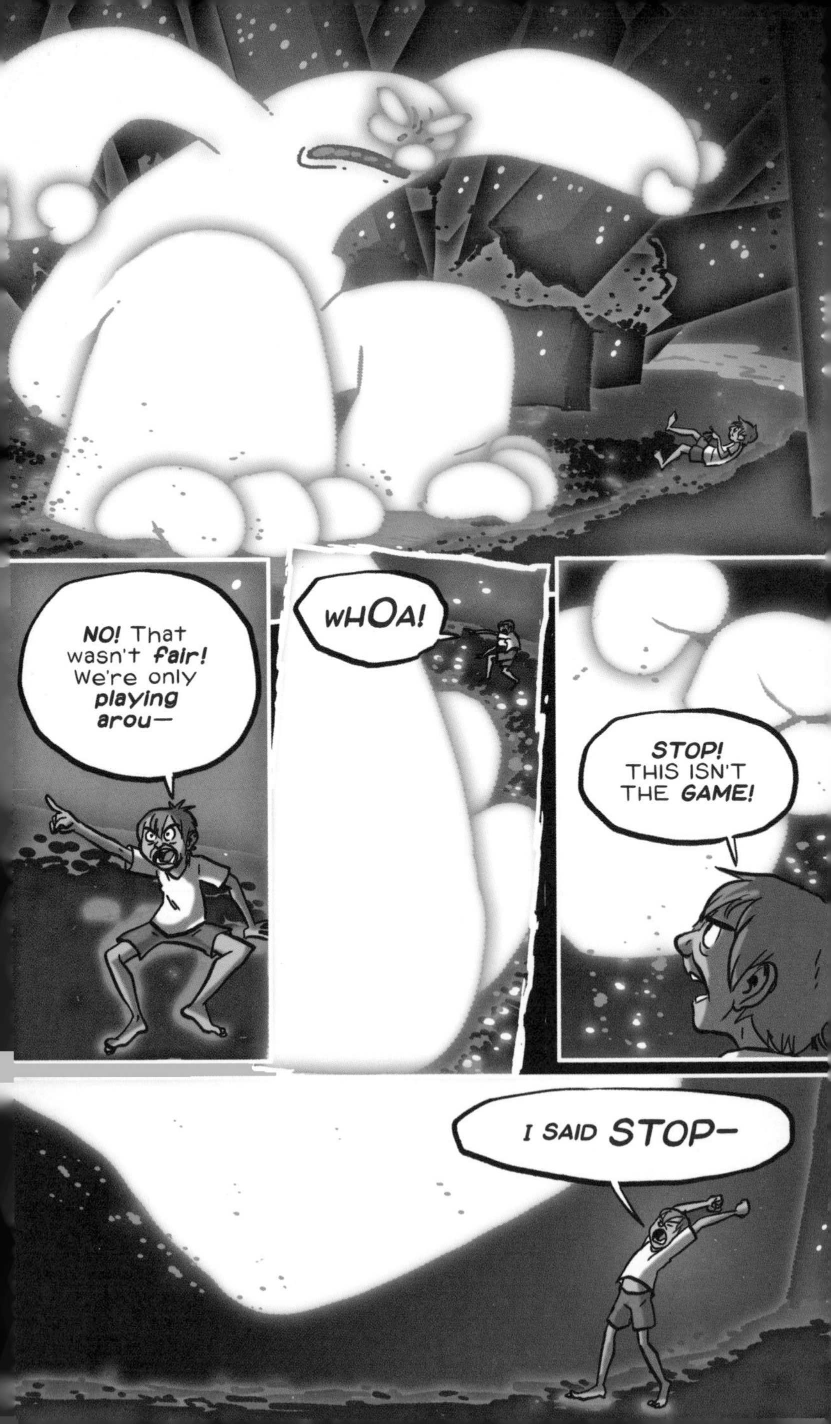
NO! That wasn't fair! We're only playing arou—
WHOA!
STOP! THIS ISN'T THE GAME!
I SAID STOP—

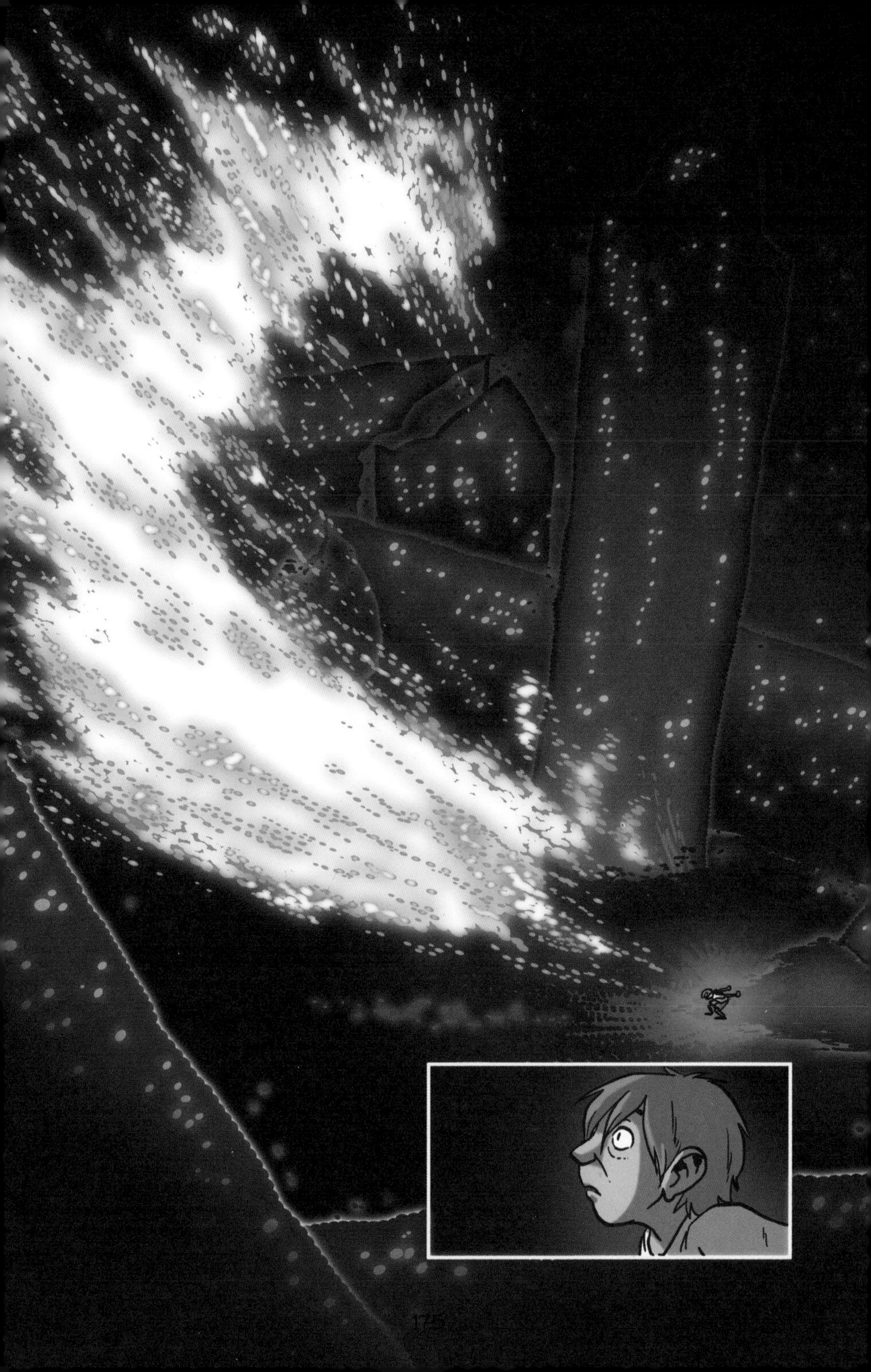

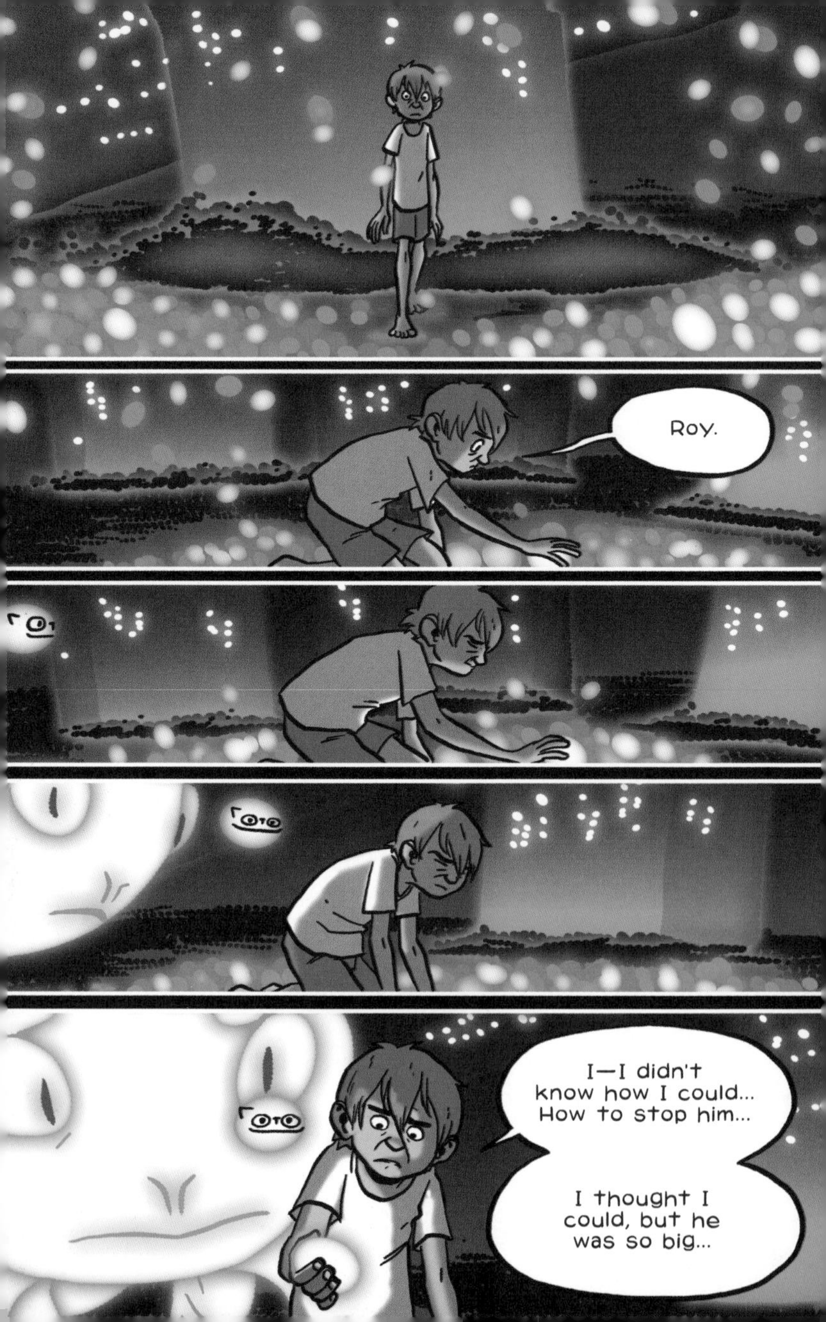
Roy.
I—I didn't know how I could... How to stop him...
I thought I could, but he was so big...

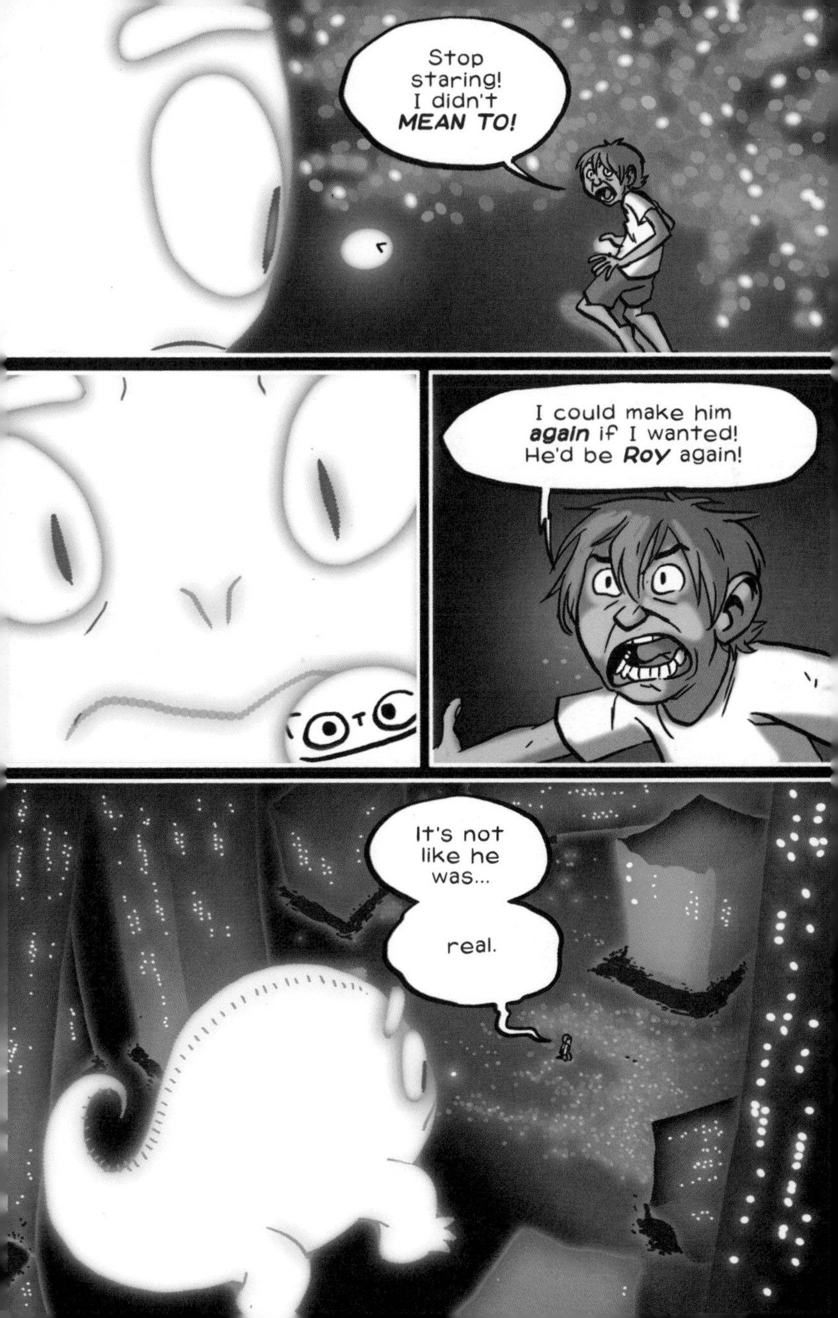
Stop staring! I didn't MEAN TO!
I could make him again if I wanted! He'd be Roy again!
It's not like he was...
real.

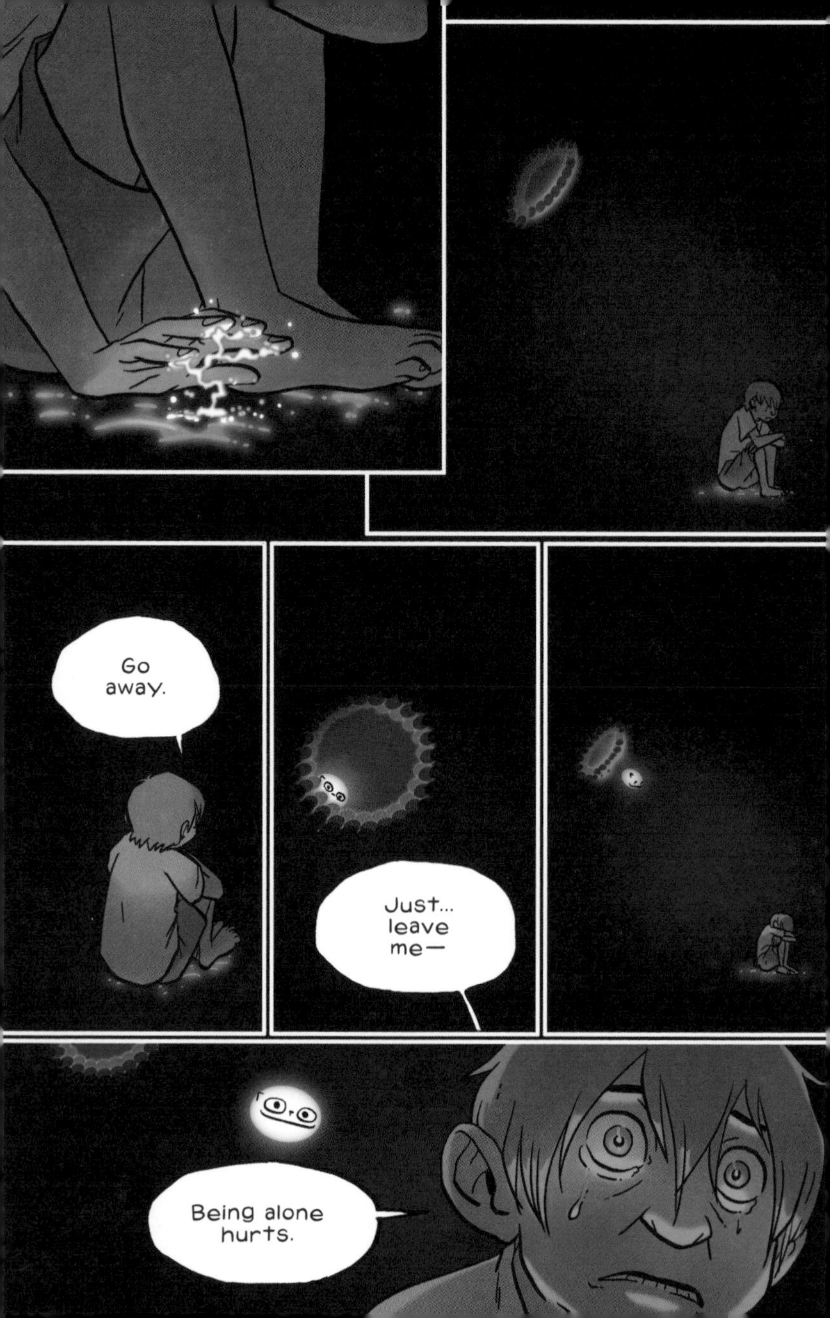
Go away.
Just... leave me—
Being alone hurts.

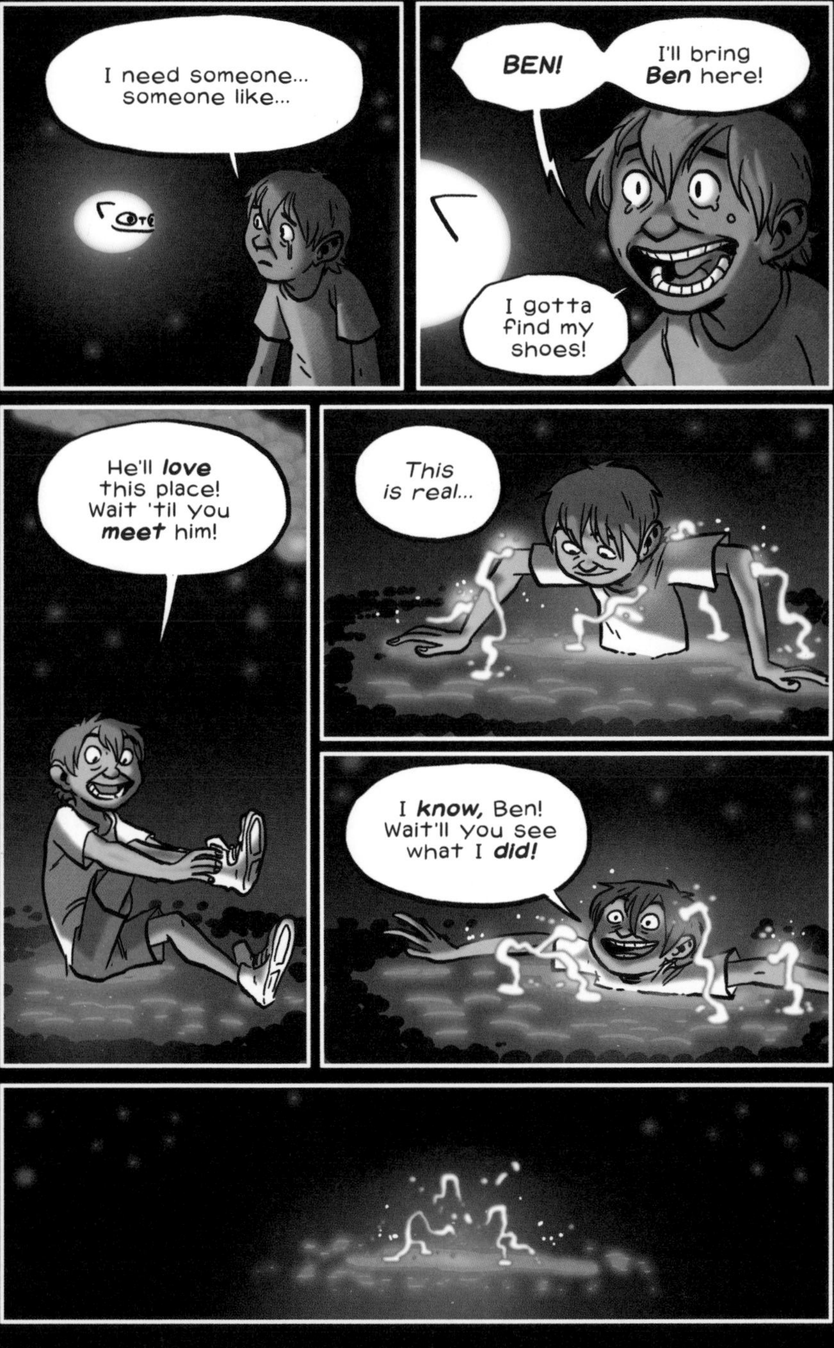
I need someone... someone like...
BEN!
I'll bring Ben here!
I gotta find my shoes!
He'll love this place! Wait 'til you meet him!
This is real...
I know, Ben! Wait'll you see what I did!

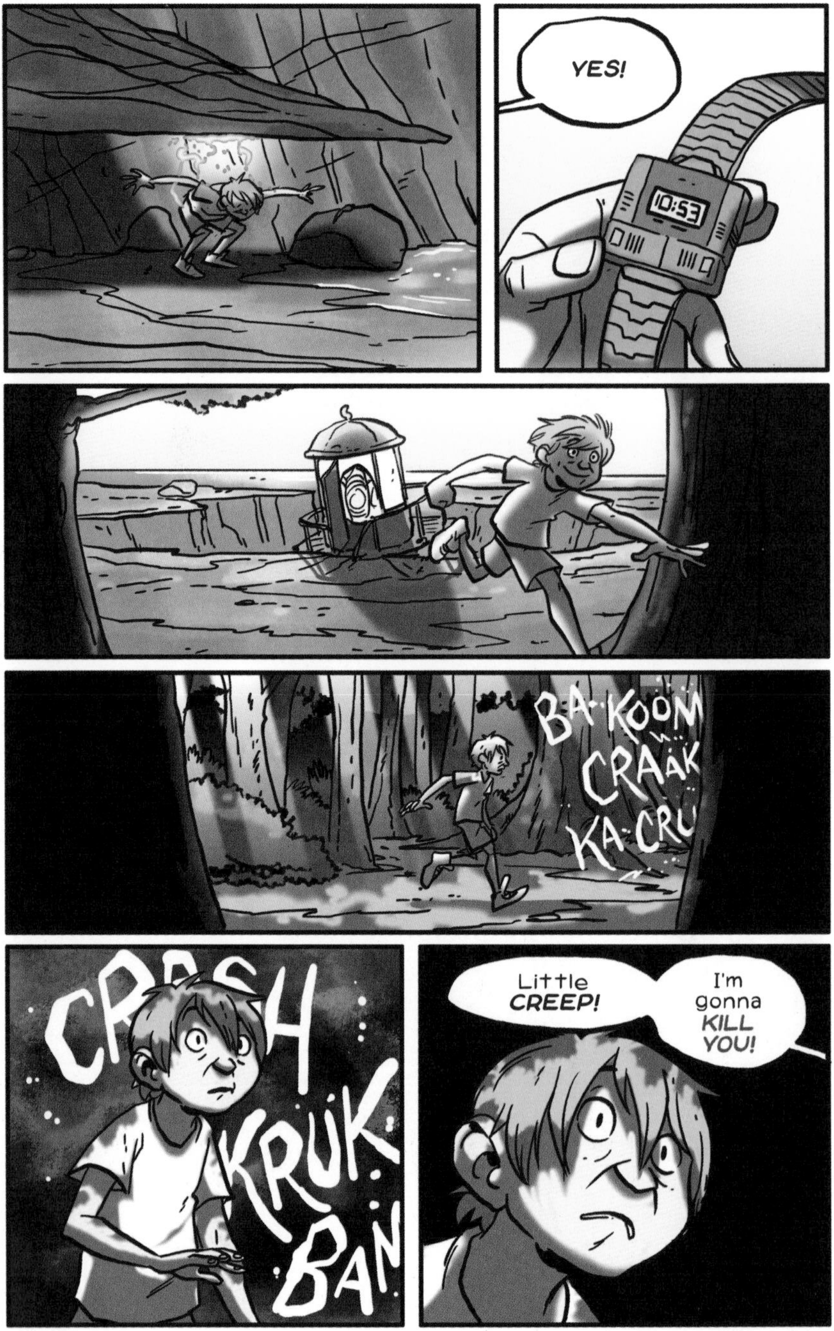
YES!
10:53
BA-KOOM
CRAAK
KA-CRU
CRASH
KRUK
BAN
Little CREEP!
I'm gonna KILL YOU!

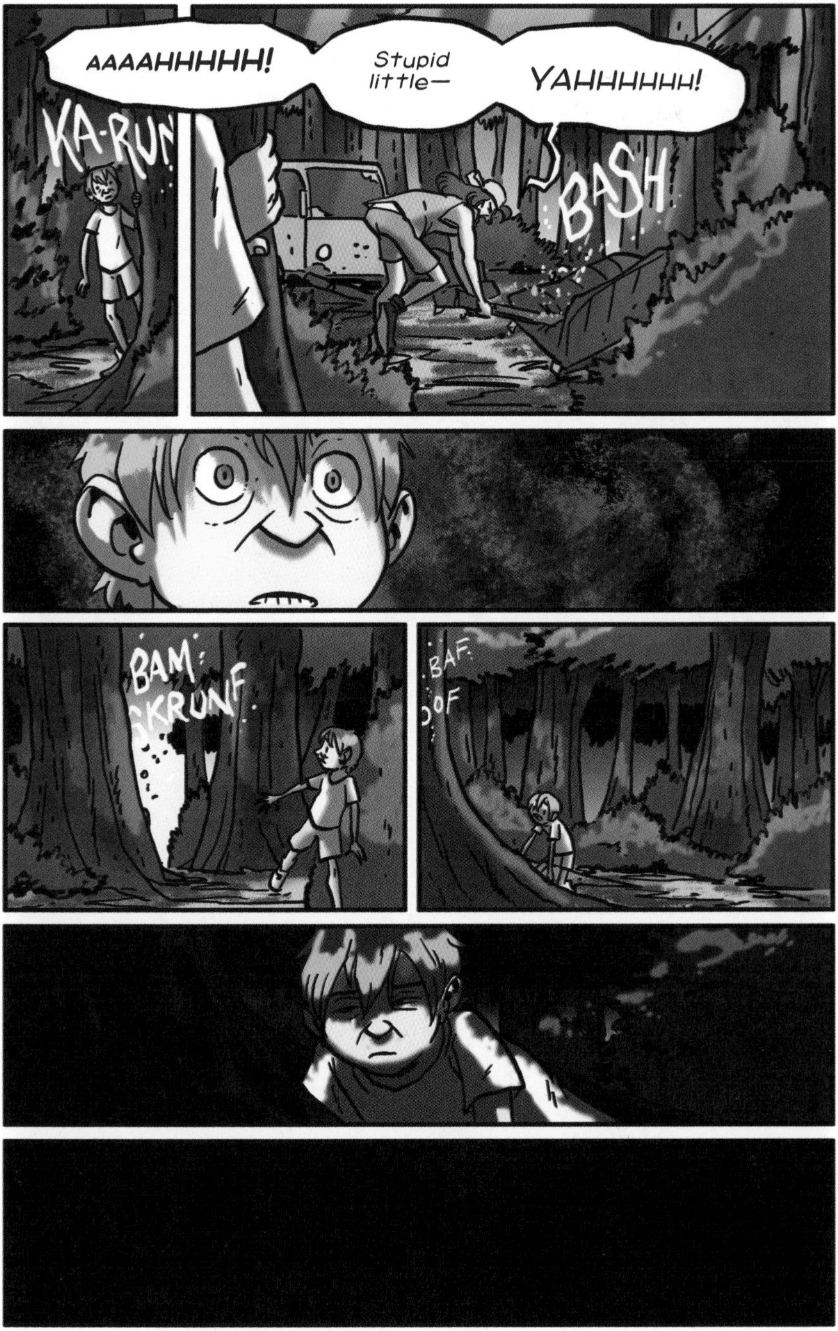
AAAAHHHHH!
KA-RUN
Stupid little—
YAHHHHHH!
BASH
BAM
SKRUNF
BAF
OOF

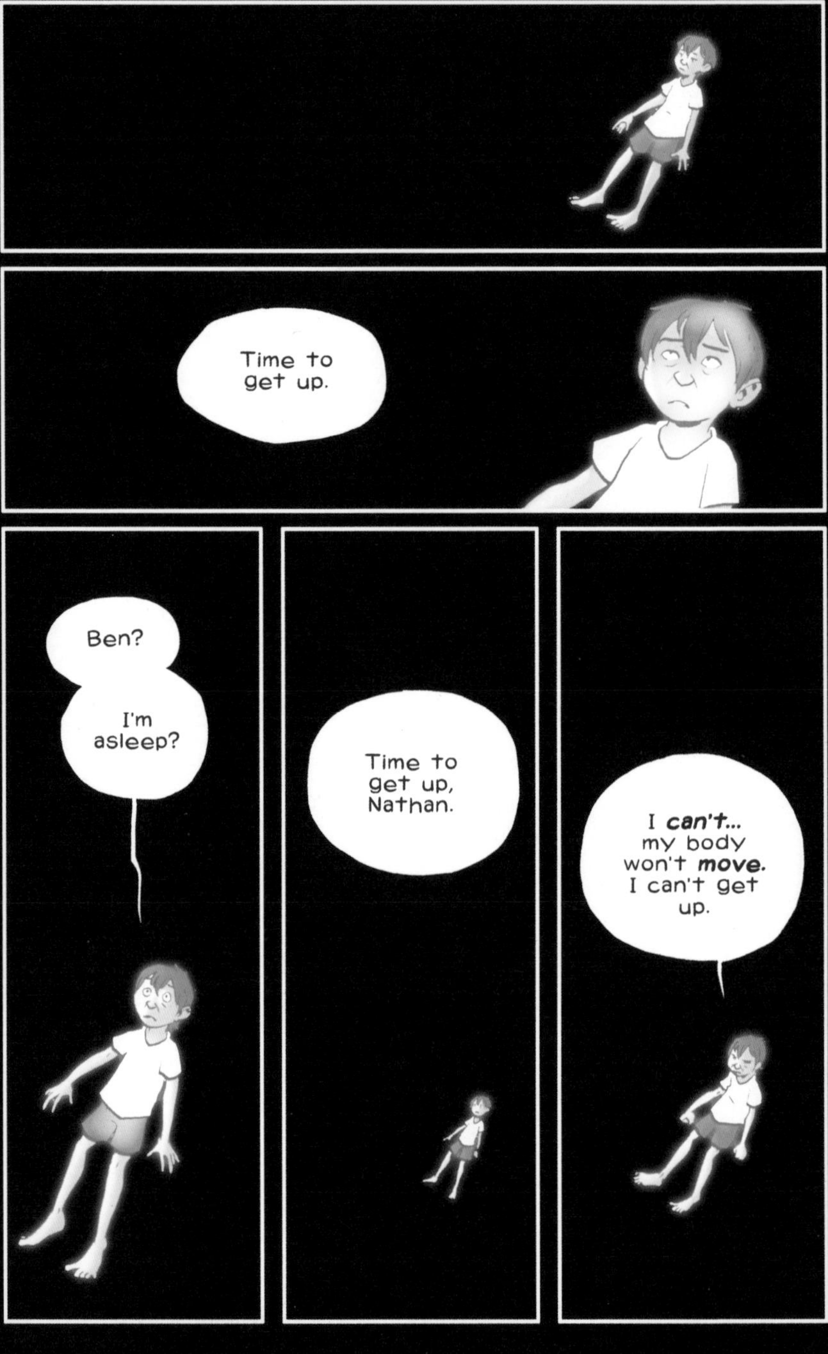
Time to get up.
Ben?
I'm asleep?
Time to get up, Nathan.
I *can't*... my body won't *move.* I can't get up.

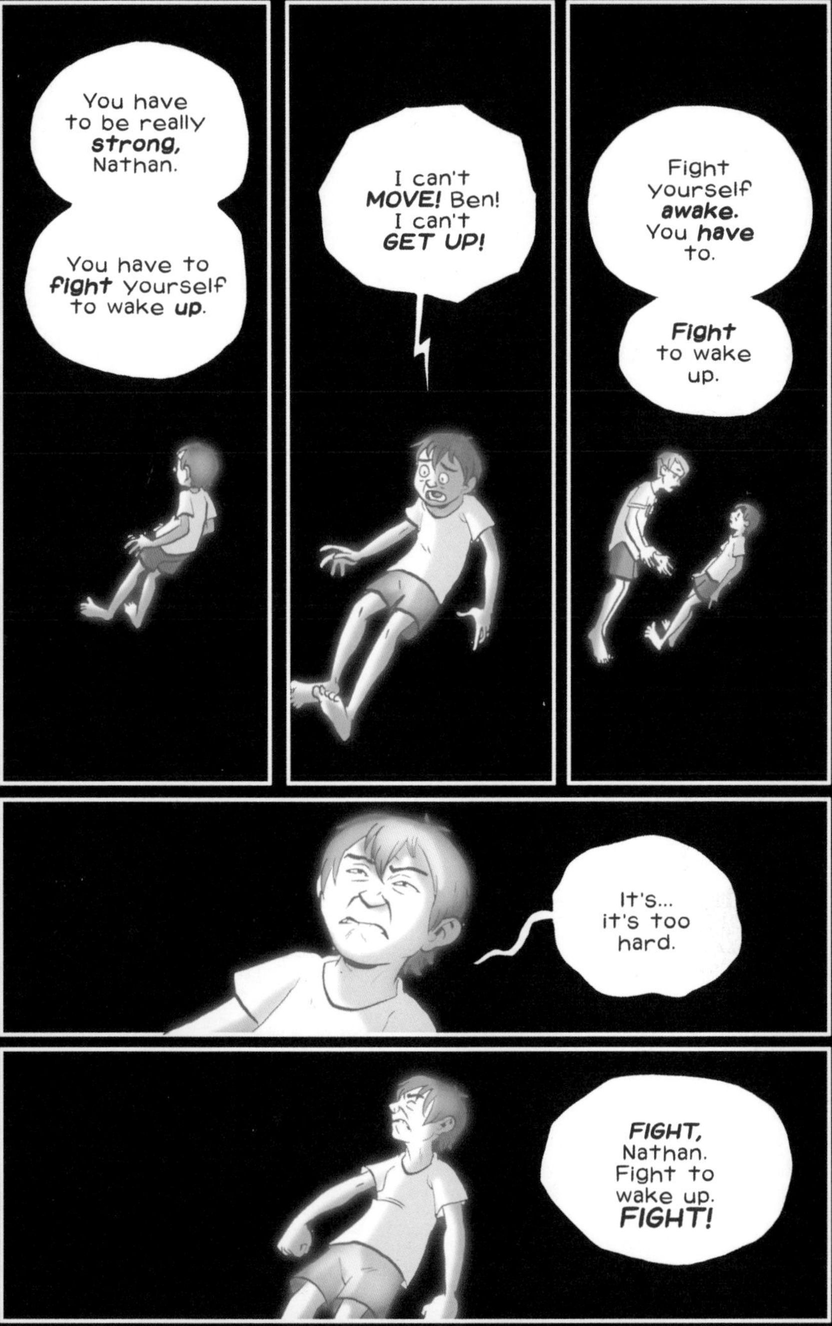
You have to be really strong, Nathan.
You have to fight yourself to wake up.
I can't MOVE! Ben! I can't GET UP!
Fight yourself awake. You have to.
Fight to wake up.
It's... it's too hard.
FIGHT, Nathan. Fight to wake up. FIGHT!

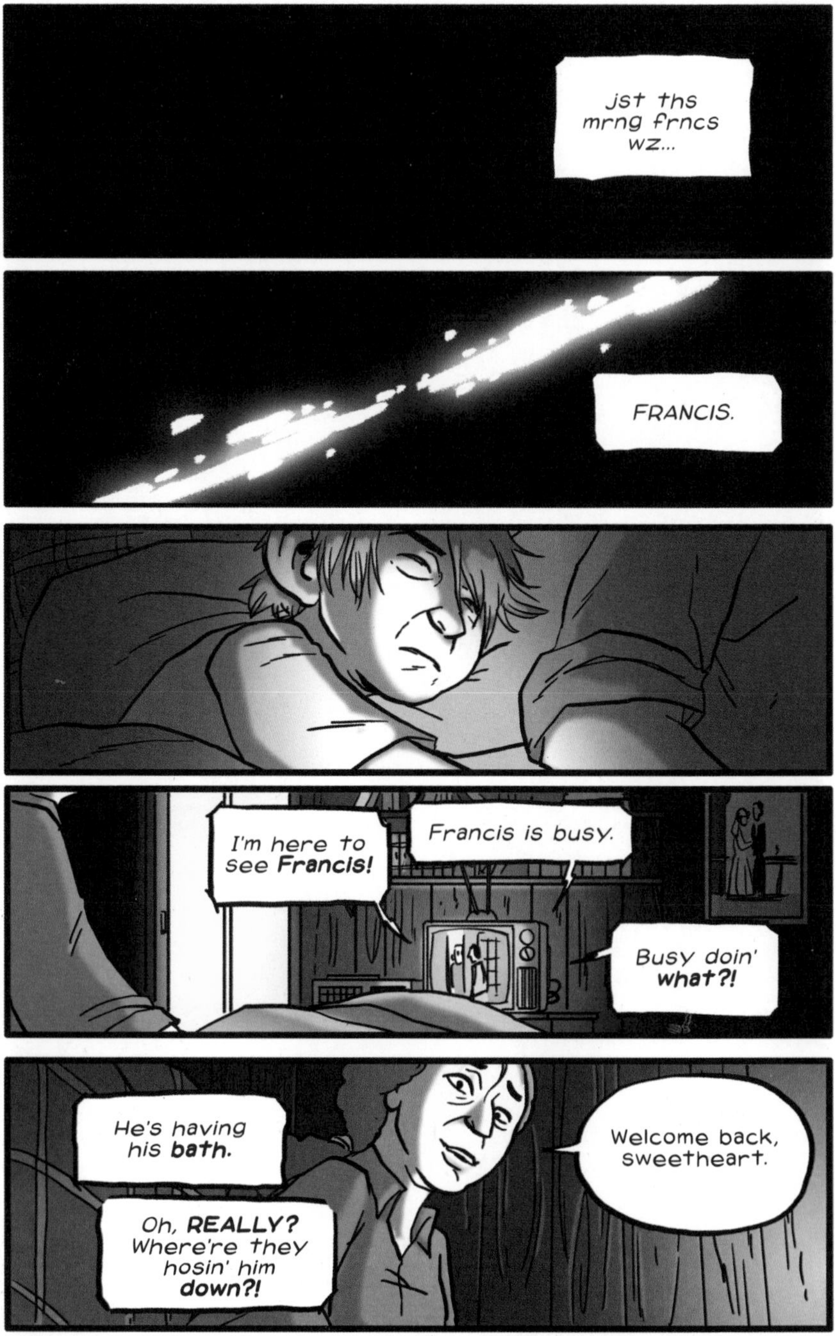
jst ths mrng frncs wz...
FRANCIS.
I'm here to see **Francis!**
Francis is busy.
Busy doin' **what?!**
He's having his **bath.**
Oh, **REALLY?** Where're they hosin' him **down?!**
Welcome back, sweetheart.

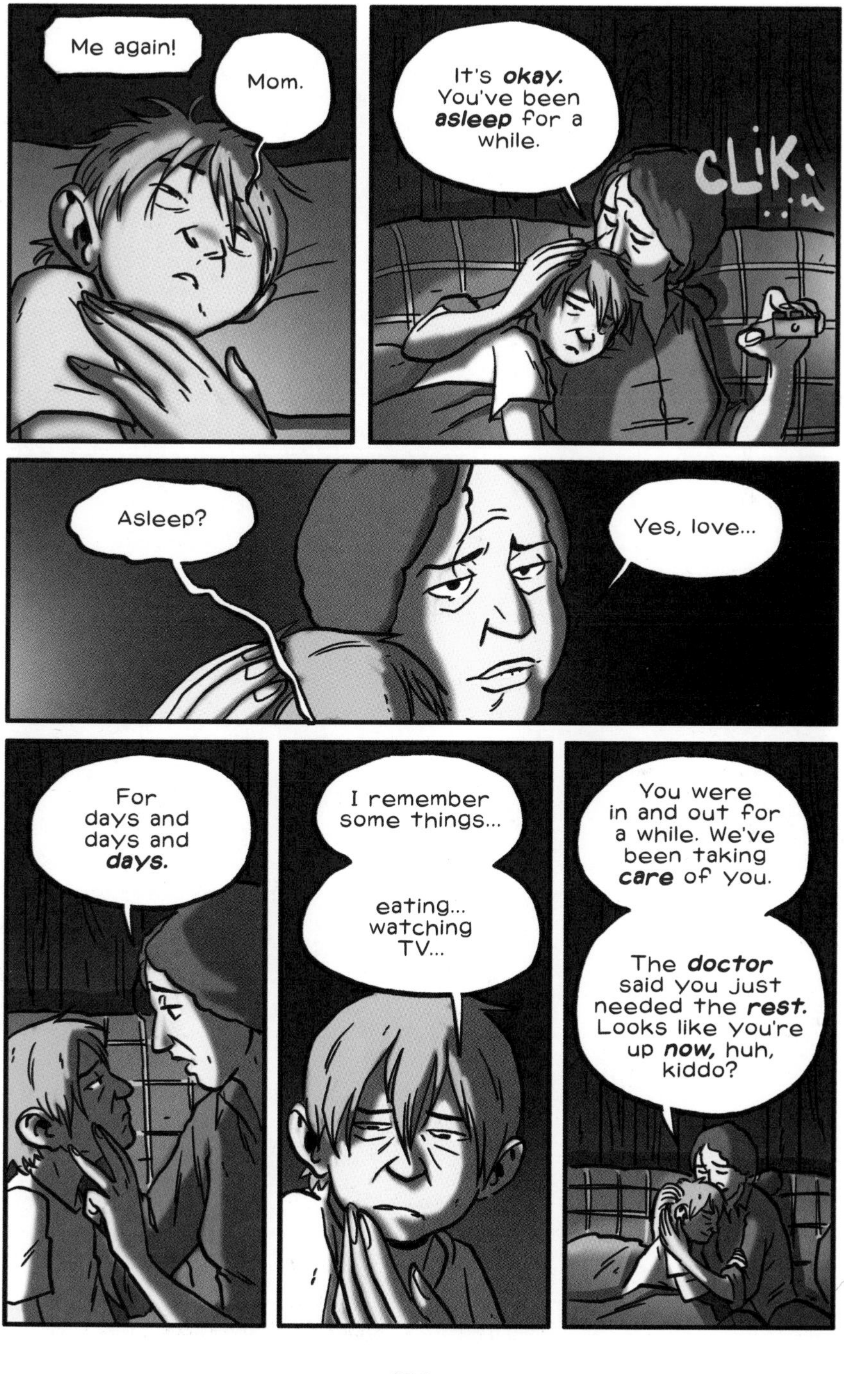
Me again!
Mom.
It's **okay.** You've been **asleep** for a while.
CLIK
Asleep?
Yes, love...
For days and days and **days.**
I remember some things...
eating... watching TV...
You were in and out for a while. We've been taking **care** of you.
The **doctor** said you just needed the **rest.** Looks like you're up **now,** huh, kiddo?

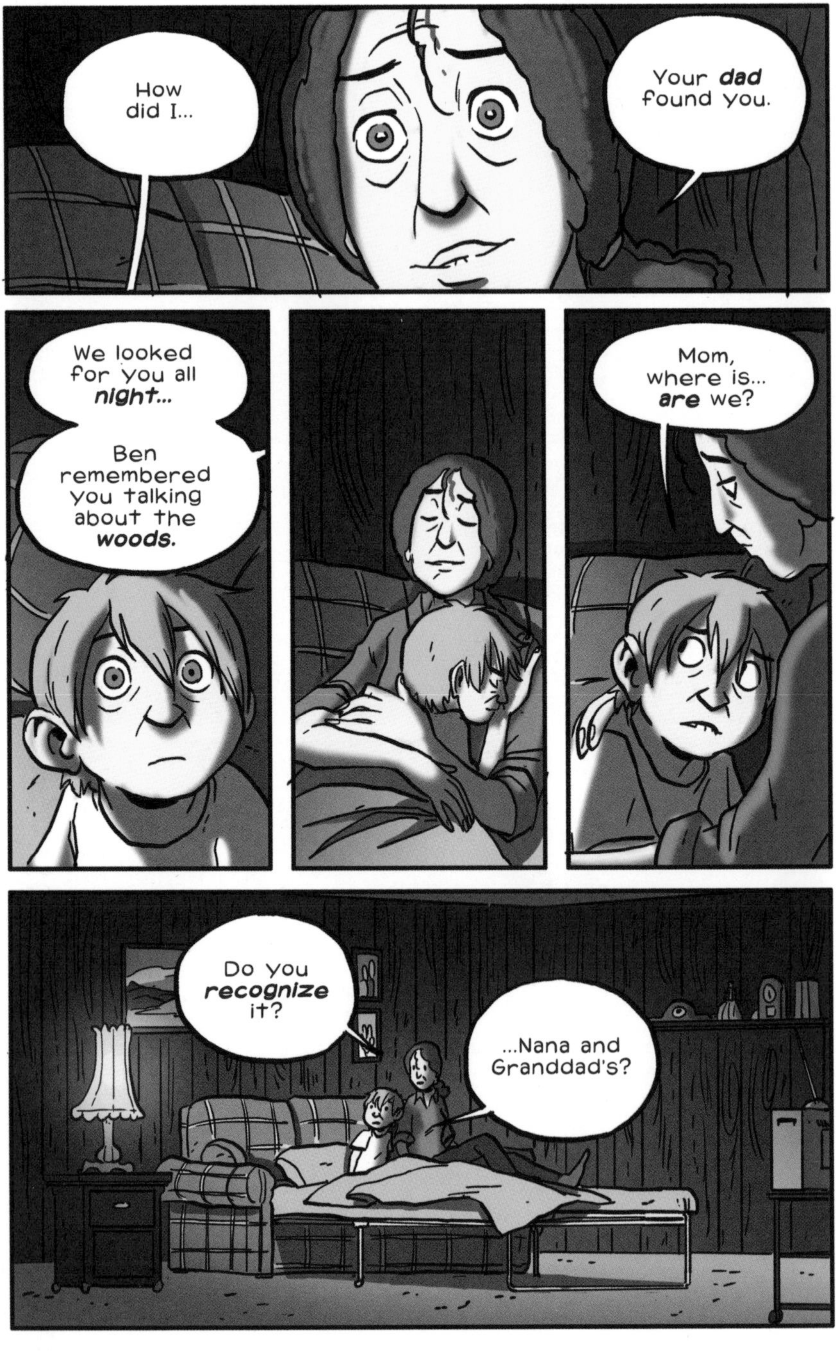
How did I...
Your **dad** found you.
We looked for you all ***night...***
Ben remembered you talking about the ***woods.***
Mom, where is... ***are*** we?
Do you ***recognize*** it?
...Nana and Granddad's?

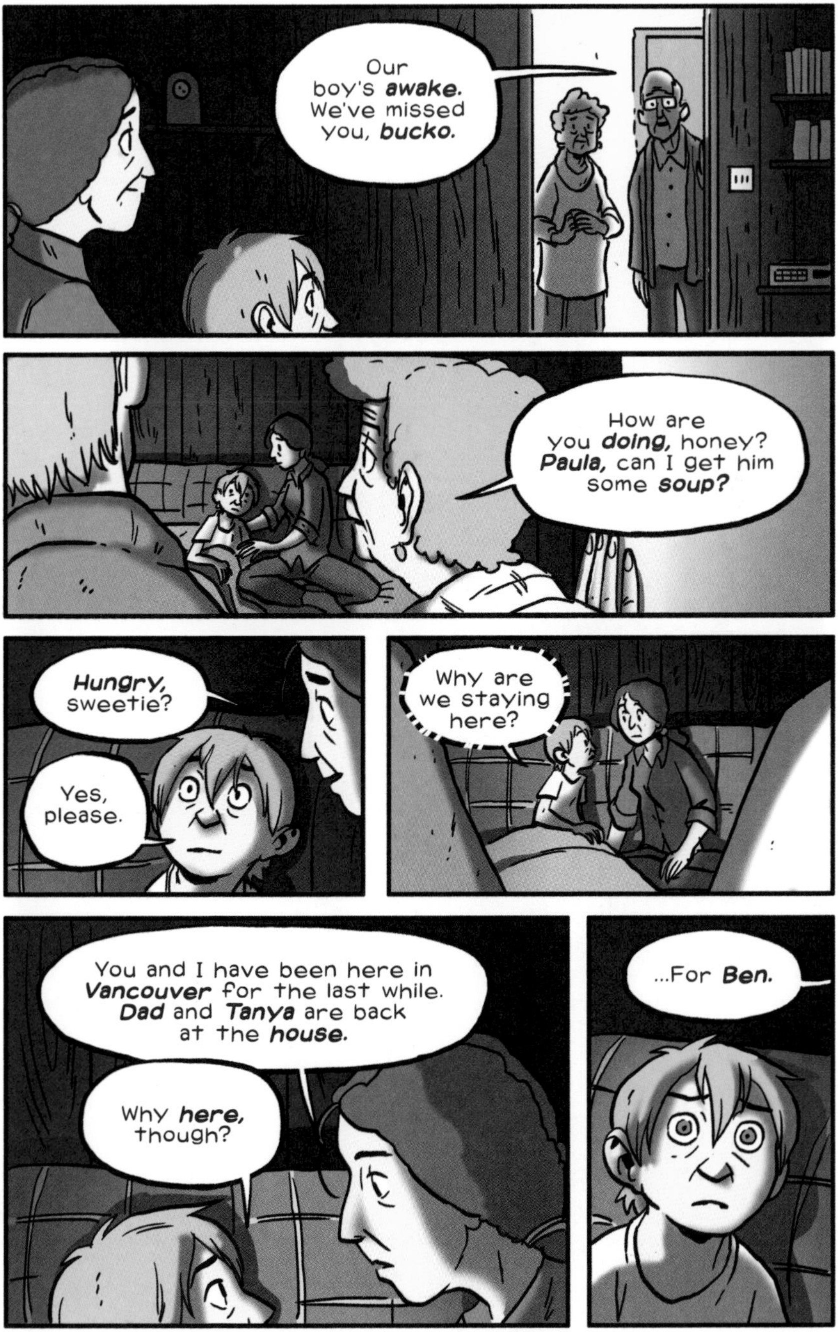
Our boy's **awake.** We've missed you, **bucko.**
How are you **doing,** honey? **Paula,** can I get him some **soup?**
Hungry, sweetie?
Yes, please.
Why are we staying here?
You and I have been here in **Vancouver** for the last while. **Dad** and **Tanya** are back at the **house.**
Why **here,** though?
...For **Ben.**

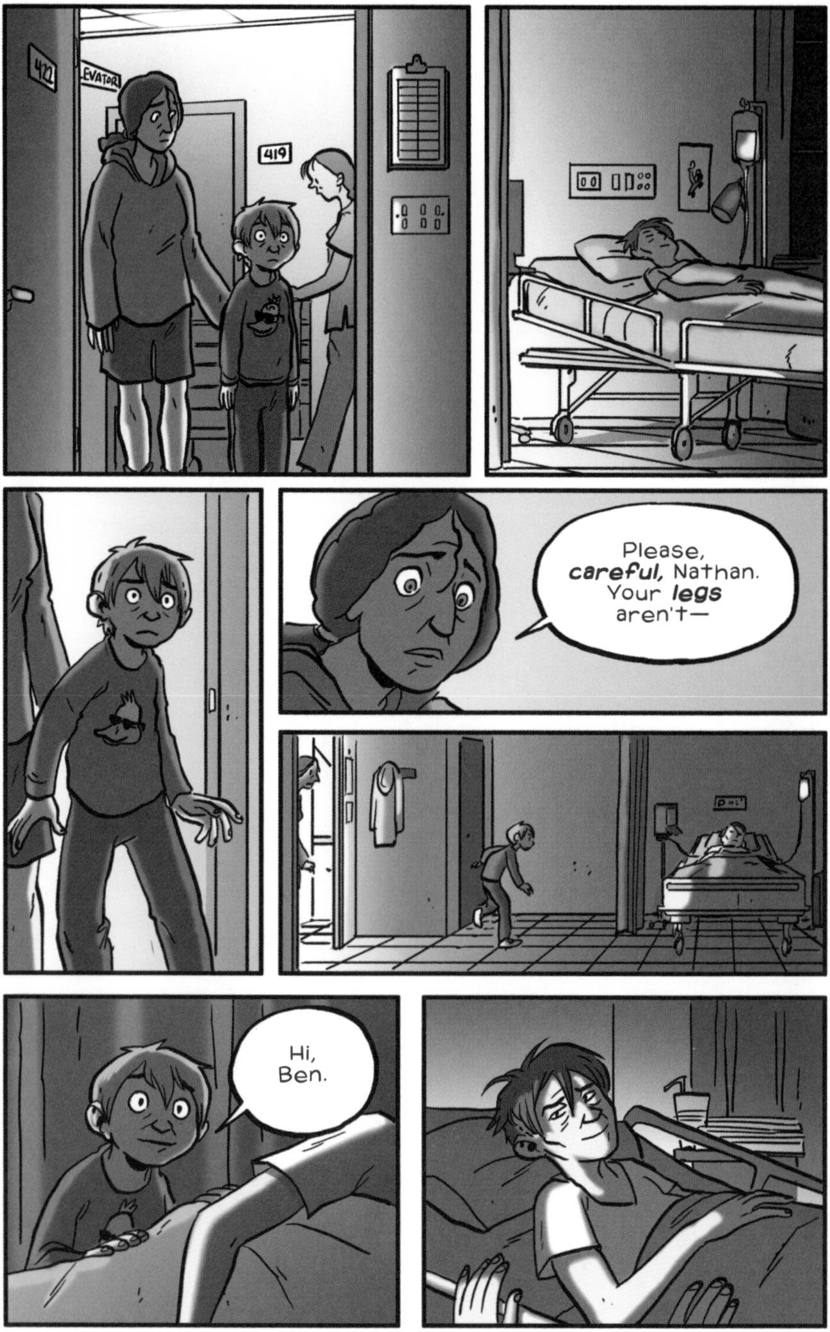
422
ELEVATOR
419
Please, **careful,** Nathan. Your **legs** aren't—
Hi, Ben.

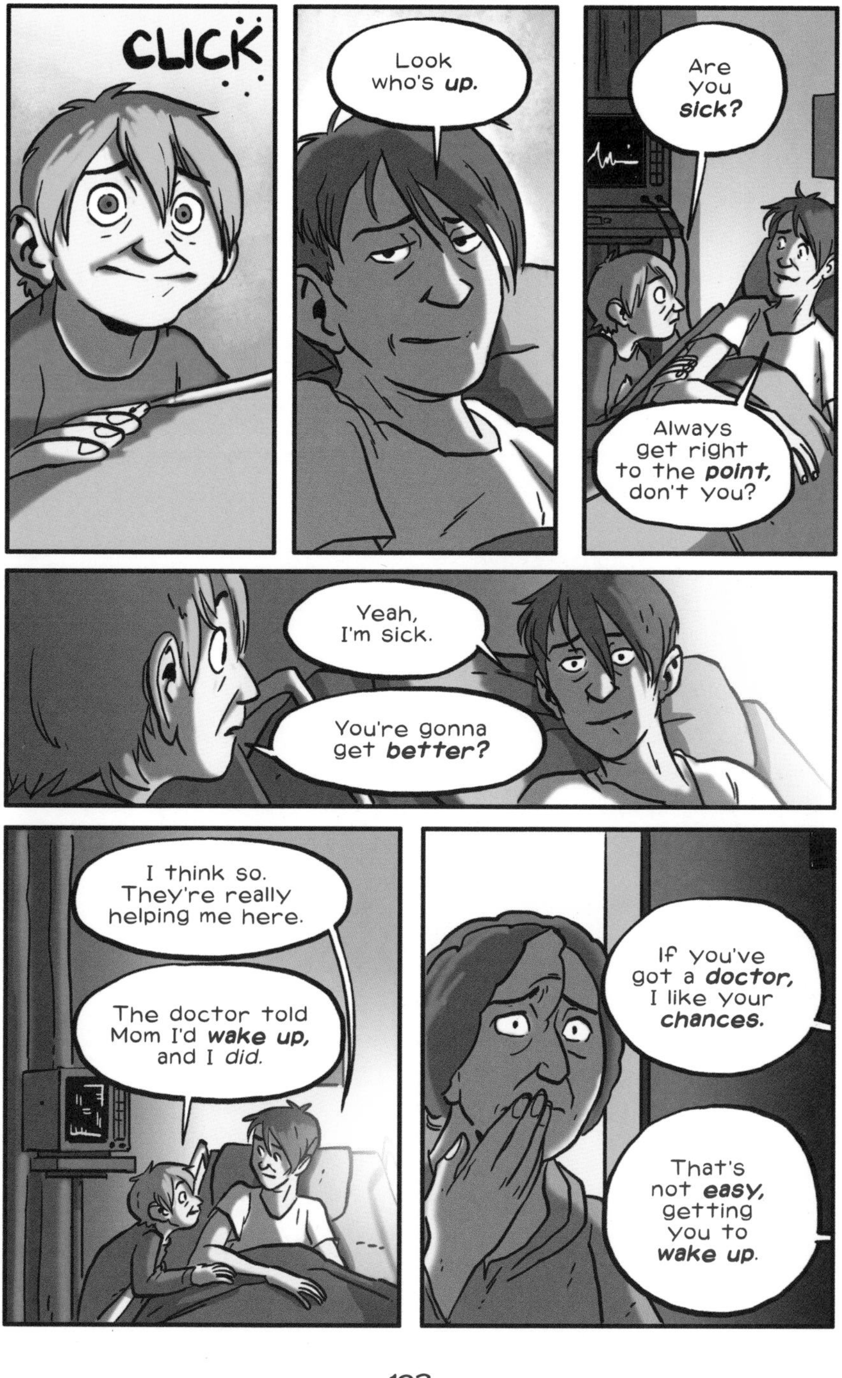
CLICK
Look who's **up.**
Are you ***sick?***
Always get right to the ***point,*** don't you?
Yeah, I'm sick.
You're gonna get ***better?***
I think so. They're really helping me here.
The doctor told Mom I'd ***wake up,*** and I *did.*
If you've got a ***doctor,*** I like your ***chances.***
That's not ***easy,*** getting you to ***wake up.***

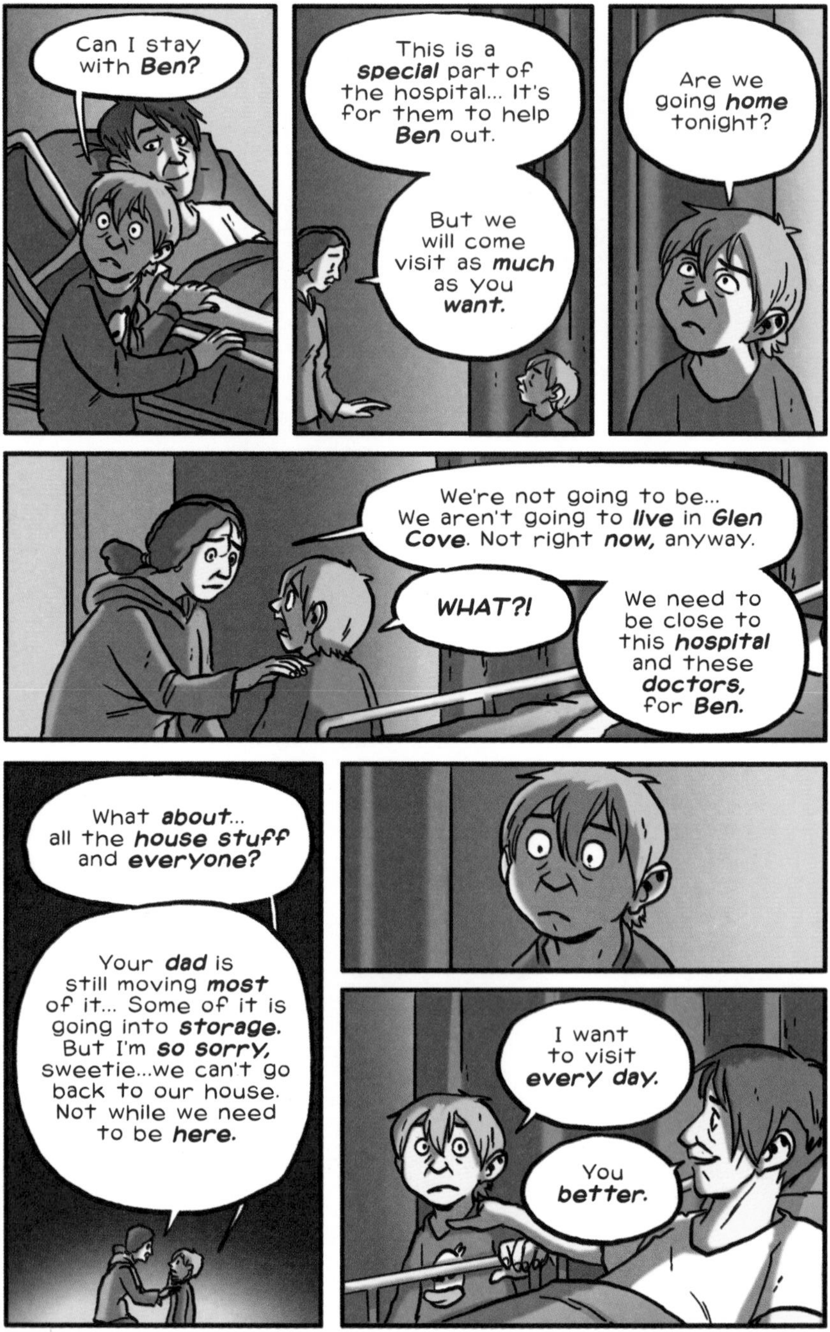
Can I stay with Ben?
This is a special part of the hospital... It's for them to help Ben out.
But we will come visit as much as you want.
Are we going home tonight?
We're not going to be... We aren't going to live in Glen Cove. Not right now, anyway.
WHAT?!
We need to be close to this hospital and these doctors, for Ben.
What about... all the house stuff and everyone?
Your dad is still moving most of it... Some of it is going into storage. But I'm so sorry, sweetie...we can't go back to our house. Not while we need to be here.
I want to visit every day.
You better.

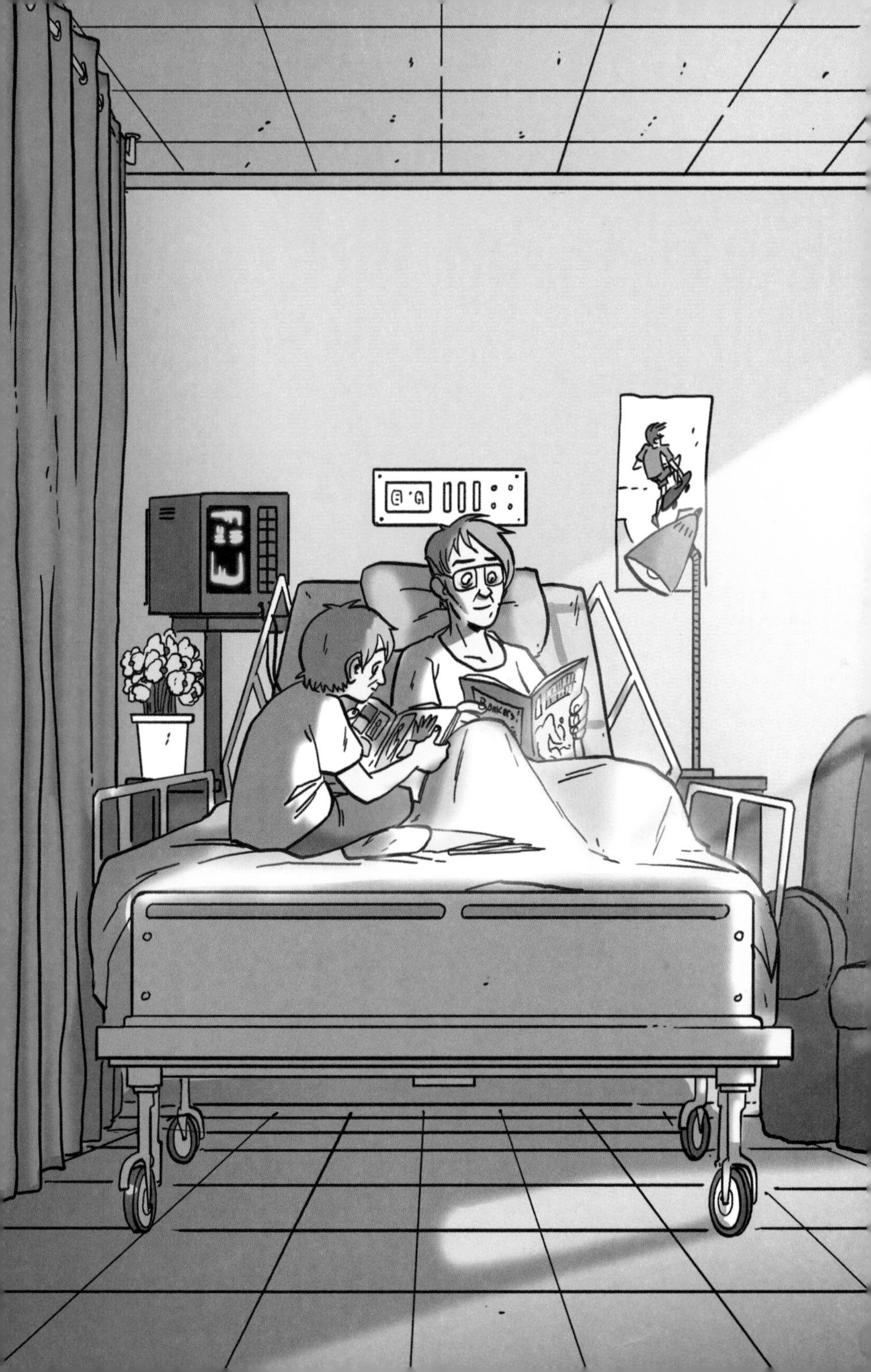
Bonkers!

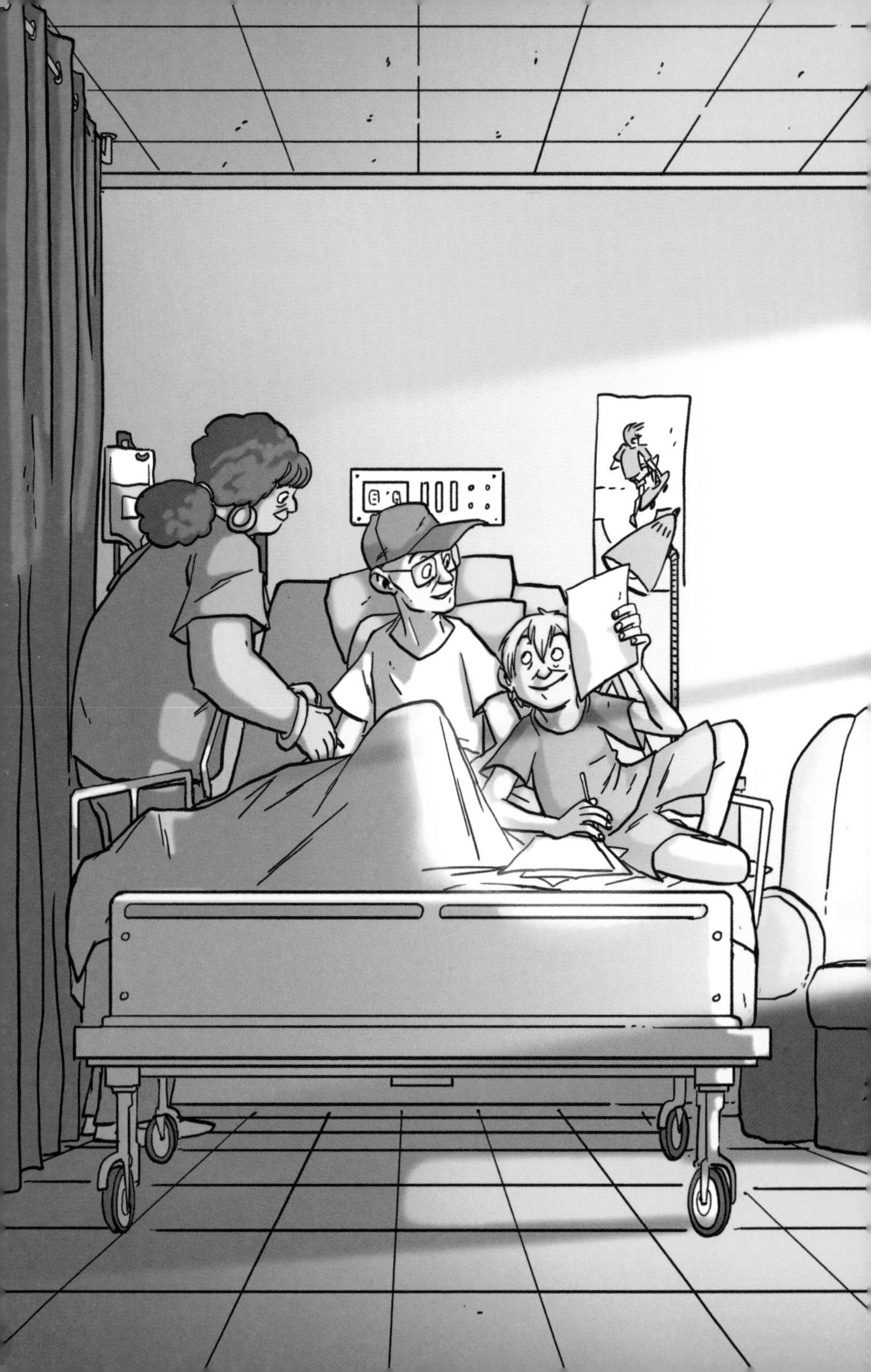

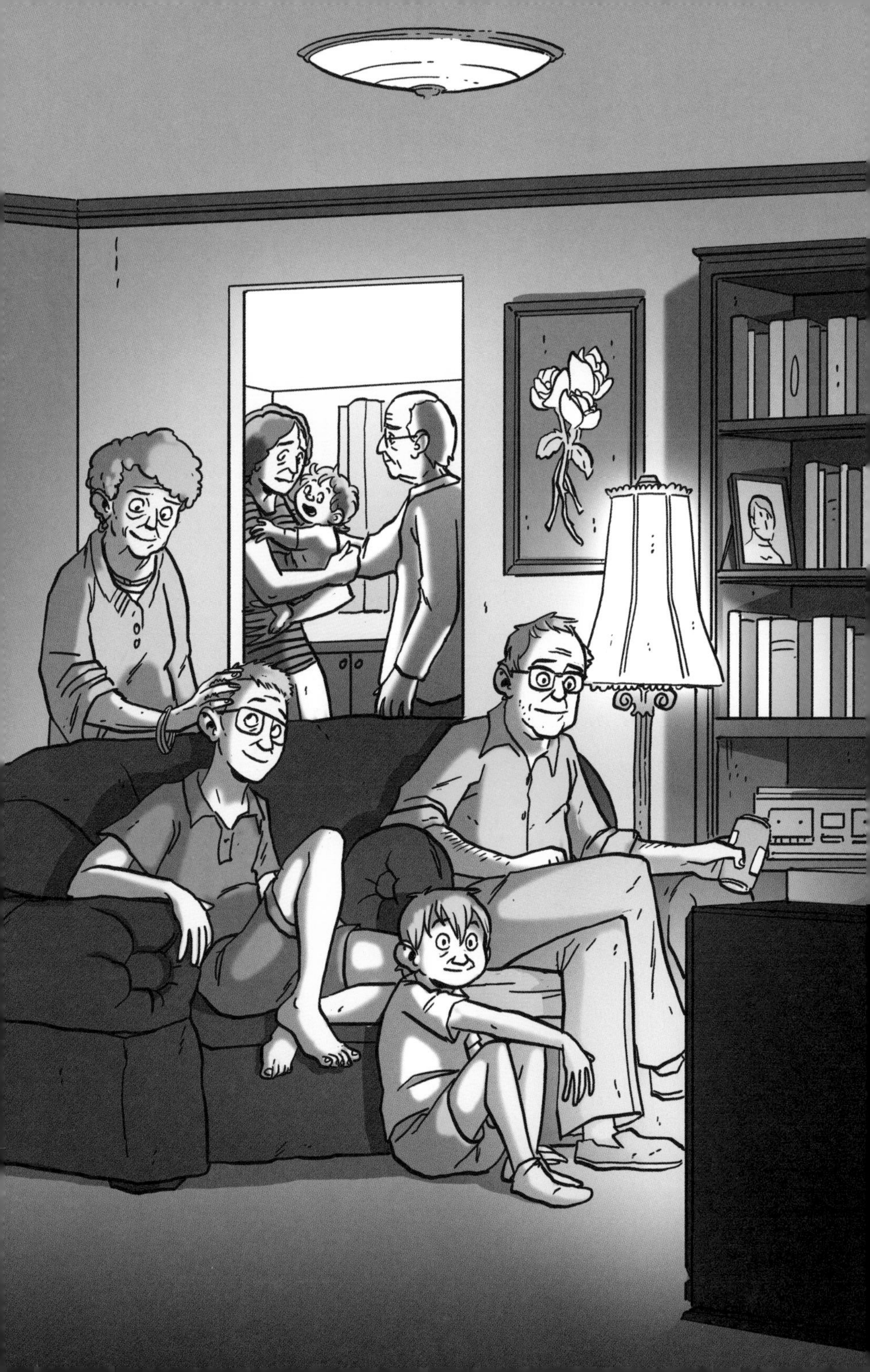

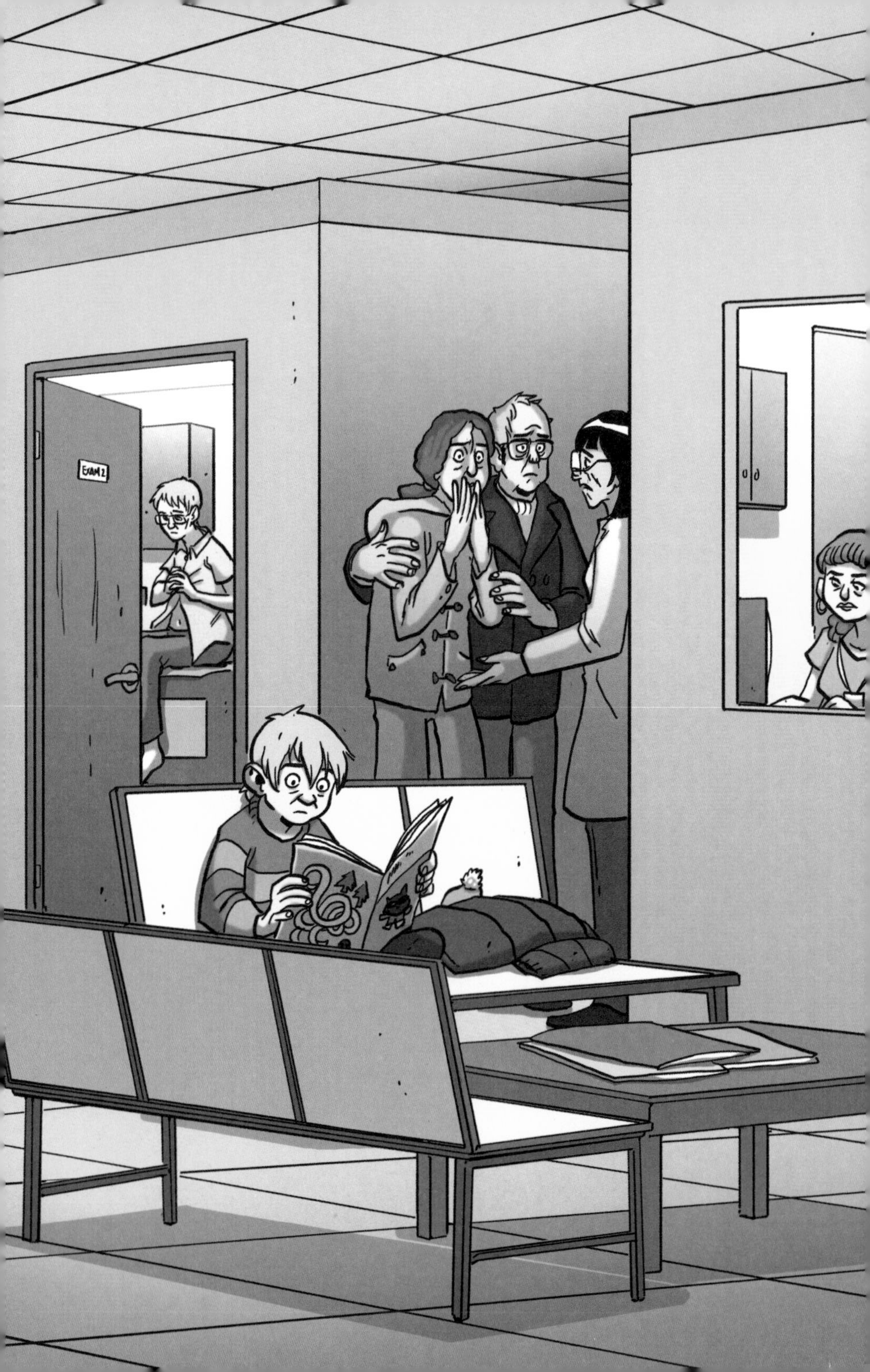
EXAM 2

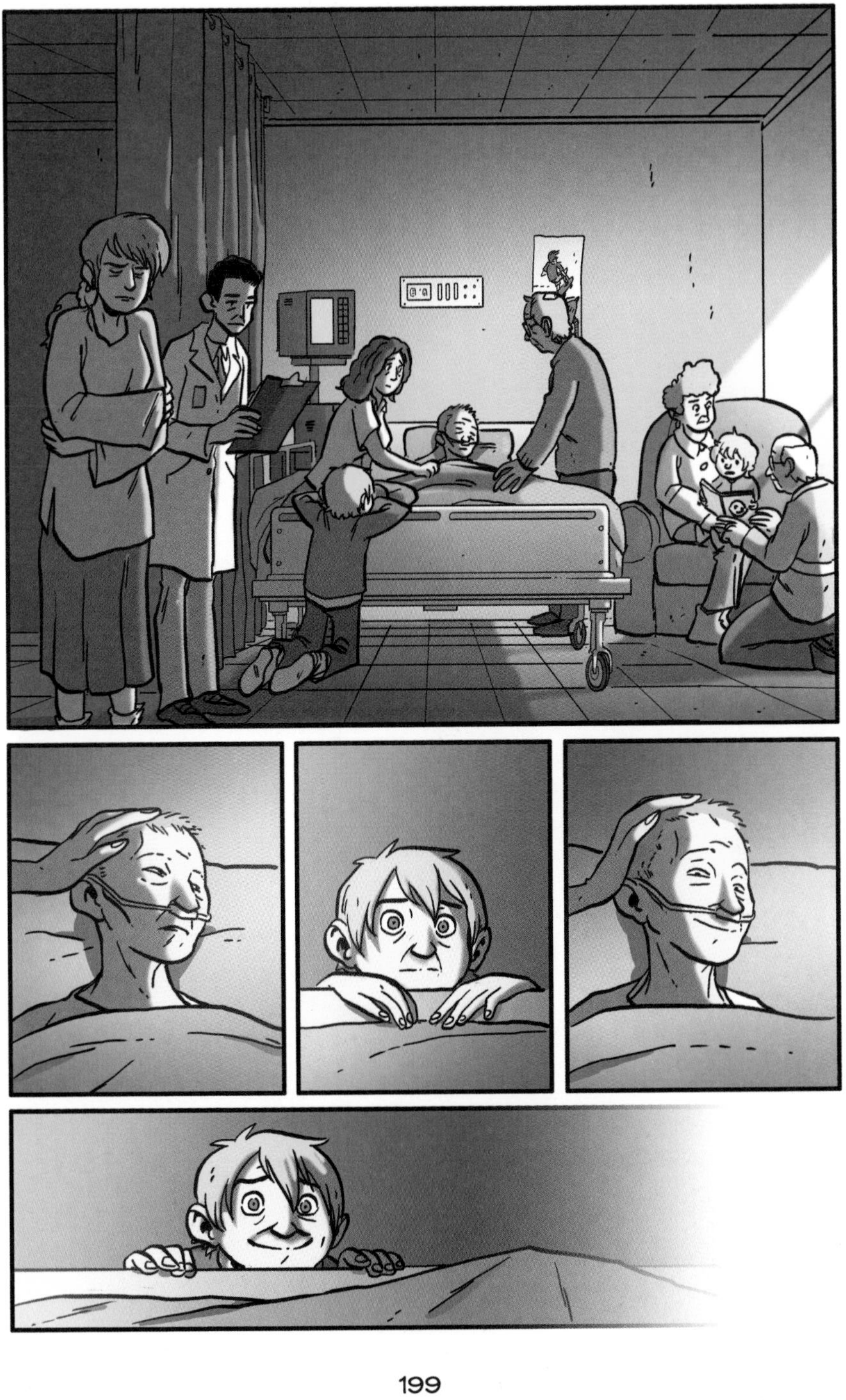

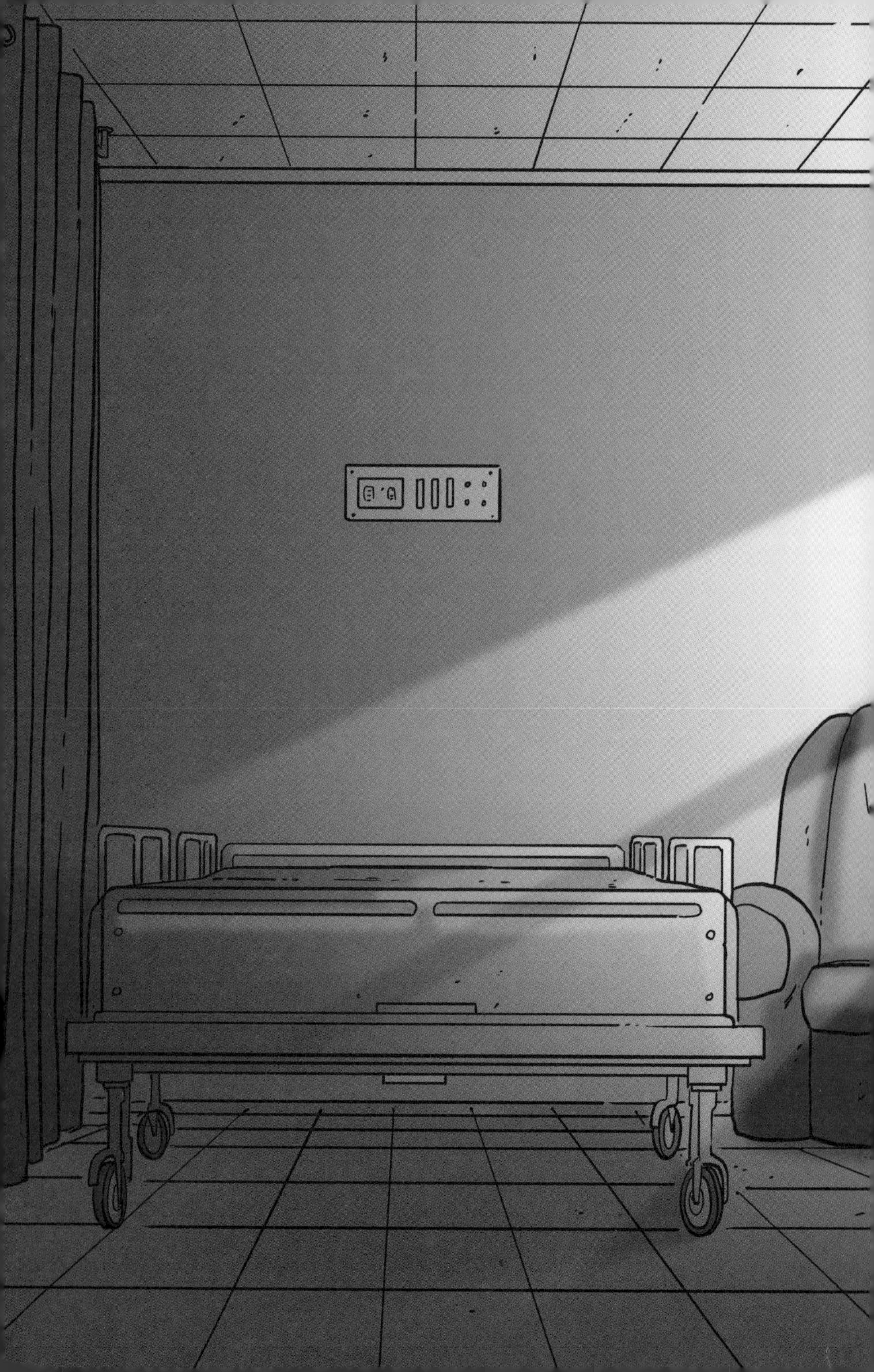

1995

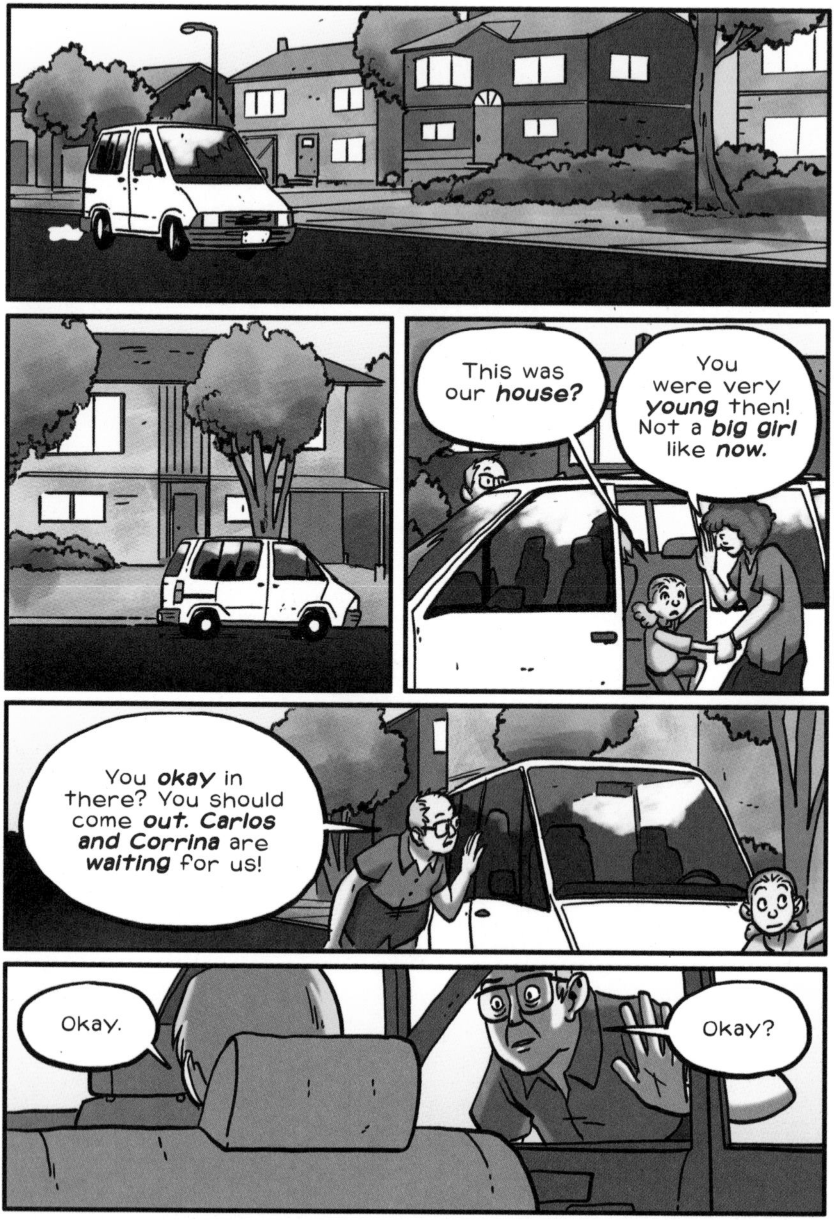

This was our house?
You were very young then! Not a big girl like now.
You okay in there? You should come out. Carlos and Corrina are waiting for us!
Okay.
Okay?

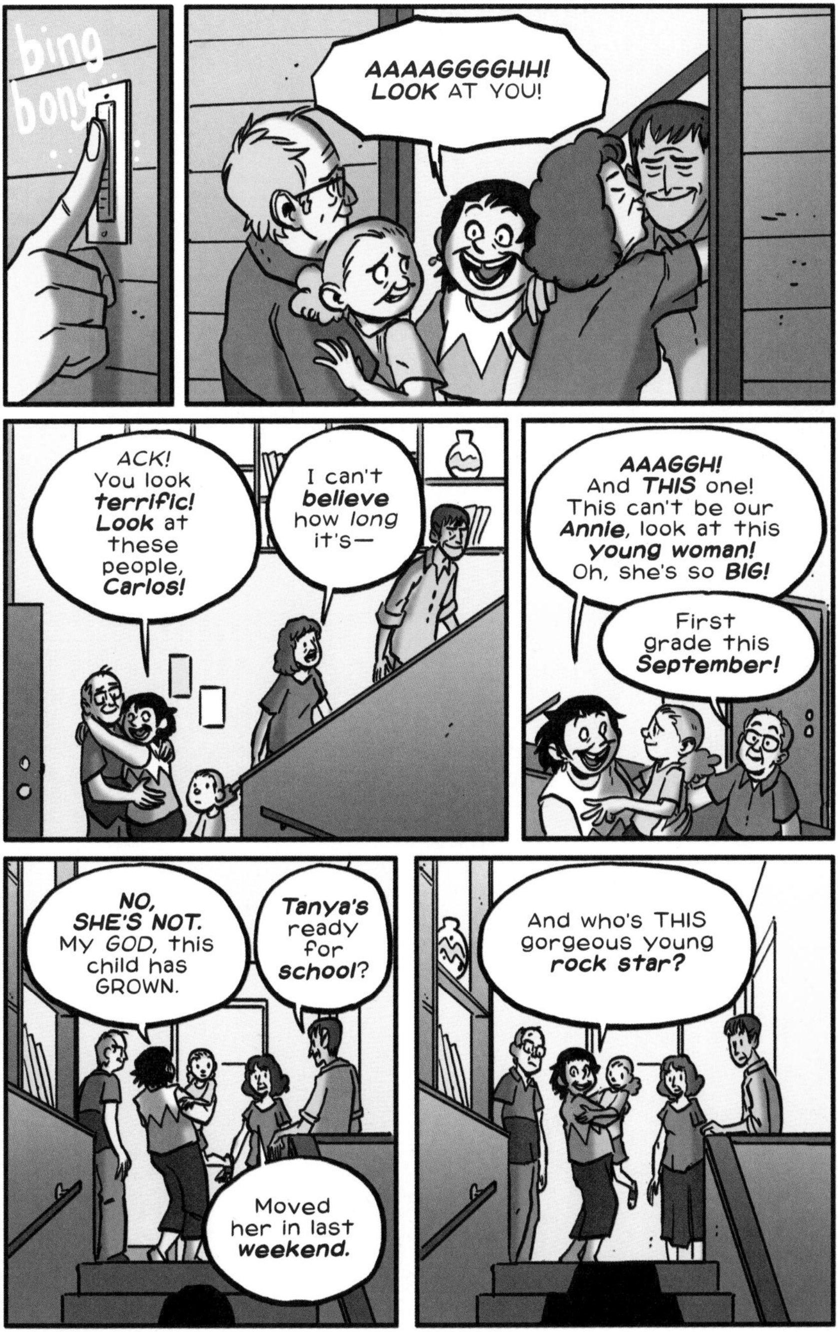
bing bong
AAAAGGGGHH! LOOK AT YOU!
ACK! You look terrific! Look at these people, Carlos!
I can't believe how long it's—
AAAGGH! And THIS one! This can't be our Annie, look at this young woman! Oh, she's so BIG!
First grade this September!
NO, SHE'S NOT. My GOD, this child has GROWN.
Tanya's ready for school?
Moved her in last weekend.
And who's THIS gorgeous young rock star?

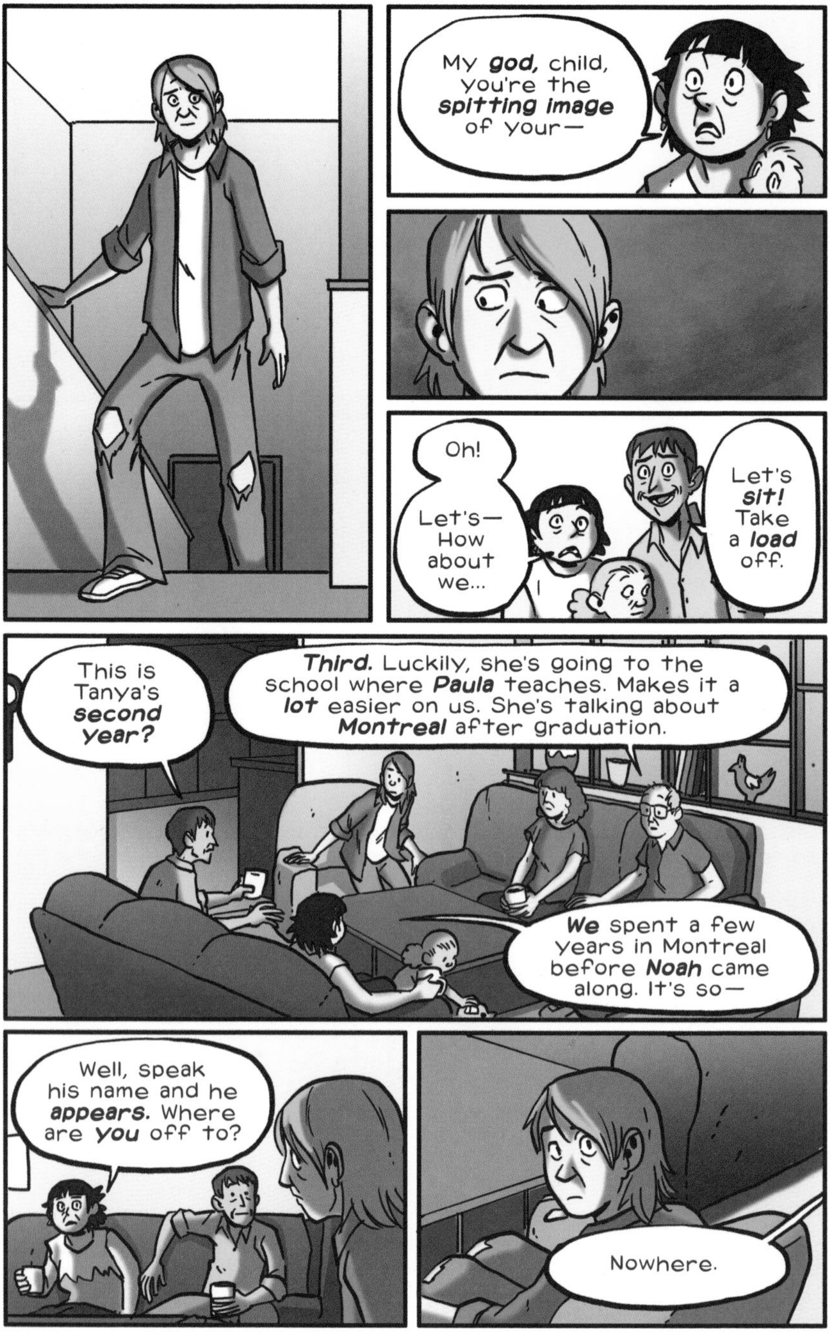
My god, child, you're the spitting image of your—
Oh!
Let's— How about we...
Let's sit! Take a load off.
This is Tanya's second year?
Third. Luckily, she's going to the school where Paula teaches. Makes it a lot easier on us. She's talking about Montreal after graduation.
We spent a few years in Montreal before Noah came along. It's so—
Well, speak his name and he appears. Where are you off to?
Nowhere.

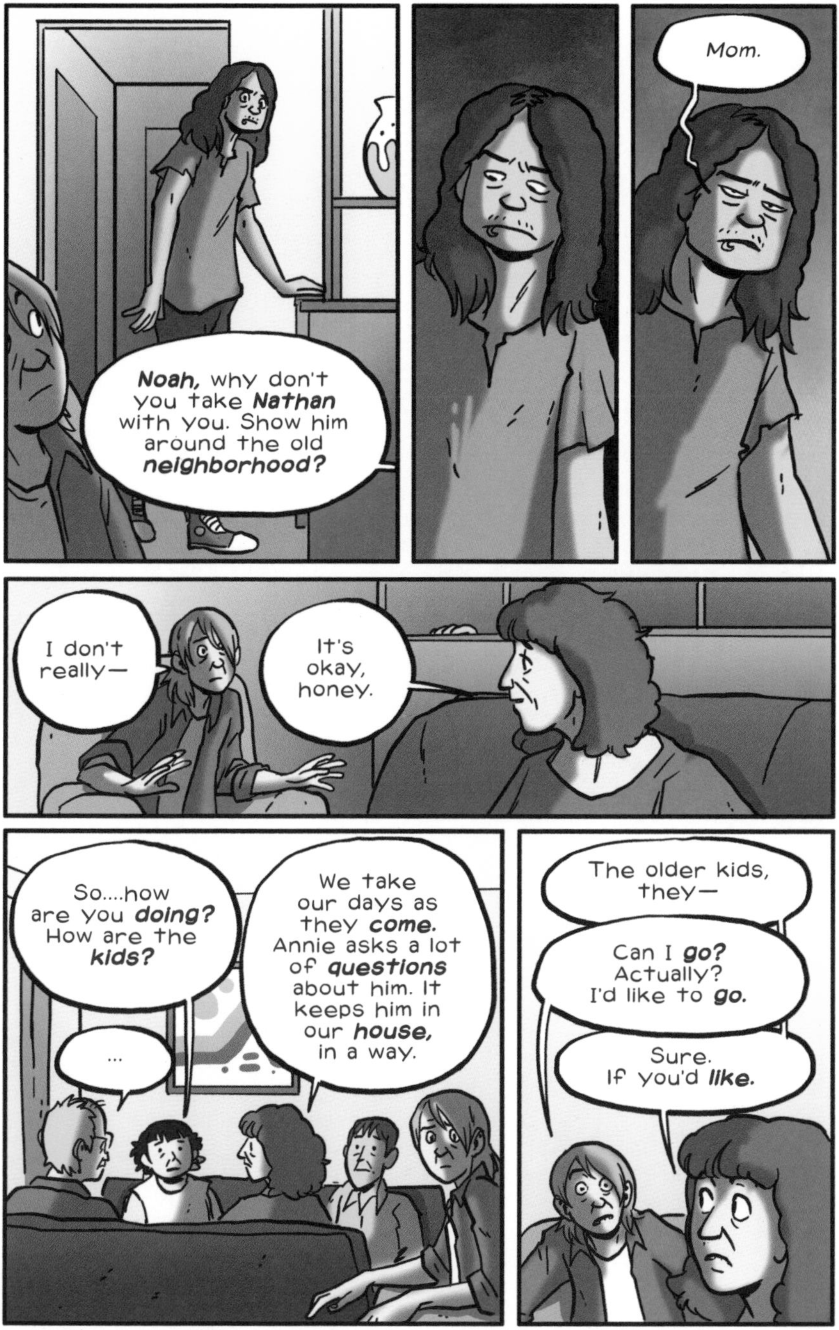

Noah, why don't you take Nathan with you. Show him around the old neighborhood?
Mom.
I don't really—
It's okay, honey.
So....how are you doing? How are the kids?
...
We take our days as they come. Annie asks a lot of questions about him. It keeps him in our house, in a way.
The older kids, they—
Can I go? Actually? I'd like to go.
Sure. If you'd like.

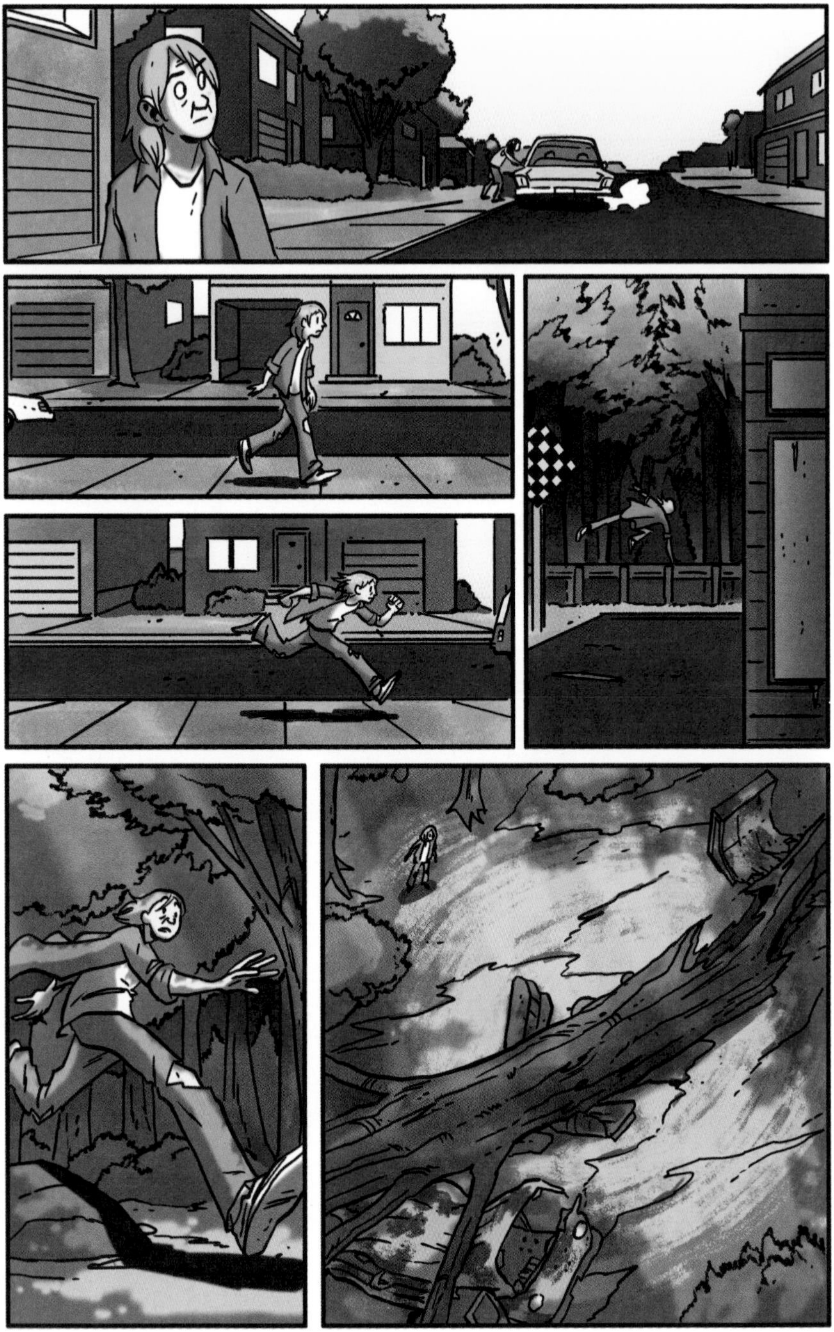

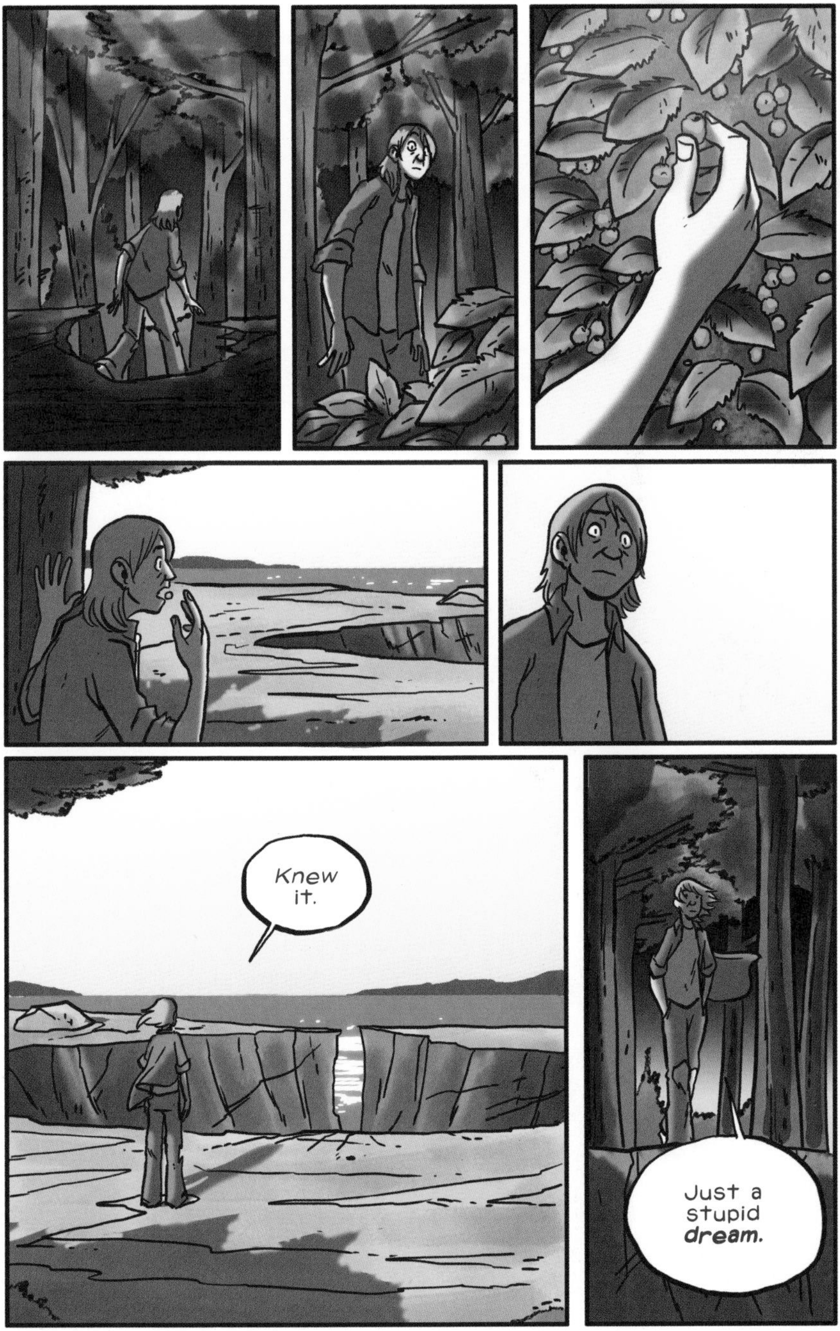
Knew it.
Just a stupid dream.

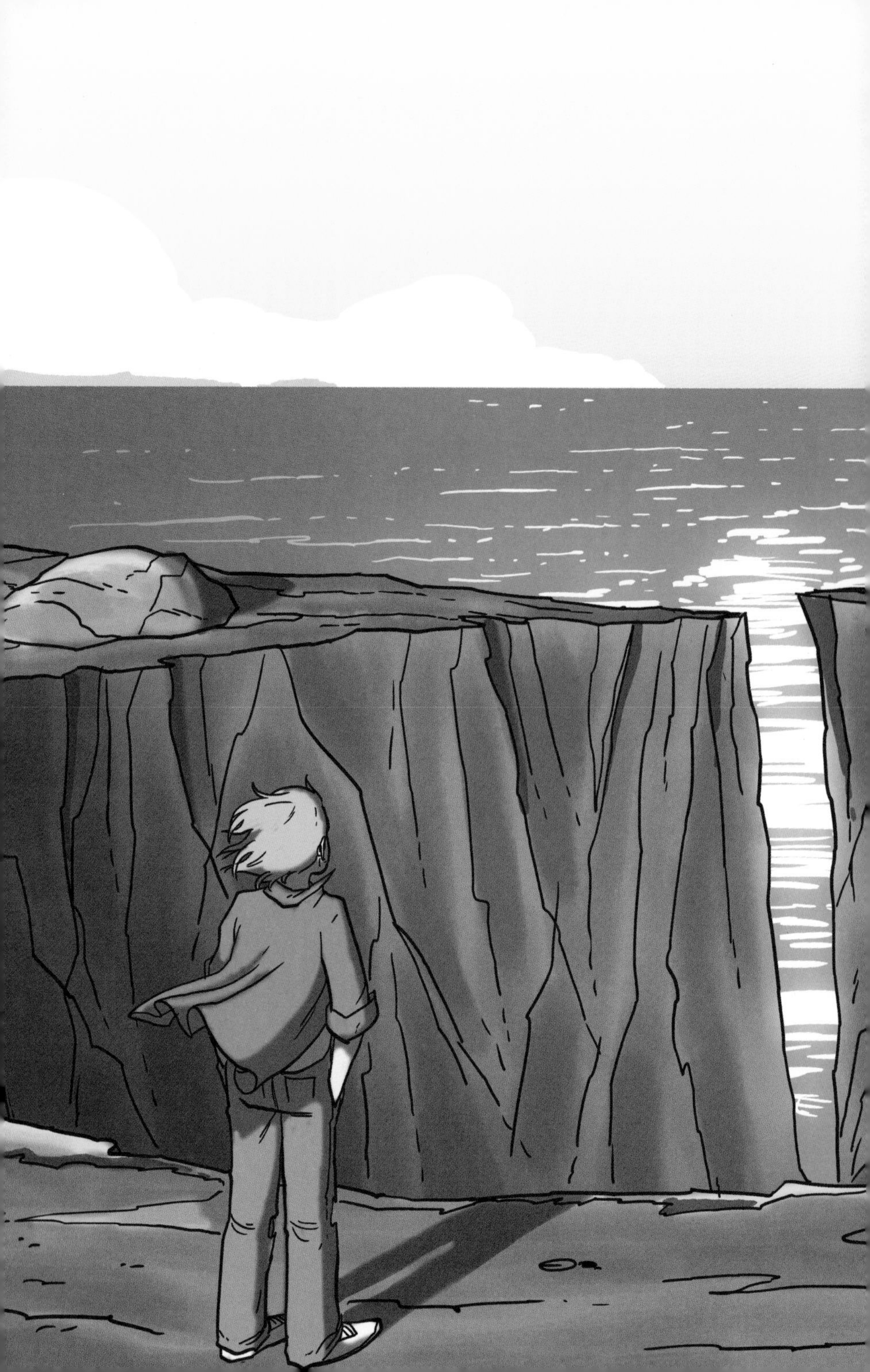

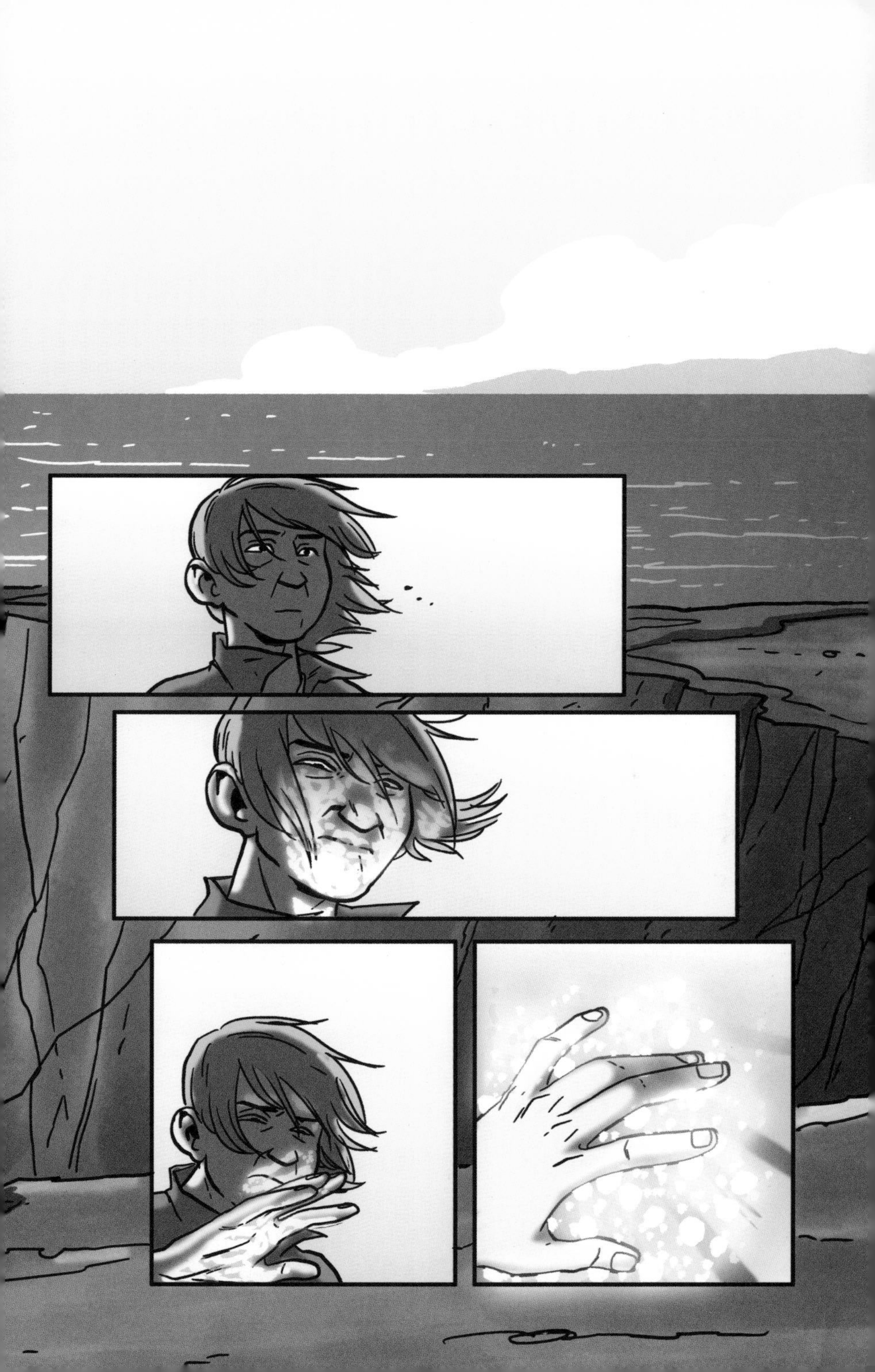

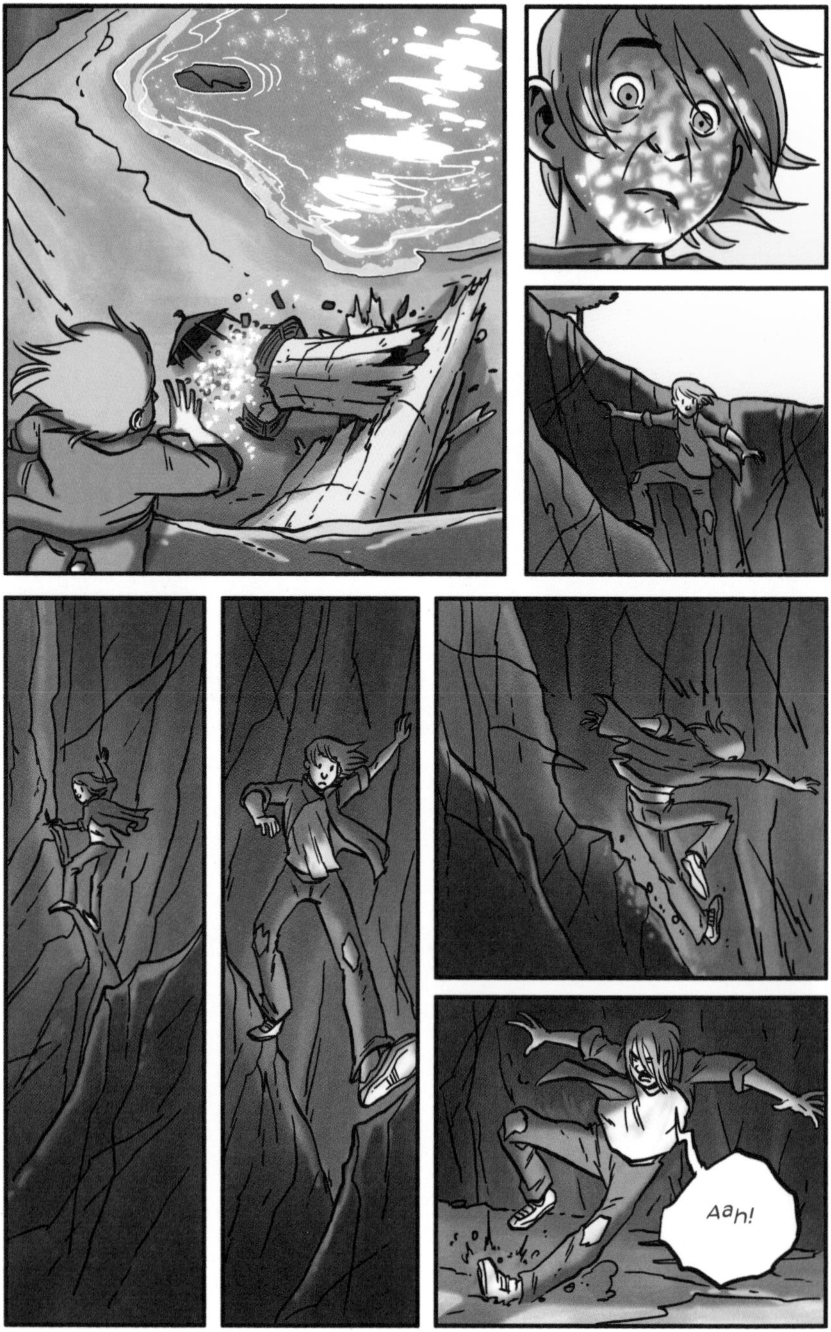
Aah!

gahhhh...

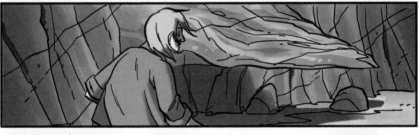

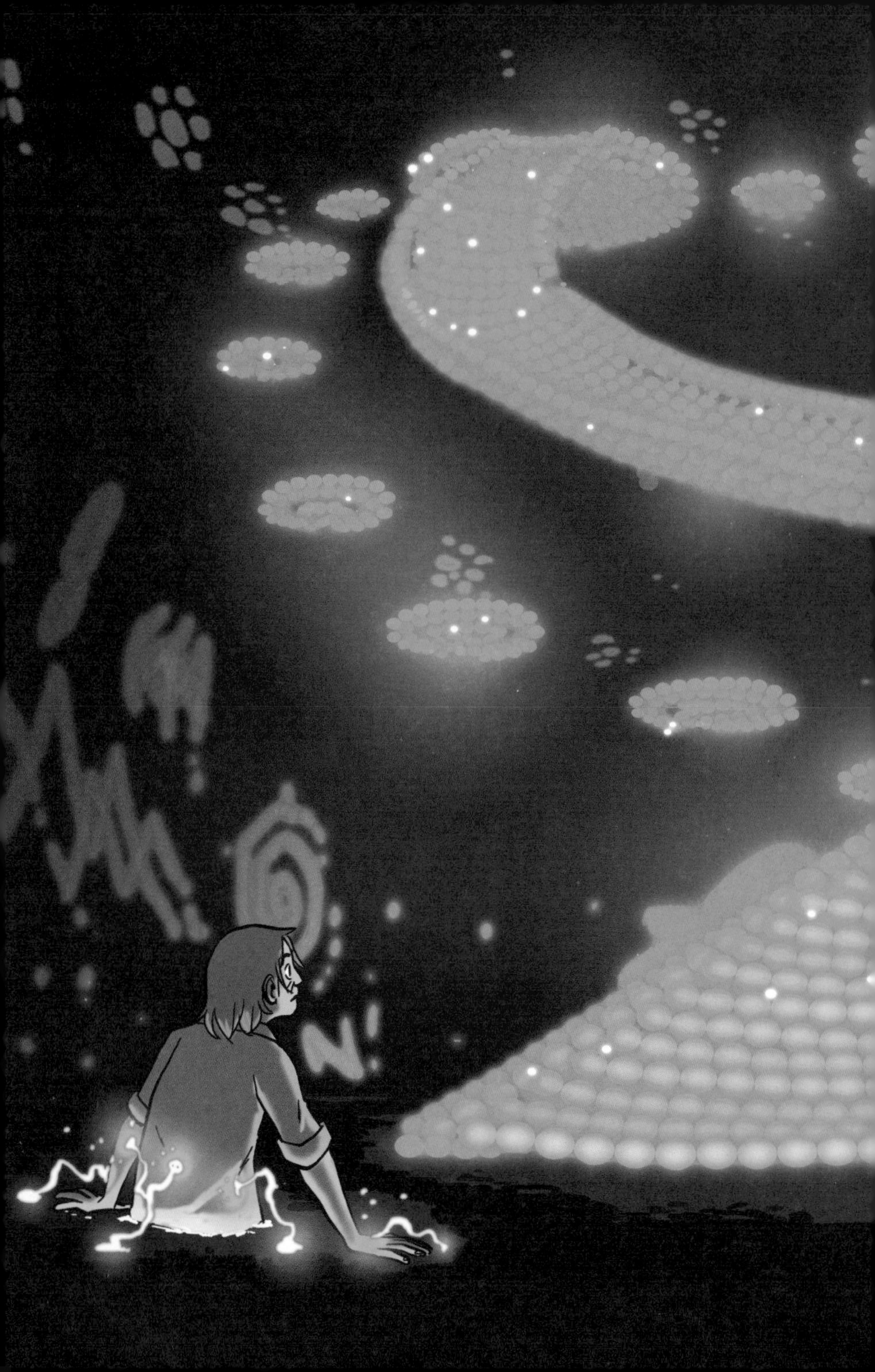

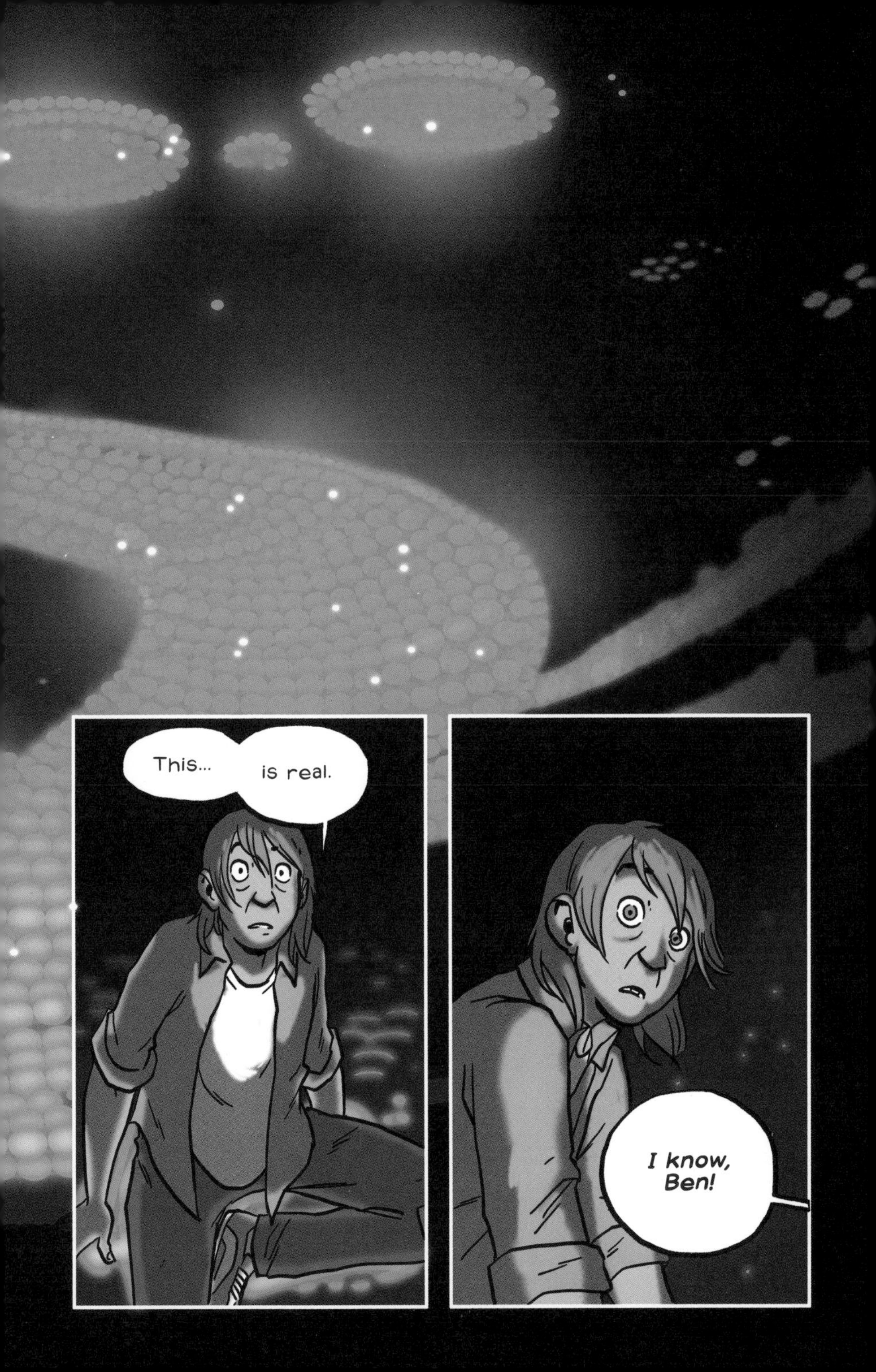
This...
is real.
I know, Ben!

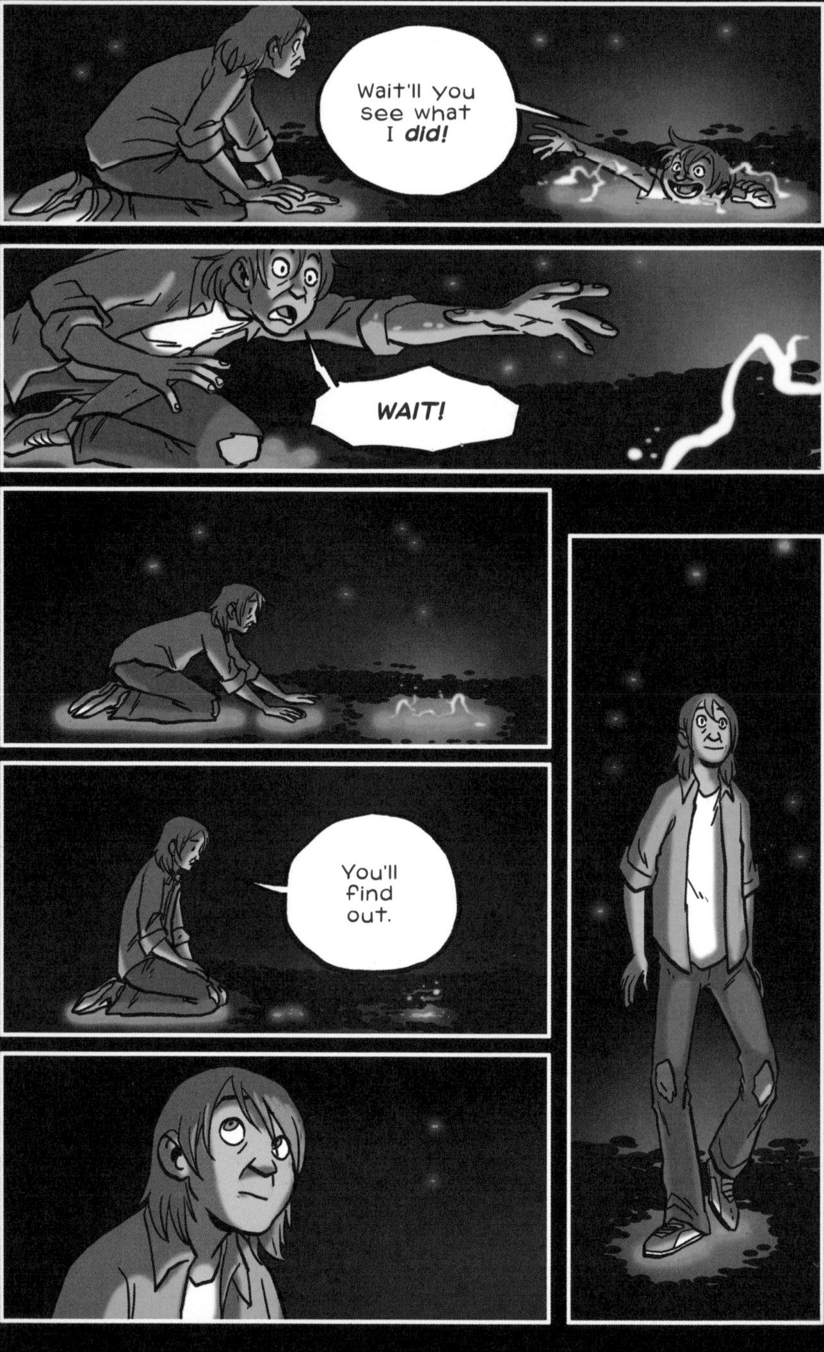
Wait'll you see what I **did!**
WAIT!
You'll find out.

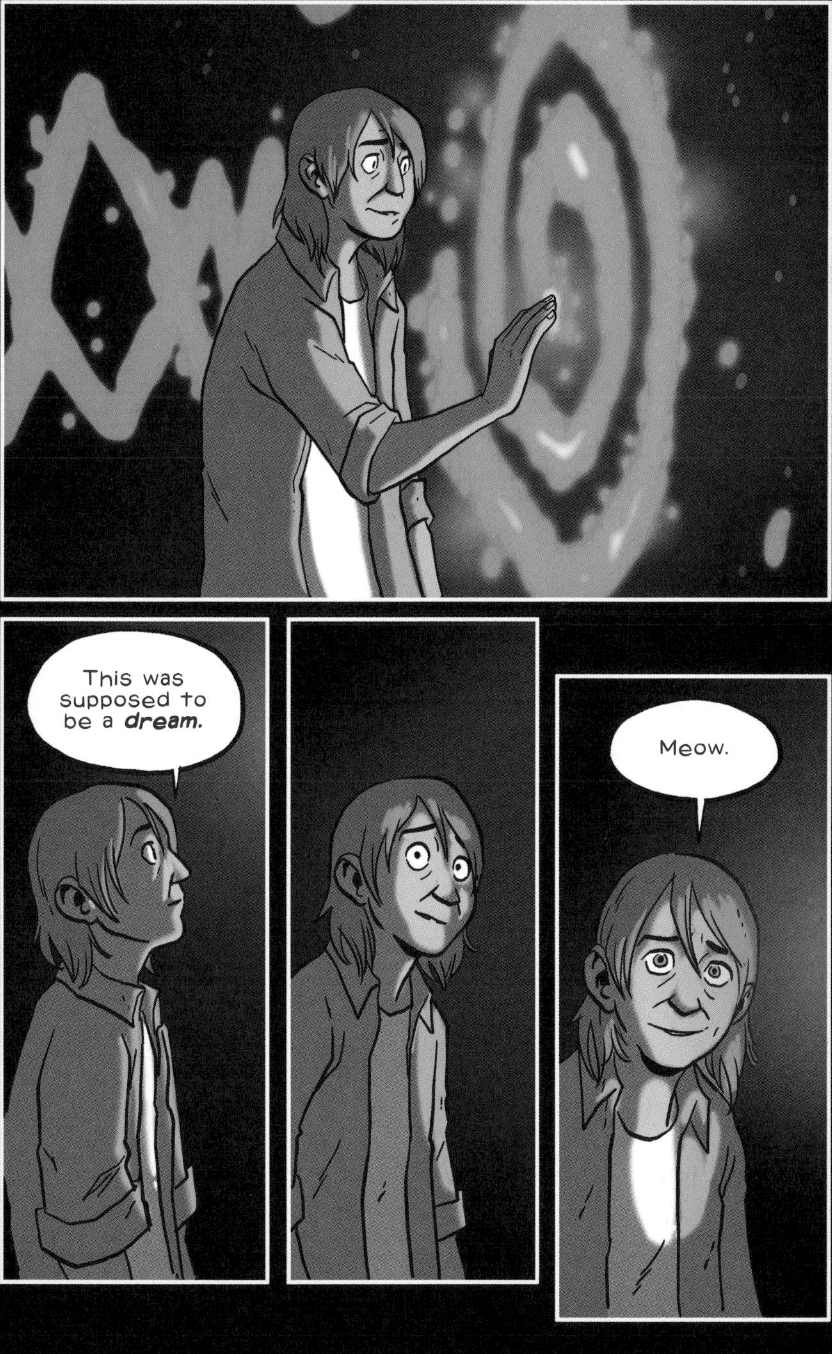
This was supposed to be a *dream.*
Meow.

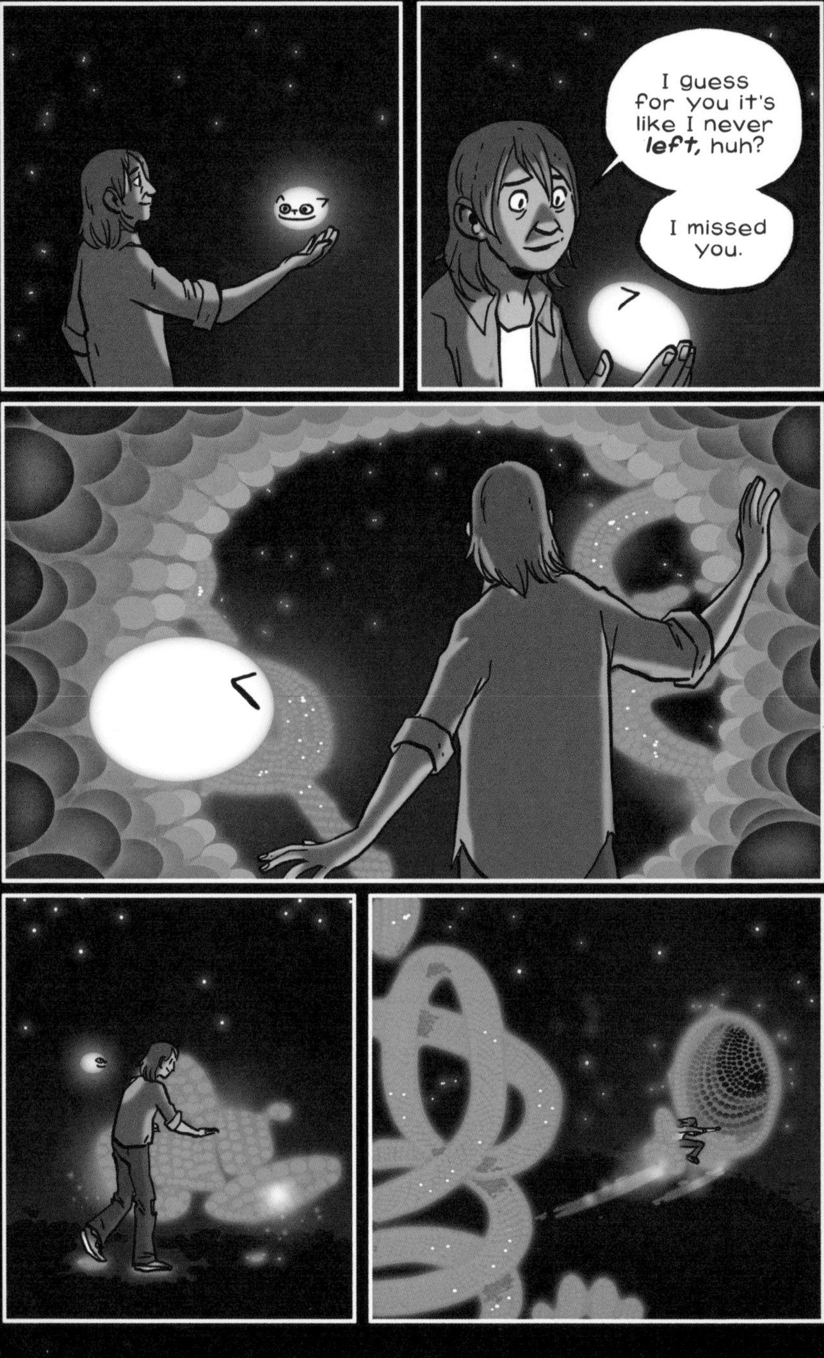
I guess for you it's like I never **left,** huh?
I missed you.

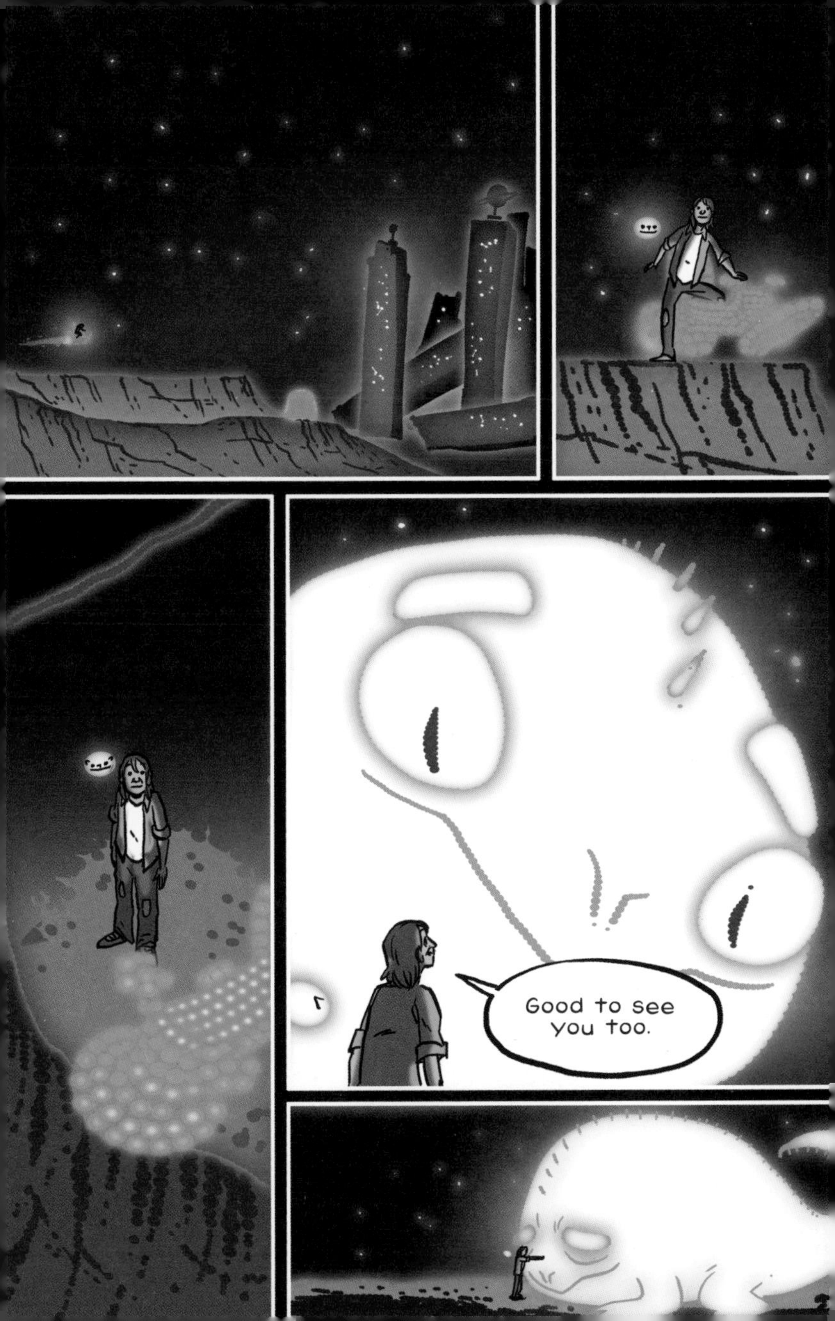
Good to see you too.

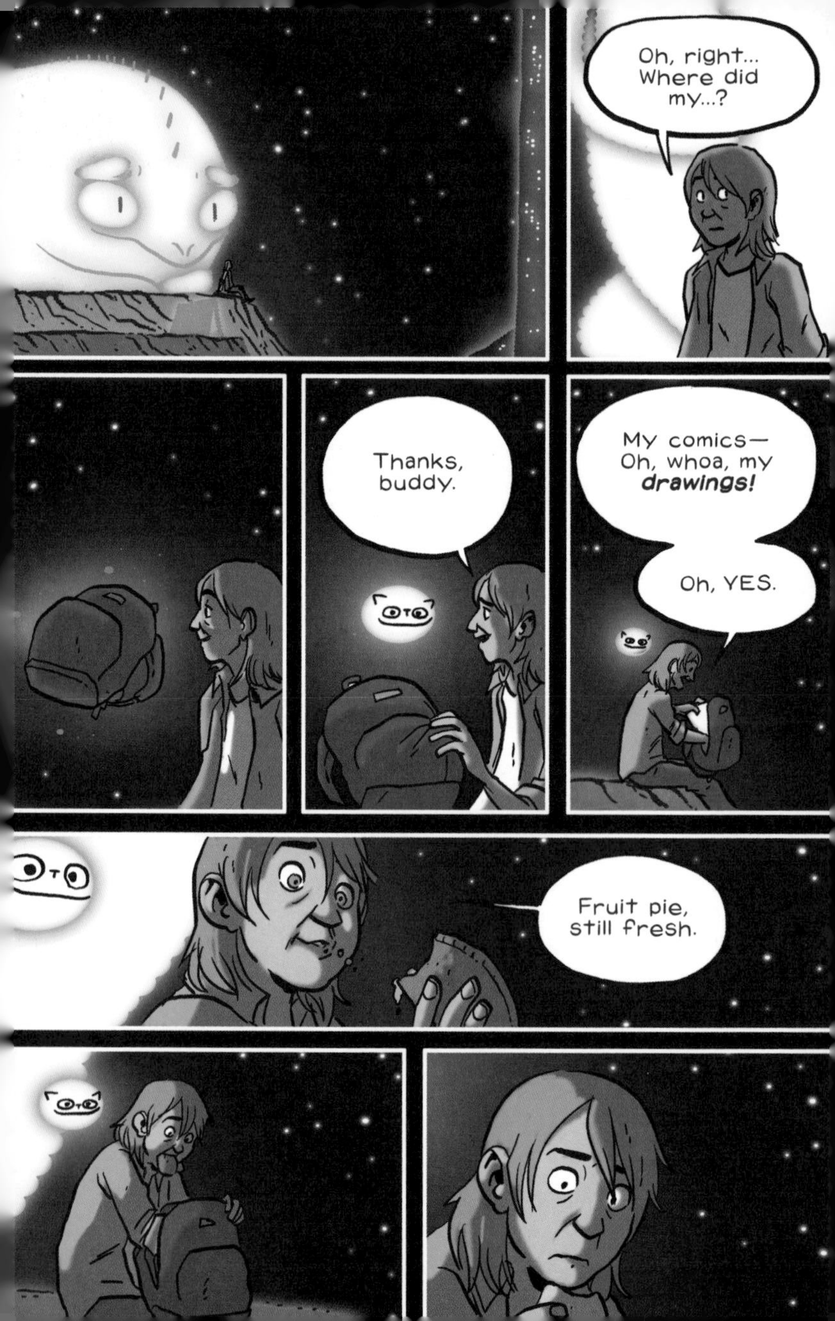
Oh, right... Where did my...?
Thanks, buddy.
My comics— Oh, whoa, my **drawings!**
Oh, YES.
Fruit pie, still fresh.

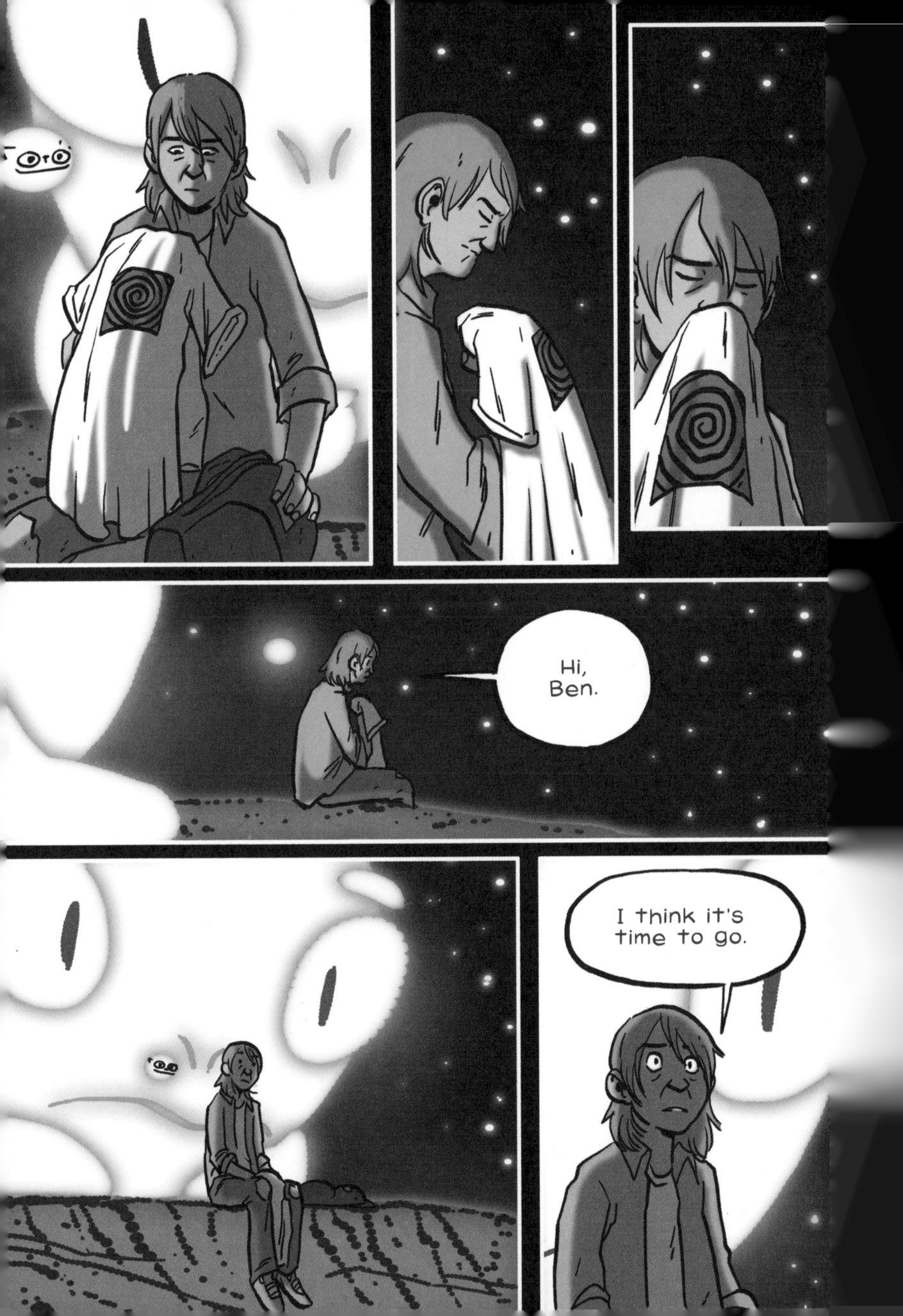
Hi, Ben.
I think it's time to go.

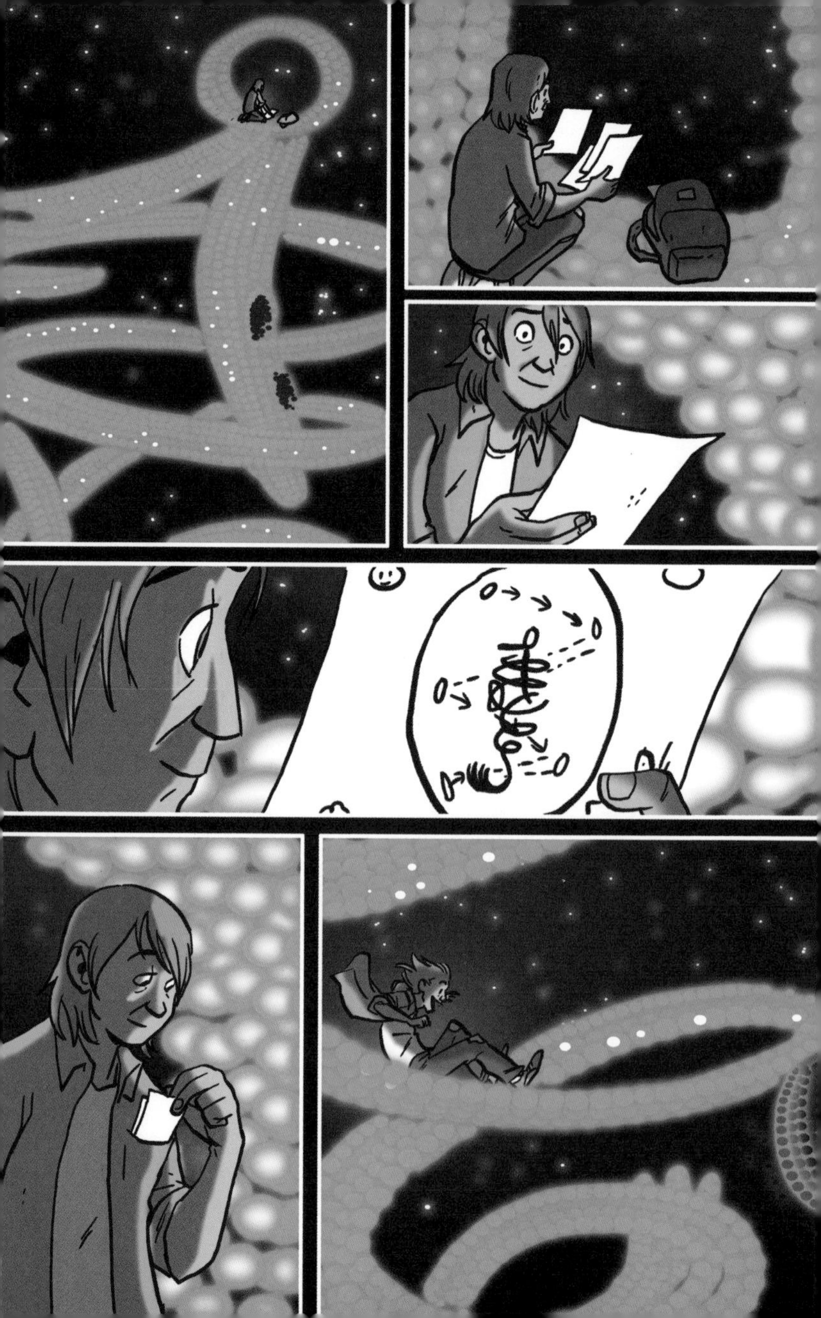

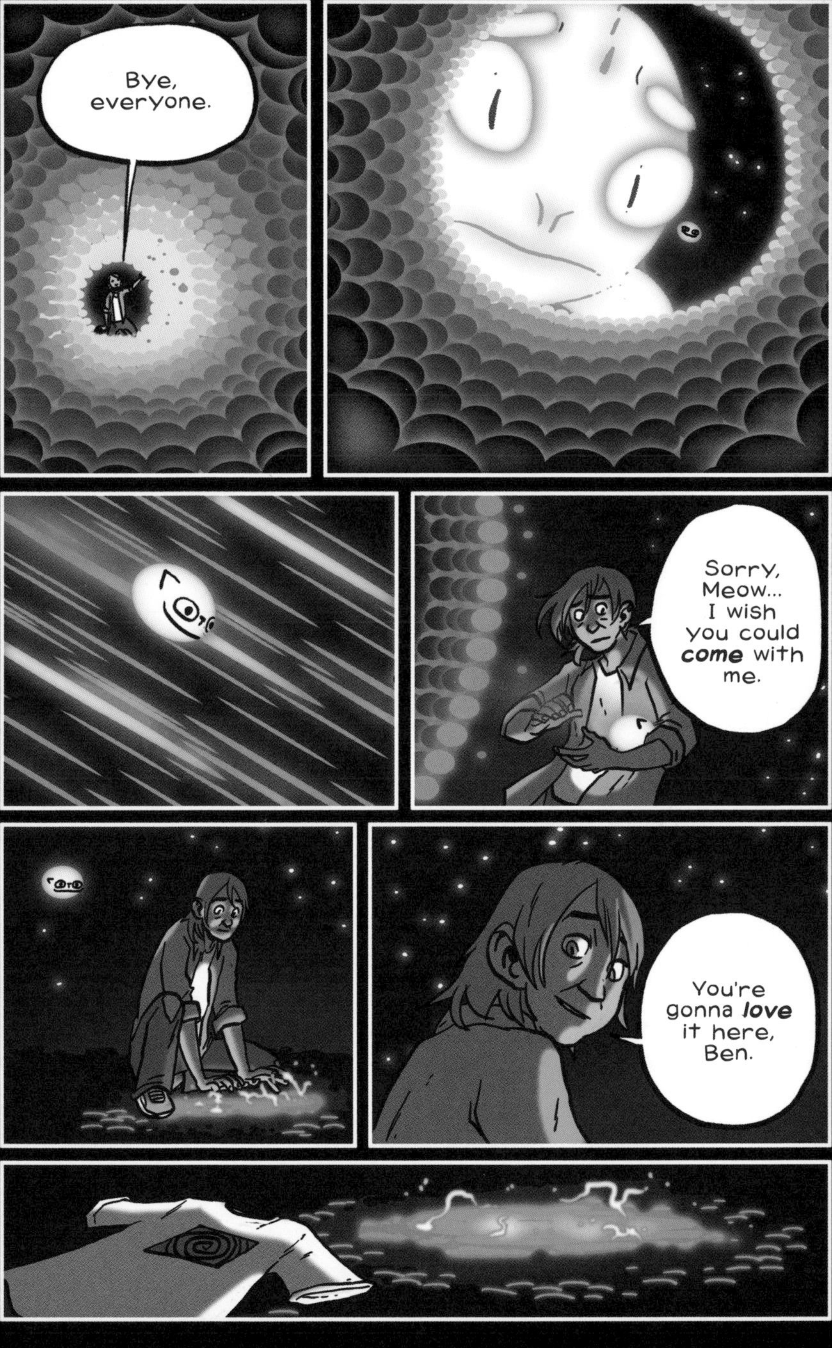

Bye, everyone.
Sorry, Meow... I wish you could **come** with me.
You're gonna **love** it here, Ben.

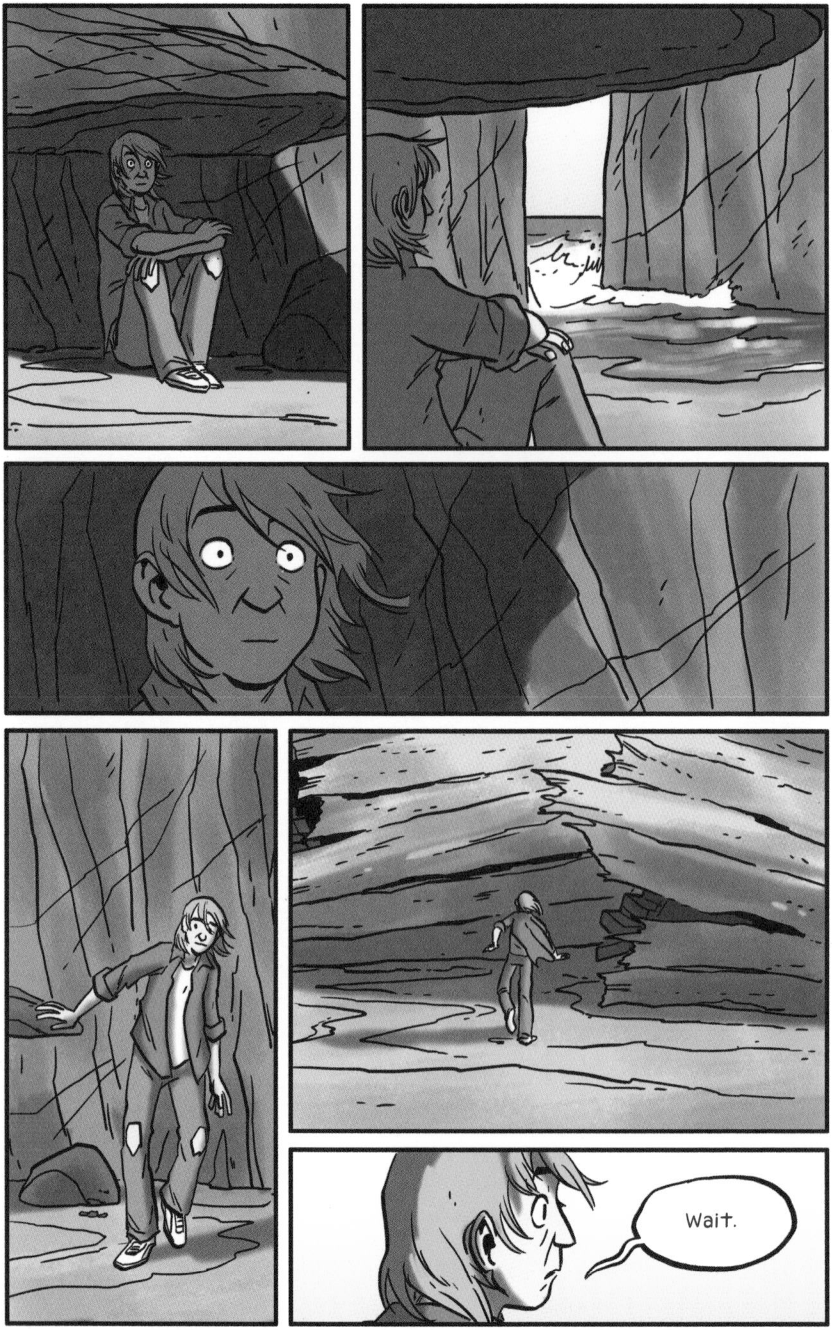
Wait.

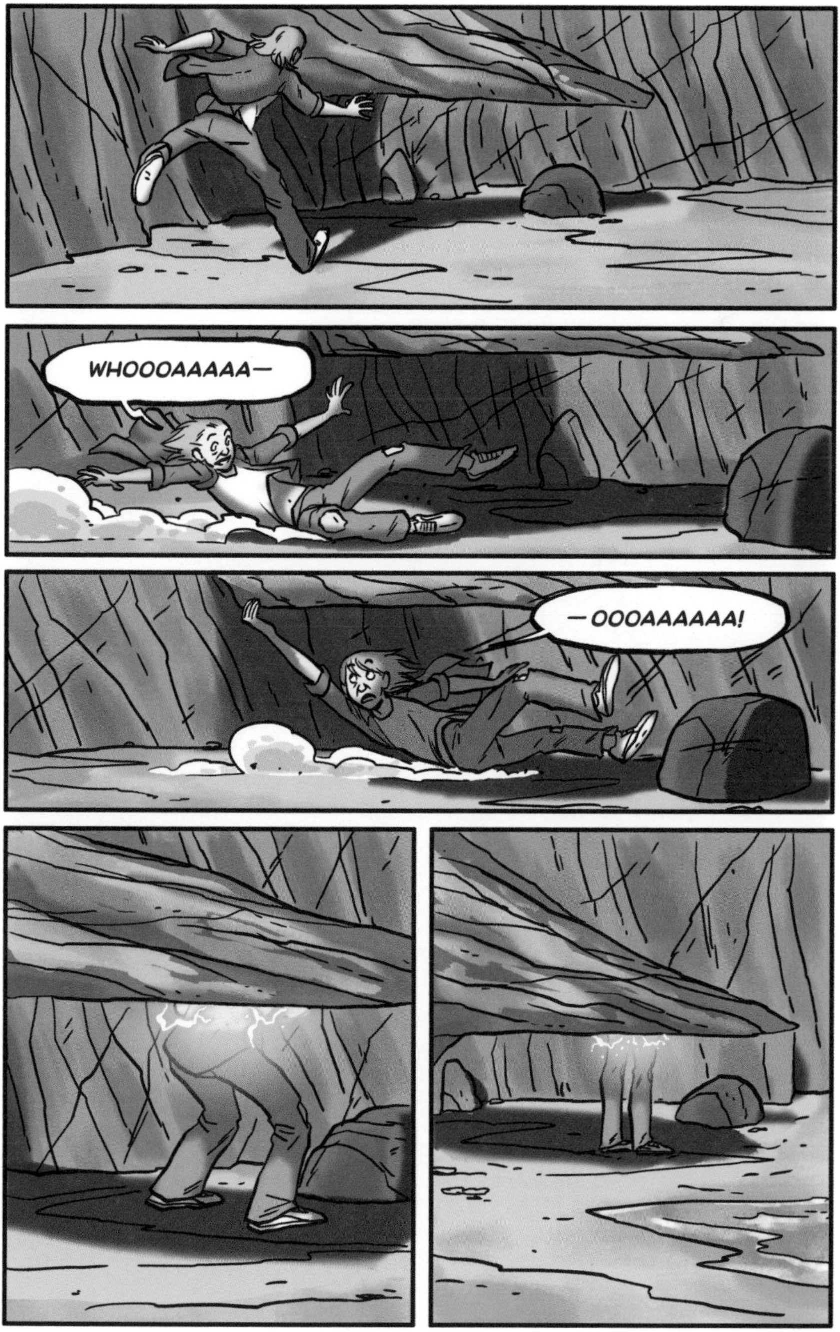
WHOOOAAAAA—
—OOOAAAAAAA!

Looks like you **can** come along.

I guess I thought...

Sorry about that, buddy.

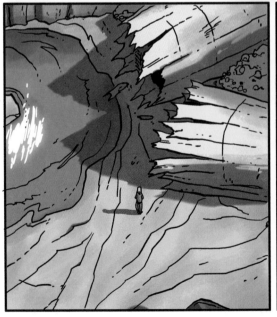

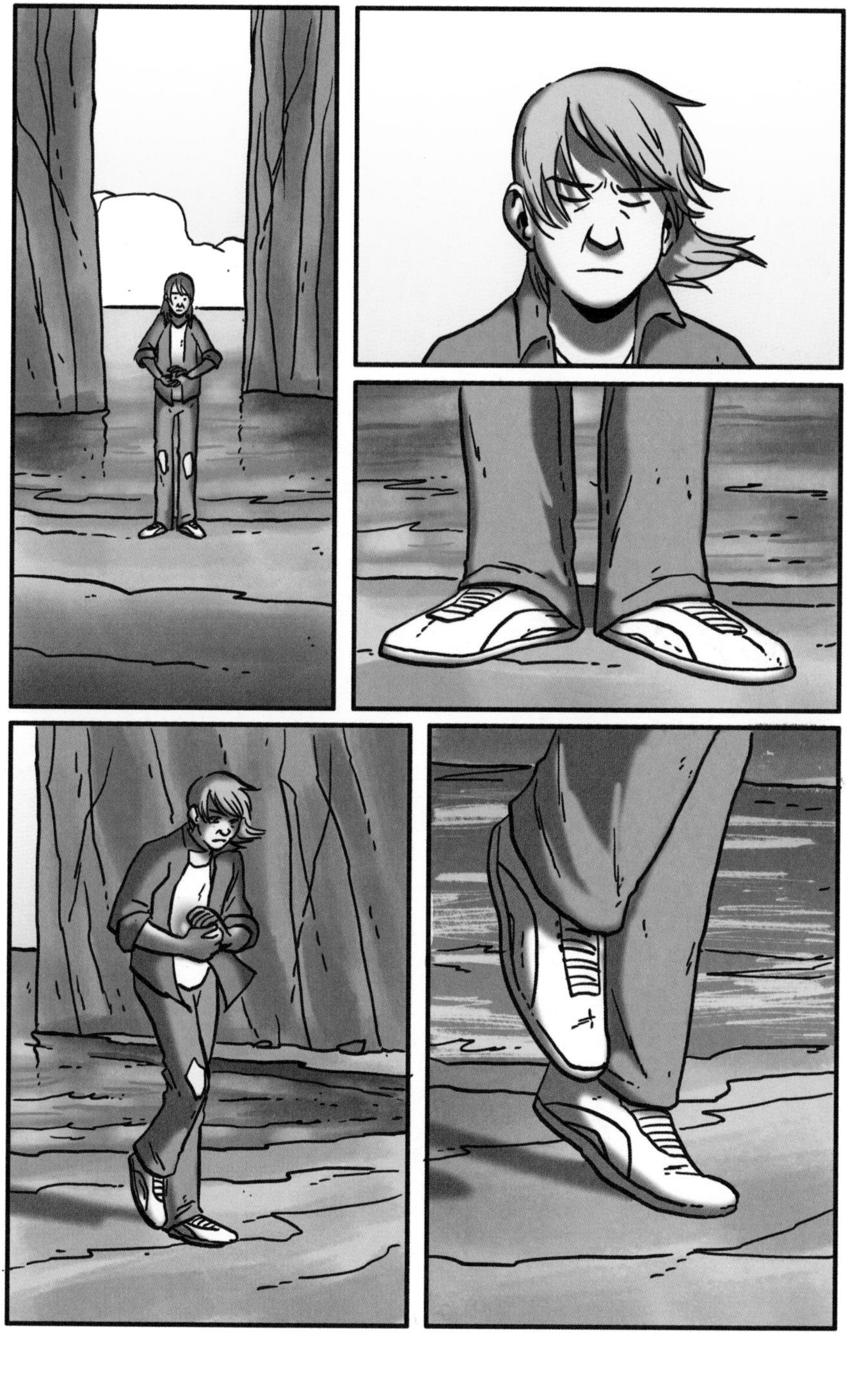

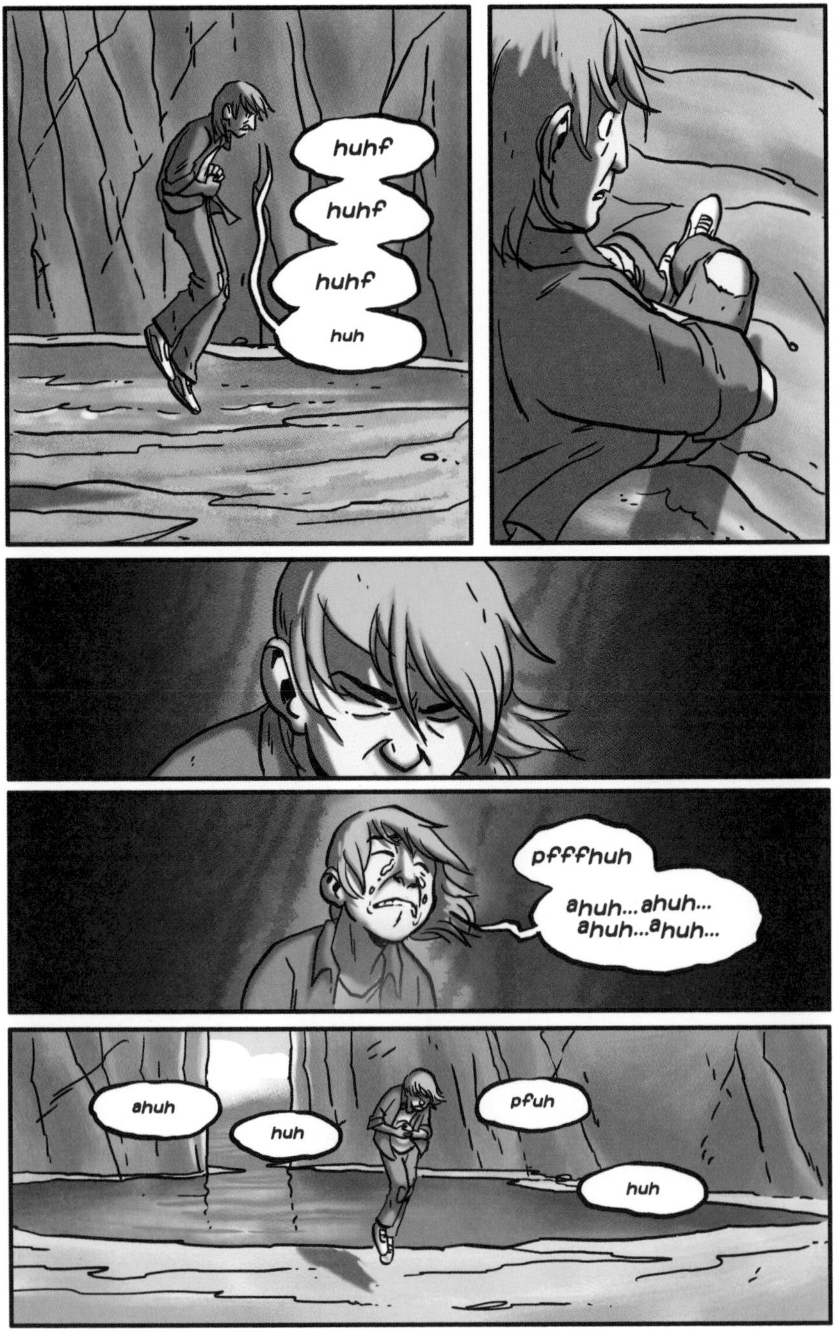
huhf
huhf
huhf
huh
pfffhuh
ahuh...ahuh... ahuh...ahuh...
ahuh
huh
pfuh
huh

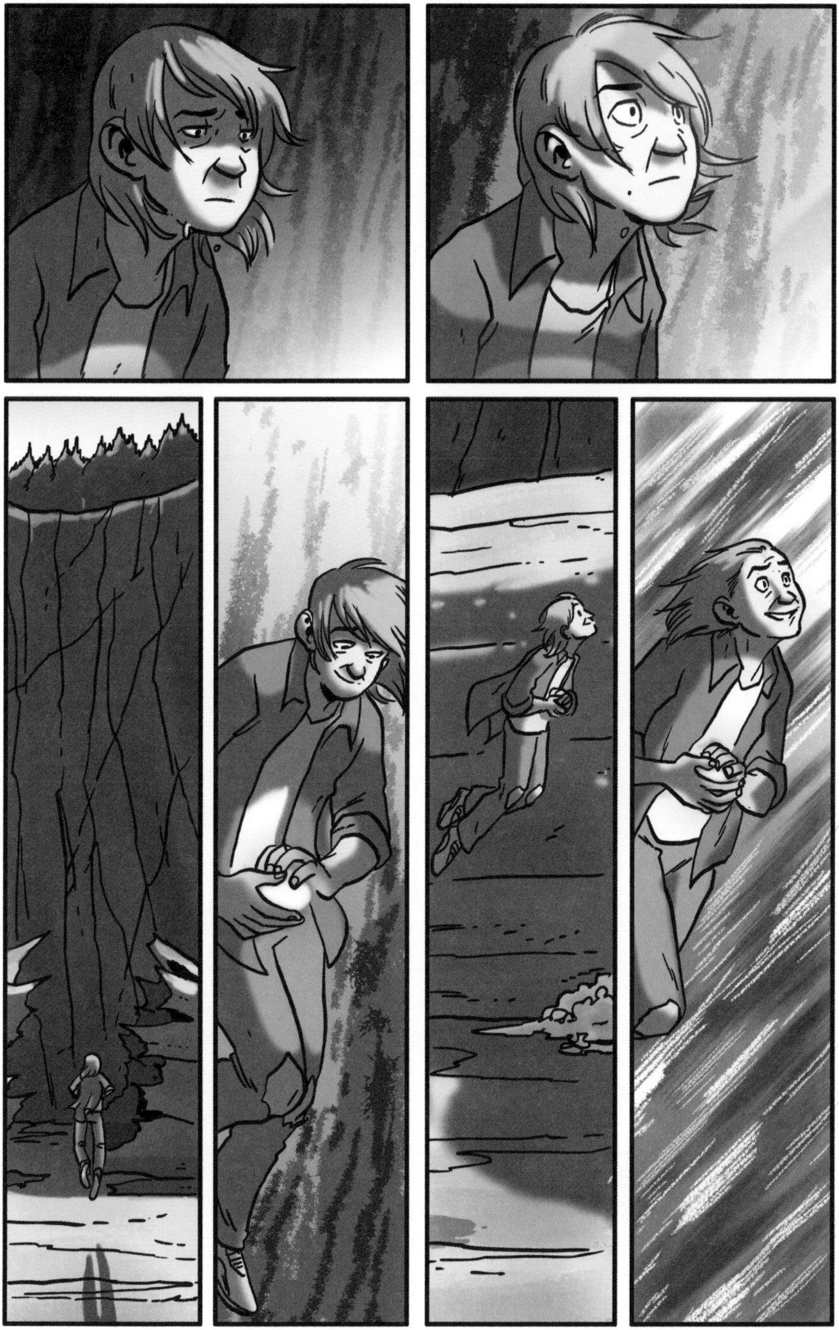

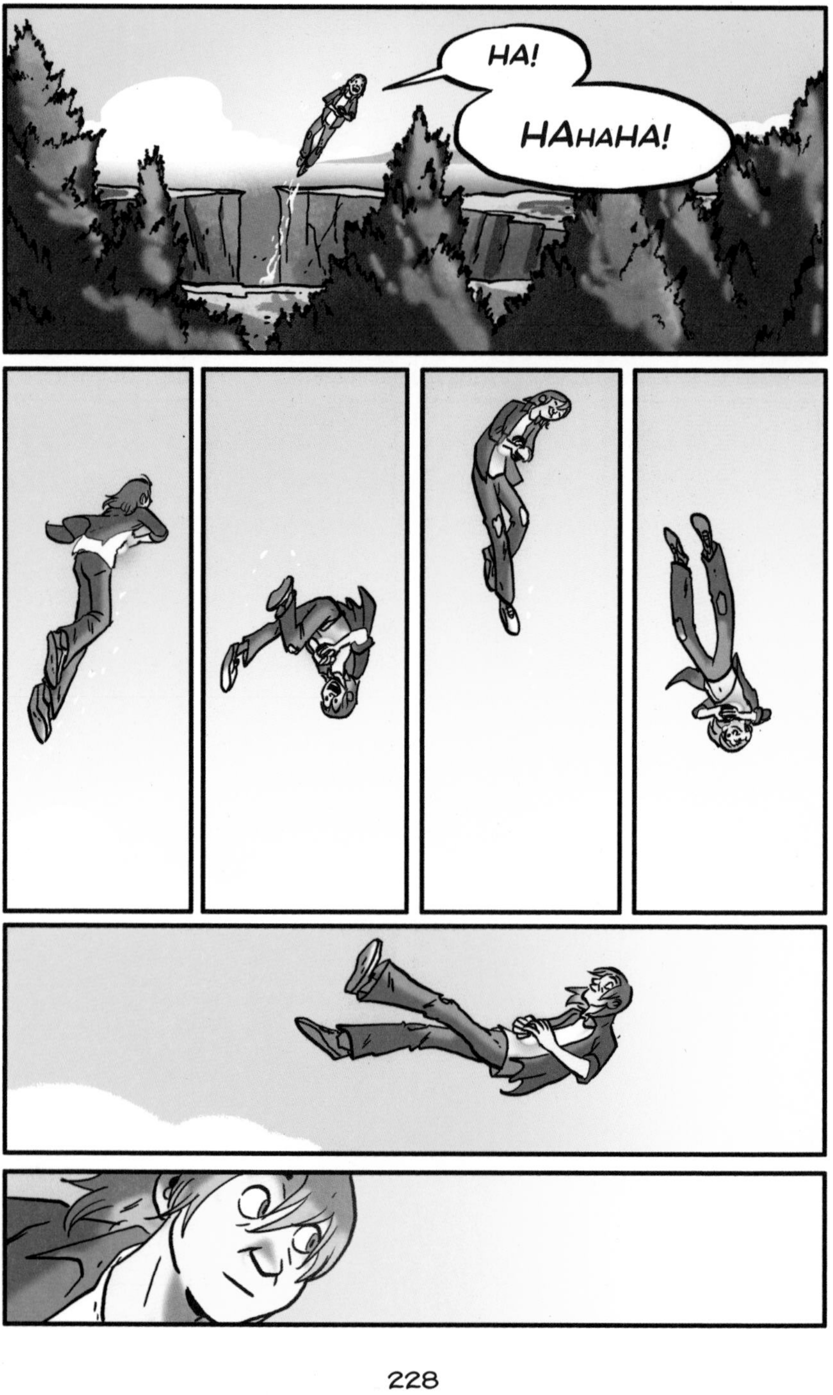
HA!
HAhaHA!

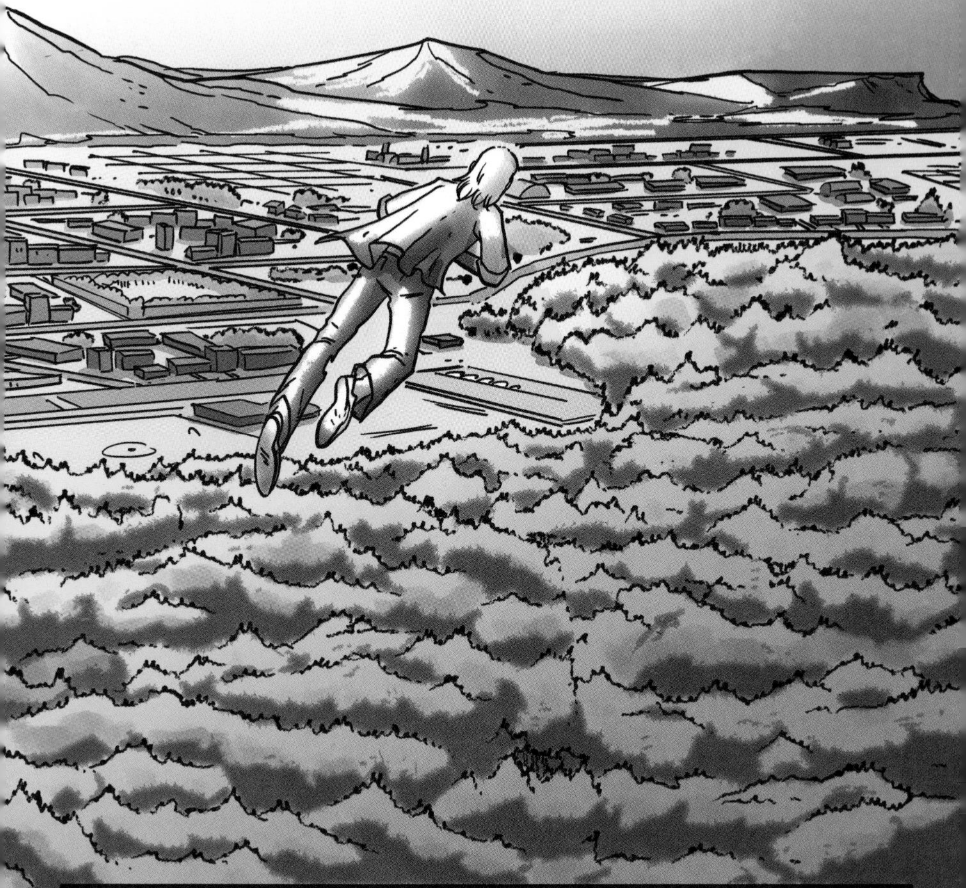

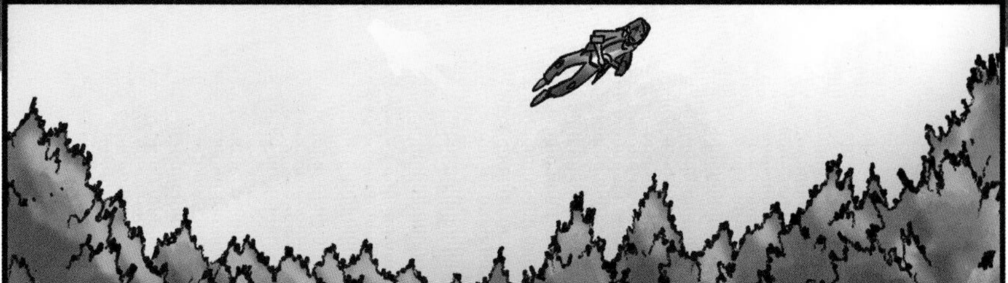

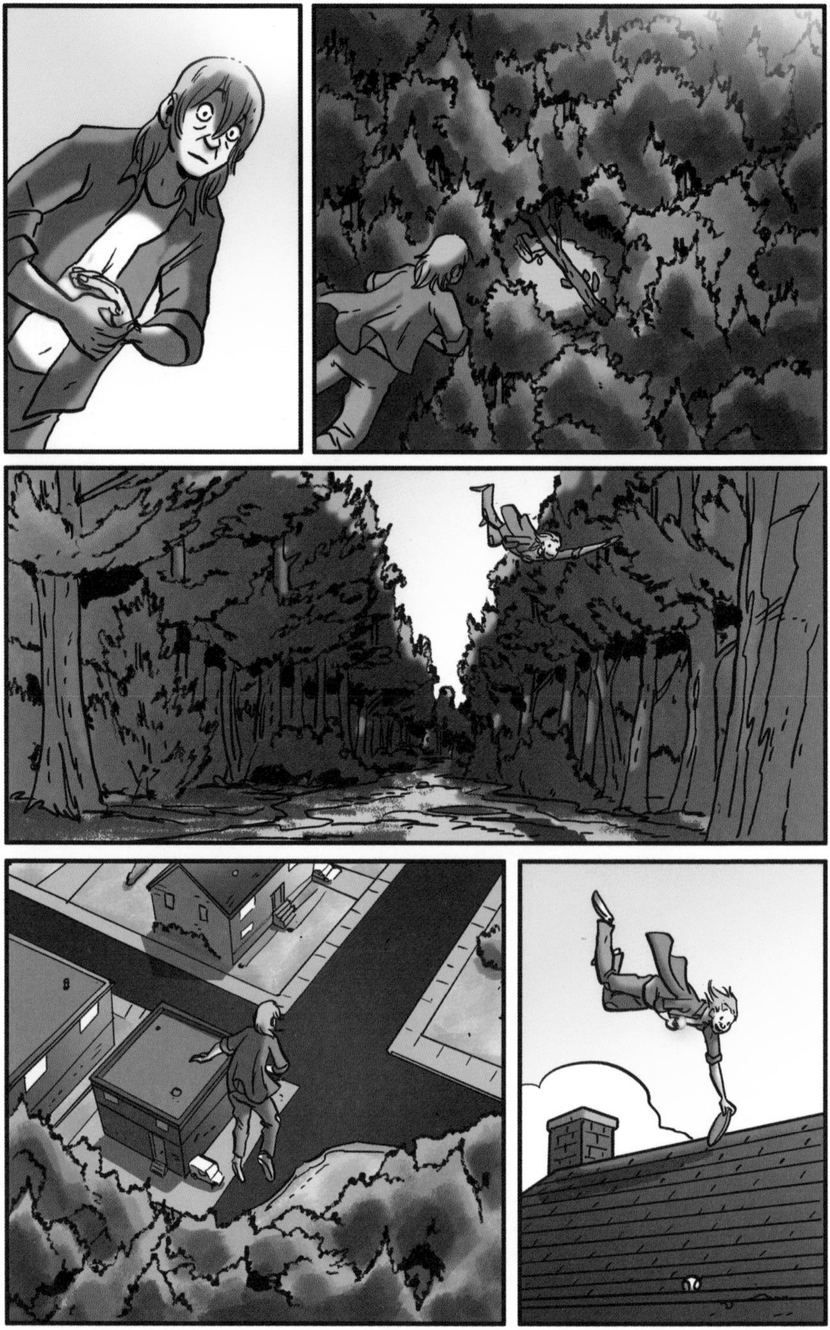

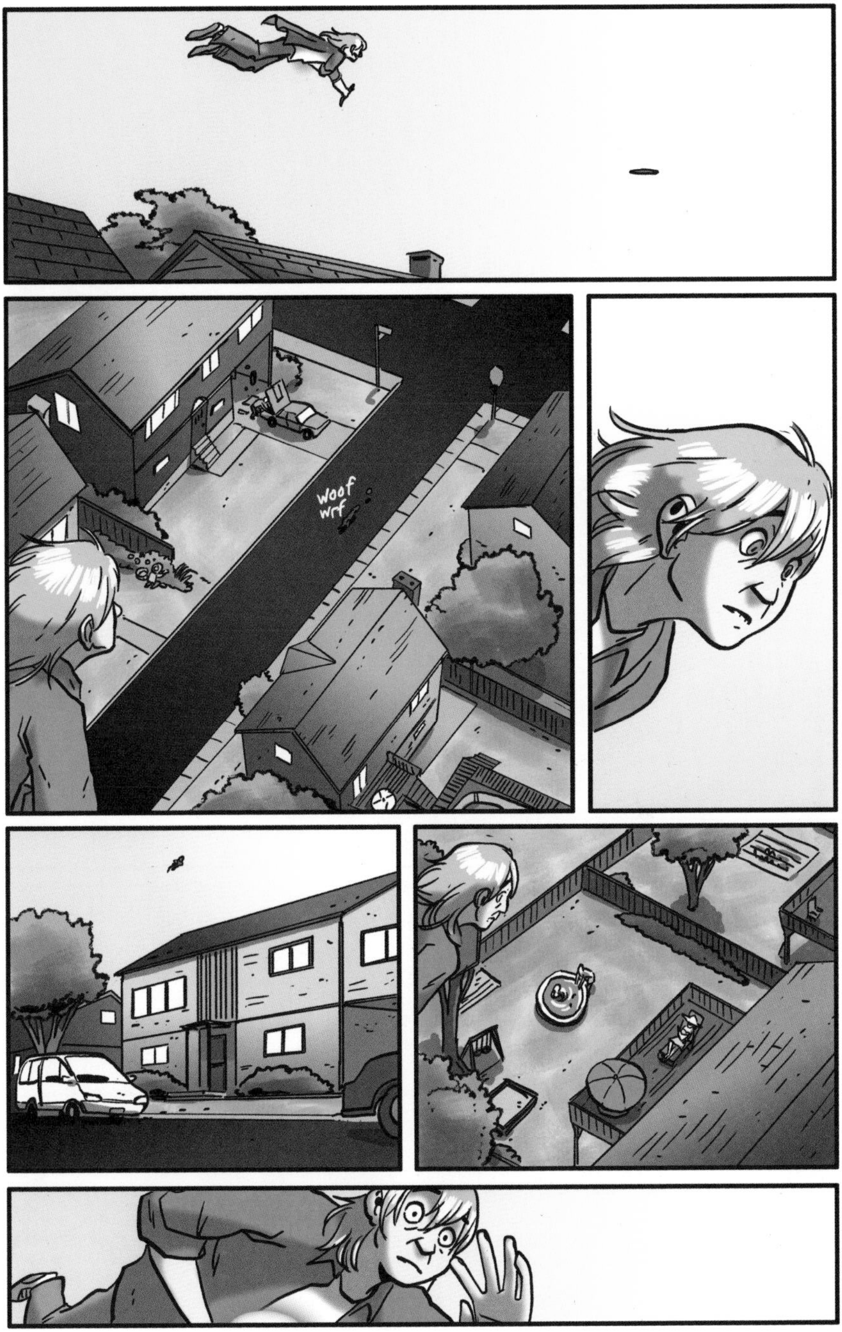
woof
wrf

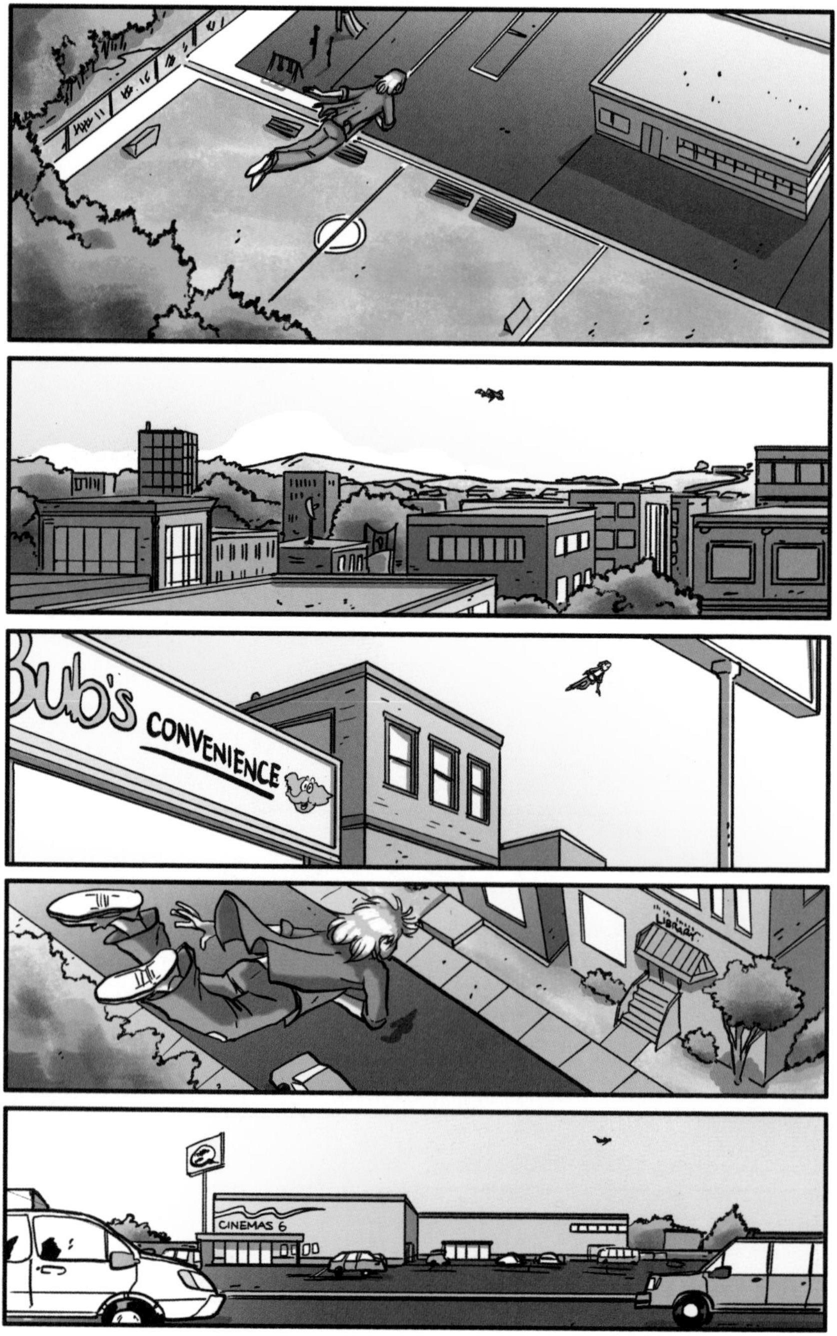
Bub's
CONVENIENCE
LIBRARY
CINEMAS 6

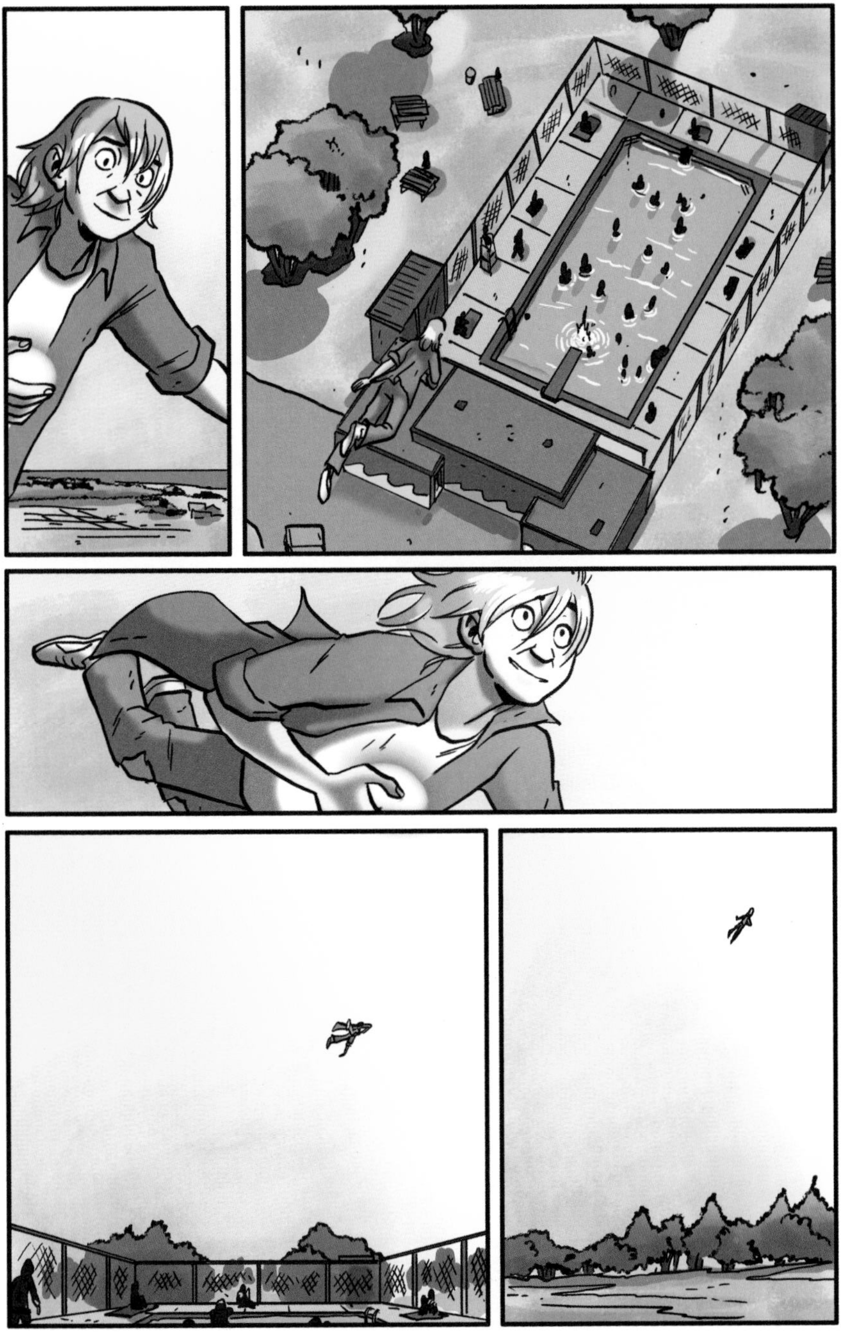

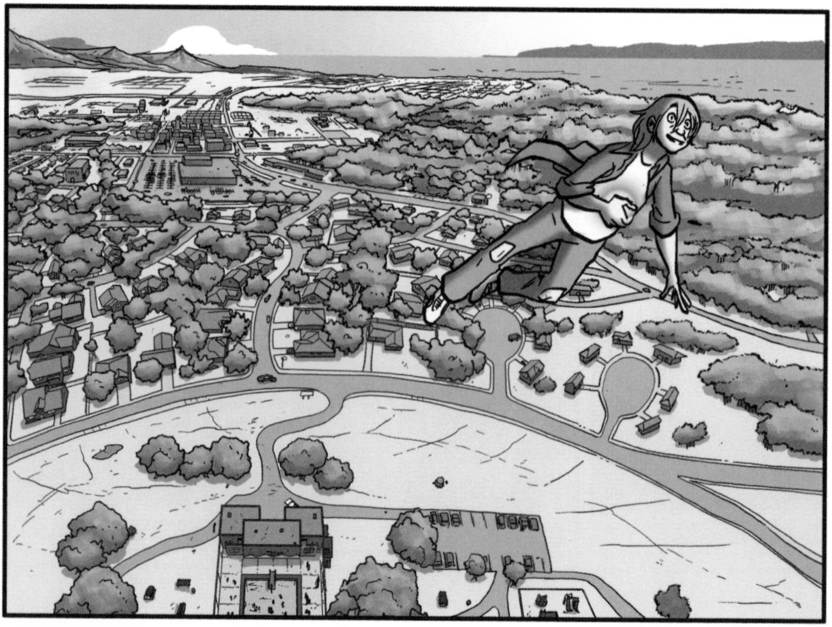

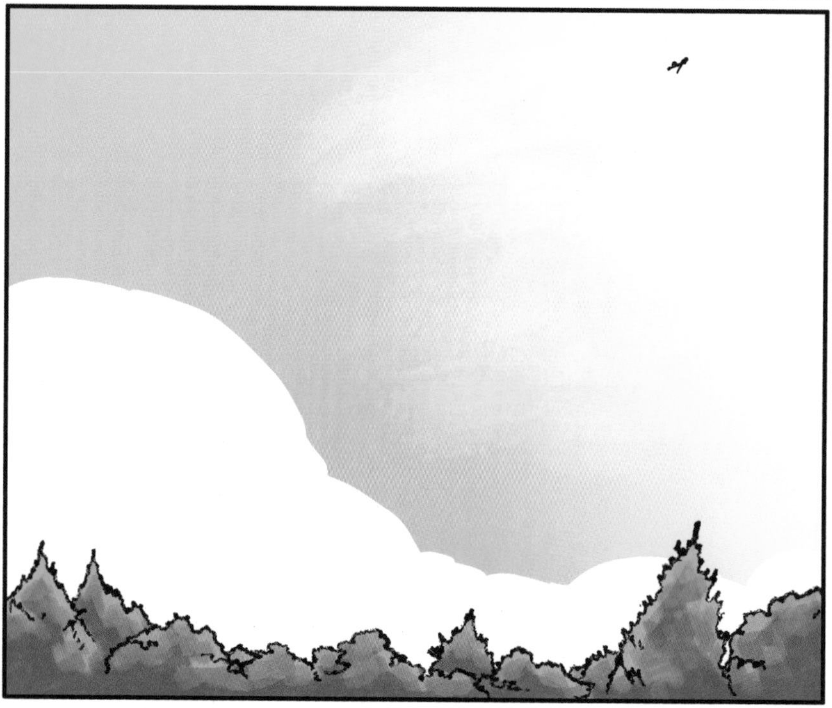

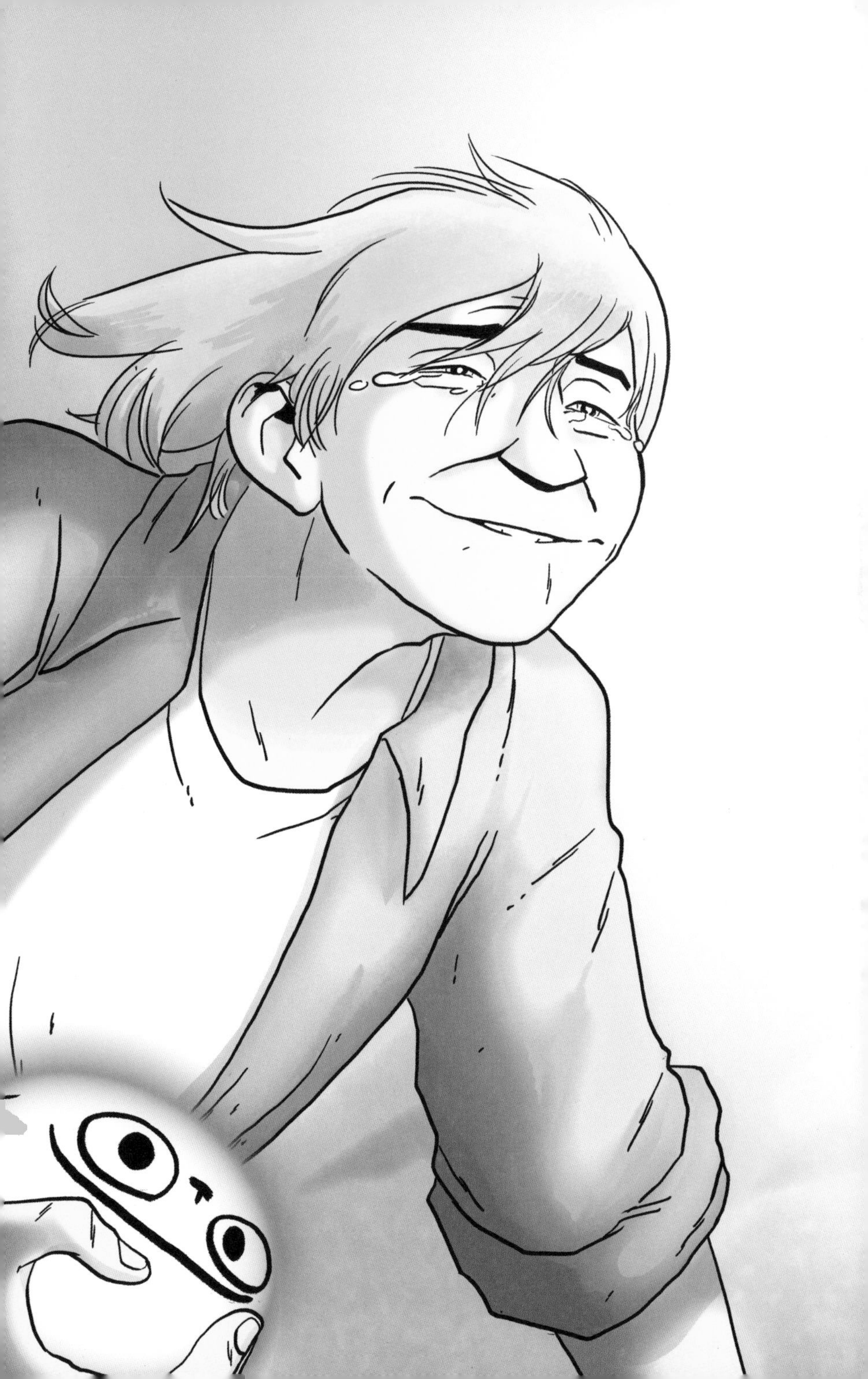

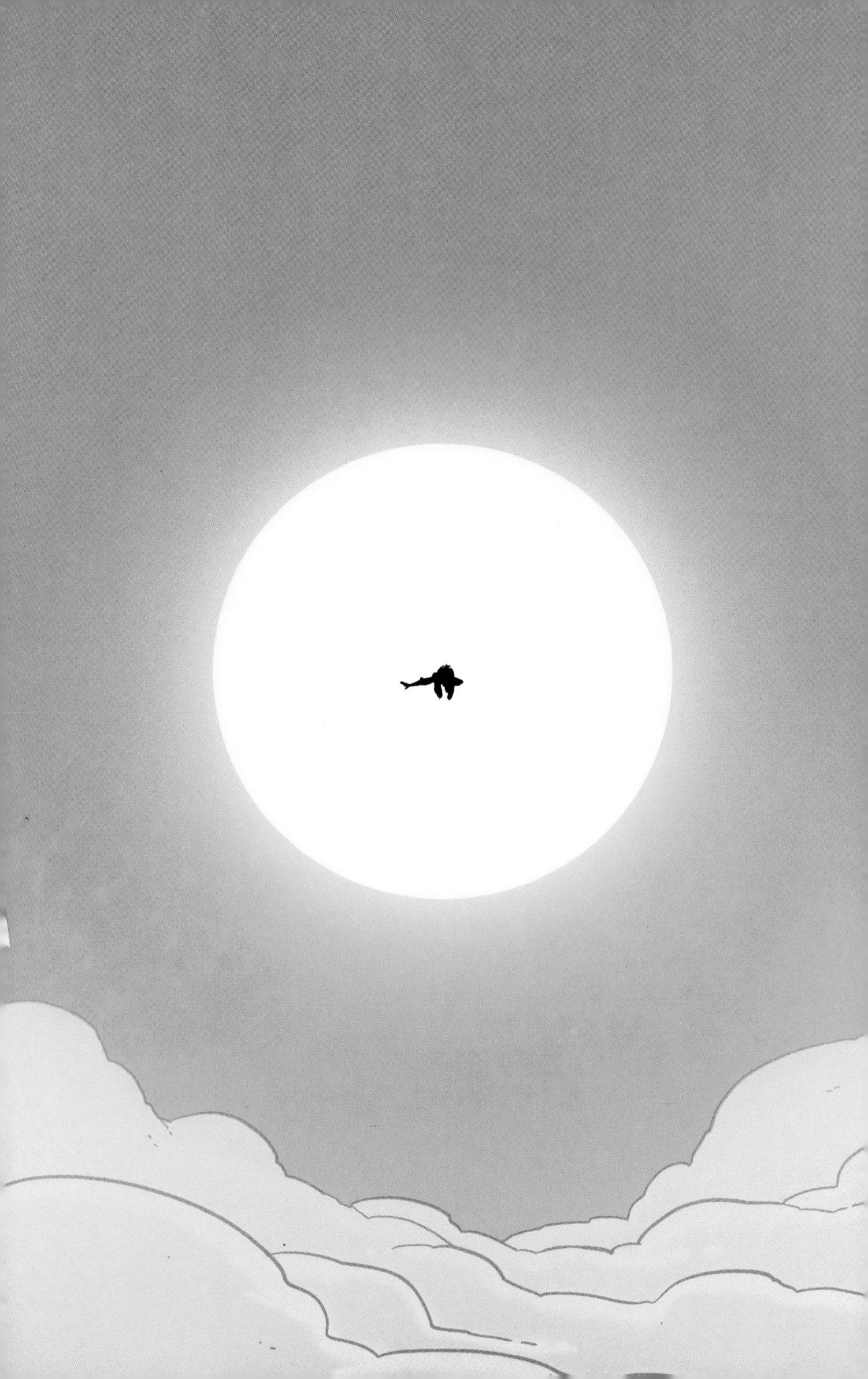

For Joseph

&

for Darwyn,

who left.

And for Oscar,

who showed up.

Acknowledgments

Meredith, stop me if you've heard this before: You're the best of people. A truly excellent example of a human being, and my greatest friend.

Oscar, you're moving up the list with lightning speed. If you don't end up liking comics all that much, it's totally cool. I have other interests, too—I'm confident we'll find common ground. I love you like no one else in the universe.

To my family—Barbara, Tom, Jeremy, Sarah, Steven, Jodi, Ruby, Gabby—thank you for being my family, for loving me and fighting with me and letting me wander off to figure out what I wanted to do. There are fewer of us than there were, but there're more of us, too, and I take an odd comfort in that. To my extended family, the Grans, I've felt welcome and like one of the clan from day one, and you're very kind for creating that feeling.

Thanks to Jason Fischer, Judy Hansen, Mark Siegel, Robyn Chapman, and Samia Fakih for helping to see this book through.

Thanks always to my friends: Rusty, Vicki, Ken, Penelope, Lee, Evan, Geoff, Tessa, David, Kate D., Kate B., Frank, Becky, Bryan, Steve, Leslie, Lacey, Philip, Dave, Jim, Ian, Ben, Cal, Will, SJ, Alex, Randeep, Anne, Liz, Damian, and the cities of Philadelphia and Halifax.

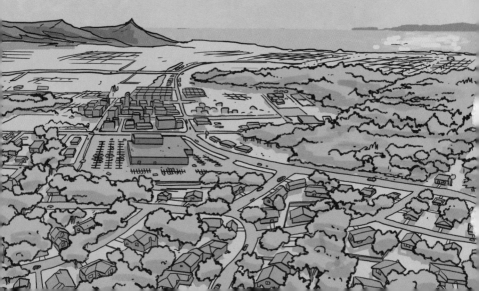